LORI FOSTER

STRONGER
THAN YOU KNOW

HQN

ISBN-13: 978-1-335-42000-8

Stronger Than You Know

Copyright © 2021 by Lori Foster

Recycling programs
for this product may
not exist in your area.

This edition published by arrangement with Harlequin Books S.A.

For questions and comments about the quality of this book,
please contact us at CustomerService@Harlequin.com.

HQN
22 Adelaide St. West, 40th Floor
Toronto, Ontario M5H 4E3, Canada
www.Harlequin.com

Printed in Lithuania

MIX
Paper from
responsible sources
FSC® C021394

Praise for *New York Times* bestselling author Lori Foster

To Kimmy Potts,

You graciously answered my request on my Facebook page for more information on Colorado, and I truly appreciate it. Not only that, you also answered all of my pesky follow-up questions! I know the Smoky Mountains, but the Rockies…not so much. You were a huge help, Kimmy, and I'm glad I didn't need to fly to Colorado for further research. (Not that I'd planned to, but still…) Thank you x 10!

I have to say, I have the absolute BEST readers in the entire world.

Big hugs,

Lori Foster

*Please note, any location errors that got through are my own!

STRONGER
THAN YOU KNOW

CHAPTER ONE

EVEN BEFORE KENNEDY BROOKS'S Uber driver turned the corner to where she lived, her skin prickled with alarm. It was well past midnight, a fact that couldn't be helped.

She should have been home at dinnertime.

One delay after another had obliterated her schedule to the point she had to rebook her flight. After hours spent sitting in the airport, exhaustion pulled at her. She wanted nothing more than to collapse in her bed, with her own sturdy locks in place.

When the scent of smoke infiltrated the closed windows of the car, her heart beat harder. She had a terrible feeling that there'd be no rest for her tonight. Maybe not even in the foreseeable future.

"What do you suppose happened?" her driver asked, pointing to the strobe of red lights that pierced the dark night.

"Fire," she breathed. And not just any fire, but in the apartment building where she lived.

Firetrucks, police and EMTs were everywhere. Neighbors she recognized clung together, many wrapped in blankets to ward off the cool Colorado evening air. Crowds of curious onlookers also lined the street, having left their own buildings to gawk.

Lifting a shaking hand to cover her mouth, Kennedy took in the enormous blaze that engulfed the entire building—including the floor where she would have been sleeping.

The driver couldn't get close, and she didn't want him to. "Stop here."

He glanced at her in the rearview mirror. "Hey, you okay? Is that your building?"

"Yes." She swallowed heavily. *What to do, what to do?*

Because she'd learned caution the hard way, Kennedy pulled additional money from her wallet. "Wait here, please."

The young man eyed the cash, glanced back at the fire and finally took the bills. "For how long?"

"I just need to make a call." She hesitated again. "I'm going to stand directly in front of your car, in the beam of the headlights." She needed privacy for the call, but she didn't want to be alone in the dark. "Leave them on, okay?"

"Sure."

Knowing she couldn't delay any longer, Kennedy hooked her purse strap over her shoulder and neck to keep it secure, dug out her phone and stepped from the car. It was an uncommonly cool September night, yet she felt flushed with heat, as if she could feel those flames touching her skin.

There was only one person she knew who might be able to deal with the present situation.

It was fortunate she had his number programmed into her phone, because her trembling hands refused to cooperate.

As the phone rang, she kept constant vigilance on her surroundings. She could almost swear someone watched her, yet when she glanced back at the driver, she couldn't see him for the glare of the lights in her eyes.

"Hello?"

Reyes McKenzie's sleep-deep voice caused her to jump,

and not for the first time. He was six feet four inches of hewn strength, thick bones and confident attitude. A man with a big, sculpted body, thanks to the gym he owned—and his voice reflected that, bringing an instant visual to mind.

Pretty sure he had other interests, as well, which would explain the edge of danger that always emanated from him.

Just what she needed right now.

Clutching the phone, hoping he'd be receptive, she whispered, "Hey. It's Kennedy."

Sharpened awareness obliterated his groggy tone. "What's wrong?"

Yes, Reyes was definitely the right person for her to call. Never mind that he had a wealth of secrets—for some inexplicable reason she trusted him. Mostly, anyway.

Tonight she had little choice in the matter. "Reyes, I need you."

She could hear him moving as he said, "I can be out the door in two minutes. Fill me in."

God bless the man, he didn't hesitate to come to her rescue. Before anything more happened, Kennedy gave him her address—something she hadn't wanted to share before now. Life had a way of upending plans, and hers had just been sucked into a treacherous whirlwind. "I'm not actually in the apartment building, though. I'm at the corner, behind a line of emergency vehicles, with an Uber driver. I don't know how long he'll let me hang out, though."

"Are you hurt?"

That no-nonsense question held a note of urgency.

"No." *Not yet.* "Could I explain everything once you're here? I'm afraid it's not safe." She felt horribly exposed.

"Forget the Uber driver, okay?" The sound of a door closing, then jogging steps, came through the line. "Get close to a firefighter. Or an EMT. *Stay there.* It'll only take me fifteen minutes if I really push it."

Nodding, Kennedy looked up the street. The officials all seemed so far away, and there was a lot of dark space between here and there. "I...I don't think I can."

"Shit." A truck door slammed. "I'm on my way, babe, okay? Get back in the car with the Uber guy and drive around in congested areas. Don't go anyplace deserted, and don't sit in one spot. Tell me you understand, Kennedy."

"I understand."

"Circle back in fifteen. I'll be waiting."

Yes, that sounded like a more viable plan. "Thank you, Reyes."

"Keep your eyes open." He disconnected, likely to concentrate on driving, and suddenly she felt very alone again. Reaching into her purse, Kennedy found the stun gun and palmed it. She'd practiced with the damn thing but had never actually used it on anyone.

She didn't want to use it tonight, either, but she felt better for having it.

All around her, smoke thickened the air and tension seemed to escalate. She opened the back door and slid into the car, saying to the driver, "Could you drive, please?"

Exasperated, he twisted back to see her. "Listen, I have to pick up another guy from the airport. I can't just—"

"I'll make it worth your while, I promise."

He eyed her anew, his gaze dipping over her body. "What's that supposed to mean?"

Oh, for the love of... Kennedy knew she was a mess. She'd pulled her hair into a haphazard ponytail, her makeup was smudged, and her clothes were sloppy-comfortable, suitable for a long flight. There was absolutely nothing appealing about her at the moment. "It's not an invitation, so forget that. Just lock the doors and drive for fifteen minutes. Stay in busy areas—no dark, empty streets—and then you can bring me back here. I'll give you another forty bucks."

Considering it, he continued to study her.

A movement beyond him drew her startled attention. There, from the long shadows, two men crept toward them. "Lock the doors and freaking drive!" she screamed.

Disconcerted, he, too, looked around, and the second he noticed the men, they broke into a jog.

Coming straight for them.

"Jesus!" Jerking the car into Reverse, he backed away with haste, almost hitting a telephone pole. Spinning around, he punched the gas and the small economy car lurched forward down the empty street. Again his gaze went to the rearview mirror. "Who the fuck was that?"

Looking over her shoulder, seeing the men fade away, Kennedy sucked in a much-needed breath. "I don't know," she whispered. *But I know they haven't given up.*

REYES DROVE LIKE a lunatic. His Harley would have been quicker, but he couldn't quite picture Kennedy strapped around him with the wind in her hair. Plus, he had no way of knowing if she'd be dressed for the cool night. Grim, he pulled up to the cross street in front of her apartment building. The road was closed off to through traffic, and the firefighters were still hard at work. Crowds had been pushed far back, held at bay by police officers.

Glancing around, he didn't see Kennedy.

But he did spot two shifty-looking dicks keeping watch on everything. Dressed all in black, with black knit hats pulled low, they watched the streets instead of the fire.

Narrowing his eyes, Reyes did a quick survey of the area and didn't see anyone else. The majority of people appeared to be enrapt with the fire—unlike these two.

Getting out his phone, he pulled up his recent call list and touched Kennedy's name. She answered before the first ring had finished.

"Reyes?" she asked with shaky urgency.

"Where are you, hon?"

"I couldn't come back. Two men are watching for me."

"Yeah, I see them. Did they bother you?"

"They charged after the Uber car, but my driver got us away. I...I don't know what they want."

"I'll find out. Give me two minutes, then circle by. I should be ready by then." Belatedly he thought to add, "I'm in my truck." Because Kennedy came to the gym he owned, and because they'd partnered in the rescue of a big alley cat, she was familiar with his ride.

"What?" With breathless panic, she screeched, "What do you mean you'll find out? You can't possibly—"

"Sure I can." For a while now, he and Kennedy had been dancing around the fact that they both had secrets. When faced with danger, she'd called him, so obviously she understood the extent of his ability.

Tonight seemed like a good night for her to learn a little more about him. "Did you hear me, Kennedy? What did I say?"

"Two minutes," she repeated blankly. "Reyes, don't you dare—"

Seeing that the guys had noticed him, Reyes smiled and disconnected. Leaving the truck, he started toward them, his attitude amicable. "What happened, do you know?"

The men looked at each other. The taller of the two said, "Looks like an apartment fire."

"Yeah, I can see that." He was only ten feet away now. "Who started it?"

They shared another glance, and Stretch spoke again. "Who says anyone did? Might've been faulty wiring."

"Nah." He continued to close the distance, his stride long and cocky—with good reason. "Pretty sure you yahoos had something to do with it." He grinned. "Ami-right?"

Stretch reached inside his jacket, and Reyes kicked out, sending him sprawling backward. He landed hard, the wind knocked out of him.

His shorter friend took an aggressive stance.

Bad move. With a short, swift kick of his booted foot, Reyes took out the guy's braced knee. He screamed in pain as his leg buckled the wrong way.

Quickly Reyes patted him down, removing both a knife and Glock. Still squatting, he shifted his attention to Stretch just as the guy got back to his feet.

Maybe hoping to mimic Reyes's moves, Stretch tried to plant his foot in his face.

Reyes ducked to the side, grabbed his ankle and yanked him off balance again.

Down he went for the second time. Unfortunately, he cracked his head and, without so much as a moan, passed out.

"Well, hell." Turning back to the shorter dude, Reyes prodded him. "Who are you and what did you want with the girl?"

Dazed with pain, his face contorted, the guy gasped, "What girl?"

"Dude, you are seriously whack. Want me to bust the other knee? I can, you know." Using the muzzle of the Glock, Reyes tapped his crotch. "Or maybe you want me to smash these instead?"

Rolling to his side, he cried, *"No."*

Heaving a sigh, Reyes stood. "What a wuss. C'mon, man. Give me something. It's not like I really *want* to hurt you, you know." *Not much, anyway.* But when he thought of these two planning to harm Kennedy…yeah. Red-hot rage. "I'll give you to the count of three. One. Two."

"All right! We were hired to grab her. That's all I know."

"Bullshit. There's always more. Like where were you going to take her? Who wants her? And why?"

"I don't know, man! We were paid half, and once we grabbed her, someone would call with an address. After we dropped her off, we'd get the other half."

"Yeah? Planned to do this whole thing blind, huh?" Reyes heard Stretch groan and knew he was coming around. Probably a good thing.

"I mean…trust only goes so far."

What a joke. Who the hell was dumb enough to trust these two? "Maybe your buddy has more info on him. If I find out you're lying, you won't like what I do."

"Bolen woulda found out same as me, when we got the call."

Sounded legit, but Reyes wasn't taking any chances. Going over to Bolen, he quickly searched him, removing another gun and also taking his wallet. Inside he found a stack of hundreds, but nothing useful. When Bolen tried to sit up, Reyes pistol-whipped him. He collapsed again.

Glancing back at the other guy, who made a failed attempt to get up, he asked, "What's your name?"

"Herman."

"Ah, dude, you said that so fast I'm not sure I believe you." When Reyes reached for him, the guy flinched away. "Man, you are seriously not cut out for this line of work." He shoved him to his side and pulled his wallet from his back pocket. It, too, was padded with bills. "You guys got a nice paycheck for kidnapping, didn't you?"

"I need an ambulance."

"Yeah, probably. Pretty sure I fucked up your kneecap. You might never walk the same." He searched through the wallet, curling his lip at a condom, a few interesting business cards for local joints, a coupon and a receipt. "Tell you what. Once I'm gone, you can try to crawl down there by the fire you set. EMTs are still caring for the people you hurt. Course that might raise questions you don't want to answer, right? One thing could lead to another, then you and your busted leg might end up rotting in prison." Reyes pulled out his driver's license. "Huh. Herman Coop. Well, Herman, now I know how to find you. And trust me, if you ever bother the girl again, I will. You won't like the outcome of that."

"God," Herman groaned, sweat soaking his face from pain.

"When good old Bolen comes around, you tell him I'm watching him, too, yeah?"

"Who the fuck are you?"

Headlights bounced around nearby, and he sensed it was Kennedy returning. With an edge of menace, he intoned, "Your worst nightmare." Seeing Herman's face, Reyes barely bit back his laugh.

He did enjoy spooking the knuckleheads.

Coming to his feet, he considered alerting the nearby cops, but he didn't know how that might implicate Kennedy. Hell, he didn't know her secrets or how serious they might be.

Should have listened to his family and researched her. In fact, he'd be willing to bet his computer-tech sister hadn't listened when he'd told her to step down.

Research was what she did, after all.

Then he and his brother followed up in whatever way was necessary.

For now, though, all he knew for sure was that there was more to Kennedy Brooks than she let on.

He nudged the thug with the edge of his boot. "On your

stomach, lace your fingers behind your head, and don't move or I'll send your balls into your throat."

It took a lot of effort for Herman to painfully maneuver around, but the balls threat often worked wonders. Choking on his every agonized breath, Herman got into position.

"Stay like that," Reyes warned again as he began moving away, one of the guns held at the ready in his right hand, the remaining weapon and wallets balanced in his left. He glanced behind him and saw Kennedy stepping out of the car, her eyes huge in the shadows. The driver lurched to the trunk, practically tossed out a rolling suitcase and allowed her to snatch a laptop case out of his hands. While she tried to get her luggage upright, the driver sped away.

Leaving her standing there alone.

Giving up on the goons, Reyes jogged to her. "Come on."

Staring at the load he carried, she whispered, "What did you do?"

"Gathered intel, that's all. Move it." He got her to his truck, dumped the confiscated items onto the floor and practically tossed her inside. "Buckle up, babe." He took her laptop case from her and shoved it to the floor as well.

After putting her enormous suitcase into the back of his truck, he gave one last look at the fallen men and a quick glance at the still-raging fire. The night had turned into a clusterfuck of the first order. But, hey, Kennedy had called him, not anyone else.

Overall, he'd claim it as a win.

TREMBLING FROM HER eyebrows to her toes, Kennedy wrapped her arms around herself as Reyes drove away, putting the fire farther and farther behind her. Physically, anyway. Emotionally? She knew what could have happened, what might have been intended, and it left her painfully aware of her own vulnerability.

Hadn't one tragedy in her life been enough? "Reyes?"

"Hmm?" As if he hadn't just annihilated two men and stowed multiple weapons near her feet, he flashed her a smile meant to reassure. "You okay?"

The interior lights created a bluish glow over his dark hair and limned his wide, muscular shoulders. No man should look as good as he did.

From the first moment she saw him, she'd made note of his physique. Every moment since then had been an exercise of resistance.

Kennedy peered down at the floor. Two big guns, a wicked-looking switchblade and a couple of wallets shared space with her laptop case, leaving her feet little room.

Those men had planned to use those weapons on her. She felt sure of it.

After adjusting the heater, Reyes patted her leg. "I've got you, honey. You're safe."

Odd, but she did feel safe. The road ahead was long and dark, and she had no idea where they were going, but Reyes wouldn't let anyone hurt her. She believed that.

"Babe? You're worrying me."

It shouldn't have surprised her, but it seemed her call had further changed the dynamic of their relationship. They already had a loose friendship, formed during the joint rescue of Chimera the alley cat, so they were beyond being merely gym member and gym owner.

They'd never dated. She'd deflected his efforts to get to know her better. Instinctively, she knew Reyes was more than a simple man running his own business. Others might take him at face value, but she'd experienced things others hadn't, and it had changed her forever.

With his secrets, as well as the lethal ability he usually tried to downplay, Reyes reeked of danger.

Plus, avoiding involvement with any man suited her just fine.

Now, that didn't seem possible.

She might be bordering on shock, but she hadn't missed the things he'd called her, like *babe* and *honey*. If he'd ever used endearments before, she didn't recall it.

Usually she wouldn't like it. Tonight? She wanted more than just his affection. She wanted his protection. She wanted his comfort.

She wanted him to promise her it would be okay.

Her eyes burned as she stared at him. She could pretend it was from the smoke, though she knew better. "I don't have anywhere to go." The enormity of the situation was sinking in, bringing a tinge of panic with it. "Almost everything I owned was in that apartment." Another thought occurred to her, and she gasped. "My car! My car was parked in the lot behind the building..."

"Shh." Reaching over, he clasped her knee, his thumb rubbing against the side of her thigh through her leggings. "I'll handle it, okay? For now, just tell me what happened."

Quickly she tried to tally her cash. She had credit cards—would it be safe to use them? "I don't know where to go."

His hold on her knee firmed. "With me. You go with me, Kennedy. We'll work it out."

Swallowing heavily, utterly relieved that she wouldn't be alone, she nodded. "I guess I'll get to see Chimera, so that'd be—what?" The way he grimaced made her fear something had happened to the cat, too. When they'd rescued her from the alley, she'd been half-starved and nursing three kittens. Reyes had taken the animals home with him, but so far she'd been joining him on the vet visits and splitting those bills.

"Chimera isn't with me right now."

Unreasonable anger swelled. "You got rid of my cat?"

"No! Damn, do you always have to think the worst of me?" He released her leg and squeezed the wheel with both hard-knuckled hands. "She's with my dad right now. Or actually, my dad's man."

"Your dad's man?" Kennedy blinked. "What exactly does that mean?"

He shook his head. "Tell you what. Let's come back to that later, okay? For now, just know that Chimera is well loved and cared for." He tipped his head to the pile of stuff he'd dumped on the floor. "Check out those wallets, see if you know either of those bozos. Keep their licenses out so I can give their names to my brother."

"Your brother? The guy who's even taller than you?" She'd seen him once at the gym, along with a woman who looked equally beautiful and badass, as if she could chew rusty nails while seducing someone.

The relationship to the brother had been plain. Both men shared superb physiques, incredible height and gorgeous faces. Reyes's eyes were a warm hazel, but his brother's had been bright blue. At six foot four, Reyes was tall, but his brother had a few inches on him. Of course she'd noticed the brother—it would have been hard not to—but unlike the other women at the gym that day, Kennedy hadn't gawked.

"Babe, if you keep questioning everything I say, we're never going to get this show on the road."

Get the show on the road? Her life was in a shambles and he cavalierly—

"I got this, okay?" He glanced at her, then returned his gaze to the dark road. "Cooperation would be nice, but you have my word, I'm not going to let anything happen to you."

And there it was, that cockiness she knew would make her feel better. "Okay. Thank you."

His grin created an over-the-top dimple in his cheek. A man like Reyes McKenzie didn't need the added charm of dimples, for God's sake.

"Licenses?" he prompted with an endless store of patience.

"Right." Having a purpose galvanized her. Her fumbling hands accidentally dumped one wallet, and she didn't care. Quickly she located both IDs, studying the faces, hopeful of making sense of what had happened. "No." Deflated, she dropped back in the seat. Damn, she really had to get a grip. "I've never seen them before."

"No big deal." He glanced at her again. "How'd you get out of the apartment?"

"I wasn't there. I was on my way home from the airport after a weekend in Texas."

With no expression at all, he asked, "Doing what?"

She really didn't feel like summing up her entire life for him, but she supposed it was necessary. "I'm a professional speaker, specifically for schools and colleges." Every muscle in her body tensed. She watched his profile, counted five beats of her heart, then made herself whisper, "I cover the dangers of human trafficking."

Slowly he nodded, as if that answered a question he hadn't yet asked. "You have that knowledge from experience?"

Five more heartbeats, each strong and steady. It was a practice she'd learned to remind herself that as long as her heart beat, she was alive.

And as long as she was alive, she had hope.

Tonight she had more than hope.

She had Reyes McKenzie.

"Should I gather from your silence that you don't want to talk about it?"

Giving up her scrutiny of his face, she stared out the passenger window. "I talk about it all the time. Professional speaker, remember?"

Accepting that, he asked, "How old were you?"

So matter-of-fact, as if she hadn't just imparted life-altering news. Most people were taken aback at the mention of something as heinous as trafficking. They balked and usually changed the subject.

None of which would help a person taken into captivity.

What victims needed, especially young people, was information. Ways to avoid being taken, and what to do if they were.

No one had ever reacted as Reyes just had. So what was his real vocation? Definitely, he did a lot more than just running a gym.

"I feel like everything I say causes you this painful introspection. I'm sorry for that, okay? But the best way for us to tackle this is to first understand it."

Kennedy knew he was right. She filled her lungs with a bracing breath. "I'd just turned twenty-one. Fresh out of college. A know-it-all." In truth, she hadn't known a damn thing, not about the real world. "I tell kids what to watch for, how important it is to have situational awareness, and what it means to risk going out alone."

"Did you get taken from Texas? Or here in Colorado?"

"Florida," she answered. Going into speaker mode, she insulated herself from harsh memories. "I was jogging on the beach, enjoying my solitude, thinking about my future…" She remembered it all in sharp-edged detail. "The next thing I knew, men had me, one with his hand so tight over my mouth I thought I would suffocate. I lost a sneaker in the sand. My shirt ripped."

Again he cupped her knee, the simple connection offering needed comfort.

"I got stuffed into a van and taken to a house with a few other women, some of them drugged unconscious." Tension gathered along her neck and upper spine. "That was punishment if you tried to get away. I saw two women held down while another woman injected them."

"The woman who injected them—she worked with the traffickers?"

"Yes." And that was something Kennedy still struggled with. How could one woman do that to another? She'd made a point of being the opposite. She helped not only women, but also children and some men.

"It's an ugly business. Anyone who's not a monster can't make sense of it."

Very true. "After a few weeks, I got away only because another one of the captives sacrificed herself. Literally." Kennedy rubbed her forehead, thinking of Sharlene and how she'd tried to mother everyone, even the women who were the same age as her. "There was one guy known for cruelty. He wasn't satisfied with rape. He..." Her throat closed. These were details she didn't share during her talks, not because they weren't important, but because they were far too personal.

Reyes lifted his hand from her knee, turning it palm up, waiting. When she put her hand in his, he enfolded it in his strength. Somehow, he seemed to know what to do to help.

Amazing.

"Her name was Sharlene. She was thirty years old and the most beautiful soul I've ever met. More than once she convinced a man that he wanted her instead of one of the other girls. She'd tell us to be really quiet, to avoid eye contact, and then she'd draw attention to herself." Kennedy stared at him. "She was used so poorly, and she did it anyway—to spare the rest of us."

"She did that the day you got away?"

"Yes." Kennedy tightened her hold on his hand. "The bastard decided he wanted Sharlene and me both, so I had to go along. So many times, when it was just us girls in the room, Sharlene would coach us on what to do, what to say, opportunities to look for."

"She gave you an opportunity," Reyes said quietly, as if he already knew.

"She did, and it saved me." The shallow breaths she'd been taking left her lungs starved, prompting her to suck in a deep, desperate inhale. "I knew that if there was a window near, I should go out it. If there was an unlocked door, I should try. If a car was moving slowly enough, I should take my chances on jumping out." That night had been dark just like this one, but instead of cool, crisp air, the skies had hung heavy with heated humidity. "We were on a busy street and the customer, who was driving, braked to avoid another car that switched lanes. I didn't know Sharlene was going to do it. I was pretty much just sitting there shaking. But all of a sudden she kicked the back of his seat hard, sending his face into the steering wheel. She kept kicking, too. I saw blood go everywhere. Then one car crashed into another, and the handler who rented us out was in the passenger seat and he reached back for her." Kennedy tightened her hold on Reyes. "He had a gun, and he was threatening to kill her, but all she did was yell for me to go." Kennedy swallowed hard, then whispered, "So I did."

After lifting her clenched fingers to his lips for the brush of a kiss, Reyes asked, "You jumped out of the car?"

"And into insane traffic. Tires screeched and horns

blared. More cars crashed. People stopped. One man came running over to help me, another couple was already on the phone to call the police. I looked back, and the guy who'd been driving was dead." Heavy remorse, forever present, settled on her shoulders. Not for the cruel bastard who'd thought he could rent women to rape. But for a friend she'd lost too soon. "Sharlene also died in the wreck."

"The prick riding shotgun?"

"He made a run for it. I don't know what happened to him, but the police were amazing. Even with me babbling and sobbing, they understood. They did this incredible coordination between departments, all while caring for me. By the time the sun came up, they'd rescued the other women at the house and had arrested the creeps who'd caused so much harm." Tears burned her eyes, and building emotion thickened her throat. "Sharlene didn't just save me, she saved them, too, and lost her life in the process." Blinking away the tears, Kennedy sniffled. "She'll always be my inspiration for bravery, selflessness and morality. To me, she'll always be my hero."

"What was the handler's name?"

She shook her head. "They were careful not to use names around us. I'd recognize him if I saw him, but that wasn't enough for the police to find him."

Sharlene had died, and that miserable excuse for a man had gotten away.

He was still out there somewhere, and that fact, more than any other, haunted her every day.

CHAPTER TWO

KNOWING KENNEDY LISTENED, that she was sharp enough to draw a lot of conclusions from his conversation with Cade, Reyes finalized his plans. After hearing her heartbreaking experience, he'd had to do something.

Something other than pulling over and holding her tight.

Other than going back to kill the two thugs he'd left disabled.

And telling her his entire backstory was a giant no-go. His family would have a fit.

So he called big brother.

Cade, a retired army ranger and one of the calmest, most take-charge people he knew, excelled at focusing on the critical data.

Plus, when he was honest with himself, Reyes could admit that Cade had an overall positive influence on his life. Yeah, Reyes had once been a hothead. From his mid-teens, he'd solved all his frustrations with fighting or fucking. And God, he'd had a lot of frustrations—many that he hid beneath caustic humor. After Cade medically retired from the military, he'd stomped the worst of Reyes's rebellious nature into the dirt. Cade wasn't unduly harsh. He definitely wasn't a bully. But, over and over, in the most impressive ways, he'd refined Reyes's ability through firm control.

To this day, his brother was the only person he knew

who could still best him. Didn't stop Reyes from challenging Cade. Often.

A man had to have some fun.

Now with Cade on the phone, and on the job, Reyes felt proactive rather than reactive to Kennedy's problem.

Cade would not only take care of her car, he'd get the names of the guys he'd disarmed to their sister, who would find out everything there was to know about them. Madison's research skills often left him awed. Before she was done, she'd know more about the two yahoos than they knew about themselves.

She'd been raised to do exactly that, and a whole lot more.

Like the rest of the family, his sister was tall and, when need be, dangerous in her own right.

In contrast to the McKenzies, Kennedy was downright tiny at around five feet five inches. She was also fierce in her attitude and independence.

At the gym, he'd watched her work hard to master a skill set that remained out of her reach. Unlike most who came to the gym, Kennedy didn't exercise to bulk up or shed weight, or even for reasons of fitness. Over and over again, day after day, she practiced offensive moves. Kicks and strikes meant to disable. From the first, Reyes had wondered what motivated her.

Now he knew, and, Christ, he hated it.

"I'll put out some feelers, see if there's any talk on the street," Cade said. "I'll check that her car isn't bugged, then store it at my place. Soon as Madison has some news, I'll let you know. Anything else?"

"No, that's it for now."

"Why am I not buying it? Why am I getting the impression you're a little more invested than usual?"

Because you're incredibly astute. Reyes shook his head.

"That's the pot calling the kettle black." After all, Cade had rushed into matrimony the last time he'd found himself assisting a woman. And not just any woman, but one that brought her own store of trouble to the table. Reyes grinned, thinking about his sister-in-law. "Not all of us fall head over ass during a mission."

"Is that what this is?" Cade asked. "A mission?"

"Notice you're not denying the head-over-ass part."

Cade ignored that. "You and I are not the same. I don't go off half-cocked, even when I'm falling hard. You, on the other hand, tend to stay in a perpetual state of boiling over."

True enough. "I got it covered. Let me know what you find out, and tell Madison not to worry."

"We'll both worry if we want to." Getting serious, Cade added, "Call if you need me. For anything."

"Will do." Reyes disconnected, then glanced at Kennedy.

"Let me guess. Your brother was warning you against any machinations on my part?" She chafed her arms. "So far your family seems far too suspicious."

"Here's the thing," he said, refusing to let her rile him. "I never take women to my house."

She snorted at that. "Yeah, right."

"Didn't say I don't get around. I do."

"Bragging? Lovely."

"It isn't bragging," he insisted, a frown forming despite his efforts to stay even-tempered. Truth was, he never lacked for female company. "Just trying to explain why my brother was…"

"Alarmed?"

"Cade? Ha. No, he doesn't get alarmed." He never missed a damned thing, either. "Big brother could be in the middle of a three-alarm fire, during a tornado, with a murderer on his heels, and he wouldn't blink."

Wide-eyed, Kennedy said, "Wow."

Yeah, he'd just spewed way more than he meant to. "Point is," he stressed, making a concerted effort to get back on course, "I take my pleasure elsewhere, not at my home."

"Is that some sort of scruple or what? No, wait," she said, her gaze discerning. "Whatever it is you *really* do, you have to keep it private. Can't manage that if you have bed partners traipsing in and out."

"Know what?" He couldn't help smirking. "That sounded so old-fashioned it should be tarnished." When she started to grumble, he spoke over her. "I'm breaking a hard rule for you, so a little appreciation would be nice."

Grudgingly she said, "Thank you."

"Just know that I'm not taking you there for any reason other than safety." He shot her a quick glance. Having her dark past confirmed, he had to consider how unsettled she might be alone in his company—especially since she didn't buy his front as a gym owner. "I won't come on to you or anything."

She slanted him a look. "I wasn't worried."

"No?" Hell, now he didn't know if he should be insulted or not.

"I've gotten good at sizing up people. Not saying I automatically trust my instincts. I still use a lot of caution. But it should be obvious I trust you overall, otherwise I wouldn't have called you tonight."

That could have been a simple lack of options. "Do you have family?"

She hesitated far too long before shrugging. "Mom and Dad. They don't live close, though, so I couldn't call them."

Wow. If what she'd described had happened to *his* kid,

he'd never again let her out of his sight. "No one you're dating? No close friends?"

She shook her head. "For the longest time I stayed on the move. Ridge Trail is the first place I've settled down since—" she flapped a hand "—everything happened."

His heart gave a hard thump in sympathy. He knew only too well how it felt to be chased by your past. "My place is secure. We'll lock down while Cade and Madison do their thing. Early tomorrow, they'll check back with what they've found, and we'll go from there."

She gave him another look of wonder. "So…that just opened up about a million more questions."

"I know, right?" Even as a part of the inner circle, the reach and ability of his family sometimes astounded him. "The important thing is that you'll be safe tonight, you can get some rest, and tomorrow we can figure out our next step. How's that sound?"

"Like I'm out of my depth."

"Yeah, you are. But I got it covered. No more questions tonight. I'm good at prioritizing, and number one is food and then sleep. Unless you're not hungry?" Some people couldn't eat when they got nervous. "If not, we can go straight to sleep."

"I'm not sure I could sleep yet, so I'll opt for food."

"You got it. Anything in particular you want? At home I can throw together a sandwich, or I have cereal. Cookies. Canned soup. Oatmeal."

"A sandwich would be great."

"Good, then we don't need to stop." He'd rather get her settled in, to know for a fact she was out of harm's way. If she'd wanted a burger or something, he'd have worked it out, but this was easier.

He was nothing if not adaptable.

This, though? Yeah, hadn't seen it coming. Knowing

Kennedy had secrets, and having those secrets burn down an apartment building and come after her with guns—two very different things.

His phone rang and, knowing it'd be family, he answered.

True to form, Madison relayed information without a greeting. "No one died in the fire. Sounds like a few people were taken to the hospital for smoke inhalation, and a whole lot of people lost everything, but Dad said he'll help with that."

Good old Dad. Parrish McKenzie never hesitated to toss around the cash. "That was quick."

"Did you expect me to be slow?"

"Nope. Just didn't know Cade had gotten hold of you already. Figured he might wait until morning."

"Don't be absurd." Madison's voice softened. "How is your lady friend?"

Lady friend? Talk about old-fashioned… "Kennedy isn't like us," he said, and figured that covered it all.

"If there's anything I can do, for her personally, I mean, let me know."

Driving one-handed, he shrugged. "She has luggage with her, so I'm guessing her immediate needs are covered."

"Luggage? She'd been on a trip?"

Feeling Kennedy's hard stare, he said, "Texas."

"I need details."

Of course she did. Madison always wanted more details. It was a trait of her talent. "Because?"

"Duh. It could be related." Suddenly she demanded, "Put her on the phone."

"Hell, no." The last thing he wanted was for his sister to chat up Kennedy, making his rescue into something it wasn't.

"I'll locate her number and call her if you don't, then you'll have to explain that one."

A frown gathered. "How the hell would you do that?"

"Easy peasy." As if ticking off the high points, Madison said, "She's registered at the gym. She likely gave her cell number there. It'd be a piece of cake to access that data—"

Growling low, Reyes said, "Fine." He knew his sister didn't make idle threats. She might be beautiful, with a deceptively delicate quality about her, but like the rest of the family, she had mad skills, plus a backbone of steel and the determination of an ox.

Lowering the phone, he said to Kennedy, "My sister wants to talk to you."

Without a word, her expression enigmatic, Kennedy held out her small hand.

Damn, these two could be difficult.

Well, they couldn't have *everything* their way. As the driver of this rescue mission, he had some rights. Defiantly hitting the speaker button with his thumb, he handed it over to Kennedy.

Proving she knew how irked he was, Kennedy smiled and held the phone loosely against her knee. "Hello?"

"First," Madison said. "You're okay?"

"Yes, I think so. Still shaking horribly, but I guess that's to be expected."

"Of course. Your voice sounds strong, though. A good thing, especially when forced into my brother's company." Sotto voce, Madison added, "He's an adorable pain in the ass."

"I've noticed."

Reyes felt his eyebrows climb. Kennedy considered him *adorable*? Screw that.

The pain-in-the-ass part he couldn't really deny.

Her tone brisk, Madison said, "I take it you've been through things like this before?"

"Unfortunately—but I'm not going into that right now."

Madison had just learned something he didn't know. "What and when?" he demanded, and was thoroughly ignored.

"Understandable," Madison said. "Though eventually I'll know it all."

Eyes narrowing, Kennedy asked, "What is it you do?"

"Reyes didn't tell you? I'm the tech guru. When he or our brother need research, I pull it together."

"Research for...?"

"I'm sure Reyes will explain in his own sweet time," Madison said smoothly. "Now, short and succinct, tell me where you've been, if there were any mishaps or you noticed anything out of the ordinary."

Without hesitation, Kennedy said, "I flew into Texas on Thursday morning early. I went first to the prearranged hotel so I could unpack, get food, rest a few minutes. A couple of hours later I was picked up by a hired driver."

Madison jumped in. "Anything off about the driver?"

"No. He took me straight to the meeting place. I caught a cab back to the hotel later."

"He didn't talk to you? Didn't watch you unduly?"

"Not that I noticed," Kennedy said. "I was busy going over my notes. For me, each talk is slightly different depending on where I give it, if it's for high school or college age audiences. I speak on human trafficking, and each location has its own unique cautions."

Madison never missed a beat. "You share what you've learned?"

"I try. The least I can do is tell young people what to look for, what to avoid. What to do if they're taken."

Reyes could practically see his sister sorting through

that information, but Kennedy pushed past any further questions Madison might have asked.

"I had speaking engagements Thursday, Friday and Saturday nights, then again on Sunday afternoon. I'd taken my luggage with me to the last location, a high school, so I could leave directly from there for the airport. Again, a hired driver picked me up."

"Nothing unusual?" Madison asked again.

"No."

"Do you remember the name of the company?"

Kennedy shared it without pause, proving she noted details. "It wasn't until I got to the airport that everything went haywire. My flight was delayed by three hours so I went for a bite to eat. Right as I was finishing up, a kid accidentally dumped a cola on me. After I assured the frazzled parents that it was fine, I went to the restroom to change."

Reyes gave a small smile. Of course Kennedy would reassure the parents. He hadn't known her that long, and still he'd recognized right off that she had a big heart. Otherwise, she wouldn't have set out to save Chimera. The alley cat hadn't been cute, but she had been hungry, and Kennedy had immediately decided to care for her.

Yes, Kennedy could be prickly, but he figured that had something to do with her past, and her understandable wariness.

"The line was long," Kennedy continued, "since a flight had just let out, so it took me forever to get into the restroom. I had to take wet paper towels into the stall with me, but it was impossible to wash properly. In fact, I'm still sticky."

"You can shower at Reyes's place."

Kennedy flashed him a lingering look. "Yes, that would be nice."

Real nice. Annnnd…now he had that image stuck in his brain. At the gym, he'd seen Kennedy working out in snug shorts and loose T-shirts, so he knew a little something about her body. She was short, toned, not overly endowed up top but she had a lush, well-rounded bottom that constantly snagged his attention.

Lately, too many of his fantasies centered on that perfect ass. Didn't matter if he'd just indulged in a sexual marathon with another woman, before the night was over, his brain focused back on Kennedy.

"Anyway," she said, unaware of his musings, "by the time I finished, I'd missed the next flight, too. At that point, I was ready to cry, I was so exhausted. Luckily, the flight attendants managed to get me on a connecting flight the next hour, but it turned into a long, frustrating night."

"And then you got home to find your apartment building burned down." Full of sympathy, Madison asked, "Anything sketchy about the Uber driver?"

"No. Poor guy was scared to death. I felt bad for him." Kennedy heaved a sigh. "I knew the minute I saw the commotion something was terribly wrong."

"Something personal?" Madison asked.

"Yes." Looking out the windshield, Kennedy hesitated. "I felt the danger. I *knew* someone was after me, and it made me ill to realize people could have died in that fire." She swallowed heavily. "Because of me."

"You're too smart to blame yourself for that," Madison assured her. "I agree it's unnerving to realize someone is so determined. I'm glad you trusted your instincts."

"Instincts are a powerful thing. I never ignore them." She bit her lip. "Not anymore."

Huh. So even if she didn't always trust her instincts, she didn't ignore them. Reyes considered that smart— because he was the same.

"I'm going to let you go now," Madison said gently. "When you get a minute, sometime in the morning, use Reyes's account to email me all the details of your trip. The names of the schools, addresses and any descriptions you can recall about the drivers. Anything, no matter how insignificant it might seem."

"Thank you. I feel better knowing I'm not alone in this."

Reyes scowled. What was he? Invisible? *He* was the one who'd rescued her. He would *personally* see that she was kept safe.

Here, in this moment, he didn't even care how long it might take.

When Kennedy's cool hand rested on his biceps, everything inside him snapped to awareness. Weird. His body had stopped reacting like that long ago. During personal introspection, he admitted that he was a sexual glutton. Apparently, all the variety had blunted the excitement of heated sex.

Yet here he was, all reactionary and overheated.

Couldn't deny it, he liked Kennedy's touch. He wanted more of it. In more interesting places.

But first... "Say goodbye, Madison, so Kennedy and I can talk."

Kennedy's smile teased. "Again, thank you, Madison. I'll get the info to you right away. In fact, I have my schedule in my laptop case. I always print it for quick reference. It has most of the details you want."

"She can take a pic with my phone," Reyes said. "I'll text it to you."

"Perfect. I know your phone isn't compromised, but I'm not sure about hers. Maybe keep her off it?"

"Ha!" said Kennedy. "I don't need Reyes to keep me off it, as long as I know it's not permanent."

"I'll sort it out quickly," Madison promised. "Be safe,

you two. And if you need anything, don't hesitate to let me know."

Kennedy handed him the phone. Instead of disconnecting, he took it off speaker and put it to his ear. "I need someone to cover for me tomorrow."

"Cade's taking care of it. He knows your employees."

"Great. I'll be in touch."

"Go easy, brother. She's strong, but some of that strength is a front."

Naturally, his sister knew this part of their call was private; otherwise, she never would have said such a thing. The three of them had worked together for so long it was easy to anticipate each and every move. "Got it. Thanks, hon."

She blew him a kiss and the call ended.

Holding out her hand to reclaim the phone, Kennedy said, "Interesting family you have."

He acknowledged that with a smile. She'd only witnessed the tip of the iceberg. Long ago his dad had made a decision that affected them all and determined their fates. Cade had rebelled and joined the military instead, but he and Madison, overall, had dutifully fallen in line with the plan.

Digging through her briefcase, Kennedy located several papers. Using Reyes's phone, and the number Madison had just called from, she sent images of each paper to his sister.

"That's quite the itinerary," he murmured.

"Which is why I keep it all typed out for easy reference." Once she'd put his phone in the console between them and stored her papers again, she got cozy in the corner and simply watched the dark scenery pass by.

Twenty minutes later, he pulled down the long winding drive to his secluded cabin. Sitting straighter in her seat, Kennedy looked around. "So…you're off the beaten path."

Did that worry her? Was she afraid to be isolated with him? Going for nonchalance, he said, "Easier to stay safe that way."

Her piercing gaze landed on him. "But we aren't that far from your gym. However did you manage it?"

Damn. He'd taken the long way around to his house with the sole purpose of throwing her off. Hadn't worked. "You know Ridge Trail. Go half an hour in any direction and you're lost in the mountains."

"We're not lost. *I'm* not lost." Looking at the towering trees that lined the drive, she mused, "I knew you were taking the long way, but I didn't realize we'd end up here."

"Here?"

"In a place like this." Hands on the dash, she leaned forward. "Oh, a rustic cabin."

In the distance, yellow lights showed through the tinted windows and outside each corner of the house. It looked warm and welcoming. "Rustic on the outside, comfortable on the inside." With every security amenity a dude like him could need.

While Kennedy darted her gaze everywhere, he pulled into the garage and parked beside his Harley. With a press of the garage door remote, a steel reinforced door slid back into place and locked with a comforting clang.

"Wow." She eyed him again. "I feel like I was just imprisoned."

"Believe me, you learn to like that sound." It meant no one could intrude and he could sleep in peace. "Each lower-level window has galvanized steel webbing that is locked in place at night."

"As it is now?"

"Yes." He sat still in the truck, his wrists resting loosely on the steering wheel, half turned toward her. He was unwilling to rush her. The last thing he wanted was for her to be skittish with him. "There are escape routes out the roof in the upper master, and under the rolling island that divides the kitchen and the dining room. It's small. Really small, I guess." He shifted, a little uncomfortable now that he thought about it. He could afford a bigger place, but what would be the point? He had to clean it, since he didn't allow anyone else into his sanctum. Well…except that now he was allowing Kennedy. "Only about fifteen hundred square feet, though it's enough for me."

With a soft sigh, she settled back in the seat and smiled at him. "It's sweet of you to give me time to adjust, but honestly, I'm beat. I'd rather see your house, take a shower, eat and then crash—if it's okay with you."

Her smile gave him one of his own. "You're not nervous?"

The rude snort she issued should have insulted him; instead, he laughed. "Got it. You don't see me as any kind of threat. Glad to hear it." Getting out of the truck, he headed around the hood to open her door, but she'd already done that and stepped out.

Over her shoulder, she slung her purse strap, then the strap for her laptop case. Both looked heavy enough to bring her low, but her posture warned him against offering to take them. Instead, he hefted her suitcase out of the bed of his truck.

Kennedy wrinkled her nose at the weapons and wallets. "I'll leave those to you."

"No problem. Here." Hastily, he stepped past her and did a quick finger press on the interior door that opened into the house. All the locks were biometric and opened only to his touch, though he could also operate them from his cell phone.

Stepping into the laundry room, he set down her luggage and offered his hand.

Kennedy ignored him as she looked through the room and into the hall. To the left was a half bath, and straight ahead was a guest bedroom and bath.

"This way." He led her up the hall and around the corner to the great room, which combined the living room, kitchen and dining area all in one big open space.

"Wow," she said again, her head tipped back to take in the high ceilings, the spiral staircase that led up to the master and the abundance of windows. "This is amazing."

Shifting again, Reyes did his own quick scrutiny. Pretty much everything was wood or rock, including the heated slate floors on the ground level. Upstairs he had wood floors with colorful rugs. "You like it?"

"It's beautiful. Somehow I never pictured you in a place like this."

"No?" Where had she pictured him? Sleeping in his gym?

"Everything is so detailed. And *clean*. My gosh, there's not a speck of dust anywhere. Not even a smudge on all these incredible windows." She turned a slow circle. "I love the spiral staircase. May I go up?" Already she'd slipped the straps from her shoulders and let the bags down to the floor.

"Sure." He trailed after her, wishing he'd had time to make his bed. He remembered tossing the quilt as soon as he'd gotten her call.

She went through the bedroom and into the master bath, staring at the dark gray slate that climbed the wall of the wide shower, the natural wood slab sink, the dark oval tub and brass fittings.

"OMG," Kennedy whispered. "This is stunning."

Tension gathered at the base of his neck. Why did he feel so dumb? "I, um, eliminated the third bedroom to make the master bath and bedroom bigger."

"Whoever put this together is a genius."

His mouth firmed. "I did."

Eyes flaring, she stared at him, then settled into a smile. "A man of many talents. You just keep amazing me." With that bizarre compliment she pivoted and headed back to the bedroom.

Reyes hurried to catch up with her.

She slowed as she entered the room. "These floors aren't heated?"

"Nah. I like it cool when I sleep."

"Me, too." Trailing her fingertips over the surface of his dresser, she strolled around the room, taking in the headboard that spanned one entire wall to accommodate the extrawide mattress. It had built-in end tables, bronze wall sconces and a niche for a few books. "You read?" she asked.

Okay, that went too far. Crossing his arms, he leaned against the wall and gave her an insolent stare. "Yeah, learned when I was four or five. I can write, too. Spell, do math, all sorts of complex shit."

Her mouth curled into a grin. "I meant do you read for pleasure?" She pulled a book to see the title. "Wood-working?"

The muscles of his shoulders drew tighter. "I made the sink in the bathroom."

"Astounding." Shaking her head, she slid the book back into place and pulled another. "Horror?"

"Why not?"

Moving on to yet another, she said, "Ah. A biography of famous and not-so-famous killers."

It always helped to understand the twisted psyche. "So?"

Done perusing his books, she lifted the quilt from the floor, shook it out and replaced it on the bed. "This is beautiful. Homemade?"

"Not by me." Damn it, if he didn't get her out of the bedroom soon, he'd do something stupid. "Local quilters. When I saw that one hanging outside, I asked if it could be doubled. Took a few months, and cost a small fortune, but I like it."

"So do I." Going to the window, she stared out. "No drapes?"

For an answer, he walked to the nightstand and picked up the remote. With a touch, the windows gradually lightened to make the interior visible from the outside. Always cautious, he immediately darkened them again. "Nifty, right?"

Keeping her back to him, she whispered, "So you're not only a physical specimen and incredibly handsome, you're a craftsman, a designer and, apparently, wealthy. No wonder I never bought the whole gym-owner bit."

"I *am* a gym owner." Physical specimen? Handsome. Those compliments drew him closer. "How else do you explain the physical fitness?"

"Some of it has to be genetics." Knowing he was nearer, she half turned her head. "Is your dad as physically perfect as you and your brother?"

"Now, how do I answer that?" Carefully, slowly, he settled his hands on her shoulders. Little by little, he thought he might be starting to understand her mood. "If I say yes, I'll be admitting that I'm perfect, and we don't want that."

She rubbed her face on a tired laugh. "You're perfectly exasperating." Surprising him, she leaned back into his body. "Reyes?"

"Hmm?"

"Your bedroom is up here, and the guest bedroom is down there, but I don't want to be that far away from you."

"No problem. As you might have noticed, the bed is huge."

"Ridiculously so." She turned to face him, staring up at him with a wealth of emotion in her eyes. "I promise to stay on my side of the bed."

"Yeah, no problem." He leaned closer to tease. "But if you wander over in the night, I promise not to mind." Straightening again, he took her hand and drew her along behind him. "Come on. You can shower in the guest bedroom while I make those sandwiches. If you don't mind, I can take a look at your phone, too."

"It's off," she promised. "Isn't that good enough?"

"For now, yeah." Turning it on just to see if anyone had contacted her wouldn't be a bad idea, though. Never knew when someone might make it easy by being too cocky. He didn't expect that—most shit like this went the hard route. Still… One look at the exhaustion on her face and he decided to let it go. "Where do you want your things? Upstairs for the night with us, or down here in the guest bedroom?"

Indecision had her gaze flicking to the suitcase, her laptop case and her purse. "The suitcase will be fine down here. The others can go up."

"You've got it." He carried the overstuffed bag into the guest room and set it on top of the bed. "Should be a few towels under the sink. You need anything else? Soap, toothbrush?"

"Thank you, but I have it all with me."

He rubbed his hands together, hesitant to leave her. She looked small and worn-out, and she had to be running on last reserves. "All right, then. I'll have sandwiches ready in ten minutes, but take your time."

For a few seconds more, she continued to stare up at him. "What would I have done tonight without you?"

Smoothing down her mussed honey-blond hair, he admitted, "I have a feeling you'd have figured it out."

"I'm glad I didn't have to."

Damn, much more of that and she wouldn't get her shower because he'd be kissing her. "Me, too." With one last brush of his thumb over her warm cheek, he walked out of the room, pulling the door closed behind him.

CHAPTER THREE

DRESSED IN LOOSE pajama pants and a baggy T-shirt, her hair caught up in a ponytail, Kennedy walked across the heated floors, listening for Reyes. When she didn't hear him right away, fear wormed in.

Incidents like what had happened tonight never failed to transport her back to that time and place when she'd been at the mercy of people who'd had none. Standing in the quiet house, out in the middle of nowhere, feeling very much alone, she became that frightened woman again.

Reflexively, she put her hand to her heart, counting the beats. One, two, three... Alive. She was still alive.

"Hey."

Her gaze shot up, and she found Reyes standing there between the kitchen and the living room. He was now barefoot, shirtless, and his jeans hung low. He also watched her closely, as if waiting for any unsettling reactions.

She had a reaction, all right. Fear immediately diverted to sizzling awareness.

Forcing a smile, she said, "I didn't hear you."

"I was texting with my brother. He has your car."

"Already?"

Reyes shrugged and turned back into the kitchen, leaving her to follow. "By the way, my sister-in-law, who until recently drove a semi, thinks your little red compact is cute."

Stomach rumbling, she went in to sit at the table. "It *is*

very cute." Two place settings were arranged, each plate holding a sandwich cut in half, chips and a few pickles. "God, I'm starved," she said as she sat.

"Dig in." He opened the fridge. "What do you want to drink?"

"A cola would be great, but then I'd never sleep, so... water?"

"Sure." He withdrew two frosty bottles and brought them to the table, cracking open the caps on each before setting them down. "I did a sort of cold cut combination. Hope that works for you. Turkey, ham and salami."

She lifted a slice of wheat bread and saw lettuce, tomato and onion. "Mmm. Lots of veggies, too."

"With cheese and mayo." He smiled at her.

She took a big bite and hummed in bliss. Once she'd swallowed, she said, "It feels like I haven't eaten for days, but I always overeat when I'm anxious."

"Anxious?"

"Nervous." She flapped a hand. "Uncertain."

He paused. "With me?" Before she could answer, he asked, "Should I grab a shirt? I should grab a shirt, shouldn't I?" He started to leave the room.

"No, goofus. This is your house and you should be comfortable." Yes, he kept her hyperaware, but she wouldn't tell him so. He was cocky enough already.

"It doesn't bother you?"

He bothered her plenty, in interesting ways. "Burned-down apartment building? Armed men? It's that stuff that put me on edge." Seeing his expression, she grinned. Had he thought she was anxious about crawling into bed with him?

She was, just a little, but it wasn't in her nature to admit to weaknesses. Not when she could help it.

"Glad to hear it." He went back to devouring his sandwich.

She didn't. "You make me grateful, Reyes. Seriously. If not for you, I'd probably be in some expensive hotel right now, scared to sleep and fretting about what to do next."

It took him a second, and finally he accepted her explanation. "You told my sister other stuff had happened. You want to tell me about that while we eat?"

She'd rather not. Not tonight. Then again, the sooner things were resolved, the sooner she'd feel safe again. She picked up her sandwich. "Could it wait until tomorrow?"

"Depends on how critical it is, and if it has anything to do with what just happened."

Always so pragmatic. "The thing is, if I start talking about all that again, the hot shower I just took will be useless. I'll be all tensed up and then I won't be able to sleep. If we wait until the morning, when I'm fresh and the sun is out, it won't feel so overwhelming."

He studied her as if looking for the lie. "You promise there's nothing I need to know tonight?"

"I honestly don't think so. It will wait." As he'd said, she was safe here.

"All right then," he decided, as if he was the one in charge.

Whereas his autocratic attitude used to rub her the wrong way, now it seemed somewhat reassuring. Still, she pretended affront. "Gee, thanks."

"Am I coming on too strong? At this point in my life, it's habit. Nothing I can do about it." He held out his arms. "You get what you get."

"You being an alpha and all that."

"Well, I am, yeah. But also, I know about this stuff, right?"

Stuff being heinous people lacking a heart and conscience?

Apparently, he didn't need confirmation. "One thing

I've learned is that the more info you have, the better you can deal with threats. If that makes me alpha, hey, I've been called worse."

She laughed. "You're nuts, Reyes, but you really do make me feel better."

Smiling with her, he let his gaze travel over her face in what felt like minute detail.

Flustered, she grabbed up a pickle and popped it into her mouth.

Finally he murmured, "I like you like this."

In so many ways she was out of her comfort zone, a common occurrence with Reyes McKenzie. "How's that?"

"Less…antagonistic? Smiling and laughing a little."

Ah. Yeah, she'd been cautious about getting to know him, at least until they'd found the cat outside his gym. "I'm imposing on you," she said. "It would hardly seem fair to be disgruntled about it."

"Is that what you call your attitude at the gym? Disgruntled?"

Her face warmed. Okay, so she hadn't been the friendliest person around. She hadn't been outright rude, either—or had she? "It was different after we found the cat, don't you think?" It had been for her. "I started to trust you a little then."

"Only a little?" He tsked. "When you ran into trouble you called me, so I have to believe you have ultimate trust."

"At least in your skill set."

"And my integrity?"

"Talk about old-fashioned." His serious expression didn't change, so she shrugged. "Sure. I assumed you'd be able to help, and I trusted that you would." He'd reacted faster than she'd expected, and with a lot more violence. Not that she'd complain.

Clearly he had a network of sorts set up with his siblings, yet she didn't know why. That, as much as his over-all carefree outlook on life, kept her guarded.

"Surprised you, didn't I?" He gestured. "With how quickly I got things done, I mean. Bet you weren't expecting that."

"No, I wasn't." Idly she nibbled on her chips, wondering what he was thinking. "Reyes?"

He glanced up. "Hmm?"

"I don't want you to feel responsible for me. Tomorrow morning, I'll work this out, whatever it is. You're not stuck with me or anything like that."

"No worries. I have big shoulders. I don't mind taking on a little responsibility."

He couldn't mean that, not when he'd set up his life as a bachelor. If she believed him, he'd never even brought another woman into his beautiful home. She cleared her throat. "Thank you, but *I* mind."

Eyeing her, he said, "I thought you wanted to wait until morning to sort things out."

"I do."

"There you go."

Exasperated, she gave up. "Fine."

Unlike most people, he didn't chime in to have the last word. He just smiled.

For the next few minutes, they finished eating in comfortable silence. She went to brush her teeth while he put things away. She felt like a slug, but if it had been up to her, she'd have left everything on the table until the morning.

This time when she stepped out of the room, he was waiting for her. "I brushed my teeth, too," he said. "Took my shower earlier before you called. So...you ready to head up?"

Hello, anxiety. She, Kennedy Brooks, was about to sleep with a certifiable hunk. Granted, it wouldn't be a sexual thing. That didn't stop her from imagining it all in a fast-rolling reel of images.

It felt incredibly momentous to nod, to allow him to take her hand, to be led up the spiral stairs and to his room.

"Did you lock up downstairs?"

"Happens automatically, and sensors tell me if anything unlocks." Releasing her, he turned back the quilt. "You're safe here, Kennedy. Swear."

Why did her mouth go dry? She nodded.

"Which side of the bed do you want?"

"Which side do you usually use?"

"The middle?"

"Oh."

He grinned. "Mind if I sleep in my boxers? It's a requirement, you know. All bachelors who live alone either sleep in the raw or in their shorts. I'm offering shorts as a concession to our sleepover. I promise it doesn't make you any more susceptible." He held up his hands. "I respect boundaries, no matter what I'm wearing." He flashed his dimple at her again. "Or not wearing."

Kennedy stared at him, awed that he'd spewed so much nonsense in a single breath. True, sleep pants wouldn't have hindered him in any way. It was just the idea of him wearing the additional barrier to his oh-so-awesome body. Unfortunately, she'd already been rattled by the idea of sleeping in the same bed with him. Rattled, yet very determined not to be alone with her unruly worries.

Now she'd have to deal with him being mostly bare?

He stood there waiting, a look of amused expectation in his eyes, and it was in that moment she realized that he hoped she would protest. Not only that, he assumed she would.

That man was never serious, not even in a life-and-death

situation like they'd experienced only hours ago. Well, she wouldn't give him the satisfaction.

"No biggie," she said, her tone all breezy and unconcerned, while anticipation hitched her heartbeat into a gallop. "I don't want you to be uncomfortable."

"Awesome."

Now she waited…but he didn't remove his jeans. Darn. She'd been braced for the impact of seeing him mostly bare and, given his grin, he knew it.

He surprised her by suggesting, "Since you're being so agreeable, how about we snuggle? That'll be a hell of a lot easier than trying to keep to my own side of the bed." Before she could mentally digest that, he asked, "You like snuggling, right?"

No way would she admit that her life had been devoid of anything even close to snuggling. Get that close to a man? No thanks. Reyes though… "I'm not sure it would be smart to—"

"I've had a shock today," he said with ludicrous gravity. "Don't know about you, but I could use some human contact. Strictly platonic. No hanky-panky." He put his nose in the air. "I'm not that easy, so don't get any ideas."

Crazy Reyes. "How many platonic relationships have you had with women?"

"A few." This time he really did look somber. "Here's the thing, Kennedy. I would never do anything to further stress a woman who was already distressed."

"And you've dealt with distressed women before?"

His voice gentled. "Pretty sure you already know the answer to that."

"I do." She didn't want either of them to get too serious, not right when they were going to bed. Not when she hoped to get some actual sleep. "Snuggling it is. I can keep my hands to myself, no problem. You're tempting, but you're not irresistible."

"You wound me." He gestured at the bed. "Climb in."

Climb was an accurate term, given the expanse of that oversize bed. She chose the side farthest from the door with the idea that if anyone did get into his house, he'd be better equipped to stop them.

Settling on her back against the downy soft pillows, she pulled the quilt up to her chin.

He gave her one long look, then switched off the light. She heard rustling and knew he was stripping down to his shorts. Inhaling deeply through her nose, Kennedy tried to relax.

When the bed dipped, she tensed all over.

"You're like a cobra, ready to strike. Is it safe for me to get comfortable?"

Nodding, she choked out, "Yes."

With great care and a deliberate lack of haste, he scooted closer, put an arm around her waist and drew her into full contact with his body.

Hot. Hard. And, great, he smelled enticing, too.

"Turn to your side." As he said it, he guided her, so that she faced away from him. One thick arm slipped under her head, the other pulled her closer still. "Now sleep."

That had to be a joke! Seconds ticked by, then minutes. His heat sank into her. Her breathing aligned with his, slow and deep. He didn't move, didn't let his hands wander, and gradually she started to relax.

Lethargy crept in.

Sleep beckoned.

Yet she knew he was still awake. She knew he'd stay awake until she dozed off. When more time passed and he hadn't done more than hold her safe and secure, she realized what he'd done. And why.

"Reyes?"

His voice sounded deep and dark behind her. "Yeah?"

"You knew I needed this, didn't you?" Even though she hadn't known it. "That's why you suggested it."

"I don't need a reason to want to cuddle with a hot babe, but yeah, I figured we both could use it."

Kennedy seriously doubted he had any such need, which made the gesture even nicer. And *hot babe*? As if. She knew she made a decent appearance, but *hot* was not a word applied to her.

"I've probably said it a dozen times today, but thank you."

He pressed a soft kiss to her temple. "Sleep."

Relaxing into him, she did just that.

REYES WOKE BEFORE she did, but then, he always woke early. Didn't matter what time he went to bed, or how much sleep he got. The sunrise triggered an inner alarm clock. Sometime during the night, Kennedy had turned to face him, and now one flannel-covered thigh was draped over his junk.

Course he had morning wood.

Luckily she slept through him gently rearranging her. Slipping from the bed, he yawned, stretched and scratched his chest. All the while his gaze remained on her.

It was a unique but not altogether unpleasant feeling to have a woman in his house. In his bed.

In this light, her golden hair looked darker, all the different shades hidden beneath murky shadow. Overall, her honey-blond hair had streaks of lighter blond, brown and even a few hints of red. All natural, he assumed, because she didn't strike him as a woman who spent much time in a salon. He'd yet to see her hair styled in any way. Sleek ponytails, the occasional braid and sloppy topknots were more her speed.

His gaze tracked down her small, sweet body.

The gentle slopes of her breasts barely showed beneath the big shirt. Her arms, one resting limply over her middle, the other turned up by her head, looked delicate and softly rounded in the most feminine way.

Despite all the work she did at the gym, it didn't show. There were no obvious muscles, definitely no bulk. He could say she was toned, without excess weight. Except when it came to her ass.

Plenty of plump curves there.

Not only was Kennedy short, she was very fine boned. Delicate hands, fingers slightly curled, were half the size of his.

Drawing a breath, his attention moved to her parted lips. That mouth was at the top of the list of things he'd noticed about her, with her attitude being first, and her stellar ass being second. Her mouth was usually set in a stern line, at least when talking to him. While trying to improve her speed at striking and kicking, she sometimes pursed her lips. When worried, she chewed her bottom lip.

She displayed a lot of emotions with her mouth, and it never failed to intrigue him.

Hell, *she* intrigued him, in ways no one else ever had.

Why she affected him so strongly, he couldn't say. It had happened the day he met her, when she'd bombarded him with her suspicious nature.

His thoughts traveled back as he recalled it, an occasion he'd locked into his memory bank because it had been so unique.

Prompted by his sister-in-law, who had insisted that Kennedy looked like a woman needing help, Reyes had approached her with the thought of offering his services.

For far too long, she'd simply ignored his presence. When he hadn't budged, she'd had no choice but to acknowledge him.

She hadn't been polite about it.

The way she'd snapped, *What?* amused him now.

At the time, it hadn't been quite so entertaining. *I'm Reyes McKenzie, owner of the gym—*

I know who you are.

She hadn't given her own name, so he'd stood there, waiting.

Until she rolled her eyes. *Kennedy Brooks. I've signed up for a year, but if there's a problem with my membership—*

There's no problem. The only problem he'd noticed was that she didn't know what she was doing. *You need any help?*

No, thank you.

Some invisible force kept him from walking away. *If you want to defend yourself—*

Just getting in shape.

That obvious lie had brought out his most forthright manner. *I don't think so.*

Instead of being impressed with his insight, she'd seemed merely curious. *Why do you say that?*

I've been watching you, he'd admitted, just to see what she'd say.

I noticed you watching, she'd countered, showing her own plainspoken ways.

Reyes had forged on. *I was watching because I see the difference between getting in shape and learning how to fend off attackers.*

Well, that confirms something for me.

For whatever reason, he'd found himself drawn to her. *Yeah? What's that?*

You're not a mere instructor.

Obviously she had her own store of acute insight. *I already told you, I own the gym.*

You're more than a mere gym owner, too.

That straight shot had leveled him, leaving him at a loss. *You think you're the only observant one here? No, Mr. McKenzie, I also notice things.*

If on that day someone had told him that Kennedy Brooks would end up in his bed, and that she'd be there not for sex but for protection… Yeah, he might've believed it. He'd known right off that she was into something, that she had deep secrets.

And that he wouldn't leave her to fend off danger on her own.

Astounding. Not that he'd save someone in need—that was his stock-in-trade. But that he'd feel compelled to make it personal? Only with Kennedy.

Studying her, Reyes smiled.

For a while now, he'd been taking note of Kennedy's every move. What time she came into the gym, how long she stayed, what she did there and how she acted as she went out. Without being too obvious to the casual observer, she was attentive to her surroundings. She had an air of alert wariness.

His sister-in-law was right, of course. Kennedy Brooks had a whole lot of *something* going on. He needed to figure out what.

Silently he headed into the bathroom, easing the door mostly closed behind him. To keep from disturbing her, he left off the light and didn't let the door click shut.

He was standing there at the toilet, lost in thought, when suddenly the light came on, blinding him. Over his shoulder, he looked back to see a sleep-rumpled Kennedy staring at him in mute, openmouthed surprise.

"Hey."

When she tried to speak, nothing came out.

Funny stuff. To fill in the silence, he said, "Had to drain the pipes, you know." She still didn't move, and he couldn't, considering he was in the middle of things. "Don't usually do this with an audience, but if you have some kink I don't know about—"

Sharply pivoting, she almost ran into the wall, staggered around and through the doorway and, all in all, fled the scene.

Smirking, Reyes finished up, then washed his hands, did a quick brush of his teeth and splashed his face. He wasn't about to waste time shaving yet.

Expecting to find her in the bedroom, he stepped out, but the rising sun proved the room was now empty. He cocked an ear and detected sounds in the downstairs bathroom.

What an interesting morning. He'd awakened with sleepy women before, but not in this house, and none who weren't comfortable with the whole scene.

Without dressing, he snatched up his cell phone from the nightstand and started down the stairs in time to hear water running. She was likely doing her own quick cleanup before facing him. Not that she needed to. The whole bedhead look and wrinkled sleep clothes worked on her.

Hell, if he let it happen, he could be half-hard already.

Determined not to spook her, he called out, "Coffee in the kitchen in ten." He didn't get a reply.

In less than one minute, he had the coffee prep done, and the smell of freshly ground beans filled the air. He set out two mugs, sugar and powdered creamer, in case she wanted either, then he took a seat at the table and switched his phone from sleep mode.

It pinged immediately, indicating one or both of his siblings had also awakened early. He saw he'd missed a call from Cade, and hit Redial.

His brother answered with, "Both are dead."

Reyes's brows shot up. To make sure he hadn't misunderstood, he asked, "The dudes I mangled?"

"Bullets to their brains. Good thing they were shot in the forehead and not the back of the head, because the ammo used blew out with an explosion."

Imagining that, he grimaced. "Meaning a shot to the back of the melon would have destroyed their faces, leaving them unrecognizable."

"Exactly." Grimly Cade said, "You need to find out who Kennedy knows that might commit execution-style murder."

"Don't tell me you feel bad for those bastards."

Cade didn't bother replying to that idiot gibe. They were both capable of offing traffickers when necessary, and neither of them would feel an ounce of remorse when it meant women would be spared their abuse. "If they weren't dead when I got there, I might have been able to interrogate them—"

Aka coerce them by whatever means into spilling their guts.

"—or at the very least I could have tracked them. Now there's nothing but cold bodies."

"Cops see you there?"

"Stop trying to provoke me."

Reyes grinned. No, Cade wouldn't be spotted. He was far too slick for that. "So now it's up to Madison to do her thing."

"She was up and at it when I got to Dad's half an hour ago. I'm not sure she went to bed last night."

"Yeah, I know how she is when she starts researching. One thing leads to another."

"And another and another, and she refuses to stop until the trail goes cold."

"If it goes cold." With Madison, that seldom happened. She could uncover stuff the FBI couldn't find. Leads that started in one direction often fanned out in new ways that kept her intrigued.

"Talk to Kennedy," Cade said. "Then let me know what you find out."

"On it." Speak of the devil, Kennedy dragged herself into the room just then. "Later," he said to Cade, disconnecting the call and coming to his feet to pull out a chair for her. The girl looked like a very appealing zombie. That sweet bottom dropped into the seat as if pulled by forceful magnets. She managed to get one hand up in time to catch her head, and then she sat there, boneless, her eyes barely open.

For some ridiculous reason, Reyes felt charmed. "Not a morning person?"

Without answering, her eyes sank shut.

He chuckled and headed for the coffee carafe. It was still sputtering when he pulled it free and filled two mugs. After setting both on the table, he asked, "How do you take it?"

Again without replying, she lifted the mug to her mouth, sipped, sipped, sipped, sighed, and said, "Cream and sugar."

On the verge of laughing, Reyes dumped in a spoonful of sugar, waited while she watched on with heavy eyes, and then dumped in another.

She murmured, "Thank you."

"I have powered creamer or milk."

"Milk, please."

Happy to wait on her, especially since it gave him insight into her preferences, he fetched the milk and dropped in a splash. Lifting one finger, she touched the bottom of the carton, urging him to pour more until the mug was full again.

Before he could use the spoon, she stirred it with her finger, then popped that finger into her mouth with an appreciative "mmm" that made him tighten all over.

Sinking back into his chair, his gaze glued to those lips, he said, "So you know, that's crazy suggestive."

As if she hadn't heard him, she brought the mug to her mouth and gulped. "Oh, *that*." Another long drink, leaving the mug half-empty. "Yeah, that'll help." Sleepy eyes finally focused on him.

He felt it with the same intensity as that sucking lick to her finger. He tried to joke, but the words came out low and gravelly. "You, lady, pack a wallop."

Her lip curled in disdain. "You must be really easy."

"Actually, I'm not." If anything, he was damned selective with his female company. First rule, the woman couldn't have designs on happy-ever-after. Not with him.

Where did that leave Kennedy? Where did he want it to leave her?

"I'm not convinced," she said. Stroking her fingers through her tangled hair, leaving the off-center part totally crooked. She indulged a giant yawn. "I know what I look like. Had to face myself in the mirror."

"After you eyeballed me." Folding his arms on the table, he watched her, then slowly smiled. "There it is. That rosy blush."

"See this?" She tipped her mug at him. "Only half a cup gone. I'll need the rest of this and two more before I verbally spar with you, so take pity on me and stop right now."

The strangest damn thing happened. Affection crowded in, taking the lead over sexual interest. Huh. The anomalous sensation left him confused, but not for long.

This was similar to what he felt with his sister-in-law, only it was different, too, because he didn't want in Sterling's pants.

Kennedy was a whole different story.

CHAPTER FOUR

REACHING OUT, REYES smoothed the hair she'd mussed, liking the softness of it, the warmth. Freed from all restraints, it skimmed just past her shoulders. "All right."

Gulping the rest of her mug, she said, "None of that, either. My sluggish system doesn't know what to make of it."

Tenderness joined the affection. "Here, let me get you a refill."

"My hero."

As he fixed his mug, he asked, "Didn't sleep well?" He couldn't recall her waking, but then, he'd slept soundly himself.

"I don't remember a thing." She sighed heavily. "Odd, right? You'd think something so unfamiliar..."

The words trailed off. Did she mean sleeping with him was unfamiliar? Or sleeping with anyone? To find out, he asked, "Unfamiliar?"

She shook her head. "Doesn't matter how I slept. I always struggle in the morning. For sure, finding a guy at the john jolted my heart, and I'm not sure I've recovered yet."

"Next time," he promised, sliding back into his seat, "I'll go downstairs so you can have the connected bath."

She was just about to sip again, but at his words, she slowly lowered the mug. Wide blue eyes stared at him agog.

"What?"

She blinked twice. "Next time?"

A slipup. He had no idea what would happen next. "Figure of speech."

For two seconds more, she continued to stare at him, then gave an accepting nod and went back to consuming her coffee.

"Breakfast? I can do bacon and eggs, or pancakes."

"I'm not a big breakfast person." She idly turned the mug. "Please don't misunderstand. I get that this was an intrusion on your private space, and it's awkward for me as well, so I'm not hinting."

Damn. Unsure what to say, Reyes just waited.

"What am I going to do today? I mean, will it be safe for me to use my credit cards? I can set up a long-stay hotel, and public transportation will be fine for a while, at least until I can get my car and get things sorted with insurance. But is it okay for me to do that?" She chewed her bottom lip. "Again, not to impose on you, but everything still feels very unsafe to me."

Tackling her points in the same manner she had, he replied, "I know you're not hinting. The number one thing, though, is that you're not alone in this." He wouldn't let her out of his sight if he didn't know it was safe. Cade would find out what he could, and then, he assumed, he'd get her set up somewhere other than the run-of-the-mill hotel scene. "I agree, it's probably not safe. I didn't have a chance to tell you this yet—" and he wasn't sure until this moment that he wanted to tell her "—but the guys who came after you last night are dead."

The coffee mug nearly slipped from her hand. She quickly set it down. "Dead? You hurt them that badly?"

"No. After we left, someone shot them." He touched his forehead. "And whoever it was wanted to make sure they wouldn't recoup."

"Oh, my God."

The ringing of his doorbell further startled Kennedy, who nearly jumped out of her seat.

"Shh. It's okay." He nodded at the security screen mounted on the wall beside a cabinet. "It's just my nosy sister."

She turned and stared. "I thought that was a TV."

"Nope." Pushing back his chair with a resigned sense of his future being forever altered, he said, "Finish up your coffee. I'll be right back."

At first she appeared ready to protest, then she glanced down at her clothes, wrinkled her nose and shrugged. "I'm not ready to move, so no arguments from me."

The second he opened his door, Madison breezed in, her laptop in hand. "What took you so long? Don't try telling me you were in bed because I know Cade already spoke with you. And being you're in your drawers, I assume you haven't showered yet."

"Haven't done much of anything yet." But, yeah, with his sis underfoot, he definitely needed some jeans. "Kennedy is in the kitchen." Which wasn't so far away that she couldn't hear their every word. "Don't spook her while I get dressed."

"I don't spook that easily," Kennedy called back.

That prompted Madison to smile. "I like her."

"You don't even know her."

She hefted her laptop. "Wanna bet?" Without expounding on that, she hurried toward the kitchen, leaving Reyes undecided on which way to go.

Should he run interference between the two women to ensure Madison didn't overstep? Or would it make sense to face the situation in more than snug boxers?

The idea of clothes won out, so he rushed up the steps, taking them two at a time. If he left them alone too long they'd probably start plotting against him.

Grabbing up his discarded jeans from yesterday, he yanked them on, and then did the same with his badly rumpled T-shirt. While zipping and snapping the jeans, he headed back down in time to hear Madison ask, "Who's Jodi Bentley?"

A lengthy pause gave him time to reenter the kitchen before Kennedy finally said, "Just a woman I know."

Having helped herself to coffee, Madison surveyed Kennedy while sipping. "Hmm. I'd say it's more than a mere acquaintance."

Still slumped in her seat, Kennedy shrugged. "We share a similar background, that's all."

"Both of you were trafficked?"

The bald way his sis tossed that out there made Reyes want to muzzle her.

Kennedy, however, merely gave her a long look. "Is this a show of your research skill?"

Pinching the air, Madison said, "A tiny example. There's more." Opening her laptop and quickly typing, she spun it around to show a shadowy figure next to a car.

Breathing a little deeper, Kennedy lost her relaxed posture. "That's Jodi."

"Yup." Touching the screen in the far right corner, Madison said, "And there's your fire."

"Jodi was there?" As if clearing away her shock, Kennedy scowled. "How and where did you get that photo?"

"There's a security camera at the all-night diner on the corner. It picked up the image."

"They gave you their footage?"

"Ah, no." Madison checked a nail. "Not exactly."

Reyes rubbed a hand over his face. Ignoring his sister, he sat down and took Kennedy's hands. "Remember, I told you that Madison is the researcher? Well, she's better than good."

"You didn't say she hacked private businesses."

Not at all bothered, Madison stated, "I hack anyone—when I think there's a good reason."

"You," Reyes said, shooting her a look, "need to pull back a little."

"No." Adamant, Kennedy freed her hands and squared her shoulders. "I want to hear it all. I need to know what I'm up against."

"Well, as to that," Madison said, "you, alone, aren't up against anything." Munificent, she spread out her arms. "You now have some of the best backup you'll ever find, short of calling out the military."

So many emotions stole over Kennedy's features. Shock, resistance, horror... And hope.

Clearing her throat and making a wild grab for composure, she asked, "Why would you want to help me?"

"I don't mean just me, since my siblings will most certainly be involved." Madison elbowed Reyes. "Now would be a good time for you to say you're in."

He held up his hands. "I'm in—but I had already told Kennedy that."

"As to why I'd help, it's because you're eyeball deep in a huge conspiracy, and I can't quite sort it all out. Jodi had something to do with it, but maybe not everything."

"Jodi is a very nice person," Kennedy insisted. "She's also a victim, and sometimes misguided."

"Yes, I have it all in my notes. Is she capable of killing two men? I believe so." She waited for Kennedy to confirm it, and when she didn't, Madison continued, "Do I think it was her? Not necessarily." Rapidly switching the photos, she pulled up another that showed a dark, ancient sedan. "I tracked your friend by the plates on her car. No such luck on this one, but notice the person returning to the car? Dressed all in black. Hand inside his jacket—as if returning a weapon to a holster."

No way could Reyes miss the relief on Kennedy's face. "So you don't think Jodi shot them?"

Madison's smile showed her triumph. "Obviously, you *know* she's capable, which puts to rest the issue of whether or not she could. But did she?" Madison shrugged. "It's also possible she was working with this other person." Again she watched Kennedy.

With no reaction at all, Kennedy waited.

"Or not. We'll have to sort it all out."

Chugging the rest of her coffee, Kennedy stood. "I need to shower, dress and figure out where I'm going, so if you two will excuse me." She didn't wait for a reply, just skirted around the table and headed into the guest room, closing the door with a firm click of the lock.

"Huh." Madison sat back. "Will she scurry out a window?"

Hell, he didn't know if that was her intent. "Not without setting off an alarm." His sister had done exactly what he'd feared. She'd come on too fast, too strong. Sometimes Madison forgot that not everyone lived in a cutthroat world of murder, mayhem and retribution.

Reyes rubbed his eyes, then dragged his hand down his face. "How bad is it?"

"Scale of one to ten? I'd say an eight or nine."

"Damn."

"Yeah. She's in deep doo-doo." Madison did a few more page scrolls. "Many of these places she went were innocuous enough. I was even able to find a few of her recorded speeches." She glanced up. "I sent those to you, as well as a digital copy of her book."

"Her book?"

"A memoir of having been trafficked. Tragic stuff, but she's sold really well."

"What do you title something like that?"

"*No One Is Safe: The Sad Truth of Human Trafficking.* There's a whole chapter on monsters among us. Very insightful stuff. I could almost feel her terror in some of those chapters, but she's also very plainspoken on how she's dealt with it."

His stomach cramped. Yes, he should probably read it to get a better understanding of what Kennedy had gone through. Not that he didn't already know the worst of it. He'd saved enough women and kids, as well as some men, to understand the harsh impact trafficking had on a person.

For that person to be Kennedy? Whole different thing.

"She's a terrific speaker," Madison said. "Very down-to-earth with workable info. She doesn't look like a celebrity, doesn't dress like one, either." Madison brought up an image of Kennedy onstage in jeans, with a nice blouse and blazer. "Because she seems like one of them, young people listen to her. They can relate. On this last trip, she got a lot of questions. Twice, after a lecture, she agreed to meet privately with students."

He'd listen to at least one of the speeches as soon as he could. "Anyone sketchy?"

"I don't think so, at least not obviously so. She also went to dinner with one of the professors at the college." Madison glanced at him. "A man." She went back to her laptop.

Everything masculine in Reyes went on alert. "What man?"

"Like I said, a professor. He seemed okay, but obviously I'll look into him more."

"Yeah, you do that." And in the meantime, he'd find out...what? Kennedy wasn't his. He didn't even want her to be his.

Ignoring his turmoil, Madison continued, "This friend of hers, Jodi Bentley, is more than a little misguided. It appears she's playing vigilante."

Since Reyes and his siblings did the same, he wouldn't condemn her out of hand for that. "Details?"

"She drove one guy off the road. I think she'd planned to kill him, but a cop was nearby and arrived before she could. Turned out the guy had outstanding warrants for kidnapping and suspected murder. Jodi claimed he'd been chasing her, and since it fit, no one questioned it."

"Sounds to me like she did the world a favor." And, yeah, it worried him.

"Another guy went home with her from a bar, and he was never seen again. Friends of his at the bar said she'd come on to him hot and heavy. She claims they went to a park to boink, he got too rough and she walked home. That time she had a black eye, so again, there weren't a lot of questions asked."

"But you're suspicious."

"I've got six or seven more stories like those, but the real kicker?" Again she spun the laptop around for Reyes to see. "This isn't the first fire she's been near."

"Holy shit." Eyes glued to the screen, Reyes took in the grainy image of a young, scrawny woman standing on the sidewalk among other spectators, watching a home go up in flames.

Madison tapped a finger over the woman. "She'd been renting the house down the street for only a month. Right after the fire, she moved."

Tension crawled into his neck, along with a rush of determination to his blood. "You think she'd want to hurt Kennedy?"

"Not really, but something isn't adding up. Is she capable of killing? Yes. Is she familiar with fires? Evidence makes it seem so. Did the poor woman have a horrific background? Most definitely. Let's just say it bears more investigation."

"What about the other guy you saw on the scene? The one who appeared to be tucking away a weapon?"

"Without plates, he's a little more difficult to track."

"Only a little?" Even though Reyes had witnessed his sister's tech magic, there were still times when she left him awed.

With a shrug, she closed her laptop. "I'll be going through other camera feeds to see if I can pick up anything else, but it's doubtful. I've already looked at the most obvious ones without luck."

"Let me know—"

"ASAP if I find anything. Naturally." Then she tipped her head. "So, you and Kennedy."

"No." Reyes pointed at her. "Do *not* do that."

Her secret little smile set off alarm bells in his head. "I hope you like her, because she'll need to stay with you for a while."

His molars clenched. "I'll find her a secure place."

"No place is secure enough if she's alone."

"Bullshit. I can tuck her into a protected facility and have her stay put." Even as he said the words, he knew he was full of it. He didn't want her on her own, alone and afraid.

Even more than that, though, he didn't want his family manipulating him. Sure, Madison might have altruistic motives, but that didn't mean she knew what was best for him.

Arms folded, Madison narrowed her eyes. "Oh? For how long, because this won't get wrapped up anytime soon. You want her 'staying put' for a month? Two?"

He shot back, "You want her to live with me *that* long?"

Clearly disappointed in him, she shook her head. "This

might be a good time to remind you that she lost nearly everything. She has a suitcase of stuff, and nothing else. Any photos, artwork, all her clothes—anything and everything personal, gone."

Shit. Turning his back on his sister, Reyes walked to the kitchen patio doors to look out. Aspens in fall shades of butter yellow, golden amber and crimson red dotted the landscape, mixed with russet scrub oak brush and backlit by a sky made vivid blue by the morning sunrise. This home was his retreat, his and his alone. It was where he worked out his frustrations, sparing the rest of the world—and his family—his occasional foul mood.

"You want me to turn my life upside down for Kennedy." Madison didn't just want it, she expected it.

"If you have a better idea, go for it. Just know that, left on her own, she doesn't stand a chance."

Pressing his forehead to the cool glass, Reyes held silent. He knew what he had to do. Hell, what he *wanted* to do. Once his sister hit the road, he'd get the ball rolling.

That didn't mean he had to embrace the damn implosion of his carefully constructed life.

When a door closed a little too loudly, he turned fast, but realized right away it wasn't an entry door, but the bedroom door.

Which had already been closed. Unless...Kennedy had come out and they hadn't heard her.

But, of course, she would have heard them.

He and Madison stared at each other.

"Oops," his sister said. "Guess the girl has stealth."

"Time for you to go." Otherwise, Kennedy really might try crawling out the window.

Already standing and gathering her purse, Madison said, "No problem. By the way, it's safe enough for her to use her phone, but she shouldn't send any texts or emails detailing her location. Whoever is on her, they're not tech savvy enough, or connected enough, to do much digital tracking, but we can't rule out a hacker. However, she should avoid all areas familiar to her because I have a feeling Jodi, or her goons, might be watching for her to pop back up. It could be dangerous."

"Unless she's with me."

Satisfaction curved Madison's mouth. "Unless she's with you." She came over to kiss Reyes on the cheek. "Good luck."

Knowing he'd need it, he said, "Thanks," and walked her out. After watching her drive away, he knew he couldn't put it off any longer.

It was time to explain things to Kennedy, whether she wanted to hear him out or not.

"Where the fuck is she?" Delbert O'Neil demanded as he paced, occasionally taking a deep draw on his cigarette. Kennedy should have been in her bed. She should now be nothing but cinders. Instead, she was unaccounted for, and that meant she was still a threat to him.

Thanks to her he'd lost everything, including his life savings. Wasn't it enough that he'd had to start over, that for weeks while hiding out he'd gone with little to eat?

By God, it should have been enough.

Yet every time she opened her damn mouth at a high school or college campus, she risked exposing him again.

"We'll find her," Golly said, despite all evidence to the contrary. "If it hadn't been for that damned ape who came after her, we'd have her right now."

Del liked the sound of that even more than her dying in her sleep. He'd get some payback on the bitch...and *then* she could die. He rubbed the snake tattoo on his neck and wondered why it felt like a tightening noose.

Twice, Kennedy had done this to him.

"Relax," Golly ordered, his twisted smile full of antici-pation. "I have a few street informants watching for her to pop up. She can't lie low forever. Even if she tries that, eventually she'll have another speaking gig and we'll be able to grab her then. That, or else Jodi will lead us to her. She's as good as yours." He prodded his tongue through a hole where two teeth should be, repulsing Del. "And the other one will be mine."

DRIVEN BY PRIDE—stupid, foolish pride—Kennedy continued stuffing her few belongings back into the suitcase.

She had to leave. Of course she did.

Reyes had made it clear that he didn't want her here. She had no right to further disrupt his life. Not only that, but his sister made her uneasy. Madison was tall, slim, incredibly beautiful—just like her blasted brothers—and she was every bit as cocky, too. Maybe not with physical ability, but the woman understood her skill. A skill she had used without apology to invade Kennedy's life.

Did the whole damn family have to be overachievers? Were they all lethal, even Madison?

She'd met Cade a few times at the gym, and it took no more than a single glance to know he owned any situa-tion he was in. The man was even taller than Reyes, so he had to be six-five. His sweeping gaze missed nothing, and calm confidence could be his middle name.

Whereas Reyes was brash, Cade was quietly in control.

And Madison was cheerfully certain.

Who *were* they anyway?

The tap at the door made her stiffen. There'd been sev-eral times in her life when she'd been horribly lost. Very alone. Frantic and uncertain what to do.

This was quickly turning into another one.

Girding herself, she walked to the door and opened it with what she considered admirable nonchalance. "I'm almost done."

His frowning gaze went over her and then to the bed, where her suitcase lay open. "Almost done with what?"

"Getting ready to leave." The nervousness sounded in her tone, though not overly. "Would you like to drive me somewhere, or should I call...someone?" She had no idea who she could call.

A muscle ticked in his jaw. Stepping in, he filled the spare bedroom with his size, his presence, the sheer magnetism of him. "Let's talk."

"I don't think so, Reyes. Truly, I appreciate all you've done. You've gone above and beyond, and it's time I quit cowering and instead acted like an adult."

Folding his arms, he leaned against the door frame. "Pretty sure you always act the adult. I've never seen otherwise. At least, not until shit went sideways, and you're not equipped to deal with it, honey."

"Yes, I know." *He* was equipped, but also unwilling. "I'll work it out."

Not moving, he asked, "How?"

Why did he have to press her? Going back to her suitcase, she jammed in the overflowing clothes and started to zip it shut. "I'll hire someone."

"No."

"No?" Temper spiking, she turned on him. "What do you mean, no? It's not up to you."

"Sure it is." He pushed away from the door frame.

Oh, hell. Kennedy backed up, which effectively froze him in his tracks, at least for a few seconds.

Quickly recovering, he strode forward. "I would never hurt you, so don't do that."

"Then quit crowding me." A dumb thing to say, since he was still a few feet away.

"This," he bit out, leaning into her space until their noses almost touched, "is crowding you."

His hazel eyes glittered gold, fascinating her. She put one hand flat to his chest and said succinctly, "Back off."

To her surprise, he did, jerking around and running a hand over his hair. "You're not going anywhere, all right? That's just dumb."

"You arrogant dick."

He turned again, this time presenting a slow grin. "What did you call me?"

"You heard me well enough." Where had she left her laptop? Her phone? "I know this is all a joke to you, and I'm aware I come off as less than savvy in dealing with the scum of the earth, but I've survived the horrors of traf-ficking, and I'll figure this out, too. The almighty Reyes McKenzie can tell me goodbye with a clear conscience."

Back to being the arrogant dick, he stared at her. "That's even dumber than talking about leaving."

For the love of... Taking a stance, she asked, "Which part?"

"All of it, but especially the part where I think you're not savvy. Saying something dumb and being dumb are two very different things. Trust me, I have no illusions about your intelligence."

Well, that was something at least. "Good. So you know I can deal with—"

"Nope."

His attitude infuriated her, and she stayed chill only by an act of sheer willpower. She even got her stiff lips to smile. "Again, it's not up to you."

"We agree you're smart, right? So," he continued before she could say a single word, "a smart woman wouldn't budge from where it's safe."

"Maybe not, but a proud woman wouldn't stay where she's not wanted." She lifted her chin. Let him deal with *that.* "I clearly heard you say you could stick me somewhere safe. Let's go with that." She unfolded her arms to hold them out in concession. "I promise I will stay put. You won't even have to twist my arm."

Reyes worked his jaw. "Here's the thing. You don't really know what I want, since I didn't know until just this second. All that bullshit earlier with my sister was just me blustering." He moved in again, this time taking her shoulders.

Why did he have to be so big? Damn near a foot taller than her. And *solid.* Good God, the man was like chiseled stone, only warm.

"I want you here, Kennedy. In fact, the only problem is that I want you a little too much."

Her eyes flared. "What's that supposed to mean?"

"I'm a dude. You're a woman. I'm sure you'll figure it out."

She shook her head. "A big fat *no* on that."

"Yeah, I already ruled it out, too, you being dependent on me and all."

"I am *not*…." No, she wouldn't lie. At the moment, she was dependent…somewhat, damn it.

"It wouldn't be ethical. And then, of course, there's your background." He eyed her. "You still struggle with that? I'm guessing you do. Who wouldn't, right? But you have to know the last thing I'd want to do is make you uncomfortable, or put you on the spot. And never, not under any circumstances, would I pressure you."

"You're pressuring me now."

"To stay." His hands kneaded her shoulders. "I meant

sexually. To keep you safe, I'll definitely pressure you if I need to." He bent his knees a little to look more directly into her eyes.

Damn him, he was potent. In fact, she found herself leaning into him a bit.

"I'll do whatever it takes then. I want you to know that, okay? Sometimes that might mean me giving orders."

"I don't think so."

"And sometimes you'll have to follow those orders."

"Like hell."

"But I'll always have a good reason, and hey, if necessary, I'll apologize once we're safe again." He tried one of his charming smiles on her. It was more effective than not. "Deal?"

Unable to help herself, Kennedy slumped forward until her forehead came into contact with his firm chest. *Holy smokes, he smelled good.* "I had just resigned myself to leaving."

Carefully his arms closed around her. "I know. Have I convinced you to stay?"

Still inhaling his delicious scent, she asked, "So now you're giving me a choice?"

"I'm not into kidnapping, so maybe."

The "maybe" made her laugh. He was so outrageous. She lifted a hand to rest against his shoulder. "I'm scared and, as you said, I'm smart enough to know I'm out of my depth. So, yes, I'd like to stay." *For now.* "I haven't yet locked down any new engagements, so my schedule is open."

"You were taking time off? A vacation?"

"Actually, I was only going to work on my next book. I can set up in here so I'm out of your way, okay? You won't even know I'm here."

He snorted. "Trust me, I'll know." His palm moved up

and down her spine, both soothing her and making her far too aware of him as a man. "You're writing another book?"

"With all the digging your sister did, you surely know that already."

He tried to lever her back so he could see her face, but when she resisted, he hugged her instead. "Yeah, I knew you'd published one book. Didn't know you were starting another."

"The results of trafficking go on and on." She still wasn't over it. She didn't think she'd ever be over it. "For anyone recovering, it might be helpful to know the resources that are available, the things I've done to help me feel more in control of my life, and to know that difficulty sleeping isn't uncommon."

He pressed his mouth to her temple. "You slept all right last night."

Because she'd been with him. Likely the difference was in not being alone, but telling him that might obligate him to keep her close each night, and she wouldn't intrude on him more than she had to. "Usually I hear every little sound, and once I do, I can't just assume it's the house settling or the wind stirring branches. I can't assume it's anything less than an intruder."

"Even though it never is?"

She went still. Knowing she had to tell him soon didn't mean she was ready to do it now. Of course, an astute guy like Reyes didn't miss much.

This time his hold on her shoulders was too firm, and she couldn't stop him from pressing her back the length of those long arms. His probing stare dissected her. Grim, he demanded, "When?"

CHAPTER FIVE

GOING OVER THE details made her nerves jangle, adding a quiver to her voice that she hated. "A month ago, I heard someone on the balcony off my apartment." That struck her with new awareness, and she gave a humorless laugh. "Or rather, what used to be my balcony. I got up to look, as I always do." Unable to hold his gaze, she stared down at his chest and whispered, "There was a man there. He'd just climbed over the railing."

"Damn." Gathering her against him once more, Reyes gently rocked her. "He didn't get in?"

Kennedy shook her head. Retelling this was so much easier while Reyes held her. "I had my gun in my hand—"

Back she went again so he could do another long stare. "You have a gun?"

She gave him a "duh" look. "That night all I had was a small .38 with a laser pointer, but now I also have a Glock." She blew out a breath. "Stupidly, I'd left my phone on the bedside table. All I could do was stand there staring at him, the gun aimed, the red dot on his chest until he smiled at me and vaulted back over the rail."

Again he hugged her. "You called the cops?"

"Yes. They came right away, took a description and looked around. In the end, they wrote it off as a likely burglar and promised to drive by often for the rest of the night, but I couldn't stay there. I went to a hotel, and the next morning I bought additional security stuff for all around the apartment. Alarms for everything. Bars for the balcony door and windows." She cleared her throat. "I also bought a screamer—one of those little handheld things where you press a button and it makes a loud, piercing noise? Plus, I got a stun gun."

His mouth firmed in disapproval, but what did she care? She'd needed protection, and she couldn't rely on anyone else.

"The cops didn't know your history or they'd have—"

"What? Protected me from the boogeyman? We both know it isn't that easy."

He smoothed a hand over her hair. "Yeah, we do." Glancing at her suitcase, he asked, "You have the weapons on you?"

"Yes." She never went anywhere without them, not even when she traveled. It was why she always checked her bags.

Moving to the suitcase, she opened it again, lifted aside a sweater and a pair of jeans, and removed the heavy firearm case that held her guns. Gingerly she set them out.

Not so gingerly, Reyes lifted them with an expert touch, looking them over. "Plenty of ammo?"

"Yes." She lifted away the egg crate foam to show the bullets beneath.

"Where's the stun gun?"

"In my purse now. I got it out of my luggage once I left the airport, before I got my ride." Exiting the room, she went up the spiral staircase on light feet to reach his bedroom. Her heart beat a little faster, now for entirely different reasons.

Reyes came in behind her. He must have returned her weapons to the case, because he was empty-handed. It didn't surprise her that he hadn't made a single sound on his approach. The man moved with stealth even when there was no reason. It seemed to be an intrinsic part of his psyche.

Being in a bedroom with him again caused her to babble. "Here it is." She put her hand in the grip to show him how she'd use it. Much like brass knuckles, it allowed her a firm grip. "I like the way this one is made. Instead of having to poke someone with a long stick, I just squeeze the handle and it works, plus it has a really bright flashlight. See the spikes? Those can be removed, but why would I?"

"Never know when you might need to gouge someone."

The deadpan way he said that put her on edge.

Carefully, he closed his hand over hers and relieved her of the weapon. "Tell me what else is going on, okay?"

She probably should, but first she needed out of the bedroom. Hurrying past him, she trotted back down the stairs and...wasn't sure where to go. Her gaze bounced around, taking in her options. The kitchen, then.

Her butt had just settled in a chair when Reyes appeared in the doorway. "So." Lifting one brow, he asked, "Are we done racing around the house?"

Feeling like a fool, Kennedy nodded.

He gestured at the chair opposite. "If I grab a seat, you won't bolt out of the room?"

"No." At least, she hoped she wouldn't.

With his hands raised to look less threatening—the ass—he came forward and eased into a chair. "I didn't mean to spook you."

Kennedy snorted. "You didn't." The memories did. The harsh reality of the threat did. The insidious fear did. Best to get it all said. "A few weeks after the prowler on my balcony, there was another incident in the grocery parking lot. Middle of the day, other people around." Her mouth went dry, remembering the brazenness of the attack. "I was loading my groceries into the back seat and a guy asked for my cart. I said sure, took the last bag, and while my hands were full he started shoving me into the back seat. Another guy was already getting behind the wheel. My car is keyless and the fob was in my purse over my shoulder, so he started the engine with no problem."

Something violent glittered in Reyes's hazel eyes. "Clearly you got away."

"I tried to scream." Her throat grew tight, so tight she couldn't seem to get enough air. "But he put his hand over my mouth and I thought he would crush my jaw. I dropped the bag I was holding. A can of peas fell onto my lap."

Quietly, calmly, Reyes listened, his gaze locked with hers as if to offer silent support.

"I used that can to bash in his face."

"Yes!" When she startled at his exclamation, he moderated his tone. "Good for you, honey."

For some reason, his praise made her feel better. "Blood went everywhere. It looked like I'd fractured his eye socket. His nose was crushed." She swallowed heavily. "I hit him again."

Slowly Reyes smiled. "Good girl."

At any other time, that patronizing phrase might have offended her. Now? It just felt nice to know he approved of her actions.

She took pleasure in saying, "*He* screamed, loudly enough to draw plenty of attention. I quickly joined him, and soon people were swarming around us. A black car screeched up next to mine, the two of them jumped in, and then they were gone. The whole thing probably lasted less than three minutes, but God, Reyes, it felt like a lifetime. I knew what would happen, what they would do, and that made it worse."

"I'm so damn proud of you," he said with gruff sincerity. Slowly, he slid his hand, palm up, across the table. Offering her his touch. A connection.

How could she resist? Clearly she couldn't, so she placed her much smaller hand in his and was immediately engulfed in his comforting strength.

"You know how hard it is to keep your head when being attacked, but you did it, Kennedy. You fought hard, and sometimes that can make all the difference."

Nodding, she squeezed his hand. "Or no difference at all."

The truth of that hung between them.

Watching her, he lifted her hand to his mouth and kissed her knuckles. "All those workout sessions at my gym are starting to make sense."

No reason to fudge the truth any longer; Reyes now knew it all. "I know I'm small, and not all that strong, but there are ways to slow a man down, right? That's what I was trying to learn. I can't best a man, but if I can thwart him, then I'd at least have a chance to get away."

He seemed to come to some decision. "No more talk about leaving here, okay? Not until we have this all wrapped up."

"That could take a long time." Or it might never happen.

"Nah. Like Madison said, you have a team at your back now. So let's come to some agreements." He turned as businesslike as Reyes could. "One, you'll stay here, and no more talk of leaving. Done and done. Two, I'll get your car for you, but you have to give me your word you won't take off."

She didn't want to go anywhere alone until she knew it was safe, so she shrugged. "No problem." The thought of ever again being held in captivity paralyzed her with fear.

"Three, we'll spend the next few days replacing things you lost, starting in about an hour. I'll be your escort-slash-bodyguard-slash-whatever, and you'll be patient with me. Agreed?"

Her mouth twitched. "You're not so hard to be around, now that I know you better."

Disbelief narrowed his eyes. "Yeah, okay. Believe that if you want."

Just by being himself, he'd lifted her mood. "Which part?"

"That you know me."

Ah, so he didn't deny being difficult. "You're still an enigma?"

"A deadly wraith in the night, capable of almost anything." He grinned.

"Almost anything, huh?"

The grin morphed into a tender smile. "I'm not capable of hurting you, Kennedy. I need you to know that."

Just as quietly, she whispered, "I do."

Satisfied by that, he said, "Four, when I have to be at the gym, you'll go with me. I can instruct you so you'll know some lethal shit, and when Cade is around, he can give you some pointers, too."

A workable solution, except that… "I can't keep up that pace for eight hours."

"I know. I have an office there with a private bathroom, comfy chair, secure browser and a small fridge. It'll be yours to use until I wrap up my day."

She honestly didn't know what to say, so she settled for, "Thank you."

"No thanks necessary. I do what I do, when and how I want to do it." He released her to stretch, which, yes, made her stare. He said, "I need to shower and shave and all that. Start a list of anything you might need. We'll knock off what we can today. First, though, we'll stop somewhere for breakfast. You might not be a fan, but I always put fuel in the tank before I tackle the day."

"All right." Thinking out loud, she said, "I have a pen and paper in my laptop case. I'll get started on that right now."

"Hey." He touched her arm. "You can use your laptop, and even your phone if you want. But don't contact Jodi. Let's see if she reaches out to you."

"She *is* a friend, you know."

"If you say so, but she was there at the fire, so why hasn't she reached out, if for no other reason than to make sure you're okay?"

"I don't know, but I'm sure there's an explanation." She really needed to make it clear about poor Jodi.

Reyes didn't give her a chance. "We'll discuss it tonight, maybe on a conference call with Cade and Madison so we can put our collective heads together. How's that sound?"

She wasn't at all keen about the idea. Yes, she trusted Reyes, but there was so much she didn't know about him, and it seemed that every new thing she learned only created more questions.

As he started out of the room, she realized he wasn't waiting for a reply anyway. "Make yourself at home. I'll be right back."

Then he was gone, and she was left thinking about Reyes. About all he was doing for her.

And about him naked in a shower.

Things were going to get horribly awkward, and she couldn't even blame Reyes. It was her own fault—for finding him so fascinating.

CADE CALLED WHILE they were still on the road, and since he wanted to talk about Jodi, Reyes put the phone on speaker. "I told Kennedy we'd go over this tonight."

"It needs to be now," Cade said. "Jodi was scoping out the gym this morning."

The hell she was! When Reyes glanced at Kennedy, he saw the same surprise on her face that he felt. "Was she watching for Kennedy?"

"That's the safe assumption. Maybe she's hoping to touch base with her."

Kennedy was already shaking her head. "I never told Jodi about the gym. If she knows, it's because…"

Reyes didn't need her to finish that thought. "She's been keeping tabs on you? I'm liking this chick less and less."

Madison interrupted, saying, "Be nice, Reyes. She's Kennedy's friend, and she was once a victim."

Very quietly, Kennedy whispered, "Being a victim isn't something that stays in your past."

Reyes gave her a sharp look. "Meaning?"

Kennedy gave a slight lift of her shoulders. "You recover, you regain your strength—but you also learn, which means you don't forget, you rarely let down your guard, and trust doesn't come easy."

"My wife would very much disagree with you," Cade said.

Kennedy's eyes widened. "Your wife was—"

"Yes." He paused. "And she's the strongest person I know."

"I'm sorry, but strength doesn't obliterate the aftereffects. We push on," Kennedy explained. "We survive, and we put a pretty face on things, but for the rest of our lives we know exactly what can happen. Most people never give the risks a thought. They go through each day with the easy assumption that they're fine, that they'll always be fine, with no grasp of how quickly their safe, normal existences can be destroyed." She drew a breath. "But I know. Those who have survived it know. And we don't let ourselves forget."

The sobering words brought down a repressive silence to hang thick and heavy in the air. Reyes reached over to clasp her knee. She covered his hand with her own.

Connected, he thought. He and Kennedy connected in ways he never had with any other woman. Damn, that was so unusual, it sort of shook him.

"You're right," Cade murmured. "It changes a person."

Reyes asked, "Is that what happened with Jodi?"

"Yes." Kennedy stroked over his hand, tracing along the hard ridges of his knuckles, then down to the sensitive skin between. The provoking touch didn't feel deliberate, but rather a necessary distraction to her own thoughts. "I met her four years ago, when she was only twenty. I'd had one of my first speaking engagements at a college, and afterward, as I was leaving, I sensed her following me. She was this sullen figure, half-hidden under an oversize hoodie. I knew something was horribly wrong. It was there when her eyes met mine, and how she looked at me."

"How was that?" Reyes asked.

"With desperation."

He appreciated that his brother and sister stayed quiet so Kennedy could forget they were listening in. Not that she would. She was too sharp for that, and far too aware of her surroundings. Their silence offered only the illusion of privacy.

"I rarely take risks with other people, regardless if they're men or women, young or more mature."

"You shouldn't." Reyes found her touch incredibly distracting. "Evil has no gender or age."

"I know." Her explorations trailed along his thumb. "But something about Jodi was different. More vulnerable. She needed me, so I invited her to lunch. She doesn't trust most people, either, and still she came with me, and we ended up talking for two hours. I got the distinct impression that she'd mostly given up on life."

"If that's so, why was she at the college?"

"My guess is that she was looking for something, anything, to give her purpose so she wouldn't dwell as often on what she'd gone through." Giving up her intent study of his hand, Kennedy shifted away and crossed her arms. "That's why I took up speaking, you know. It makes me feel like I'm helping."

"Is that also why you write?"

"It's cathartic," she said. "Spelling it all out helps me understand it, and gives me a sense of control. Jodi hadn't found a direction yet. She was still floundering in her fear and hatred. Once we became friends, I think it helped her."

"You're not sure?" Reyes asked.

"Jodi disappears for long stretches. Sometimes a month will go by before I hear from her. Then I'll get texts for three days in a row. I just never know with her."

"So," Cade said, "we can't be certain why she was checking out the gym."

"She was stealthy about it," Madison said. "Hanging out across the street, trying not to be obvious."

Kennedy stared at Reyes. "There have been times when Jodi thought I was in trouble, and she acted without discussing it with me."

"Example?" Cade prompted.

"One time after I'd spoken with this gigantic group, a guy asked me out. He was loud and obnoxious about it, saying he'd help me through all my troubles, like I was a joke." Her mouth firmed. "Overall, I ignored him. Things like that happen sometimes. A lot of people get uncomfortable with my story. Guys try to laugh it off. Girls make snide comments about it, as if I'd brought it on myself."

"Immature, clueless brats," Madison commented, though not with any heat.

Kennedy agreed. "They're young and dumb, and thankfully, reality hasn't yet knocked them down. What they say doesn't matter much to me."

Much? In that moment, Reyes wanted to protect her from everyone and everything, even mouthy college knuckleheads.

"Jodi takes the insults to me more personally. Apparently, she was there that day, and she waited until she found the boy—"

"Man," Cade corrected. "If he's college age, he's a man and should behave like one."

Kennedy's amused smile slipped into place. "I get the feeling that being a man might mean something different to you and Reyes."

Reyes couldn't deny that. His father had treated him like a man before he'd ever become a teenager. From a young age he'd been taught that stupidity wouldn't be tolerated and cruelty was an unforgivable sin, most especially where women were concerned.

"Anyway," Kennedy said, exasperated with them all now that his siblings were speaking up. "Later that night, she caught him alone and hit him in the back of the head. He ended up with a concussion and twelve stitches."

Damn. Reyes didn't blame Jodi for wanting to defend her friend, but that was a pretty harsh way to go about it.

"You know it was her?" Madison asked.

"I didn't, not at first. The police contacted me after some of the other students told them the guy had been hassling me. I was at the hotel restaurant having dinner, so they knew I hadn't done it. At the time I didn't have a clue what might have actually happened. Later, though, when I thought about it, I got a... I don't know. A hunch?

I contacted Jodi the next morning and found out she'd been in the audience when she told me how much she'd enjoyed my talk."

Reyes frowned. "Does she live near the college where you were speaking?"

"Honestly, I'm not sure where she lives. She seems to travel a lot."

Maybe, Reyes thought, she traveled to follow Kennedy. Creepy. "You asked her flat out about the guy?"

"Yes. She didn't confirm it, but neither did she deny it. Basically she repeated back to me one of the things I often say in my lectures—that no one has the right to treat you as if you don't matter."

None of them said anything for far too long.

Finally Madison spoke up, directing her comment to Reyes. "I've put a few safeguards in place. When she comes near the gym again—and she will—we'll know it right away."

"I suggest the direct approach," Cade said.

Kennedy stiffened. "What does that mean?"

"I'll go up to her and find out what she's doing." Reyes lifted a shoulder. "No biggie."

"Absolutely not!" Turning to half face him, Kennedy insisted, "I'll call her and—"

"No," Reyes said.

At almost the same time, Cade and Madison echoed him.

"If she's involved in the fire," Madison explained, "our way is better."

"And if she isn't, no harm done," Cade said.

Kennedy gave him a dark frown. "You and I will discuss this later."

"My brother is smart, Kennedy. You can't strong-arm him just by getting him alone."

Reyes grinned at Cade's observation. Would Kennedy try to badger him into doing things her way? Probably.

Less blunt than Cade, Madison said, "We really do know what we're doing. Trust us, okay?"

Kennedy's eyes narrowed. "Actually, I have no idea what you're doing. Now might be a good time to tell me."

Of course, no one spoke up. Grunting, Reyes muttered, "Thank you for nothing" to his brother and sister. "I'll handle it, okay?"

"Sounds like a plan," Madison said. "Enjoy your day."

"Don't go overboard," Cade warned. "And keep me posted."

With the call ended, Reyes put his mind to choosing a place for breakfast. He scanned the streets, looking for somewhere that wasn't too busy.

"Well?" Impatience crackled in that single word Kennedy threw at him.

How come everything she said or did made him want to grin? For such a small woman, she sure packed a lot of attitude. Even in such an untenable position—with thugs after her, a sketchy friend and the loss of her possessions.

"How about I give you the broad strokes?" Hopefully, that would appease her. No way could he share the nitty-gritty. Other than immediate family and, of course, Bernard, his father's assistant, chef, butler—and now cat kidnapper—no one knew the details of their operation. Yes, Cade had confided in Sterling, but only because he'd fallen in love with her.

Even thinking it made Reyes curl his lip.

He and Cade were alike in many ways, but they also had a lot of differences. For one thing, Reyes had no intention of getting married. Not now, maybe not ever.

"If you're thinking of lies to tell me, don't bother."

Her derision tickled him even more. He was grateful to

see that all the turmoil hadn't dented her dominant persona. "Nah, I wasn't. Just ruminating on my life, I guess." He glanced at her, saw she looked more confused than ever, and laughed. "So here's the big picture. My family works to rescue trafficked victims, sometimes with the law, sometimes not." *Often* not, but yeah, he probably shouldn't go into that yet. "It's like a task force, covering a lot of ground. Rescue, counsel, financial assistance, all that."

Cutting right to the chase, Kennedy asked, "Have you killed anyone?"

Damn, way to throw a guy off guard. "I'm not sure that's part of the broad strokes."

"I'd like to know."

"Yes?" He rushed to add, "Only assholes who really deserved it."

The funniest thing happened. Instead of being outraged, Kennedy gave him a firm nod, and whispered, "Good."

Whew. What a relief to know she wasn't horrified.

Then she said, "Of course, you'll understand that Jodi feels the same way." She gave him a placid smile. "She feels everyone she's hurt also deserved it."

Everyone she'd hurt? Well, hell. The day just totally soured.

EVEN AS KENNEDY wondered what Jodi might have gotten into, she felt the need to defend her. Dread warred with loyalty. If Reyes knew it all, would he feel honor bound to see Jodi locked away? She'd never be able to bear that.

With the hope of making Reyes really understand, she formulated her thoughts. Luckily, Reyes didn't press her. Not yet anyway. He waited until they were seated on the terrace of a trendy local restaurant outside Ridge Trail before ramping up the questions.

"Let's hear it, but keep your voice low."

Looking around, Kennedy wondered who he thought might hear. It was a cool morning and few people were lured by the mountain views. Those who had ventured outside were at the other end of the terrace.

"Isn't it amazing how quickly people grow accustomed to things? It's absolutely beautiful out here, yet the crowd is inside." She shook her head.

"Have you gotten used to the scenery?"

"No. I'm still in awe whenever I look at the mountains."

"Me, too." He waited while a young man brought them water, offered coffee and left behind menus. "You shouldn't drink so much caffeine."

"I lost everything last night. No bitching about my coffee."

He grinned. Without perusing the menu, he asked, "Know what you want to eat?"

She'd never been here before, but obviously he had. As she skimmed the selection, the pricing staggered her. "Um…you remember that I'm currently penniless, right?"

His expression softened. "We'll get that sorted out later, okay? For now, it's my treat."

Glancing at the French toast, she winced. On top of his offer to replace her necessities, the meal seemed extravagant. "Not to be crass, but covering my expenses—for now—won't strain your finances?"

"Nah. It's all good."

Giving up on the concern, she laid aside the menu. Fine. He'd chosen the place, and he seemed familiar with it, so why should she grovel over breakfast? "Yes, I know what I want."

"Perfect. I'm starved." He lifted a hand and within seconds the young man was back.

Kennedy ordered the French toast, fresh berries and bacon.

Reyes requested the same, and added scrambled eggs and home fries.

How he stayed so ripped while consuming so much food, she couldn't imagine. Of course, he ran a gym and was physical all day long, which probably explained it.

"Now, before our food gets here, spill the beans. What nefarious stuff has Jodi gotten into? Don't fudge the truth or leave out anything. I need to know what I'm up against."

Yes, to be fair, he needed to know everything. After a fortifying sip of her coffee, she cleared her throat. "First, let me explain something about Jodi, okay? Unlike the place where I was held—" and basically rented out "—Jodi was outright bought and owned by a man who was, from what she's said, pure evil."

"Any man who participates in trafficking is evil." He held up a hand. "Still, I get your meaning."

"There were times he closed Jodi in a small room in the basement. It was his idea of punishment if she wasn't performing up to his standards. Once, he left her there for two days. No food or water. By the time he let her out, she said her spirit was broken. She only wanted to eat, bathe—and to never go back to that room." Fingers of red-hot rage clenched around her windpipe, forcing her voice to a ragged whisper. "No matter what she did, though, he found reasons to lock her away again and again. She never knew if she'd be punished for an hour, a day, or if he'd leave her there to die. Jodi said that was the worst torture of all. Not knowing."

As he often did, Reyes reached out to her. His strong fingers closed oh-so-gently around her forearm, then trailed down until he could hold her hand in his own.

It astounded her that his touch helped so much. For a second there, she'd gotten lost in the details of what Jodi had suffered.

Putting her left hand to her chest, she counted her heart-beats. The combined facts that she was alive and that Reyes planned to keep her that way helped her to find her composure.

"You do that often," he said softly.

She'd been staring blindly at the table. At his observation, her gaze snapped up to his.

When he nodded at her left hand, she realized his meaning.

Never before, not even to Jodi, had Kennedy explained the small gesture that signified so much. It was private to her, central to her struggle with a past that still haunted her today.

"Containing your heart?" he asked, his tone still amazingly gentle.

With his hand offering safety, his hazel eyes showing so much understanding, the words just came out. "I'm feeling my heart beat."

His thumb moved over her fingers, but he didn't say anything.

"It's dumb," she said, feeling a little self-conscious.

"No, it's not. Anything that reminds you you're alive is a good thing."

Oh, wow. He actually got it. An emotional tsunami hit her. She couldn't speak, so she nodded, and Reyes didn't press her. He continued to watch her, almost like he'd never seen a woman before—or maybe like she fascinated him in some way.

A bizarre way? She hoped not.

Just then, their food arrived, relieving her of the awkward moment. He took care of thanking the server, commenting that it smelled good, asking for more coffee and, in the process, giving her a much-needed moment to clear her head.

When they were alone again, she said, "Thank you."

He chided her with a half smile. "No more of that, remember?"

"I can't help it." He was just that wonderful. Far more than she knew a man could be, especially a big buff alpha like him. "You can't know how much I appreciate… everything." Most especially the way he grasped her innermost thoughts.

"Does that make it better?" he asked, shaking out her napkin and leaning over to put it in her lap, overall pretending that she wasn't frozen still. "Talking about it, I mean."

"I don't know." The speaker in her came forth, and while she cut into her French toast, she began to ramble. "I've never really talked about my personal experiences. What I share in my speeches is a general impression that applies to a lot of people, in a lot of situations. The specifics of what happened to me… I've put some of them in my book. Writing things and saying them aloud are very different."

"Maybe you need to talk about them more." He forked up a bite of egg. "With me."

Yes, with him, she probably could. From the start, Reyes had been different. Cocky, yes, but with the ability to back it up. Assured, but in a very nice, take-charge way.

Concerned, and that was what had worried her most. She'd worked hard to regain her life, and Reyes saw right through the facade to the hyperaware, ever-vigilant, still very afraid girl who knew that, alone, she didn't stand a chance against the cruelty of the world.

CHAPTER SIX

THE IDEA OF sharing her innermost thoughts, her basest fears and most humiliating moments left her shaken, so she deflected. "I thought you wanted to know about Jodi."

"That, too." As usual, Reyes let her off the hook. "Go ahead and eat. We're not in a rush. I have the whole day free."

No problem there. She was finally hungry, and the breakfast really was delicious. In between bites, she shared some of Jodi's characteristics. Like her brusque insistence of going it alone. Her staunch defense of any woman injured by a man. The very meager way she lived.

"How long was she with the bastard?"

"A few months. She's never said exactly, but I know it was long enough that she'd given up hope. Unlike my situation, she was alone. At least I had Sharlene and the other women. We made a unique sort of family, weird as that sounds."

"Not weird at all. Even in terrible circumstances, there's comfort in numbers."

See, how could she not be impressed with his insight? "Jodi was alone, mistreated, desperate, and I hope you don't blame her for—"

"If she killed the fucker, I'll cheer her on."

"She did." Once the blurted words left her mouth, Kennedy went still, anxiously waiting to see how Reyes would react. He surprised her by *not* reacting.

Around eating, he asked, "How'd she do it?"

This was Jodi's secret, and Kennedy had never shared it before. "You can't tell anyone."

"Okay." He nodded at her food. "You need to eat, hon."

No, she wasn't buying it. "Just like that? You won't say anything to Cade or Madison?"

"No reason. They already suspect she's crossed a few lines, and if Madison wants to know details, she'll figure it out." He rolled one shoulder. "Just know that you never have to question my word. If I can't keep something secret, I'll say so. If I say I will, then I will."

Had she offended him? She didn't think so. It felt more like he wanted to reassure her. Again. "I wasn't questioning you, not really."

"Good. So how'd she do it? I'm guessing he didn't leave any weapons around."

"No. He'd had weapons, some that he'd used to threaten Jodi, but they were always locked away where she couldn't get them."

Right up until the tide had turned.

Her heart beat a little faster. Nervousness did that to her. Reyes might treat this little convo as no big deal, but to Jodi, it would be the biggest betrayal imaginable. Unfortunately, Kennedy wasn't sure what else to do. "The room he put her in was small and dark. The door locked on the outside. She said it was bare concrete, with damp walls. Always cold." Imagining it made her shiver. "All she had was a bucket for a toilet, and a wooden pallet to keep her off the floor. No blanket, no water or food. No way to stay warm." Feeling more of the chill Jodi must have suffered, Kennedy lifted her coffee cup in both hands, cradling it close.

Reyes's eyes narrowed. "I hope he didn't have an easy death."

She glanced around the restaurant. No one was near. No one paid them any attention other than a few women giving Reyes sly glances. Not that she could blame them. He owned the space by his presence alone, not to mention his size and that too-handsome face.

Dropping her voice to a barely there whisper, Kennedy continued the gruesome tale. "Jodi managed to break up the pallet by busting it against the wall. Then she dragged the edges against the rough concrete wall to sharpen them."

"Clever."

She'd always thought so. "Jodi could have starved before he returned, but she used her misery to build her rage. She was waiting next to the door when he finally came in."

"And?" he prompted.

Again, images formed in her mind, turning her stomach with the ugliness of it all. "She stabbed him with a jagged piece of wood. She said it wasn't a fatal blow, but the wood broke off in his side, and she had several pieces that she'd gotten ready. She…slashed and stabbed until he went down and didn't get up."

"Grisly," he said, not at all disturbed. "She got out of there, then?"

Kennedy shook her head. "She locked him in the room first, then yelled through the door that she'd call an ambulance for him if he gave her the combination to his safe. Jodi said he could barely talk, that he was hurting bad, bleeding everywhere. She'd… Apparently she'd cut across his face, laying open his cheek and injuring his eye. She said he was begging for help, afraid he'd go blind."

"*Fuuuuck,*" Reyes said, sounding impressed. "Guess she got a little payback."

"He was desperate, and he gave her what she wanted. She found cash and weapons in the safe, and also her purse, which still had her ID and stuff. She grabbed some of his clothes so she could change once she was well away. Then she found the keys to his car, and…" Kennedy shook her head. "She left."

"No ambulance, huh?"

Still, Reyes didn't seem disturbed. "She never told anyone, and she never went back. Unless someone found him, he died in that room."

"A fitting end for him."

"There were times when Jodi wanted to check the house, to make sure he was dead and gone. I always managed to talk her out of it."

"Good." He went back to eating. "It's risky to revisit a site."

"Know something about that, do you?"

Scoffing, Reyes didn't take the bait. He just nudged her plate at her. "There've been times since then that Jodi went after people?"

Kennedy really hated to share this part, even knowing she had to. "I don't have names, or even many details, but she told me about a guy who'd been abusing his wife. She sabotaged his car somehow and he ended up going over a bridge. He survived, but hurt his back, and Jodi was satisfied that he wouldn't walk again, so he couldn't hurt his wife."

Reyes offered no judgment.

Rubbing her forehead, Kennedy said, "She also took credit for a few pimps who were found dead, as well as a guy who'd paid one of the pimps for time with a seventeen-year-old girl."

"Is that it?" he asked without inflection.

Kennedy shook her head. "She went after a drug dealer who was preying on kids. He's dead, too. OD."

Softly Reyes said, "Jodi's gotten around."

"If the stories are all true, yes she has. I've done everything I could to convince her to stop. I've urged her to start building a better life for herself."

"She doesn't yet know how."

"No, she doesn't. And the longer she plays vigilante, the more concerned I am that she won't stop—until someone stops her."

"A worry for you, I'm sure." He again nudged her plate. "If that's it, will you please eat before your food gets any colder? We have a lot of shopping ahead of us."

She had a feeling Reyes wanted time to think. He was certainly quiet for a while after that.

Once they'd finished up their food, Kennedy accepted a refill on her coffee.

"Seriously, hon, you consume way too much caffeine," he commented.

"You can have your vices and I'll have mine."

"My vices are more fun."

Assuming his were all sexually related, she shook her head. "Jodi said she'd never admitted what she'd done to anyone other than me. With the first guy, I don't blame her."

"Of course not."

Kennedy knew if she'd been braver, stronger, she'd have done the same thing. Instead, she'd allowed herself to be intimidated until Sharlene gave her life to free her.

No, she didn't blame Jodi. Too often, she blamed herself.

And the rest of it? The other people Jodi claimed to have hurt or killed? Honestly, she just didn't know.

A WEEK WENT by in an incredible rush. Having a woman in his house was, at times, more pleasant than he could have imagined, and other times beyond frustrating. Like the way Kennedy slept in the guest room now.

Reyes hated it.

He'd *liked* holding her, but the very next night, she'd quietly made her preferences known and had slept apart from him ever since.

His subtle suggestions that she might be more comfortable with him, that his bed was big enough, the mattress more comfortable, had only brought out her infuriating manners.

She'd politely say, "The guest room is very comfortable, but thank you," and he didn't know how to press the issue without also pressing her.

That, he wouldn't do.

Why did she have to get all stubborn now and deny them both?

Other than their sleeping arrangements, everything else was easier than he'd expected. He, Reyes McKenzie, a man who'd put careful boundaries around his privacy, now relished having a woman in his space.

And not just any woman, but a woman he couldn't touch.

Never in his life had he thought he'd be in a situation like this—and liking it.

She'd damn near shopped him to death those first few days, saying it was his own fault since he wouldn't let her out of his sight. True enough, she'd offered to let him sit in the mall restaurant while she gathered everything she needed, but he, being a glutton for punishment and feeling over-the-top protective of her, had stuck as close as her shadow.

He'd also covered those expenses, and it seemed like Kennedy would never get over it. Hadn't anyone ever helped her? Didn't matter how many times he assured her he could afford it, she got touchy about paying him back once she could access her funds.

He was independent, too, so he got it. But in some

strange, chauvinistic way, he'd savored the act of providing for her.

So he had some caveman genes? Go figure.

In the end, all her careful selections, based on price and comfort, worked out. She now had warmer clothes for the chillier fall weather, plus hiking boots for their evening walks, which had become routine.

Kennedy shared his fascination with the mountains. She could walk forever, discovering creeks, exploring shallow caves and memorizing birds. Sometimes they followed easy paths, and other times they labored over rough terrain. He loved it all, and sharing with Kennedy made it somehow special.

His cabinets now held her favorite snacks, which were mostly things he didn't eat, but he enjoyed watching her enjoy them.

How twisted was that? Here he was, a grown-ass man, sexual in the extreme, but the way Kennedy licked her lips while eating a cookie made him hot.

He really needed to get laid, and soon.

But he wouldn't leave her alone to see to that, so... celibacy ruled his immediate future. Which wasn't to say he didn't appreciate his time with her.

"I need a shower," she said, as she climbed into his truck.

"You can use the showers at the gym, you know." They spent each morning and afternoon there together. Already Kennedy had gotten better at a few basic moves, though she wasn't a natural like his sister-in-law, Sterling. Overall, Kennedy didn't have the same killer instinct or a rabid desire to hone deadly skills. For her, it was more about survival. She didn't want to maim, as Jodi had done. Or stay and fight, as Sterling would insist on doing.

Kennedy wanted enough advantage to flee.

"I'm not big on group showers." She wrinkled her nose. "There are always other people there." She gave him a look. "Do you realize the women walk around naked like it's no big deal? They dry their hair, chat with their friends and apply makeup, all while entirely nude."

No, he hadn't known that. Interesting. "You're shy, huh?" Or was it that the trauma of her past made her more private about her body?

Yeah, that would make sense. Frowning, he got behind the wheel, all the while checking the area to ensure no one, including Jodi, was looming around.

"I've always been reserved when it came to my body."

"There's no reason," he said with total honesty.

Half smiling, she ducked her face. "I used the sink in your bathroom to clean up, and I changed clothes, but it's not the same as a nice long shower."

No, he supposed it wasn't. And damn it, he didn't want to think about Kennedy lingering under a warm spray.

In more ways than he could count, she was the total opposite of his brother's wife. Put in a similar situation, Sterling would have owned the showers and anyone in them. In part, her alpha attitude made her perfect for Cade.

But Reyes wouldn't like having a chick around who was every bit as ruthless as him.

"I mean it, you know. You have a nice body."

Her eyes flared. "You've never seen my body."

"I've seen you in snug shorts." He rolled a shoulder. "You have a really nice ass."

Kennedy almost choked. "That's…" She shook her head. "Um, thanks."

Her modesty was kind of cute, now that he knew it was just part of her nature and not something wrought from abuse. "Did I embarrass you? Sorry. I don't know a lot of shy women."

"I'm not really shy. Not about most things."

"Just your ass?"

Laughing, she slugged him in the shoulder. "I got a lot of work done today. Your office is comfortable."

Often while at the gym, after a few hours of instruction from him, Kennedy would retreat to his office to write her book. He'd read most of the one already published, and that made it even more difficult for him to be apart from her.

He was most at ease when he had eyes on the woman.

"Glad to hear it."

Once they were on the main road to his house, Kennedy retrieved her phone from her purse and checked her messages. That was a pattern for her. While doing drills, or writing, she kept the phone in her bag so it wouldn't distract her.

Now, as she flipped through texts, he immediately sensed that something was wrong.

The urge to pull over, to give her his undivided attention, warred with the need to secure her in his home. He wasn't Cade, all even-tempered and shit. Hell, he was the opposite of Cade. "What is it?"

"You're not going to like it."

Probably not. Anything that put that worried expression onto Kennedy's face automatically irked him. "Tell me anyway."

She nodded, looked at the phone again, and said, "I just got a text from Jodi."

Well, that wasn't horrible. At least he hoped it wasn't. "Took her long enough. What does she have to say?"

Kennedy chewed her bottom lip. "She, um, is warning me that you're dangerous."

"She's right." He gave her another quick glance. "But remember, I'm not dangerous to you."

"She said you wreak destruction wherever you go."

He snorted. *How the hell would Jodi know?* "A little dramatic, but whatever."

"None of that bothers me, Reyes. I'm glad you can be ruthless."

"So what's the problem?"

"Jodi wants to meet me tonight."

"No."

"She said I can stay with her—"

"No fucking way."

Frowning, Kennedy said, "You realize that your vocabulary deteriorates whenever you get annoyed or when you're taken by surprise."

"I'm not taken by surprise." He scowled, letting her know what he thought of that notion. "But I don't want you going anywhere. Your friend might be unbalanced."

Kennedy didn't deny that.

What would he do if she decided to bail on him? It wasn't yet safe. Hell, they still hadn't discovered anything pertinent, and until they did, he couldn't resolve jack shit, which meant she was still in danger. "You remember she was at the fire, right?"

"It's not like I'd forget."

That was something, at least. He gave the situation quick thought, trying to gauge what his family would say about it, then he shrugged. They weren't here, and he had to make a decision. Once they got home, Kennedy would barricade herself in the guest room again and he'd lose his chance to persuade her to his way of thinking. "Now might be a good time to ask her why she was there, to see her reaction."

Kennedy considered that for a moment. "If I do, she's going to ask me how I know."

"Or she'll deny it."

"No, I don't think she'd lie to me. As far as I know, she never has."

"So you'll tell her the truth that a security camera off another business picked up her image. You don't need to mention Madison, though."

"I'm not sure I'm good with half-truths."

"Sorry, honey, but it's necessary. Until we know how Jodi is involved, you can't trust her."

She stared at the phone, her troubled thoughts showing in her frown. "All right. Should I call or text?"

"Call. And put her on speaker."

Her chest expanded on a deep breath. "God, this feels like such a betrayal."

"I'm sorry." He meant it. "Your safety comes first, okay?"

Nodding, she let her thumb hover over the screen...and finally pressed the phone icon.

It rang only once before a frantic voice answered. "Kennedy, thank God. Tell me you're all right."

"Yes, I'm fine."

"People deliberately burned down your apartment building."

She shot Reyes a look as if to say, *See? She's transparent.* "I know. I'd just gotten home from a trip. It spooked me."

"That's why you're with the big guy?"

"I met him at the gym where I work out." She cradled the phone closer. "Jodi, what were you doing at my building that night?"

"Trying to watch out for you. Jesus, Kennedy, I didn't know you were still out of town and when I saw the whole thing burning, I panicked. I thought you were inside."

"But how did you know to be there?" she pressed.

"So here's the thing. You can't tell that hulk, okay? I don't trust him. He's incredibly shifty."

"He's not, actually," Kennedy replied. "He's one of the good guys, Jodi."

"There are no good guys. They're all creeps, as you should know by now!"

Reyes reached over to touch Kennedy's knee, letting her know he wasn't insulted, that in fact he got Jodi's anger.

She nodded, then said gently, "You trust me, Jodi. So trust me to know a monster from a protector. Reyes won't hurt me, I promise."

"Maybe not physically," Jodi sneered. "Some just use women as conveniences. He's that type of man, Kennedy. Do you know he's banging several women already? While he's with you?"

Kennedy's brows shot up. "While I've been with him, he hasn't gone anywhere, and what he does in his free time is his own business. We're not together that way."

For some reason, it irked Reyes to hear Kennedy say that. It was true, but still...

Sharp with disbelief, Jodi hissed, "You don't care that he's using them?"

It bothered Reyes that the woman's voice had risen. She teetered on the brink of rage, and it wouldn't take much to push her over the edge.

"You don't know him, Jodi, but I do. If he's sexually involved with anyone, it's consensual. I don't think he'd lie to them, either. Odds are they're as satisfied with an open-ended agreement as he is."

He noticed that Kennedy avoided his gaze.

New concerns intruded. There were only three women he'd seen lately, and if Jodi knew about them, then it meant she'd been spying on him for a while.

Which likely meant she'd been spying on Kennedy, too, and had seen her with him at the gym.

Kennedy must have figured the same thing, because she said, "Listen to me, Jodi. I need you to explain a few things, all right? First, *why* were you at my apartment?"

All the heat evaporated from her voice. "You're like family to me. The only family I have. I've watched over you for a while."

Pressing back into her seat, Kennedy paled. "By hanging outside my apartment? By following me?"

"Sometimes, yeah. You remember that jerk that was hassling you, right? I want to make sure no one else bothers you. You're not like me. You don't fight."

Briefly closing her eyes, Kennedy nodded. "That's true. I've tried to get better, and I'm more in shape. I'm just not much of a fighter."

Now wait a minute! Reyes hated the hint of shame he heard in her voice. Of course she was a damn fighter. Anyone could see that.

"I knew you'd been out of town," Jodi continued. "I try to keep up with your schedule."

Kennedy's gaze met his.

Disturbed, Reyes turned down the drive to his house. The fine hairs on the back of his neck stood on end, and he used extra caution surveying the area.

"All right," Kennedy said, trying to soothe her. "You were there and you saw something?"

"I thought you were already back. You were supposed to be back."

"I had delays." Kennedy rubbed at her forehead.

"I'm glad, because if you hadn't, you'd…" The words trailed off, then renewed with a vengeance. "I saw those assholes dicking around your apartment! I *knew* they were up to something, and I was right."

"When I saw the fire," Kennedy said, "I called Reyes. He picked me up. You didn't see that?"

"No, I left once everyone was out of the building. That's when I figured you weren't in there."

If she'd already left, then who killed the two men?

Kennedy asked her exactly that, being more direct than Reyes expected. "Those two men were found with bullets in their heads."

"I know," Jodi said. "Good riddance."

Kennedy stiffened. "Did you…?"

"No, but I would have." Her voice lowered with grave determination. "The world is better off without their kind. I didn't have a chance to get to them, so I'm glad someone else did."

"But *who*?"

"I figured it was your boyfriend."

"He is not my boyfriend, Jodi. I already explained this to you."

"Okay, okay. Don't get your panties in a bunch. I'm just saying. He seems like he's capable, right? Who's to say he didn't off them?"

"I say he didn't. Remember, he was with me."

"Yeah, okay. So someone else did us a favor."

By the second, Kennedy got more frazzled. "You've been following Reyes, too?"

"Sometimes. I mean, I'm not going to trust him with my girl, am I?" Her attempt at levity fell flat. "He's a creep."

Dark with suspicion, Kennedy asked, "Do you know the women he's been with?"

"No. Want me to check into them more?"

"No! Absolutely not."

Reyes squeezed her knee, then pressed the garage door opener so he could pull inside. Immediately, he shut it again.

Already he felt better, knowing Kennedy wasn't exposed to her lunatic friend. He hadn't seen anyone following them, but there was a chance Jodi was good enough to be somewhere on the property and not get spotted.

After a steadying breath, Kennedy reclaimed her calm. "I don't want you to do anything else, Jodi, okay? I mean it. I'm an adult and I can take care of myself."

"Yeah, right," she said with caustic sarcasm.

In contrast, Kennedy softly chided, "That's not kind, Jodi."

Seconds ticked by, then Jodi said, "Sorry. I just don't want to see you hurt again."

"Then don't assume the worst about Reyes, don't spy on his girlfriends and, please, trust in my instincts and intelligence."

"I guess this means you're going to stay with him."

"Do you know where he lives?" Kennedy whispered, her spine going rigid. "Have you followed him home?"

"No, but I've seen him at the gym, and I've seen him visit women." She paused. "He's cagey, you know? Not easy to tail." Jodi huffed out a breath. "When can I see you?"

Reyes shook his head, not wanting her to commit.

She accepted that without question. "I don't know. Right now I'm working on my book and trying to get my life reorganized after the fire and everything."

"Plus, it's not really safe for you to be out alone."

"No, it's not."

"Okay, so stay with the hulk. But promise me, if he does anything he shouldn't, if he hurts you in any way, you'll let me know. I swear to you, I'll end him."

Jesus, the girl was unhinged. Reyes met Kennedy's horrified gaze. Again he shook his head. He wasn't worried, so Kennedy shouldn't worry, either.

Keeping her gaze locked with his, Kennedy stated, "If you attempt to hurt him in any way, I won't forgive you, Jodi. Do you understand?"

"No sweat. I've got my hands full with another jerk anyway."

"Wait. *What?*"

"I'll be in touch, okay? And remember. You need me, all you gotta do is call."

Kennedy sat forward. "Jodi, don't—"

The call ended with all the subtlety of a thunderclap. Kennedy redialed immediately, but this time Jodi didn't answer.

"It's okay," Reyes said, hating that the girl had upset her. "Take a breath, babe."

Gulping in air, Kennedy visibly struggled with everything she'd just heard. Reyes gave her plenty of time, until the automatic overhead light flicked off, filling the garage with shadows.

Galvanized, he opened the truck door and got out. The look on Kennedy's face bothered him. She had enough worries without adding Jodi to the list.

With a long, purposeful stride, he circled the hood. For once, Kennedy was still sitting there. Not waiting for him to do the gentlemanly thing, but rather in a fog of dread.

He unhooked her seat belt. "Come on, hon, it's going to be okay." He took her purse and gym bag, and when he closed his fingers around her arm, she finally reacted.

Looking at him, Kennedy whispered, "She's irrational."

"Sounds like." He eased her out of the truck, more cognizant than ever of her small frame. With his arm around her waist, he led her inside. "It's not your problem."

"She's my friend."

"She's obsessed with you." Someone had to state the obvious. "That's not healthy."

"You heard her." Kennedy halted in the mudroom to kick off her sneakers, then she took the gym bag from him, and her purse. "She doesn't have anyone else."

Reyes smoothed her hair, left unruly from her activity at the gym. Her blue eyes were big and soft, her lips trembling.

And he wanted her like he'd never wanted another woman.

"We'll figure it out, okay? First things first, though. We need to let Madison know Jodi has been following me, that she knows about…" Shit. He rubbed the back of his neck.

"Your women?" Kennedy asked, her tone just a tad too detached to sound authentic. "Yes, you should let Madison know about that." She pivoted away. "I need that shower, now more than ever."

He let her go, mostly because he wasn't sure what to say.

She'd staunchly defended him to Jodi, stating unequivocally that he wouldn't misuse women. Hell, she'd even defended Annette, Cathy and Lili, correctly assuming that they were strong women who made their own decisions.

He'd never lied to a woman to get her into bed.

He never would.

If anyone wanted more than just sex, he walked away.

Yet here he was with Kennedy, who wanted nothing at all except his protection.

At the moment, that didn't seem to matter. She *knew* him, better than any other woman. In some ways, better than his family.

On top of that, there was a lot to unravel with everything Jodi had admitted.

Keeping Kennedy safe remained his top priority. Getting closer to her felt vital.

As he went through the house, he thought about everything he had to juggle, including his own confusion, but for the moment, he felt uncommonly…content.

It was because of Kennedy, and damn, he wasn't sure what to do about it. He was still a die-hard bachelor. Cade had made the whole relationship thing work, but as he often reminded himself, he wasn't Cade. A woman didn't fit into his life, the life groomed for him by his father.

But then, he didn't think Kennedy wanted to be a part of his life. So why was he tormenting himself about it?

Because he wanted her. Bad.

And that, he could have…if only she wanted it, too.

CHAPTER SEVEN

"YOU SURE YOU know what you're doing?" Del asked. He was damned tired of hanging around this run-down excuse for a cabin with nothing to do but smoke and think. He wanted to get back on the street, get his connections going and start acquiring girls he could rent out. Until then, he was bleeding what little cash he'd saved.

"You need to learn patience," Golly said, probably for the hundredth time. "With patience comes great rewards."

Hearing that nonsense, Del was fairly certain he and Golly had little in common. To him, selling women was a business. Not so for his cohort in this miserable scheme. Golly was obsessed with a scrawny girl and had some sick, twisted plans for when he captured her.

He was also completely repulsive. Throughout his life, Del had met some real disgusting characters, but none were as unbalanced as this one. It was bad enough that many of his teeth had rotted out, that his bald head was perpetually sweaty and that his shirts seldom covered his gut. Did he have to continually smile as if his brain had malfunctioned?

Sick prick.

Making a decision, Del stubbed out his cigarette and stood glaring at the man. "I'll wait a little longer, then I need to move on." Yes, he wanted Kennedy. He wanted to make her sorry for having crossed him. Mostly he wanted to remove her as a threat. The rest of the world had forgotten about him, but Kennedy?

She would never forget; he was fairly certain of that. It had taken him a while, but he'd finally located her here in Colorado. He was *that* close to ending her for good, but he had to move with caution, which was why he'd agreed to team up with the sick fuck now rocking in a wooden chair and humming.

What bothered him even more than the unnatural manner of the guy? That face. Del would bet the man had always been butt ugly, but an unhealthy fixation gave him the appearance of a demon from hell.

And that goddamned smile made it all the worse.

Yeah, if they didn't find Kennedy soon, Del would cut his losses and move on. He lit another cigarette.

No bitch was worth this much trouble.

THAT NIGHT, AFTER debating with herself for far too long, Kennedy reluctantly returned to the living room instead of staying in the guest room, as was her norm. She'd tried to stick to her plan of giving Reyes as much space as she could so her time spent at his home wouldn't feel so invasive.

Already he'd reordered his life to accommodate her. She'd never known anyone like him. Who did that for a mere acquaintance?

Obviously, a man of Reyes's caliber.

He might act irreverent at times, and there was no denying he had a high opinion of his ability, plus his blatant sexuality was as much a part of him as his height and good looks.

And he was so much more than that. Smart, caring, gentle, practical, efficient.

Proud.

Gorgeous.

She'd brought so much trouble to his door, and it was all amplified by Jodi's volatility. Asking for anything more was unforgivably selfish, and yet here she was.

She found Reyes half sprawled over the couch, his head in the corner of the armrest, one muscled leg stretched along the cushions, the other braced on the floor. He had a laptop balanced on his hard abdomen and was focused on something he read.

Of course he noticed her silent approach. He missed nothing.

Glancing up, his expression went wary. "Hey."

After dinner, she'd insisted on doing cleanup, where she'd lingered as long as she could, too unsettled to want to be alone. Finally, around eight thirty, she'd gone to the guest room. That was over an hour ago. Clearly, given her current habits, he hadn't expected to see her again until the morning. But for every second she'd spent pacing the room, her agitation had grown. She'd been unable to calm her rioting emotions.

And she'd been unable to stop thinking about Reyes.

It wasn't that she didn't trust Jodi, because overall she did. She didn't think Jodi would ever hurt her. As Reyes had said, Jodi was clearly obsessed with her.

But what if she hurt Reyes? He'd deny even the possibility, though people couldn't dodge bullets. Did Jodi own a high-powered rifle?

She honestly didn't know.

Another worry worm that had crawled into her brain was the idea that Jodi didn't understand boundaries, and she was so single-minded about protecting Kennedy that she didn't seem to distinguish right from wrong.

Would Jodi do something completely over-the-top that, in effect, could end up hurting her? Yes.

Now here she was, afraid for Reyes, riddled with guilt, worried for Jodi—and for the women Reyes visited.

Closing his laptop and setting it aside, Reyes sat up. "Everything okay?"

Now that she stood before him, she felt far more awkward than she'd anticipated.

She shook her head. No, she wasn't okay.

He was on his feet instantly, his hands clasping her shoulders, drawing her close. "Jodi has you rattled?"

"Yes." God, it felt good to let him hold her. *Too* good. It would be dangerous to depend on him that much, so she pressed back, robbing herself of his physical comfort. "I've been thinking."

He waited, and when she couldn't seem to vocalize the rest, he prompted her with, "Okay."

That made her smile. Silly Reyes. Always trying to comfort her. Always succeeding. "Can we sit?"

"Sure, yeah." He cleared a spot, then eased down with her, still keeping her close.

Such a big, badass guy, who always took care with her. Knowing she'd confused him—heck, she had herself confused, too—Kennedy leaned into his side.

So warm and strong. Resting one hand on his chest, she settled against the curve of his shoulder. "Let me get this said, okay?"

"All right."

"If you want to visit a woman, you should."

Arrested, he went perfectly still. But not for long. "Damn it, Kennedy—"

"Let me finish," she urged.

Frowning down at her, his mouth flattened, he gave one firm, annoyed nod.

"I know you think you need to stay here with me, but it's enough that you let *me* stay. Even if you're not here, it's safe, right? I promise I won't step outside. You shouldn't be locked down just because I am."

"My turn, yet?"

"No." God, this was difficult. "If you're staying in to-night—"

"You know I am."

Yup, that was relief turning her bones to noodles. Had she really thought he might race out the door just because she gave him permission?

Maybe she should do more than that.

Maybe she should encourage him to go…have his needs met.

God, that idea galled her, but she was determined to be fair to him. "I already knew you didn't spend your nights at home. Jodi confirmed it, therefore there's no reason for you to be discreet about it. You have a right to live your life."

"Damn right I do." He levered her up and across his lap as easily as he would have moved a throw pillow. She landed on his hard thighs with startling awareness. "No one tells me what to do or not do. Cade tries sometimes. Dad often gives it his best shot. Even Bernard has put in the effort a time or two."

She was on Reyes's lap. Everything he'd just said breezed in one ear and out the other.

The position was unlike anything she'd known. When was the last time anyone had held her?

So long ago that she couldn't remember.

"Are you listening to me?"

Not really. For some reason, he was running down the list of his family members as if they had some bearing on the situation. For the life of her, she didn't know why.

Kennedy sat stiffly, trying to give him the attention he demanded. But…

This was not at all what she'd expected when she ventured from the guest room.

His big hand came up to cradle the side of her face. "Pay attention, okay?"

She nodded. "Yes, okay."

Showing his doubt, he slipped his thumb under her chin and tilted her face up more. "If I wanted to go out, I'd go out."

"You can't *want* to stay cooped up here with me."

"Why not? You're good company." The thumb under her chin began a slow caress. "At least you are when you're not hiding in the other room."

Hiding. That summed it up nicely. "This is all so different. I'm used to being alone. I don't know what to do."

"With me?"

The way he asked that, it sounded sexual. Funny, but it caused a flutter in her stomach that didn't come close to resembling panic or even discomfort. "I don't date, Reyes. I don't sit around having casual conversations with men. I never sit on a guy's lap."

"So?"

Right. What exactly was her point? "I do my speaking, I engage with the audience, I answer questions, and then I go home to work on my book."

"Alone."

"It's what I prefer." Or rather, what she used to prefer. The fact that she was here now, *sitting on Reyes's lap*, proved that being alone didn't appeal as much at the moment.

His gaze searched hers. "Are you saying you'd rather I go out? That you want time away from me?"

"No!" Good God, running him out of his own home was the very last thing she wanted. Unsure what to do with her hands, she folded them together in her lap. He might be casual about their current position, but she wasn't. "Actually, I was going to ask you something."

"Shoot."

It would be better to just get it out there rather than keep agonizing over it. In a rush of words, she asked, "Since you're staying in, could I sleep with you again?"

The house got so quiet Kennedy could hear the steady thumping of her heart.

He cleared his throat. "You're ready for bed now?"

It was barely ten, but... "Yes?"

"No problem." In rapid order, he set her on her feet, moved his laptop to a table and began turning off lights.

Watching him, Kennedy said, "I guess after speaking with Jodi, I'm a little more nervous than I thought."

"That chick could spook anyone." He stood beneath the only remaining light near the stairs.

"I don't think I'd be able to sleep on my own. My brain would just keep churning over problems. But that first night here, with you, I slept well."

He held out a hand. "I know what you're saying, and what you're not. Don't worry that I'll take it the wrong way, okay?"

She took two steps toward him before pausing again. "I know it doesn't make sense for me to tell you to go out, then ask you to sleep with me."

"Makes perfect sense because I'm not going out, so we might as well share the bed."

He was the most confounding man ever, the way he just rolled with a situation, no questions asked. Surely, nothing like this had happened to him before.

Could he really know her that well?

She couldn't resist taking his hand. God knew he offered it often enough.

They started up the steps, with him measuring his stride to match her own.

Part of her shopping expedition had included warm pajamas. She wore the snug-fitting thermal bottoms with a looser matching top. After her shower, she'd left her hair free to ward off the headache trying to claim her. Her teeth were brushed, she'd applied lotion to her skin, and now…now she really wanted her thoughts to settle instead of jumping in a dozen different directions, each one more unsettling than the last.

At the bedroom door, he said, "I need to brush my teeth. Go ahead and get under the covers." He stepped into the bathroom and closed the door.

She knew he'd showered at the gym, and she assumed he wore his jeans out of deference to her. He'd adopted that habit ever since she'd moved into the guest room.

Maybe he thought she'd opted for a different room because his casual near-nudity made her feel threatened.

In truth, she enjoyed looking at him. Sure, she might be forever affected by her experience, but that didn't make her blind. In many ways, Reyes was like a work of art. A living sculpture of long bones, pronounced muscles and delectable body hair.

The door opened and he stepped back into the room to find her still standing there.

Smile going crooked, he chided, "You haven't moved."

"I got lost in thought."

"Yeah? About Jodi?"

Shaking her head, she asked, "Why are you wearing jeans all the time?"

Coming to a halt, he looked down at his jeans as if he'd forgotten he had them on, then he scratched his jaw. "I figured it was the polite thing to do."

She gave an exasperated sigh. "Because you think it makes me uncomfortable?"

"I thought it might, and didn't want to take the chance."

Heading to the bed, she said, "Well, it doesn't. But even if it did, I don't want you adjusting things for me. Your comfort should come first. That's what I'd prefer, okay?"

"So if I just go naked around the house, you're okay with that?"

She had the covers lifted in her hand, one knee on the mattress about to climb in, but at his statement she almost fell in face-first. "Naked?" Straightening back to her feet, she dropped her hands to her hips and eyed him with suspicion. "You're just messing with me. No way do you prance around here naked."

"Prance, no."

Her mind conjured an image… "Be serious, Reyes."

He laughed at her sharp tone. "Sorry. Gotta take my pleasures where I can." Sporting a big grin, he shucked off his jeans but left on his boxers, turned off the light and got into bed.

Leaving her standing there feeling foolish. "So you don't walk around here without clothes?"

"Not often."

This time she rudely huffed, sure that he was only baiting her to get a reaction. She slid between the cool sheets, and immediately Reyes tugged her close, curving his body around hers.

His minty breath teased her cheek. "Get comfortable in whatever way works for you, as long as it's near me, and then we can get some sleep."

"I want you comfortable, too," she whispered.

"So you know, I'm a hell of a lot more comfortable like this than with us sleeping in separate rooms."

She turned her head enough to face him, but her eyes

hadn't yet adjusted. She had the sense of him being very near, yet she couldn't make out his features. "You said you've never brought a woman here."

"Haven't." His hand smoothed over her hair, then tucked it back behind her ear with a tenderness she felt in her heart. "There's a difference in being home alone and knowing a woman sleeps just downstairs."

His temperature seemed to have risen, sending his heated scent to envelope her. "This is nice," she murmured.

"Very." He pressed a kiss to the top of her head. "Now sleep."

Held against his body, listening to his deepening breaths, Kennedy felt his hold loosen as he fell asleep.

There couldn't be another man like Reyes anywhere.

Without thinking about it, she whispered, "It's a good thing you don't want me, or we wouldn't be able to do this."

His arm immediately snuggled her closer, and his husky voice, low and rough, sounded very near to her ear. "I've wanted you from the first time I saw you. Make no mistake about that."

Her eyes popped open wide.

"Since we enjoy sharing the bed, from now on you sleep with me. Only sleep. And if you ever want more, just let me know." Putting a final kiss to her ear, he breathed, "Now sleep. If we talk about this much longer, I'm gonna get hard and that'll bother you and we'll never get any rest."

He wanted her. Enough that he could get an erection from talking? Kennedy had no idea what to say. She stared into the darkness, her eyes rounded, her heart galloping… and the strangest sort of thrill curling around her heart.

Huh. Reyes McKenzie had done the impossible.

He'd sparked her interest. Now she needed to figure out what to do about it.

THE WEEKEND ROLLED AROUND, and Reyes walked through the house whistling. Who knew he could be so happy with sexual frustration? Being celibate with Kennedy made all the difference. For several days now she'd slept with him each night.

Each day, she tried to figure out when and how she could leave. He understood that. Their investigation had come to a grinding halt with no new clues and no new leads to follow. She wanted to get on with her life.

Each day he became more determined to keep her around a little longer.

How long, he didn't know. Sooner or later, she'd need her own place, yet every time he thought of it he got a bad feeling. Something wasn't right. Whoever had come after her was just lying low. Eventually they'd crawl out of the shadows again, and when they did, he wanted to be with Kennedy so he could ensure her safety.

Sitting at the kitchen table, sipping yet another cup of coffee, Kennedy looked lost in thought.

He'd learned to make an entire pot instead of only a few cups. Sometimes it seemed she sustained herself on worry and caffeine, along with the determination to help others avoid her fate.

"It's Saturday," he said, aware of her gaze lifting to his body. As she'd requested, he'd gone back to wearing only his boxers in the morning, at least until he dressed for the day. More than a few times, he'd caught her looking him over.

He wasn't quite sure what her intense scrutiny meant. With another woman, yeah, he could assume. But this was Kennedy, and she had a troubled past.

"I know." She smiled at him. "The pancakes were amazing. Give me a few more minutes and I'll clean up."

"You've done all the cleanup, lately. It's my turn."

"I clean because you always cook." As if that bugged her, she said, "I know how to cook, too, you know."

As he carried plates to the dishwasher, he said, "No biggie. You can do dinner whenever you want."

"That's not what you said the last five times I asked."

He shrugged. "I didn't want you to feel obligated. But sure, if it means that much to you, I don't mind. Just not tonight. It's Saturday, so I figured we'd go out."

She perked up at that. "Out? Out where?"

He heard the excitement in her voice and felt like a dope. Of course she wanted to get out. Other than their one breakfast at a restaurant, the entirety of her social life had been going to the gym and back. Her life was literally on hold, the danger still out there with no way for them to address it.

"Dinner and a movie?" he suggested.

Standing, she carried her now-empty cup to him. "I'd rather visit this Bernard person so I could see Chimera. You keep telling me you still have the cat, but in all this time, I haven't seen her. *And*," she stressed, when he started to speak, "you refuse to take me to see her."

"Because it's complicated."

Adorably cute in her pajamas, she growled, "Either you have the cat or you don't."

"Fine." He gave up. "You want to see Chimera? I'll talk to Bernard today and see when we can visit."

Narrowing her eyes, she looked at him askance. "You make it sound like some grand concession."

Yeah, because he'd wanted to take her out, not drag her to his father's house, where she'd be dissected and where his relationship with her would be up for discussion. He could already hear his dad lecturing him.

Who needed that shit?

"Look," he said, ready to launch into something, probably something obnoxious, that was interrupted by the doorbell.

Before Kennedy could get all panicky, he cursed. "My sister. And damn it, it looks like she has Sterling with her." More or less stomping out of the kitchen, he went to the door and shouted through the intercom, "I'm not dressed. Give me five."

"I won't look," Sterling said, then she snickered.

Aware of a blur behind him, Reyes watched Kennedy dart toward the guest room. "No hiding," he called after her.

"Just getting dressed," she assured him, seconds before she disappeared from sight.

Fuck it. He opened the door to let in his sister and sister-in-law. "Coffee's in the kitchen. Kennedy is changing out of her pj's. I'll be right back."

Sterling boldly stared at him, then snorted. "Those boxers are no different than the shorts you wear for working out."

Madison, not in the least interested in what her brother wore, headed to the couch with her laptop. "I'm here to see Kennedy anyway."

That brought him away from the stairs and back into the living room area. "Why?"

"The cops did a massive, coordinated statewide search of missing youths. Found a lot of them, too, and in the process, they also arrested several suspected traffickers. I want Kennedy to check out the photos to see if anyone looks familiar."

That sounded interesting. "Got it." He rushed upstairs to take a speed shower, clean his teeth and shave. He dressed in a long-sleeved pullover and worn jeans. Carrying his shoes and socks, he headed back down.

Kennedy was already neatly dressed in a flannel shirt,

skinny jeans and thick socks. She'd pulled her hair into a high ponytail and put on a touch of makeup.

Cute. She wanted to impress his family.

She was going about it the wrong way, but he wouldn't tell her so.

Sterling now had a cola, and Madison had a bottle of water. Curled in a chair, Kennedy asked numerous questions, which Sterling fielded like a pro, telling her only so much without admitting to anything private.

They were mostly questions on fighting styles, and Kennedy seemed duly impressed with their answers.

Reaching to the small of her back, Sterling pulled a wicked blade from a sheath. "Check out my new knife."

Gingerly Kennedy accepted it, handling it like a live grenade.

Madison's laptop was open, but so far no one was looking at it. Reyes lifted it, going through the photos with a practiced eye. He didn't see anyone familiar to him, but then, that was the problem with the ever-growing trade.

When the women started talking about fashion or, in Sterling's case, the lack thereof, Reyes decided this might be a good time for him to dodge out. He could talk to his dad, let him know that he might have to bring Kennedy by, and he could warn Bernard not to be so damned possessive of the cat.

Yes, the cat *was* Bernard's now. Reyes had relinquished ownership when Bernard turned to comical mush over the critter. Pretty sure if he'd pressed the issue, Bernard would have challenged him.

Then his dad would be pissed, and probably Madison, too, because they all considered Bernard one of the family.

Shaking his head, Reyes said, "If you ladies are going to hang out here awhile, I think I'll head over to Dad's to check on…things."

Madison shooed him away. "I'll give you three hours while Kennedy and I get better acquainted."

Better acquainted? What the hell did that have to do with searching through arrest photos? He didn't like the sound of it and was about to protest when Sterling got to her feet in a rush.

"No way." She pointed at Reyes. "You're going to the house to spar with Cade and I want to take part."

Why couldn't his sister-in-law just go along like Madison had? She never let anything slide, and she never missed an opportunity to sharpen her edge.

Reyes tried a smile that felt like a snarl. "I thought you were going to visit."

"Ha!" Sterling narrowed her eyes on him. It was an effective look for her, both mocking and, for some, intimidating. "You know I don't get into the whole girl-talk thing."

Madison glanced up with indignation. "I hardly think researching traffickers fits that description."

"You're talking clothes, not creeps."

"They're going to search through arrest photos," Reyes reminded, trying to divert her.

Sterling huffed. "And that'll take how long? Once they're done, we both know the chitchat is going to veer to female stuff."

"News flash, Sterling. You're female."

She rolled her eyes. "Barely."

Of all the... "My brother would disagree with that assessment."

"Your brother is incredibly unique." She shrugged it off. "So far, he's the only one I know who makes it worthwhile to be female."

Kennedy's fascinated gaze took it all in. "Why don't you like being female?"

Just to irritate Sterling, Reyes answered before she

could. "Being smaller and weaker grates on her. She'd rather kick ass than fix her hair."

"Hey." Madison glared at him. "Some of us enjoy doing both."

"Yeah, I get it," Reyes said, with enough inflection to insinuate that Sterling did not. "You happen to be both lethal and feminine. Apparently, most can't figure out that balance."

Slowly smiling, Sterling said, "Oh, now I'm really going to enjoy sparring. Plan to bleed."

He groaned. When Sterling got in that particular mood, she could be a total bear. He wouldn't actually bleed, but he would be wearing a few new bruises before they wrapped it up. "I didn't agree to spar with you."

"You will."

He narrowed his eyes. "So maybe I'll give as good as I get."

"You can try."

Damn it, they both knew he could flatten her—if he wanted. The problem was that she *was* his brother's wife. Cade loved her more than life, and if his scuffling got too rough, Cade would take it out on him. "I'm *sparring* with you," Reyes stated, emphasis on *sparring*. "Save that painful shit for your husband."

"Chicken."

Ignoring Sterling, he made an impulse decision and bent to press a kiss to Kennedy's forehead. "Call if you need me, otherwise I'll be back before Madison is ready to go."

It took her a few seconds to recover from the affectionate peck. She blinked several times, then lifted her chin. "I'm getting curious about all this sparring stuff. I think watching would be fun."

"Another day," he said easily, and moved on before she

could challenge that dismissal. He leveled a severe look on his sister. "Don't overdo it."

After giving him another airy wave, Madison situated the laptop on the coffee table and gestured Kennedy over to sit beside her so they could look at the images together.

Sterling turned to Kennedy with a quick apology. "Sorry to visit and run—"

"I understand," Kennedy assured her.

Still, Sterling explained, "Sparring with the guys is special. I always learn something new."

"I'm in no way offended," Kennedy promised. "Go have fun."

Fun. Frustrated, Reyes walked out of the room with Sterling dogging his heels. He literally *felt* her behind him as he went down the hall and out into the garage. If he thought he could leave her behind, he would.

But one thing he'd learned about Sterling—dealing with her was never easy. In her current challenging mood?

It'd be downright impossible.

CHAPTER EIGHT

"I CAME OVER with Madison," Sterling said. "Since I hadn't planned to leave—until you offered better entertainment— you'll have to give me a lift back."

Great. More isolated time with her. *If only he'd kept his mouth shut.* Reyes plastered on an insincere smile. If she knew she'd irked him, she'd only dig in more. "No problem."

His lack of enthusiasm made Sterling laugh out loud. "You are so transparent, you big fraud." When he started around to open her door, she made a sound of derision and hauled herself up into the truck.

Stopping to stare at her, Reyes propped his fists on his hips. "What if I'd planned to take my bike?" He hadn't had the Harley out recently. The day was cool, but the sun was bright.

Already jumping back out of the truck, Sterling said, "Awesome. Let's do it."

Figured she'd like that idea. Cade would kick his ass for real if he had Sterling strapped around him on the drive to his father's place. For such a calm, in-control guy, his brother was ridiculously territorial with his wife. "No, I don't think so."

"Spoilsport." Again she jumped easily into the truck. As he pulled out of the driveway, she added, "Reyes has a girlfriend," in a low and annoying singsong voice.

The truth was, he loved his sister-in-law, most especially because she had brought Cade back into the family. His big brother had avoided that duty by joining the army rangers. When he medically retired with a bad knee from too many jumps out of moving planes, he'd reluctantly returned to the family...yet an emotional distance had remained.

From the start, Cade had bucked their father's iron will. He wanted to choose his own destiny, not fall in line with his father's plans.

When he met Sterling, though, he got a whole new perspective on what family meant, mostly because she didn't have one and therefore appreciated his.

They'd all pulled together to get her bacon out of the fire. Of course, that hadn't stopped Reyes from teasing her mercilessly. He'd at first considered her a pushy broad who'd played at being a badass. Hadn't taken him long to realize she wasn't playing.

The lady had endless stamina, a backbone of steel, a streak of bravery a mile wide and endless determination to learn. He liked her. More than that, he respected her.

Maybe he should tell her that to end their not-so-subtle war.

Nah. Pretty sure she enjoyed it as much as he did. Or at least, as much as he did when he wasn't worried for Kennedy.

"Not denying it, huh?"

Reyes took his sunglasses from the visor and slipped them on. "What's that? Did you say something?"

Sterling grinned. She was a tall, bold woman with strong features, a sturdy, rockin' body, and a lack of fashion sense. When she smiled? Downright beautiful.

"You like her. Admit it."

"I like her." He more than liked her. Not that he'd do anything about it.

"Wow." Clearly Sterling hadn't expected that reply. "So how does she feel about you?"

It occurred to him that his sister-in-law might make a good sounding board. She'd been through a devastating experience similar to what Kennedy had endured. The big difference was that Sterling appeared to bounce back. Like a boxer, she refused to show weakness in any way. Long before she'd met Cade, she'd had some understandable hang-ups concerning sex—but she'd forged onward, involving herself in sexual situations until she no longer froze, for the sole purpose of ensuring she wouldn't cower when threatened. Her whole focus had been on helping others, and she knew she couldn't do that if the threat of sex left her emotionally paralyzed.

Because of her resolve, she'd learned to "get through it" without anyone realizing how she disliked the whole physical thing.

Now with Cade... The two of them could barely keep their hands off each other. Sterling had gone from tolerating sex to wallowing in the pleasure of it.

Which meant his brother did a fair amount of smiling these days.

"Trust me," Sterling said, "if it takes that much thought trying to figure it out, she's not into you. Women aren't that subtle."

Never a dull moment with his prickly sister-in-law. She had a razor-sharp wit that he couldn't help admiring. "I could use some advice."

Slapping a hand over her heart, Sterling pretended to swoon back against the door.

"Knock it off. I'm serious."

As if she didn't believe her ears, she said, "You want *my* advice?"

Damn, couldn't she ever let up? "Never mind. It was a bad idea."

"No way, now I want to hear this. Behold, a serious woman. Tell me what's troubling you. I'm all ears."

The humor caught him off guard, making him snicker. "I don't know how Cade tolerates your sarcasm."

"He doesn't earn it, that's how." Shifting to better face him, she grew serious. "Come on, give. All ribbing aside, you're my brother now and I care about you. I'll help if I can."

Yeah, that was the sister-in-law he loved. She could charge into danger with the best of them, and she also had a heart of gold. "You know what Kennedy went through."

"Yeah. Hope the dick who did that to her is buried deep."

One guy was. The other? He didn't know. "She's... guarded still."

Plainspoken as always, Sterling asked, "You mean about sex? With you?"

Reyes frowned. "You're jumping the gun."

"So you don't mean sex?"

Why in the world had he thought she'd be subtle about the topic? "Damn it, will you let me talk?"

She pretended to zip her lips.

After shooting her a quelling glance, she remained silent and waiting, and Reyes released a deep breath. "Sex between us hasn't come up. I'm not an idiot where women are concerned. I pick up on stuff. Kennedy's not into it, not just with me, but I think with anyone. I think she's..." Not damaged. Never that. "I don't think she's given sex a thought since she got away."

"Can I speak now?"

Why not? "Have at it."

"Kennedy obviously doesn't know what she's missing. In her mind, sex is still all about humiliation, lack of choices and pain—basically the total opposite of fun. Given what she's been through, she's probably not looking to change that."

"You did."

"Yeah, well, you know I can't stand being cowed by anyone or anything. To me, sex was a handicap to overcome."

"And you managed that." Could Kennedy?

"Yeah, I did. Scx was no longer an agony, but it was a far shot from enjoyable." She bobbed her eyebrows. "Whole different story with your oh-so-amazing brother."

"I figured." It felt both strange and natural to have this discussion with Sterling. "The last thing I want to do is spook Kennedy, you know? I want her to feel safe with me."

"She does. Guaranteed."

"Yeah? You really think so?"

"She's smart, right? She would have moved on already if she didn't trust you."

At least that was something.

"Here's what I'd do," Sterling said. "Build on that trust. Like the way you kissed her goodbye today? Totally took her by surprise, but she didn't mind. It just wasn't something in her wheelhouse. I doubt she's let any guy get close enough for an affectionate peck. Do that a few more times."

Not a problem. "And?"

"Trust opens the door to other things. Right now, she's got her guard up, even with you. I mean, a smart woman doesn't want to take the chance on being hurt twice. So while she doesn't think you'd do anything heinous to harm her, she's still protecting herself. When she lets down those walls, she'll notice things."

"Like?"

"Like your very fine physique and sexy attitude. Actually, she's probably already been clued in on that, she's just not sure what to do about it."

Reyes felt heat burn up the back of his neck. A compliment from Sterling was a damned uncomfortable thing.

Either she didn't notice his unease, or she flat out didn't care. "You know how to seduce, right? I mean, you are Cade's brother, so I assume—"

Affronted, he growled, "Knowing how and thinking I should are two different things."

In a soothing tone, Sterling explained, "I'm not saying to come on hot and heavy. That'd be all wrong. Just help her ease into things. I know if she gives you a back-off signal, you'll respect that."

"Yes."

"So there you go. When she realizes she likes the contact, that a kiss isn't an ugly, unwanted thing, that it makes her want more, then you can deliver. Little by little, though, okay?" She landed a friendly punch to his shoulder. "I know this family has some superior genes coursing through the bloodline, but a guy is a guy is a guy. Don't think she's all enthused when she might not be. Wait until she makes it clear it's what she wants."

"I wouldn't pressure her." For some reason, it was important to him for Sterling to understand that.

"I know that, Reyes." Briefly she touched his forearm, as if to emphasize the sincerity of her words, then she retreated again. "I guess that's why you want to spar? Have some pent-up frustrations to work out?"

Something like that. "Just keeping my edge."

"If you say so."

Which translated to: *You are so full of it.*

He liked Sterling, he really did. If nothing else, she always kept it real.

Now that they were alone, Madison launched right into work. "Over the past month, our local Human Trafficking task force teamed up with the state and did a huge sting. They not only rounded up a bunch of missing kids, they got multiple traffickers."

Freezing in horror, Kennedy breathed, "The kids are okay?"

"They are now, yeah. Many of them were runaways and such, and they're getting help. Some were being groomed to be prostitutes, but for most, it hadn't happened yet."

Thank God.

Madison scooted closer. "Not every situation is like yours."

"I know that, but they're all awful."

"I agree. But what I meant is that sometimes the kids are coaxed into it, not forced. They have someone taking care of them when no one else has—and sometimes just because they think they're misunderstood and they're rebelling against their parents. Being out with a 'protector' who ensures they have food and pretty clothes, it's seductive. Then the sexual favors start, and pretty soon, once they're used to that—"

"The trafficker asks for more." Kennedy hated them all. Each and every one of the monsters who preyed on the vulnerable, either through emotional control or physical abuse.

"Yes." She touched Kennedy's hand. "But they're rescued now, and the ones responsible will be prosecuted. What I need you to do is look through these images and see if you recognize anyone."

Kennedy took the laptop from her and settled back on the couch. Photos of men, and a few women, both facing forward and in profile, filled the screen. "How did you get these?" They looked like official police photos.

Madison smiled but didn't answer. "Click on each image

to enlarge it." With a pat to Kennedy's hand, she stood. "I could use a cup of coffee and maybe a few cookies. You?"

"Sounds good. You want me to make it?" She now felt fairly comfortable in Reyes's home. A dangerous thing, that. A part of her knew she should be expending every ounce of free time trying to figure out how to leave; instead, every day she became more settled.

"No, you look through those. I'll be right back."

An hour later, with a looming headache and eyestrain, Kennedy admitted defeat. "I'm sorry, but I don't recognize any of them." Which only meant there were too many horrible people in the world.

"That's okay. It was worth a shot."

Another hour passed while they talked and strategized. Kennedy liked Madison. The woman was far too pretty with her fawn-colored hair and wide hazel eyes that matched Reyes's. She had to be six feet tall, slender but toned, and though she had a fragile femininity about her, Kennedy believed she could do serious damage.

Never would she underestimate any of the McKenzies.

When the doorbell rang, Kennedy nearly leaped off her seat.

"Oops." Madison glanced up at the nearest monitor. "I was enjoying our visit so much, I didn't even notice someone approaching."

Far less cavalier, Kennedy's heart lodged in her throat, making her rasp when she asked, "Who do you think it is?"

"Oh, look. He's staring right into the security camera. Isn't that clever of him?"

Kennedy gaped at her.

"It's hidden, you know, but he spotted it." Finally realizing that Kennedy was frozen beside her, Madison smiled. "No worries. It's just Detective Albertson. What a surprise."

"You know him?" Kennedy started to relax.

"We've never met. He's been keeping tabs on my family, so I've been keeping tabs on him."

As she headed for the door, Kennedy panicked. "Wait! Should you open that?"

Gently, and with understanding, Madison said, "It'll be okay, I promise. I won't let anyone hurt you."

She wouldn't let... Good grief. Was everyone in the McKenzie family so cocksure of themselves? Of course, she believed Madison was capable, but the man was big, muscular, and he just might have his own set of skills.

Launching from her seat, Kennedy quickly backed up to the kitchen entry, which also put her in line with the hall. If she had to make a run for it, she'd go to the guest room she used, lock the door and dig out her weapons. In fact, maybe she should do that now.

Too late.

Madison swung open the door to reveal a... Wow. Seeing him for real instead of through the camera, the guy looked like a male model. Not as tall as Reyes and Cade, but then who was? He was still six-two, with broad shoulders beneath an expensive suit.

Sandy-brown hair, with gold streaks that made it a few shades lighter than Madison's, and dark-as-sin eyes, made him a devastatingly handsome man.

Madison smiled. "Hello, Detective Albertson. How nice to see you."

The detective had been staring at Madison in a surprised yet absorbed way—until her words registered. Then he straightened, on alert. "We haven't met."

"No," Madison confirmed. "We haven't."

He looked past her into the house, locked on to Kennedy for a heart-stopping moment, then gave his attention back to Madison. "Miss Madison McKenzie."

Madison actually seemed pleased that he'd said her name. "That's Ms., if you don't mind."

He acknowledged that with a nod. "I wanted to speak to your brother."

"Which one?"

"The one who lives here?"

She laughed. Kennedy couldn't credit it.

And, damn it, she was still tempted to run.

"Unfortunately, Detective, he's away at the moment. Would you like to come in?"

Kennedy almost choked. She didn't want a stranger in the house!

Sensing her unease, Madison glanced back. "It's okay. Detective Albertson is a very good, honest cop. Isn't that right, Detective?"

Confused by the familiar way she addressed him, he ran a hand over his mouth. "You've been studying up on me."

"Tit for tat, you know."

Flirting? Was Madison actually *flirting* with the man? They were all certifiable…but also proficient, damn it. She trusted that Madison knew what she was doing. Sort of.

Maybe.

Still undecided, Albertson hesitated, then finally nodded and stepped in. "Thank you."

"Coffee?" Madison asked as she headed to the couch and casually closed her laptop.

Not missing a thing, the detective's suspicious gaze zeroed in on the device. "Sure, thanks."

Madison looked to Kennedy. "Would you mind?"

"Oh." Shaking herself, Kennedy said, "Sure," and hurried away. She needed a minute to herself, and this would help. As she poured the coffee, she tried to think.

Reyes would be furious, she didn't doubt that. Would he be mad at her, or just his sister?

Didn't matter. Reyes was the one she trusted—his sister, she barely knew. So she used her phone to quickly send a text to Reyes.

your sis just let in Detective Albertson. They R talking & it seems ok but thought you should know

Immediately she got a reply: On my way. She was about to put the phone in her pocket when another text came in: Stay behind Madison.

Obviously, he believed his sister could protect her. For the moment, that was good enough for her.

"So." MADISON COULDN'T help admiring the handsome detective. His sandy-brown hair was a bit too long, curling at the ends in what might have created a boyish look if it wasn't for his strong jaw and sinfully dark eyes. Such a stunning contrast, that lighter hair with the dark chocolate gaze. With brothers like hers, most men seemed far too ordinary in comparison.

Not so with Crosby. Having never experienced lust at first sight, she sighed.

The good detective shot her a suspicious look, to which she smiled...and yes, that only made him more wary.

It wasn't only his looks worth noting. Since he'd been checking into them, he had to know that her brothers were very dangerous people. So was she. Yet here he stood, in Reyes's house, gazing at *her* with cautious interest—something most men didn't dare to do.

That dark stare did funny things to her insides. She'd have to get used to the detective in small doses. "If you're here for a reason, I suggest we get to it."

Now he smiled. "Suddenly in a rush?"

"Well, since Kennedy surely texted Reyes, and since

he'll race over here just to throw you out—and I do mean *throw*—yes, it might be wise to find out the reason for your visit."

That took care of his smile. Annoyance gathered his brows together. They were a few shades darker than his hair and added even more interesting dimensions to his face.

"You're threatening me with your brother?" he growled.

"Oh, no, I'm happy to finally meet you in person. Remember, I offered you coffee." Louder, so that Kennedy would hear, she said, "Although I'm starting to wonder if that meant making a new pot, since it's taking so long."

Wearing a hot blush, Kennedy finally slunk back. She set the cup on a coaster on the coffee table, then backed a safe distance away.

Clearly she didn't trust Albertson, which sort of amused Madison. "Crosby—may I call you Crosby?" She didn't wait for him to answer before continuing to Kennedy. "Crosby is fine, I promise. You can trust my judgment. That said, I don't mind that you contacted Reyes, I promise. No reason to blush."

Now Kennedy frowned, too. "I think you're trying to embarrass me."

"Not at all. I just want us all to be honest." She turned back to Crosby. "Now, why are you here?"

He rubbed a big-knuckled hand over his mouth. "We've arrested a lot of shady men lately—"

"I'm aware."

"Yeah, well, maybe you don't know that there was one particular man I want, but he wasn't in the mix. I thought you might know something about that."

Madison almost clapped her hands. "We're collaborating? Oh, how fun! Do you have an image?"

"I do. So you know, it's inside my jacket pocket."

"Not going for a gun, huh?"

"No, I'm not, so don't overreact."

That he understood her capability flattered her. Few men would even acknowledge her talents, much less respect them.

Slowly he withdrew a small, crinkled photo and handed it over.

"Hmm." Madison studied the black-and-white of a balding guy in slight profile, which showed a scraggly ponytail hanging down his neck. He had a very weak chin, an ugly smile and a few missing teeth. "I'm sorry, but he doesn't look familiar."

Kennedy gave up her suspicion of Crosby in favor of seeing the photo for herself. Silently, she stared at it. "Are you able to give a name to go with the image?"

Madison watched Kennedy more closely. She saw... maybe not actual recognition, but definitely a flash of something.

As if delivering a curse, Crosby muttered, "Rob Golly."

Kennedy's head jerked up. She stared in horror at Crosby, which brought him closer to her in a rush.

"You know him, don't you?"

"No," she said, stepping closer to Madison. "No, I don't."

Madison touched her arm. "But you've heard of him?" Was his a name she'd learned during her time being trafficked?

Or...was the bastard somehow tied to Jodi?

Starting to tremble, Kennedy asked, "Why are you looking for him?"

Crosby noted Kennedy's unease and he solicitously indicated the chair.

Gripping the photo enough to add new wrinkles to it, Kennedy sank onto the cushion.

Madison chose a spot on the couch and patted the seat beside her.

Ignoring that, Crosby sat at the other end, as far from her as he could get, and retrieved the coffee. He sipped, no doubt using that time to formulate how much he wanted to share.

"You can tell me, you know," Madison assured him. "I'm completely trustworthy."

He shot her an incredulous look. "You're completely... something. *Trustworthy* isn't the word I'd use."

Smart man. "Okay, give. Who is Rob Golly and why do you want him?"

Keeping his gaze on Kennedy, Crosby said, "I've been tracking him for a while. Over two years, actually. He's a known abuser of women, the worst sort of scum you can imagine."

"Oh, I don't know," Madison murmured. "I have a very developed imagination."

Kennedy gaped at her in horrified disbelief. "You're treating this like a joke."

Oh, my. Kennedy definitely knew something about the man. "I'm sincerely sorry," she said, keeping her tone soft. "I never meant to make light of it."

Kennedy firmed her lips and nodded.

Glancing at Crosby, Madison felt sure that he, too, saw how tightly strung Kennedy had gotten over the man. "Go on."

He gave a small nod. "Golly moves around a lot, renting old houses where he'd keep women as prisoners. I finally tracked down his last house."

Kennedy literally held her breath.

Until Crosby added, "But he wasn't there."

Covering her mouth with one hand, Kennedy frowned.

"What do you mean, he wasn't there? You had the wrong house?"

"Right house, but Golly was nowhere to be found."

"How do you know it was the right house?" Madison asked.

"All the signs were there. A room in the basement meant to be a cell. A door with too damn many locks on it." His right hand curled into a fist, and he rasped, "Blood on the floor."

"That sounds horrid," Madison whispered, no longer in a flirting mood.

"The worst nightmare a person could imagine." Crosby sat forward, all his attention on Kennedy. "I had the right place, I know it. But Golly was gone, and so was his last victim."

Kennedy said nothing, but her eyes went glassy with unshed tears.

Falling back on her training, Madison asked, "Did you check the yard? Sounds like old Golly might have a few bodies buried around the property."

"Nothing at that house, but at another we found remains."

Madison didn't know how much longer Kennedy could hang on. She looked ready to implode, with fear, anger. Any minute now, Reyes would come crashing in and all hell would break loose. She would wait for him outside to warn him to behave, except that would mean leaving Kennedy alone with Crosby, and Reyes would be furious if she did that. If she took Kennedy with her, that would leave Crosby alone in Reyes's house. Another sin in her brother's eyes.

What to do?

"Tell me, Detective, when did you join the trafficking task force, and why were you tracking Golly in particular?" In her experience, most men enjoyed bragging. Not her brothers, not to strangers anyway, but for most other men it appeared to be a basic masculine trait.

Crosby surprised her silly by saying, "I'm not on a task force. My interest is personal, and you won't distract me with your questions." His smile looked the opposite of friendly, more like an issue of clear challenge. "I'd rather hear about you, your brothers and the head of it all, your father."

CHAPTER NINE

REYES KEPT HIS foot pressed hard on the gas pedal, weaving in and out of traffic. With every minute that passed, every mile he covered, his blood burned hotter.

How fucking *dare* his sister let a stranger into his house? She knew better.

After he'd finished sparring with Cade, they'd both gone to their respective suites within their father's immense mountain mansion to shower and change before meeting upstairs for drinks with Parrish. His father was keenly curious about Kennedy, and more than a little concerned about Reyes's involvement with her.

He'd denied any involvement, of course.

Neither Cade nor Parrish had bought his denials. The McKenzies were razor-sharp and cut through BS like a hot knife through butter.

Reyes had geared up for the inquisition, especially when he informed Bernard that he'd be bringing Kennedy over to visit Chimera the cat. Then her text had come in, and his only thought had been getting to her.

Cade had made the spur-of-the-moment decision to follow him home, just in case there was real trouble, while Parrish had told Reyes to trust Madison.

Right. Logic told him that the cop likely wasn't a stranger to his sister, but at the moment he didn't care.

Finally he turned into the long drive to his home, going so fast that the truck tires kicked up dirt and gravel. He screeched to a halt outside the garage, next to the silver sedan.

Fuming, he jogged up the walk—and the front door opened.

Kennedy said, "I'm sorry I overreacted," and then launched at him, her arms going tight around his neck.

Just as quickly, he moved her safely behind him and lifted his Glock.

Madison appeared next in the doorway. "I'd really prefer you not shoot the detective. Overall, he's been very helpful."

"Get out of the way, Madison."

She crossed her arms. "No, I don't think so. You're running on emotion and you know that's not wise."

Yeah, he did know it, but feeling Kennedy tremble behind him, he didn't give a shit.

Then she stepped around in front of him again, whispering, "Please don't do anything dumb. I'm fine, but I desperately need to talk to you, and I can't do that until Crosby and Madison are gone."

Crosby? Now why the hell did that fry his ass? "You know the fucker's first name?"

"Reyes," Madison sighed, making the sound long and aggrieved. "Get a grip, will you?"

Behind him, Cade pulled up. The door of his SUV slammed with foreboding.

Madison threw up her hands. "I know Kennedy texted you. I know she was worried." She came closer, stepping onto the walk, too. "But, Reyes, I promise there's no reason."

He was just about convinced when a man came out the door. "Honest to God, I've never before had two women trying to protect me."

"Trying?" Madison repeated. "If it weren't for me, you'd be eating dirt right now."

"Maybe I'm not the slouch you think I am."

Jesus, Joseph and Mary. He'd stepped into bedlam. Lowering the gun to his side, Reyes asked, "Do I need to kill him or not?"

Together, Madison and Kennedy said, *"Not."*

"Fine." He turned and shoved the gun into Kennedy's hand. Horrified, she accepted it with the same enthusiasm she might give a cockroach.

To Cade, Reyes said, "Back off."

Cade held up his hands. "No problem. I, at least, trust our sister."

"Thank you," Madison stated primly.

In two long strides, Reyes reached the handsome bastard standing just outside his front door. Smiling in evil anticipation, he threw a punch too fast for the other man to duck and clocked him right in the jaw.

Staggering back, cursing, Crosby caught himself and took an aggressive stance. "That's not necessary, McKenzie."

"It is if you don't want me to rip you apart." He grabbed Crosby's arm and propelled him off the front porch to the yard.

This time Crosby went down from the sheer momentum of the attack, but he didn't stay down.

Bounding back to his feet, he surprised Reyes by snapping to Madison, "Stay out of it."

"I don't take orders from you," she informed him without heat, and stepped into Reyes's path.

Frustrated, Reyes looked to Cade. "A little help?"

Cade cocked a brow. "You want her pissed at me, too?"

Curses burned the back of his throat. "I won't kill him," he promised Madison.

"He's being helpful, you idiot. Why don't you just cool down and listen?"

"Because he dared to come to *my* house." Reyes advanced on his sister. "And *you* dared to let him in."

Suddenly, somehow, Crosby was in front of Madison. It so astonished Reyes that he came to an abrupt halt. "What the fuck?" He looked past Crosby to Madison, then almost laughed at her expression of chagrin. Grinning at the interloper, Reyes asked, "You're trying to protect my sister?" If Crosby admitted it, Madison would probably flatten him herself. "From *me*?"

"I'm the one you're pissed at," Crosby stated. "Focus on me. Not her."

Cade snorted a laugh.

Kennedy stood there wide-eyed.

"How sweet," Madison said, immediately hooking her arm through Crosby's and more or less stealing his attention. "Since I know your intent is in the right place, I won't take offense." She grinned triumphantly at Reyes. "There, you see? He's an honorable cop, which is something I already knew, and which I wanted to explain to you, but you wouldn't listen."

Reyes eyed them all—then held out a hand to Kennedy. Carrying his gun gingerly, proof that she wasn't all that comfortable with firearms, she immediately hurried to his side. Voice low, she urged again, "Let it go, please. We need to talk."

Nodding, he took the gun and slid it into his back holster, then said to the others, "Go home." Holding Kennedy's hand, he turned and walked into the house. She kept trying to look back, but he didn't let her.

Cade, intuitive brother that he was, got to the door before Reyes could secure it. "Not on your life," he said, pushing his way over the threshold. Giving Madison a look, Cade said, "Inside. Now."

For Cade, she did as she was told.

Unfortunately, she brought Crosby with her.

Kennedy kept both of her arms locked around one of his—like she thought she could restrain him?—and said, "If you'll all excuse us a moment?" She began hauling him toward the guest room.

Over his shoulder, Reyes glared at Cade. "Stay put."

"I'm not about to budge," he promised. And, in fact, he stationed himself between Crosby and Madison.

"Damn, he's smooth," Reyes complained right before he closed the door behind him.

Kennedy immediately began explaining. "The detective brought a photo with him. Reyes, I think it's the man who had Jodi."

Wow. Not at all what he'd been expecting. Quickly reevaluating the situation, he asked, "What makes you think so?"

"Back when I first met her, Jodi described Rob Golly to me. He's one of those balding men with a ponytail. Missing teeth. A weak chin. The photo matched all that."

Sadly, that description matched a lot of dudes. "That doesn't mean—"

She shook her head. "His name is unique enough to stick, right? And then there's Crosby's description of the house where Jodi was taken." She turned away, her arms hugged around her middle. "He said he's been tracking Golly for a while. The things he shared…" She shuddered. "Horrible, horrible monster. Jodi's held it together only because she believed she'd killed him. If he somehow survived, if he's still alive, it'll destroy her."

"Or," Reyes said, his thoughts scrambling ahead, "she already knows he didn't die, and that's why she's worried for you. Whoever knows her might be exposed to his vengeance. Worse, anyone she cares about could be used against her."

Kennedy blinked at him. "I'm not worried about me."

He gave her a level look. "No reason you should be since I won't let anyone hurt you." He'd kill Golly and all his cronies before he'd let them lay a finger on Kennedy.

She started pacing. "I need to copy that photo so I can ask Jodi if it's him."

"Done. I'll take care of it."

Staring at him, her jaw loosened. "It can't be that easy. I got the feeling that Crosby suspects your whole family. He even made a veiled accusation about your father."

Ice skated down Reyes's spine. His voice lowered to a rough growl. "What did he say?"

"Just something vague really, but it was how he said it."

"Tell me."

She licked her lips, thinking. "Madison was trying to engage him in small talk. I think she was flirting."

"Doesn't sound like my sister." What the hell could Madison be up to? "She pays no attention to men."

"Well, she's been paying a lot of interested attention to Crosby."

Probably Madison's way of softening the guy up, taking him off guard, getting him to say too much. "How did that lead to my father?"

"Madison wanted him to tell her more about himself, about the task force or something like that. He said he wasn't on a task force, that his interest in Golly was personal. Instead of going into it, he wanted to hear more about her, you and Cade and your father, too. Something about your father being the head of it all."

Son of a bitch. "I should have killed him," he snarled. Still might.

Exasperated, Kennedy demanded, "Do you, or do you not, trust your sister?"

"Do." *But she'd been flirting?*

"And you don't indiscriminately kill men for asking questions, especially police officers."

No, but he could start. When she glared at him, he confirmed, "No, I don't."

"Madison isn't worried about him. When she saw him on the security cam, she recognized him. She opened the door and let him in without a qualm. I just... I don't know him, and I didn't think you'd want him here." She shrugged helplessly. "So I texted you."

"Hey." Reyes drew her against his chest. God, it felt good to hold her. On the drive back, he'd been running on a potent combo of instinct and adrenaline, anger and worry, unable to consider the possibilities of an intruder. "You did the right thing, babe. Anytime something feels off, even a little, I want you to let me know."

She dropped her forehead against him. "I've been here nearly a month, Reyes. This can't go on indefinitely."

His first impulse was to ask, *Why not?* He bit back that automatic response real fast. Why not? There were a million reasons, number one being that he didn't want a significant other. He liked his life of kicking ass when necessary, indulging in sex without emotional constraints, and fulfilling his father's edicts efficiently while never allowing the grisly details of the enterprise to overtake him.

"Shush." Holding Kennedy's shoulders, he stepped back and bent his knees to look into her pretty blue eyes. "You can't talk about leaving when we finally have something to go on. First thing we'll do is reach out to Jodi. I'll get that image from the cop, then we'll meet with her somewhere safe where I can control things."

"Jodi will never agree to meet with you."

"So we'll keep that part from her. Cade can be backup." Madison would, of course, provide necessary surveillance and digital security. "It'll be safe." Come hell or high water, he wouldn't let her be hurt. *Not ever again.*

Undecided, Kennedy visibly shored up her courage. "All right. But first you need that image. I won't upset Jodi without something concrete to show her."

Reyes cupped a hand to her cheek. "I don't want you to worry."

"Even you, Reyes McKenzie, don't get everything you want."

He grinned at her retreating back as she left the room. No, he wouldn't get everything. Pretty sure he might get Kennedy, though, at least long enough for them both to have a really good time.

Today, right now, that felt like enough.

DEL DIDN'T LIKE hiring others to do the dirty work, not when it was usually his favorite part. Imagining Kennedy's expression when he got his hands on her... It was all he'd had to think about lately, so yeah, he'd like to be there, upfront and real fucking personal.

Instead, he was stuck waiting with Mr. Butt-ugly, who kept grinning without saying anything.

Fucker got weirder by the day.

"Look, there's no reason to keep paying punks to handle things I could handle myself."

"Is that so?" Golly asked, still rocking, still smiling. "You're familiar with murder?"

"I don't want to *murder* Kennedy." Not right off, not after all this trouble. For a day or two he wanted her alive and kicking—then he'd gladly snuff her.

"You think *he'd* just let you take her?" Shaking his head, Golly said, "Don't be stupid. That one won't die easily. It'll take having more than one shooter on him, and even if they fail, I have two others in a truck, ready to ambush them on the road."

"Jesus, how many people are we paying?"

"Enough to get the job done."

Del *really* didn't like him. Worse, he sort of feared him—and that feeling grew more unsettling every day that he was stuck in Golly's company, witnessing his unhinged behavior.

There was no way of knowing when the prick might snap and kill everyone in sight.

The rocking abruptly stopped. "If it wasn't for me, you wouldn't even be close to getting your hands on that woman. *I'm* the one who knew to follow Jodi. I'm the one who discovered she was friends with Kennedy. The only reason you're involved at all is because I want Jodi to see what happened to her so-called friend. I want her to know what you're going to do to that bitch."

For about the hundredth time, Del regretted ever meeting the whack job, and he really wished he hadn't agreed to partner up with him.

It was pure happenstance that they'd discovered their connection. Del had lingered late one night at a truck stop to shop the wares. He'd picked out a sweet little honey who'd looked strung out and willing to chance a ride with any stranger. Yet once he'd gotten her in the car, Golly had come out of nowhere and joined them.

The plan, he knew, had been to kill him, then rob him.

Instead, Del had done some fast talking, explaining that he didn't give a shit what happened with the chick. He had run his own business once, so he got it.

One thing had led to another, they'd ended up sharing a meal while bragging on their ruthlessness… At the time, Golly had managed to act sane enough. A dupe, for sure.

Now here he was, becoming more embroiled by the day with a certifiable maniac. There was no guarantee that Jodi would meet up with Kennedy tonight, but so far, following her was their only chance.

Kennedy, the conniving bitch, had all but disappeared off the face of the earth. Once her apartment had burned to the ground: poof. No more Kennedy.

"Why do you want Jodi so bad?" Del asked, watching the man through a veil of smoke while he sucked on his cigarette. "She ain't much to look at. You could grab another broad easy enough."

He rocked faster. "She took from me. Stole things she can never give back. For that, she'll pay."

Shit. He was back to sounding off the rails. Del moved away to look out the window, hoping that tonight would be the night.

"I'm going to make her pay," Golly promised from behind him. The rocking chair began to squeak. He was so agitated, he even laughed. "She'll pay, and pay, and pay until I'm satisfied she's paid enough. It's as easy as that."

Misgivings growing, Del asked, "What the hell did she take that was so important?"

And once Golly explained, yeah, he understood.

Now he almost felt sorry for the scrawny girl—but he still felt sorrier for himself. Del needed away from Golly and soon, before he too became a target.

KENNEDY SAT STIFFLY beside Reyes as he pulled into the remote area at eight o'clock. The rough ground was bumpy and his truck headlights sent deep shadows stretching from tall fir trees and pinyon junipers.

It felt eerie and dangerous. And, damn it, Reyes was too silent.

She wasn't ready.

From the moment he'd started making his plans, everything had moved at lightning speed.

He'd talked a bit with Crosby, enough to get his measure, or so Reyes had said. Madison and Cade had taken part.

Never in her life had she felt more like an outsider. It was obvious that the siblings worked as a team, that they had an uncommon knowledge of things that went beyond even what Crosby had learned as a detective.

She'd tried to ask Reyes about it, but he'd gotten all hush-hush, doling out only a select few details that didn't really answer any of her questions.

Now here she was, ready to meet with Jodi if her friend showed.

Like Kennedy, Jodi had been uncertain of the whole thing.

With Reyes listening in, she'd called Jodi. Twice. No answer either time. It wasn't until the middle of last night that Jodi had finally called back, waking her from a sound sleep.

She'd been groggy and confused, but not Reyes. He'd pressed her away from his body, where she'd been snugly held, and quickly prepped her on what to say and not say.

He'd stayed silent beside her while she answered the call, but having him there had made it easier.

She'd told Jodi that she had to see her, and to her surprise, Jodi hadn't argued.

Instead, as if she'd been expecting the request, Jodi had arranged for the meeting at this remote location in the mountains. At one time it had been camping grounds, but the owner hadn't maintained the property, so other than a rut-filled road leading to what had once been a clearing, there was nothing around.

And the sun had set some time ago.

"Take a breath, babe. Everything is fine. Cade came in on foot and he's the best backup around. We have eyes on the truck so Madison can not only track us, she can see anyone else who might get near us. Remember, I won't let anything happen to you."

See, all *that*? Who the hell talked about eyes on a truck, meaning some high-tech surveillance stuff, and solid backup, meaning his brother was armed and ready to shoot if necessary?

Clenching her hands together, Kennedy asked, "Who are you people?"

"Shh. I'm gonna kill the lights now, okay? Then we'll go the rest of the way on foot."

And when they got near to the center of the clearing, Reyes would hang back.

She'd be alone, exposed.

No. He said he'd protect her and she believed him. God, she wished she was stronger, as clever as Madison or as fearless as Sterling. But she wasn't. She was just Kennedy Brooks, traumatized girl unable to move out of the past, trying to be a confident woman and failing far too often.

Reyes stopped the truck in a copse of tall trees. Everything went dark.

"Hey." He pried one of her hands loose, carrying it over to his mouth, where he pressed a warm kiss to her knuckles. "You've got this, babe. And I've got you. I swear, I won't let anything happen to you."

She nodded, knew he couldn't see her in the dark, and whispered, "I know. I'm just..." So cold and empty. "I'm fine."

"Yeah, you are. Extra fine." This time, he leaned in and his mouth brushed over her cheek, her jaw, down to the corner of her lips.

Holy smokes. That chased away the ice in her veins. "What are you doing?"

"Warming you up. Did it work?"

"Actually…yes." She exhaled a long breath. Funny, she did feel steadier. Who knew a kiss could accomplish that much? "Thank you."

"You and your gratitude." He flashed her a grin that did more to reassure her than all the words in the world. "Stay put until I come around. You have your flashlight?"

"Yes." She lifted the heavy utility light off the floor of the truck.

"Warm enough?"

No, but that had more to do with her nerves than the October temperatures in the mountains. She'd dressed appropriately, even had a stocking hat for her ears. "I'm—" She started to say *fine* again, but after his silly flattery with the word, she adjusted to, "Ready."

Without another word, Reyes got out and somehow, without making a single sound, came to her side of the truck and opened the door.

Wow, the man was a wraith. More and more, she wanted to know the backstory of what he and his family did.

Accepting his hand, she climbed from the truck. She, of course, made far too much noise as her hiking boots crunched over fallen leaves, twigs and rocks. Without the flashlight, she couldn't see, but apparently Reyes had no problem. He led, she followed, and with every step she tried to calm her rioting pulse.

They walked for maybe five minutes before he pulled her to a halt. Keeping his mouth close to her ear, he breathed, "I'm waiting right here behind this outcrop of rock. Go about ten steps and then turn on the flashlight. You'll see the fallen tree. That's where Jodi wants you to wait."

She remembered. Jodi had been adamant that she come alone. Reyes had flatly refused, promising to wait at the base of the road.

Obviously, a lie.

Supposedly, Cade was already in place, and Madison felt confident that Jodi would approach from a different direction. Reyes had agreed with her assessment.

It all seemed far too clandestine for her peace of mind.

Cautiously stepping away from Reyes, Kennedy counted her steps, tripped once, felt a juniper branch scratch her cheek and finally was able to turn on the flashlight.

She spotted the fallen tree right off. She also heard night sounds she hadn't noticed while standing so close to Reyes. Wind, animals, insects. The urge to look back, to prove he was still there, tested her resolve, but he'd schooled her on what not to do, and that was a biggie. He didn't want her giving him away.

What if a bear showed up? Or even a big spider?

The snap of twigs lodged her heart in her throat, and then Jodi stepped out from behind a tree.

Her friend kept her distance, her mistrust palpable. "Where's your boyfriend?"

The caustic question unfroze something inside Kennedy. This was Jodi, and that tone of voice was so familiar that it worked wonders for relieving her fears. "He's nearby if I need him," she admitted, and she could almost hear Reyes groaning his disappointment that she hadn't stuck to the plan. "Jodi, how are you?" Despite her worries, a genuine smile slipped up on her. "It's good to see you."

Lifting her chin, Jodi asked, "Do you mean that?"

"Yes, I do." Taking a few more steps, Kennedy bounced the flashlight around the area. "This is a weird place for a meeting. It feels creepy."

"To me, it feels safe."

"Safe from what?"

"Anyone. Everyone."

The reminder of Jodi's fear broke Kennedy's heart. Whereas she had, overall, moved on with her life, Jodi hadn't—and probably never would.

"Have you lost weight?" Jodi was a short woman, always on the thin side, yet with enough attitude for an Amazon. Tonight she looked positively frail. Even bundled up beneath a sweatshirt, Kennedy could see that she was at least ten pounds lighter. Her black leggings hung loose around her knees and bunched above her boots. The sweatshirt slouched off shoulders that were far too narrow.

Chin notching up even more, Jodi shook back her messy brown hair and sneered, "Someone's been following me, so yeah, I've skipped a few meals."

Oh, God. "Why didn't you tell me?" Taking two more steps toward her, Kennedy reached out. "You know I would help you however I can."

"Yeah? Glad to hear it." Jodi came closer.

Kennedy expected an embrace even though Jodi wasn't usually the hugging type.

Instead, Jodi took her by surprise by snaking an arm around her neck, snatching her back against a tree. Her shoulder thumped against the trunk and the flashlight nearly fell from her hand.

It took a second for the gesture to register, for Kennedy to realize that Jodi had her in a bruising choke hold. "What are you doing?" Not only was Jodi's arm clamped so tight under her chin that Kennedy could barely draw breath, but now Jodi had a gun in her hand, and she aimed it in the direction of where Reyes waited.

"I know you're out there," Jodi said, her voice hard and filled with anger. "Come out."

Kennedy frantically tried to twist away, which only

prompted Jodi to tighten her hold. Obviously, this was a familiar move to her friend, and she had it fairly well perfected.

Kennedy was a few inches taller than Jodi, and probably had twenty pounds on her, yet she couldn't get free. Not without trying to hurt Jodi, and she didn't want to do that. Not yet anyway...

This was ridiculous! She thought about tossing the flashlight so she'd have both hands to work with, but that might make it difficult for Reyes to see her.

Reyes stepped out with his own gun at the ready. "Loosen up," he ordered. "You're hurting her."

Ignoring that, Jodi asked, "Why are you here?"

Unconcerned with his own safety, Reyes strode closer. "Try to hurt her," he warned, "and I'll put a bullet through your brain."

"I don't want to hurt *her*," Jodi shouted, sounding genuinely appalled by the accusation.

"Terrific. Then we should be able to get along because I don't want to hurt you."

"Says the big man with a weapon," she sneered.

"To protect Kennedy," he promised evenly. "And Jodi, if necessary, I'd protect you, too."

"Liar," she screamed.

"You don't have to take my word for it." Reyes stopped, his gaze unflinching. "Do you think Kennedy would lie to you?"

Her arm tightened in reaction. "Now that you've corrupted her, who knows?"

"Jodi." Little stars started to dance before Kennedy's eyes. "Can't...breathe."

"Oh, God." Immediately, Jodi released her, then had to help support her as she started to slump.

The flashlight fell from her hand with a thud. In the next

second, Reyes was there, first taking Jodi's gun from her and then putting his strong arm around Kennedy's waist. "I've got you, babe. It's okay."

"Reyes." Finally able to gulp in enough air, she wheezed, "She's my friend."

"I know. Here, sit down." He lowered her to the fallen log and crouched in front of her. "Okay now?"

Her throat ached, but otherwise she felt okay. Her gaze sought out Jodi. The beam of the fallen flashlight skimmed over the ground, stopping at the toes of Jodi's boots and barely illuminating her face. One hand pressed to her mouth, the other to her middle. She looked devastated. Wounded, guilty, horrified...

"I'm okay, Jodi." Seeing the terror in her friend's eyes, Kennedy pleaded, "Please don't run. I really do need to talk to you."

Jodi was undecided, her muscles shifting, her eyes darting around.

Reyes looked up and beyond her, and then gave a soft curse. Almost at the same time, his phone buzzed.

"Stay low," he said to Kennedy, pulled out his phone to glance at the screen, then palmed his gun again. "Jodi, listen to me. We've got company."

"No." Frantically, she searched the area.

"My brother spotted three people coming up from the same direction you used."

"Brother?" she snarled, and then in the next breath, "I wasn't followed! I couldn't have been."

Keeping his voice calm and even, he said, "We need to get to my truck. Now."

A shot sounded, then sounded again and again in a terrible echo that split the quiet of the night. Immediately, footfalls thumped over the ground, shaking bushes and disturbing brambles.

"Assuming you can shoot, you need your gun," Reyes said. "Now get your ass over here, but stay low."

Oddly enough, Jodi did just that.

She stationed herself in front of Kennedy.

Well, that was embarrassing. "What should I do?" Kennedy asked. She desperately needed to feel useful.

Without answering, Reyes pressed them both down and used his own body as a shield. Silence descended, and somehow that was almost worse. There were two more shots, each coming from a different direction.

"They've fanned out," Reyes murmured, but he didn't look or sound worried.

Bully for him. She was worried enough for everyone. For Cade. For Jodi.

And especially for Reyes.

When his phone buzzed again, he withdrew it, used his thumb to unlock the screen and handed it to Kennedy.

Surprised, she quickly read the message aloud. "Retreating. Go now."

Just like that, he surged to his feet, swiped up the flashlight and said, "Hustle, babe, while we have the chance." He urged Kennedy forward with a hand around her upper arm.

"Jodi," she said, resisting just enough to grab for her friend.

Jodi ducked away. "My car—"

"For the love of sanity…" Reyes released Kennedy to snatch hold of Jodi's sweatshirt and then propelled them both along. "There's something you have to see, Jodi, so stop fighting. I'm not a threat to you."

Kennedy quickly took Jodi's other arm. "I swear it's true."

Subsiding, Jodi picked up the pace. "That was your brother who texted?"

"Yeah. He'll follow us out of here." Reyes drew the flashlight over and around his four-door Ram truck, likely ensuring no one was near it, and then he killed the light.

"Where's your brother's car?"

"Where no one will see it." He opened the rear door of the cab and hoisted Kennedy up into the narrow back seat with more haste than care, dropping the flashlight into her lap. "Figured you two would want to sit close so you can share that image on your phone."

"What image?" Jodi hauled herself in and scooted closer to Kennedy, which put her away from Reyes.

"No lights yet, okay?" Competence personified, Reyes got behind the wheel and started the truck in what felt like a single motion. The doors locked. "I'll tell you when."

"Okay, Reyes." Yes, Kennedy was rattled, but he was so calm and efficient about the whole process, she wasn't nearly as scared as she'd thought she'd be.

"I'm proud of you," he said suddenly. Leaving off the headlights, he turned a wide circle and easily made his way back to the uneven road.

"Me?" Kennedy asked. "Whatever for?"

"You kept it together," he said, while being vigilant to their surroundings. "You kept your priorities straight. You even understood your friend when I didn't. If it hadn't been for that, I might have…" The truck bumped along. "I didn't like seeing her restrain you."

Both women were silent, until Jodi whispered, "I'm sorry about that. I didn't mean to hurt her. I just… It was a reaction. To a threat, I mean."

"She knew that, I guess." Reyes blew out a breath. "I didn't."

"You don't trust me?" Jodi guessed.

"'Bout as much as you trust me, I'd say. Difference is

that I trust Kennedy, and if she says you're okay, I believe her."

Knowing how confusing this had to be for Jodi, Kennedy patted her forearm. "Where are we going, Reyes?" To Jodi, information was power. She'd feel better with more details.

"Convenience mart or something. A place where there's plenty of light. Then you and Jodi can…talk."

"Without you giving me the evil eye?" Jodi asked.

"You'll get the eye," he said, "and everything that comes with it, because no matter who you are, no matter how much she trusts you, you've got trouble on your tail and I'm not letting it anywhere near Kennedy."

Jodi gave her the most comically bemused expression. "Who the hell *is* he?"

A good question. There were many layers to Reyes McKenzie, and Kennedy wanted to uncover each one. "He's a good man," she said simply, because that much she knew one hundred percent.

Jodi snorted. "Yeah, like Bigfoot and unicorns, huh?" She crossed her arms and slumped into the corner of the cab. "I think I'll wait and judge for myself."

Reyes left the dirt road and flipped on his headlights right before he turned onto pavement and accelerated, leaving the spooky campgrounds and danger behind.

Or so Kennedy thought.

CHAPTER TEN

KENNEDY WAS ABOUT to ask Reyes if she could now use the light from her phone when he gave a low curse.

Glancing in the rearview mirror, he asked, "You two buckled up?"

Kennedy watched Jodi quickly hook her seat belt, then she answered, "Yes. Why?"

"Hang on." He swerved sharply to the right.

Kennedy knocked into Jodi, with only the seat belt keeping her upright. The blinding glare of high beam headlights flashed into the back window of the truck, causing her heart to jump into her throat.

Reyes jerked the truck into the left lane and hit the brakes. Another truck went barreling past them and then immediately screeched into the middle of the road, stopping sideways.

He punched the gas and shot past them again, going half off the road and narrowly missing the front fender.

Kennedy felt like her teeth had been jarred loose. Knowing Reyes had his hands full, she kept as silent as possible so she wouldn't distract him, her body tense from her toes to her eyebrows.

"Are...are they after me?" Jodi asked.

"Or me," Reyes said. "Maybe Kennedy. Who the fuck knows? No worries, though, I've got this."

Again Jodi gave her an incredulous look, one that asked, *Is he insane?*

Kennedy shrugged.

Reyes drove faster and faster, but on this stretch of road, there was no other traffic, no exits—and no one to help.

"There's Cade," he said.

She looked back and realized another vehicle was now behind them.

"Do me a favor, babe? Duck down."

Confused, Kennedy asked, "Duck…?"

"Down," he barked.

When Jodi bent forward in the seat, Kennedy copied her.

A second later, gunshots rang out, followed by the screaming of tires and finally an awful crash.

Reyes pulled to the side of the road. Before Kennedy could get her wits about her, he said, "Lock up behind me," and then he…

He left the truck!

"Reyes!" Scrambling for the door, Kennedy opened it enough to shout, "What in the world are you doing?"

"Taking care of business." He pushed the door shut again. "Lock it."

With his eyes ablaze and his expression hard, Kennedy obediently hit the lock.

He gave one firm nod and turned away.

Good heavens. She'd never seen him like that. Peeking over the back seat, she watched him, utterly fascinated and scared to death for him.

In a long, purposeful stride, he approached their pursuers, staying just outside the direct beam of the other truck. It was twisted, the front end smashed against the rise of the mountain. Kennedy didn't see any movement.

Unhooking her seat belt, Jodi twisted about on her knees and watched, too. "Is that his brother coming up the other side?"

Until Jodi said it, Kennedy hadn't noticed Cade—strange, since he was so incredibly large. "Yes."

"They're unusual."

An understatement.

Jodi nudged her. "I think they can be just as dangerous as the goons who were chasing us."

"Most definitely." So far, Reyes was the most lethal person she'd ever known, and, given her background, that was saying something.

Together they saw Reyes and Cade look into the truck, then around it. Reyes pried open the damaged front door and leaned inside. The headlights went out and the grinding from the engine died.

When Reyes straightened again, he and Cade shared a short conversation. Apparently the danger was over?

Not that she'd believe it—until Reyes told her so.

"You wanted to show me something?" Jodi glanced around, wary as always, squinting into shadows and searching the long, empty stretch of road. "That's why we're here, right?"

Shoot. After all that, Kennedy almost didn't want to. "It's going to upset you, but I want you to know, I'm here with you every step of the way."

Stoic, Jodi straightened her shoulders. "What will the big guy have to say about that?"

Being honest, she said, "There's a lot I don't know about Reyes."

"Yeah, well, I thought I knew him, but clearly I only skimmed the tip of the iceberg."

Her cocky attitude didn't fool Kennedy. Jodi was afraid, the type of bone-deep fear felt by a woman who'd once been in hell. It'd be better for her if Kennedy cut to the chase instead of letting her dread build.

Pulling her cell phone from her pocket, Kennedy adjusted the settings. Earlier, she'd silenced it and turned down the brightness, and now she adjusted it back. "A detective came to see us. He's been hunting someone, and he thought Reyes might know something about him. Unfortunately, he didn't—but I think I may have recognized him."

"Him?" Expression changing, Jodi demanded, "Is it the man who had you? The one who got away?"

"No." Somehow, she thought that man was small-time when compared to Rob Golly.

And yet, both men were almost insignificant when compared to Reyes. They were pure evil, but Reyes was bigger, braver, smarter, stronger. Also kinder, more caring, funnier.

He was all things good, which made him a perfect counterbalance to their cruelty.

She pulled up the photo on her phone. Thanks to Madison, it was a clearer, neater image than the one Crosby had carried. Glancing back at Reyes again, Kennedy saw that he stared toward her, keeping her in sight, ever vigilant, while speaking on his phone. Maybe talking to his sister? That'd make sense, given that Madison would be able to tell them a lot about this stretch of road.

Unable to put it off any longer, she took Jodi's hand in her own, locking their fingers together, and then turned the phone so she could see it.

A low sound, like that a wounded animal would make, slipped past Jodi's parted lips.

Heart breaking, Kennedy knew she had her answer.

"He's *dead*," Jodi rasped.

Maybe. "Shh. Let me explain, okay?" Jodi continued to stare at the photo. "The detective said he went to the house—I think the one where Golly kept you."

Jodi shook her head. "His body—"

"There was no body."

"I *killed* him," she growled, the words barely audible.

"Honey…are you sure?"

"Yes!" She tried to snap her hand away, but Kennedy held on.

If she released Jodi, her friend would probably leap from the truck and disappear. It's what Jodi did. She ran when threatened, and only reappeared when she thought Kennedy might need her.

Using that to her advantage, Kennedy whispered, "I need you here, Jodi. Whatever is going on, we can sort it out together."

"You don't need me!" She hitched her chin toward the window. "You have *them*, now."

Startled, Kennedy glanced back and found Cade and Reyes watching them, equal expressions of concern on their faces.

Ignoring them for the moment, Kennedy scooted closer to Jodi and lowered her voice. "They're men and they haven't been through what we have. We back each other up, remember? You're stronger than me, Jodi. I can help sort this out, but I need to be able to reach you when necessary. I need to know you're safe."

Settling her shoulders back against the seat, Jodi whispered, "You're strong, too, otherwise you wouldn't be crushing my fingers."

"Oh, my God, I'm sorry." Quickly she freed Jodi, and, as she'd assumed, Jodi was out of the truck in a heartbeat.

Kennedy heard Cade say, "Don't make me chase you. It's getting damned cold out here and cops could show up any minute."

"Or more thugs," Reyes added.

Kennedy slid across the seat to get out on Jodi's side. By God, if Jodi took off, she'd chase her down herself.

Trying to be as casual as everyone else, Kennedy got

close to Jodi, then asked over the truck bed, "The driver of the truck?"

"Dead," Reyes said, already walking around to her. "We've made a plan."

"My plan," Jodi said, "is to get my car and get out of here."

Cade casually approached around the other side, but Kennedy wasn't fooled. There was a coiled readiness about both brothers, and she didn't think it was on her behalf. Shoot, they both knew she wasn't about to charge away from safety.

But Jodi? Yep, Jodi looked ready to take on the world. Alone.

"I know where your car is," Cade said. "The plan is for me to take you to it—"

"No."

As if Jodi hadn't interrupted, Cade continued with, "—so I can make sure no one else is lurking around. Then I'll follow you to a main highway. At that point, you can do as you please."

"But Jodi?" Reyes gave her a long look. "You need some backup. If Golly is out there, he might be the one who set the fire to Kennedy's apartment building."

"To get to me," she rasped, her hands clenched into fists at her sides, her expression grim.

"It's possible. I can't go into everything now. We're not safe standing here, so how about you keep us informed of where you'll be at all times?"

"I don't know." She pushed her hair from her face. "I'll think about it."

"Think while I drive you back to your car," Cade suggested.

Kennedy was impressed that Cade sounded so reasonable, so nonthreatening when anyone could see he was a walking weapon.

Just like Reyes.

When Jodi looked at her with indecision, Kennedy stepped forward. "Please? I won't be able to bear it if anything happens to you. You're like family."

"Family," Jodi repeated, as if weighing the word.

"Sisters," Kennedy stressed.

Jodi's mouth quirked. "I'd be the black sheep of the family, you know. The weirdo that everyone dreaded seeing."

"Not true." Kennedy moved closer, saying again, "Please, Jodi."

It took her far too long before Jodi found a flippant way to give in. "Yeah, sure. Why not? These two can't be more dangerous than Golly, or whoever is pretending to be him."

Oh, Kennedy hadn't even considered that. Someone pretending to be Golly? Was it possible?

"We need to roll." Reyes took her hand and tugged her to the front seat.

"Come on," Cade said to Jodi, gesturing toward his SUV. "Time to end this miserable night. The problems will still be there in the morning."

Kennedy looked over her shoulder.

Jodi walked backward to keep her in sight.

Near her ear, Reyes said, "She'll be okay, honey. I promise."

Wondering how he could guarantee such a thing, Kennedy nodded. "We'll talk in the morning," she called to Jodi.

"Sure thing." And with that, Jodi turned and fell into step beside Cade.

MISERABLE, INCOMPETENT FUCKS. Del glared as Golly disconnected his call and carefully set the phone on the table.

"What do you mean, they were both there but got away?"

At first, laughter was the only answer.

At the end of his rope, Del snapped, "Answer me, damn it!"

"He's better than we thought."

We? So far, Del hadn't been allowed much input at all. "Yeah? How's that?"

"We thought we had a setup, but it was the other way around. Somehow, that bodyguard of hers anticipated us being there."

"I wasn't anywhere except in this stupid dump!"

"It's a lovely cabin, not a dump, and you complain too much."

Del would have killed another man for that offhand insult, but this man? No, the way he watched Del made his skin crawl. "So what happened?"

"Shots were fired. My men were pinned down. The drivers I set to ambush them should have had it in hand, but that didn't work out, either, apparently."

Taking a chance, Del suggested, "So maybe I should plan the next—"

"No!" Slamming his hands down on the table, Golly rose to his feet and stared hard at Del, his protruding gut nearly busting the seams of his shirt. "She won't get away again."

"Jodi? Yeah, that's fine for you. But I need to stop Kennedy before she gets the cops on my ass again."

"I'll get them both," he promised, relaxing again, his twisted smile back in place. "Kennedy will be my gift to you."

Fuck that. Del didn't want to owe this man anything. It was past time he started making his own plans—separate from the lunatic. "Yeah, sure." Del decided it'd be easiest to just placate him. "Sounds good. Thanks." First chance he got, probably early tomorrow morning, he'd take off on his own. Once he did, he'd never again make a bargain with the devil—especially a devil who was bat-shit crazy.

ONCE THEY WERE ALONE, Reyes made haste getting them away from the area. He constantly checked the rearview mirror, regardless of how far they drove. Used to be, that would have made her nervous. Now she understood that it was just his way of using extra caution.

They were almost to his house when his cell rang. Driving one-handed, he held the phone to his ear and said, "All done? Great. Yeah, we'll be home in five. Tell Madison thanks for me, too." For a few seconds Reyes listened, then glanced at her and shrugged. "Sure, we can do that. All right, I'll see you both then."

"What?" she immediately asked.

"Cade tailed Jodi home. Jodi doesn't know that, though, so don't tell her. She thought he dropped back once they got to a more congested area."

"But he didn't?"

"No, he didn't. He circled back and followed her to a dive motel on the outskirts of town, to make sure no one else bothered her. We're nothing if not thorough. The motel, by the way, is near an I-70 on-ramp, not more than thirty minutes from Cade's bar, The Tipsy Wolverine."

Kennedy blinked at the name. *The Tipsy Wolverine?* "You're making that up."

"Nope." For only the briefest moment, he hesitated, then seemed to give a mental shrug. "I have a gym, Cade has a bar, we hear shit at both—that's part of how we operate."

A nugget of info? Desperately needing a new focus, Kennedy jumped on that. "Operate?"

"Patience, doll. For now, I need to tell you something else, but I need your word you won't say anything to Jodi."

If she didn't trust Reyes so much, his serious tone might really bother her. "All right."

"Cade tagged Jodi's car before he came after us. We'll have GPS on her wherever she goes. Usually that's something I'd keep to myself, but I'm telling you so you won't worry too much. She might get spooked and run, but we'll be able to find her."

Her heart, her emotions, softened. "To make sure she's safe?"

"Yeah."

Could he be more wonderful? "Thank you."

"You're not pissed?"

How could he think that? "I'm incredibly grateful that you're helping her."

"Whether she wants my help or not?"

Yes, Jodi had given that impression. And on the surface, she might even believe that she'd rather go it alone. But deep down?

Deep down, she desperately needed help. For a multitude of reasons, Kennedy was fairly certain that Reyes would understand. "She's so wounded," Kennedy explained. "So suspicious of everyone, I'm not sure she'd ever ask for help no matter how badly she needed it. It'd take a lot to earn her trust."

"You managed it."

"Only because we share a similar background."

He seemed pained by that reminder. "We're going to rendezvous with Cade and Madison at my dad's place tomorrow."

"Your dad?" she choked.

"Don't let him scare you, okay? No matter how much he scowls."

"Why would he scowl at me?" Even the possibility made

her irate. She'd been through hell lately. She wouldn't let anyone, not even Reyes's father, treat her badly.

"Dad's just gruff, that's all. But hey, you'll finally get to see Chimera again, and you'll get to meet Bernard. I think you'll like him, mostly because he worships that cat."

"So I'll like Bernard but not your father?"

"Bernard, when he's not stealing cats, is a pretty likable guy."

Her mouth twitched. "He stole our cat?"

Reyes rolled his eyes. "That was humor. Sort of. None of us knew Bernard liked animals until I brought Chimera home and he went bonkers over her. When you meet him, you'll know how funny this is, but he was doing the whole baby-talk thing to her. Crazy. And those kittens? It was love at first sight. He did more or less steal the cat, but it made him so happy, I didn't really mind. I just act like I do to give Bernard a hard time, you know?"

No, she didn't know. It seemed that irritating people, especially family, was one of Reyes's favorite pastimes.

The whole idea of meeting his father and Bernard concerned her. It wouldn't be for the typical reasons a guy brought a woman home to meet the rest of his family. Not in her situation. It was more likely a safety issue, since that was his number one reason for keeping her around.

Alarming for sure. She'd already accepted that her life was on the line, but for them all to be involved... Maybe it was even worse than she'd thought.

To give herself some time, Kennedy turned to stare out the window, barely noticing the passing scenery, until Reyes pulled into the garage. It had been such an eventful day. Her stomach was still uneasy and every nerve seemed to be twitching.

Her world was again a scary place, but she wasn't facing it alone. And neither was Jodi.

That gave her more comfort than she could explain, and it was all because of Reyes.

Such a remarkable man he was.

Continually glancing at her, he turned off the truck and came around to her side, gently assisting her out of the truck as if he thought she might fall apart at any minute.

She *was* a little emotional, mostly with gratitude.

Everything he'd done for her made her want to hold him tight—so he'd hold her tight in return. While he and Cade, and even Jodi, had handled the threats fearlessly, she'd been a jittery mess.

They stepped into the house together, and, God, it felt good to be home. Maybe not her home, not long-term, but for now it felt more like home than anything had since her kidnapping.

"Jodi's right, you know." Reyes led her to the living room. "You're stronger than you think."

She gave a small laugh. "I was so nervous, I nearly crushed her fingers."

"That's not what I'm talking about." He tipped up her chin. "That shit tonight could have rattled anyone. Another woman might have been hysterical. But you, babe, you followed instructions without arguing, you didn't cry or fall apart and, not only that, you helped take care of Jodi." He threaded his fingers into her hair. "She thinks she's a badass, but that girl is shook. Being on her own would be a terrible thing, and you, with your big heart and logic, reached her when I'm not sure anyone else could have."

"Reyes." Giving in to her need, she put her arms tightly around him and borrowed some of his strength. Being this near to him, feeling his heat and breathing his scent, went a long way toward leveling her nerves, yet she continued to tremble.

Reyes didn't judge her, though. Nope, he saw the best

in her. And damn it, she was starting to fall in love with him because of it.

"You're amazing," she whispered, and then confessed, "I don't know what I'd do without you right now."

REYES HAD NEVER had a woman cling to him like that, not without the addition of sex, but even then, it was different. Hungry or playful.

Not appreciative.

Kennedy's desperate hold, the tripping of her heartbeat and the feathering of her breath against his neck did something to him. Something unfamiliar. He tucked her closer, reassuring her. "You're all right."

"Because of you." She burrowed into him. "I know you don't want to hear it, but thank you."

"Shush. It's all right." Without meaning to, he pressed his mouth to the tender skin of her temple.

Her face turned toward him, and suddenly they were nose to nose, sharing breath and staring into each other's eyes.

A sexual moment for him, but he seriously doubted she viewed it the same way.

When he started to move away, she held him tighter. "I'm not upset."

"No?" She had every right to be. Someone was after her, Jodi or both of them. If the two fucks in the truck hadn't died, he could have questioned them. As it was, he'd removed their wallets and passed them to Cade. Hopefully, Madison would have plenty to share with him tomorrow.

"I was," Kennedy admitted. "The gunshots—"

"Cade had that in hand, and if one of the idiots got by him, I'd have taken care of it."

"So self-assured," she teased.

"I'm prepared," he said seriously. "Well trained."

And...he cared about her.

"Yes, it's been easy to see that you can handle yourself. But, Reyes, they tried to drive us off the road."

"And how did that turn out?" With two dead bodies, that's how.

She shook her head. "You amaze me. You stayed so blasted calm through all of it."

Taking her hand, he led her to the couch. He didn't pull her onto his lap this time, not when he was feeling so oddly territorial. Instead, he put his arm around her shoulders and drew her comfortably into his side. "Since you'll meet Dad tomorrow, I figure I better explain a few things."

"What things?"

"Long ago..." Hell, he sounded like the start of a *Star Wars* movie. "When I was thirteen, actually, my mother was taken, trafficked—and that changed Dad."

Horrified, she bit her lips. "God, I'm so sorry."

"He found her. Dad would have charged through hell for her, and a few times I think he did."

Kennedy rested a hand on his chest. "Is she okay now?"

He shook his head. "A year later, she committed suicide." He didn't want to dwell on that memory for too long. "I know what that type of abuse does to a person. I saw it in my mom—and I saw it in my dad. It changed him. He and Mom both came from money, then they made more of their own. Not bragging about finances or anything, just saying Dad had the funds and the motivation to turn his focus almost solely to taking down traffickers." He rested his chin against her silky hair, breathing in the scent of her while forcing all emotion from his tone. "That focus included grooming us—Cade, me and Madison— into weapons. We started learning every fighting technique there is, usually from the best trainers in the world.

Hand-to-hand combat, grappling, boxing, mixed martial arts. We're versed in it all."

"Madison, too?"

"Yep. Though Dad groomed her for computer work, he wanted each of us to have a well-rounded education."

"Was there room for affection?" she asked softly.

"I guess. It was a difficult time, you know? Cade rebelled." Smiling, Reyes said, "He doesn't do well with orders, which is funny, since he joined the military to escape Dad's regimen. There, he excelled. With Dad? They're so much alike, they always butted heads."

"And now?"

"Sterling changed things. I think she blunted a bunch of Cade's anger and resistance."

"It sounds like you like her, but I got the impression you two don't get along."

"She's my sister-in-law and I love her, but yeah, I enjoy twitting her."

"You," Kennedy said, poking him in the stomach, "enjoy twitting everyone."

"Maybe." This whole discussion was easier than he'd expected, because Kennedy was so easy to be around. "Cade trained, the same as we all did. His pride demanded he be the best."

"How old was he?"

"Fifteen." Now that he'd started talking, Reyes wanted to share other things, too, things he'd never discussed with anyone, not even his siblings. "Cade is a half brother. Maybe that has something to do with how he's always been."

"Different mothers?"

"Yeah. When he was born, his mom gave him to Dad and moved on, and that was that. He's never met her. But to Madison and me, he's our big brother and nothing will ever change that."

"Of course. You were all raised together?"

He nodded. "My mom was basically his mom, too, until we lost her. We were all devastated, you know? And then Dad made his decision and we didn't really have time to grieve. On top of learning to fight, we're experts with weapons, from every improvised implement you'd find on the street to military grade."

"And that tricky driving you did?"

"Dad's covered every scenario," he confirmed. "Before you start thinking he's too mercenary, he also started a task force to help ensure victims are legally represented, that they get any counseling they need, and enough financial aid to start over."

"Wow. Your dad sounds pretty phenomenal."

"He is." He could also be overbearing, dictatorial and downright cold at times. Except that... Sterling had changed him some, too. Maybe it was getting Cade back as his son that made the difference. Reyes admitted, "I used to be a real hell-raiser."

"No?" she said with facetious surprise.

Reyes gave her a squeeze. "Dad didn't seem to care as long as I channeled my anger and energy into what he considered the right direction, which basically meant defending someone. But Cade? That dude is military through and through, and he's all about personal control. He put the stomp on my bad attitude real quick."

Rearing up, Kennedy frowned at him. "What does that mean?"

Her automatic defense made him grin. "It means anytime I got too froggy, Cade showed me that his quiet control trumped my rage every time. He always made it into a lesson. Like he'd block one of my punches, give me a smack, and explain why he'd managed it so easily."

Her scowl darkened. "I don't think I like the idea of him putting hands on you."

"Ah, hon, Cade and I have been sparring since we were early teens. This was no different. And I did learn. Funny thing, too, was that Dad would watch on with a satisfied smile, as if it made him proud to see Cade school me." He shook his head with a short laugh. "It's the truth, I'm a better man because of Cade. Better fighter, better strategist, probably a better son and brother."

"Did he teach you to shoot, too?"

"Actually, that's the one place where I'm better than him. I'm a top-notch marksman. Cade is good, better than many, but I have the edge there."

"Your family sounds absolutely fascinating."

He enjoyed this more than was wise. Having Kennedy curled up against him, her hand idly resting over his abs, her frowns and her smiles, her trust, felt like an amazing gift.

"What about your family?"

She ducked her face again. "There's just my mom and dad. They're both terrific."

"You haven't told them everything that's going on now?"

"They'd just worry." Her fingertips toyed with the buttons of his flannel shirt, stopping near his navel—and making him nuts. "They're quiet people, very involved in their church, and they were hurt so badly when I was taken."

Eyes narrowing, Reyes lifted her face. "Don't tell me they blamed you."

"No, of course not. Mom and Dad both cried for days when I returned. They'd aged so much, all from grief." She lowered her eyes. "They love me and I love them, but I couldn't stay in Florida. Not anymore. It was hard for them to grasp that type of evil. Mom would look at me and then suddenly crumble again. It was heartbreaking, for both of us. Dad couldn't bear seeing my mother so upset, and he felt like he'd somehow failed me."

"So you moved on?"

"Not the way you're saying it. I stayed long enough to convince them I was fine, then I moved away with a lot of happy fanfare, letting them think I was on an adventure for life." She sighed. "We talk often, and I try to get home at least once a year to see them, but I will never again deliberately worry them."

"Hey." He couldn't stop himself from pressing a kiss in between her brows, where a fretful frown lingered. "You were a victim, and parents are supposed to worry for their kids. That's not on you. It's on the bastards who took you."

Her gaze relaxed...then dipped down to his mouth. Yeah, much more of that and instincts would take over. He'd be kissing her hot and hungry before he had time to talk himself down.

He sat forward and, in a voice as casual as he could make it, he said, "It's getting late." He stood and pulled her to her feet. "I can be ready for bed in twenty minutes. How about you?"

She searched his face, her expression confused, a little embarrassed, but she managed a smile that didn't reach her eyes. "I need thirty minutes, so don't rush."

Reyes watched her head to the guest room, and he knew—oh, yeah, he knew—it was going to be a very long night sleeping beside her.

CHAPTER ELEVEN

WELL, HE HADN'T been wrong. An hour had passed and still he stared up at the ceiling, full of conflicts and hunger, both horny and swamped with tenderness.

Seeing that look on Kennedy's face when he'd abruptly moved away... He'd done that to her.

What should he have done instead?

He thought back to Sterling's advice, about how he should ease into things. He'd agreed to give it a try, and then instead he'd blown it.

There wasn't much he feared in life, but he detested the idea of pushing Kennedy, maybe making her uncomfortable with his lust.

"Reyes?"

Her voice was husky with sleep, and she shifted a little, turning to face him. "Hmm."

"Why are you still awake?"

Because I want you so damn much, and you're here, all sweet and soft beside me, and I can smell the scent of your shampoo and lotion, and the warmer, muskier scent of your skin, and it's making me nuts.

Of course, he didn't say any of that. "Just thinking."

"About?"

And...there went his brain again, pondering all the things he wanted to do with her. He turned on his side and levered up to his forearm. "Why aren't you sleeping? I thought you were out."

"Close, but I keep thinking about earlier."

"At the campsite? That's over, babe. You're here with me, safe."

Smiling, she touched his cheek, then his bare shoulder. "I meant on the couch, when I made you uncomfortable."

What the hell? "You didn't."

"It's just…the way you looked at me, well, I thought you were going to kiss me."

He'd been thinking of a hell of a lot more than mere kissing, but all he said was, "I would never take advantage of you."

"I know." Her fingers drifted across his chest. "But did I totally misread that? It's been forever since I paid attention to a guy, and now I'm worried I got my signals crossed. If so, that'd be really embarrassing." After all that, she drew a breath, and asked, "So were you thinking about it?"

Damn. He couldn't lie to her, not when she sounded so vulnerable. With a mental shrug, he admitted, "Yeah, I was thinking about kissing you—and more. Can't seem to help it around you. Just remember, you don't have to worry that I'll—"

"What if I wanted you to?" she interrupted. "Because I do. And it's the strangest feeling, wanting something I haven't even thought about for so long."

Reyes swallowed heavily. *What exactly did she want from him?*

"If you'd rather not, I understand."

"That's not the problem." God, he wished the room were lighter so he could really see her, not just the shadows and outlines of her features from the moonlight filtering through the darkened windows. "Why don't you tell me why you'd want me to?" Once the words left his mouth, they sounded lame.

Never in his life had he asked a woman to explain desire.

She scooted closer, opening her hand over his left pectoral muscle. "Until recently, the thought of getting that close to a man was repugnant."

"Things have changed, though?"

"With you, yes." Stroking over him, she seemed to relish the texture of his chest hair. She explored him—and it was sexy as hell. "Now I think about it all the time. Not just kissing you, but more."

Way to level him. "Kennedy—"

"I promise it won't mean anything," she rushed out. "I know it could be awkward if I got ideas, since I'm staying with you. Still… I just thought maybe you wouldn't mind." Her breasts pressed against his upper arm. "It doesn't have to be more than a kiss—"

He touched his mouth to hers, as light and easy as he could, but damn, a roaring sounded in his ears.

This was Kennedy.

This was red-hot hunger.

Go slow. Be easy.

Don't scare her.

Gently he framed her face in his hands and shifted her to her back. "I want you to tell me if at any point—"

She lifted up enough to seal her mouth to his, and he forgot what he was going to say.

In fact, he forgot his own name. As her mouth moved under his, he forgot that she'd been a victim, that he was her protector…

That this was only supposed to be a kiss.

Her arms snaked around his neck, and her lips parted to the touch of his tongue.

Half atop her now, Reyes slanted his head for a better

fit and ate at her mouth with all the need burning up inside him.

With a soft groan, she shifted one of her legs alongside his hip, creating a cradle with her body. He liked that enough to trail a hand down her side until he could cup one full, soft cheek, lifting her more firmly against him.

His brain couldn't seem to wrap around the reality of what was happening. He'd wanted Kennedy forever, and here he was, one big hand stroking over the generous curves of her ass, his tongue in her mouth, their groans mingling.

This was *Kennedy*.

Being so fucking hot.

She wasn't at all like a woman caught up in past abuse. She wasn't timid or reserved. She gave and she took, and it was the most natural thing in the world.

Even when he had a fleeting moment of sanity, she quickly pushed him beyond it again. He left her mouth to kiss her throat and made a desperate attempt at control. "Babe—"

"Don't stop. Please don't." Her fingers tunneled into his hair and tightened. "Please."

"I won't unless you tell me to."

"Perfect," she purred, and steered his mouth back to hers.

Holy hell, she apparently wanted him every bit as much as he wanted her. Definitely not something he'd expected, but damn, it set him on fire.

Suddenly he had to touch and kiss every part of her. He wanted light enough to see, and he wanted nakedness to finally sate his imagination.

He wanted everything Kennedy Brooks could give, and then some.

Holding her face in his hands, he slowed her down. "I'm

onboard one hundred percent, but I want your word that if anything bothers you, if you want me to ease up, or stop altogether, or—"

She smashed her fingers to his lips. "Do you have a condom?"

"Yup." He didn't mean to be abrupt, but the more agreeable she was, the hotter he got.

"Get it, then no more talking." She gave that quick thought, reconsidering apparently, because she added, "Unless you want to tell me something to do, something that you like."

He'd never survive this. Shifting her small, cool hand to his cheek, he whispered, "I like *you*, Kennedy." And that was more than enough.

Her expression softened. "I like you, too, Reyes." She brushed a tender kiss to his mouth. "Thank you for giving me this."

His eyes flared. She was thanking him for agreeing to have sex? "You are the most..." What? Sweetest? Funniest? Craziest woman he'd ever known? All of the above. "You're welcome," he said, then quickly slid to the side and turned on a lamp. He was already hard as granite and breathing too fast, but who cared?

Kennedy liked him.

He knew the truth—he more than liked her. His brain shied away from dwelling on that disquieting thought. At the closet, he got down a box of condoms, turned—and completely froze.

Her back to him, Kennedy pushed down her pajama pants, giving him a stellar view of the ass of his dreams.

His mouth went dry.

Straightening again, she tossed the bottoms toward the top already on the floor, and turned toward him wearing only minuscule rose-colored panties.

A wet dream, that's what she was.

When he continued to stare, she shifted.

"I'm not very endowed in the boob department."

"Babe, seriously, you're perfect." Proud shoulders led down to small, high breasts, her rosy nipples already pebbled tight. A narrow waist flared into generous hips and full thighs, down to shapely calves.

Visually, he devoured her.

Holding the box of condoms loosely in his hand, he strode over to her. "I've thought about you naked from that first day we met."

Her lips lifted into a cheeky smile. "I didn't think about you naked until we rescued Chimera."

Ah, that alley cat had proved most instrumental in his relationship with Kennedy. And, damn it, it was a relationship. That of friends, and soon lovers.

By far the closest relationship he'd ever had with a woman who wasn't related.

Reaching past her, he set the box on the bookcase headboard. He touched her hair, sifting the silky blond strands through his fingers and then settling them behind her shoulder. Leaning down, he kissed her throat, filling himself with the warm scent of her, absorbing her softness and accepting that she was his.

On a breathy sigh, she tipped her face up and away to give him more room. He cupped both her breasts, loving how they fit into his palms. Against her throat, he suggested, "Let's lose the panties, too."

She nodded but otherwise didn't move, so he did the honors, trailing his hands over her body, tracking all those sweet curves and the silkiness of her skin, down to her waist, her hips, then around to her bottom—and inside her panties.

Stepping against him, she opened her mouth on his

chest, her hot little tongue tasting his skin, her sharp teeth scraping gently over him.

While stroking her, he eased her panties down. His arms were long enough, and she was short enough, that it was an easy thing to get them over her hips, and from there, they dropped on their own.

He was a visual man, and he absolutely loved women's bodies, so he held her back enough to look her over again.

"It's not going to change," she whispered with the first hint of nervousness. "This is it."

His gaze locked on hers. "Just so we're clear, you're the sexiest fucking thing I've ever seen, and I'm going to want to look at you a lot."

"Oh." Her chin angled up. "I'd like to look at you, too, so drop the boxers."

Ah, there was the confident, no-nonsense woman he knew. "Yes, ma'am." He took two steps back and quickly shucked off his shorts. Holding out his arms, he said, "I'm not shy. Look your fill, just make it fast because I'm dying to get you under me."

With her eyes on his dick, she murmured, "What if I want you under me?"

Was that nervousness, or just pure challenge? Was she saying it'd be easier for her in the dominant position?

He couldn't tell, so he said, "Whatever you want is fine by me." More serious now, he gathered her close for a devastating kiss. Yes, *this*. Skin to skin, heat combining… It couldn't be more perfect.

By silent agreement, they moved to the bed, both of them touching, stroking, exploring. Reyes drew her right nipple into his mouth, flicking with his tongue, then leisurely sucking, and she went a little wild. Her fingertips bit into his shoulders and her hips rose in a frantic rhythm against his.

Nice. He could have spent hours just doing this, but she wasn't patient enough for that. Her legs were shifting, her feet sliding over the sheets restlessly. Relieved that she wasn't having any bad memories, at least not so far, he lowered a hand to her sex.

That got her still real quick, mostly in bated anticipation. Smiling against her nipple, he stroked over her, parted her and teased her soft, damp lips with one finger.

Her body arched in response.

Her hand covered his and she pressed, urging him to move more quickly than he'd planned.

She was already wet enough that his finger pressed deep, even as her muscles squeezed around him.

Watching her, turned on even more by her need, he murmured, "It's like that, huh?"

"Shut up, Reyes," she groaned, already sounding near release.

Her long abstinence had left her incredibly tight, and apparently hungry. Taking her mouth again, he kissed her with every bit of finesse he possessed while rocking his palm against her mound in coordination with his thrusting finger. He was hard enough to be lethal, but he wanted to experience her pleasure first, to know he'd accomplished that much before he let himself go. He wasn't a bastard— her release mattered a lot to him—and so he concentrated on her, on each small reaction, the catch of her breath and every vibrating moan.

The problem was that as she got closer to the edge, so did he. Knowing he wouldn't last much longer, he brought his thumb up to her clitoris, and that almost did it for her. She gave a harsh groan and clenched around him, her heels digging into the mattress.

Beautiful. Urging her on with whispered words, he found a rhythm that pushed her ever closer. He added a second finger, stretching her carefully, spreading her slick moisture, then pressing his fingers as deeply as he could while continuing to tease her clit with the rough pad of his thumb.

She grew tighter and tighter, more restless, her breaths fast and shallow. He loved it, every freaking second of it. After a few minutes more, she came with a low, intense groan that absolutely did him in.

The second Kennedy went limp, he literally lurched over to grab a condom, rolled it on in haste, and parted her legs to settle over her.

"Yes?" he asked, needing her confirmation, needing to know she was still with him.

"Yes," she whispered, getting her eyes open and giving him a dreamy smile. "Definitely—"

He pressed into her in one long, smooth thrust.

"Yes." Gripping his shoulders, Kennedy caught her breath.

Yeah, maybe he should have gone a little slower. He was larger than a lot of guys, something other women had enjoyed. But this was Kennedy, and other women didn't matter anymore. It was what she felt, how she responded, that mattered to him.

"You okay?" She held him in a snug, wet vise, making speech near impossible. "Tell me you're okay, babe."

"Fine," she breathed, tightening around him even more, followed by a shifting of her hips.

"Ah, hell." Balanced on his forearms, he tipped his head back and drove into her with urgent need. Worry hovered around the periphery of his consciousness, because no matter the naturalness of her response, she had a dark past that could dredge up memories at any second.

But lust, tinged with something softer, stronger, drove

him on despite that. As long as she didn't call a halt, he *had* to have her.

It helped that she moaned, that she hitched her legs around his hips and lifted into his every heavy thrust.

When he felt her tightening yet again, he wanted to shout with pure male satisfaction. Stiffening, her head back and her body arching, she cried out with another, stronger release.

That was it. Reyes couldn't wait a second more, so he let himself go.

Gone. Lost.

Probably a little in love.

And even that revelation didn't unsettle him. As he sank down against her, utterly replete, his world seemed at peace.

All because he had Kennedy in it.

ONCE DURING THE NIGHT, Reyes awoke to find her propped on an elbow, staring down at him.

"Hey," he said, still half asleep. "You okay?"

"Perfectly fine." She drifted a hand over his chest.

"Then why are you awake?"

"We forgot to turn out the light. The rain woke me and I remembered you were right here, that I could look my fill, and sleep didn't seem as interesting."

He lifted his head from the pillow and glanced at the window to see steady trickles of rain tracking over the panes. "What time is it?"

"I don't know." She leaned down to kiss him. "Go back to sleep."

The lecherous look on her face amused him. "So you can ogle me?"

"Sure."

He grinned. "I have a better idea." Pulling her up and

over him, he kissed her and wanted to go on kissing her. "We'll sleep after, okay?"

Instead of answering, she took his mouth again.

Yeah, he could get used to this, all right.

THE NEXT TIME Reyes woke, it was to see Kennedy's naked rump sneaking from the bed. Damn, but that was an eye-opener for sure. Tiptoeing, she slipped into his bathroom. Seconds later he heard the toilet flush, then the water running, and he glanced at the clock. Seven o'clock.

With a family meeting on the agenda, it was time to rise and shine. Indulging an elaborate stretch, he came fully awake.

A deep contentment had invaded his bones. Hell, he was smiling. Who woke with a smile?

Obviously, any guy lucky enough to have phenomenal sex with Kennedy.

Creeping over to the door, he peeked in and saw her cleaning her teeth with a toothpaste-covered finger.

Still naked.

Lord love the girl, she looked fine at his sink.

"You're welcome to use my toothbrush."

She blanched, jerked around to face him—finger still in her mouth—and glared. Turning back to the sink, she rinsed and spit before saying, "You were supposed to stay in bed."

"Why?" Eyeing her body, he propped a shoulder on the door frame. "You didn't."

Color suddenly tinged her cheeks. "I was trying to wake up enough to truly appreciate you." She indicated the toothpaste. "And I didn't want to have morning breath."

Reyes grinned... *Truly appreciate you.* Kennedy was absolutely the most unique woman he'd ever met. "Sorry to have spoiled your fun, but we can head back to bed if you want."

Her brows lifted over blurry eyes, her expression that of someone offered a gift. "Really?"

His grin widened. She truly amused him in the mornings with her sluggishness. "We have a little time before we need to head over to Dad's. We can sneak in a quickie if you want, but we can't linger. I'm sure Bernard is putting together a big breakfast."

"So early?"

He shrugged. "We'd be cutting it close, but I can manage if you can." It was his experience that women generally took longer getting ready than men did.

"Blast." Looking very disappointed, Kennedy said, "If you want me verbally functional, I need coffee before I meet anyone. Lots and lots of coffee." She huffed a sigh, then strode up to him and stood, defiantly staring into his eyes. "Look, I know I started this with wanting just a kiss, but we shot past that last night, right?"

"Er...right." Where was she going with this? Hopefully, she didn't have regrets now.

Then again, she'd just been cleaning her teeth with a finger and planning on keeping him in bed, so...

"Good, we're agreed." She opened her hand over his chest, lightly petting him, testing the strength of his pec muscle, using her thumb to brush over his left nipple.

"Kennedy—" Much more of that and she wouldn't get a single sip of coffee.

Smiling up at him, she whispered, "Last night was a surprise. You're a surprise." She pursed her mouth thoughtfully. "Actually, I was the biggest surprise."

His heart softened. "Because you enjoyed yourself?"

"Far, far more than I knew was even possible," she confirmed. "And now that I've had a taste, I'm not done."

Catching on, he asked, "You want more, is that it?" Definitely not a problem for him.

"I really do. But actually, waiting until tonight might be a good idea." She scrunched her nose. "I'm more alert in the evening, and honestly... I'm a little sore."

Had he been too enthusiastic? "A shower would probably help."

"After coffee. But for now, can I count on a repeat?"

That quickie was sounding better and better. "Guaranteed."

A beautiful smile bloomed on her face. "Perfect." She stretched up on tiptoe to peck his lips, then headed for her top and bottoms. "Let's do coffee before I perish. It took all my resolve to accomplish cleaning my teeth without it. The rest might have been wishful thinking."

Reyes stood there grinning inside and out. He'd had sex, varied and often, but knowing he'd pleased Kennedy, that he'd overcome the ugly memories of her past, was a gift he'd always cherish.

Funny that, good as the sex had been, he still couldn't compete with caffeine. Should have known there wouldn't be a typical "morning after" with Kennedy.

She was different, so it figured this would be different, too.

With her, it was also better.

YES, REYES HAD SAID, in an offhand way, that his dad was loaded. She still hadn't expected *this*.

Good God, it appeared the man owned a mountain, or at least a good chunk of it, so that he had complete privacy.

And his house... Her eyes were round enough to drop out of her head as Reyes drove up higher and higher along the private road. When she spotted the smaller house to the right, she let out a breath of relief. Maybe his father lived there, and the other building was an upscale lodge or something.

But no, he went right past the very nice, moderately sized home.

"Who lives there?" Kennedy asked, thinking the smaller home felt cozier.

"That's Madison's place, though she, as well as Cade and I, have private suites in Dad's house just in case there's ever an emergency. His security is the best."

Kennedy stared at him, agog by that notion since Reyes had his place completely locked down. "Better than yours?"

Snorting, he said, "No comparison. Everything at Dad's is state-of-the-art shit, like the government would use, you know? Most of it isn't even available to the public. He has some crazy-cool stuff."

And Reyes's weird darkening windows weren't crazy cool? "If you say so."

He gave her a quick, knowing look. "Don't be nervous, honey."

"Oh, right. You tell me your father is an ogre and that he'll likely try to intimidate me, you say he has equipment not available to the rest of us mere mortals, and I can see he's insanely wealthy—but I shouldn't worry about any of that."

"No," he said gently, "you shouldn't. Dad is just...my dad, you know? Sure, the situation is a little different, but you'll hold your own, I don't doubt it."

"Cade and Madison will be there?"

"Sterling, too."

That was something, at least. Safety in numbers and all that. Being among his family would serve as a buffer against her new, somewhat raw awareness of Reyes as a sexual man. Left alone with him, she'd probably keep him in the bed all day.

He'd probably like the sex, but would he start to feel smothered? Already she'd practically insisted that he keep on sleeping with her, when that had never been his intent. He'd been very up-front about avoiding commitments.

Shame that her heart hadn't listened.

But even that, the sweet ache that filled her chest every time she looked at his impossibly handsome face, could probably be written off as lust. For so long she'd believed the scum who'd kidnapped her had stolen her sexuality in the process. In her mind, intercourse was something to be suffered, not enjoyed.

Yet with Reyes, the pleasure had been so intense she didn't know how to describe it.

"You have a certain look about you," Reyes mused aloud. "Want to share your thoughts?"

"Sex," she blurted, seeing no reason not to share. "It was all so hot and powerful and—"

"Wet," he agreed, his voice low and deep.

It felt like her stomach tumbled over in a very pleasant way. She fanned her face, feeling flushed. "Topic switch, okay? I don't want to be flustered when I meet your dad."

His satisfied smile nearly did her in, but he obliged her by asking, "What do you think of the house?"

"It's big enough to be a lodge that could hold a few hundred people." Not only did it sit partially in the mountain, but colorful aspens were everywhere, as well as giant boulders. Who needed landscaping when Mother Nature did such a remarkable job?

"You should see it at night, with all the exterior lights shining like amber along the stone columns. It's pretty. And the sunsets here are spectacular."

The sunsets at Reyes's house were beautiful, too. When

she left there—because eventually she would—she'd miss it so much. The fresh air, the sounds of nature all around, sunrises and sunsets, the privacy. To her, Reyes had the perfect setup, and it was much nicer than this massive structure.

She didn't care if that wasn't fair. Yes, the house was beautiful, stunningly so, but herein lived Reyes's father, and she already disliked the man based on Reyes's descriptions.

He pulled right up near the front door instead of using one of the many parking spaces. After he turned off his truck, he asked, "Ready?"

Not even. Forcing her mouth into a smile, she nodded.

As usual, Reyes walked around to her side and played the gentleman while she continued to take in the grandeur of the place.

A circular deck on the second floor created a covered porch at the front double doors. Wings extended in both directions, sort of hugging the mountain, with the entirety of the house enclosed by a smooth stone wall. The same stone was used in the giant pillars that supported the second-floor deck.

She was still craning her head around, taking it all in, when the front doors opened.

Sterling stood there grinning at her, while a tall, elegant man fussed behind her. "My job," he stated in lofty tones, reaching past Sterling to wrest the doorknob from her hands so he could sweep the double doors wide. "Reyes," he said, and then he smiled at Kennedy. "And you must be Ms. Brooks."

She almost said, *Guilty*, but caught herself in time. "Hello. You have a beautiful home."

"Thank you. Though it's actually Parrish's, I claim it as well."

Ah, so this wasn't Reyes's father. He had to be mid-sixties, tall, thin, with silver hair and a reserved expression—except for his eyes. Those eyes were full of mischief. "You're Bernard?"

He surprised her by saying, "None other. And so we're clear right off, Chimera is mine."

Grousing, Reyes took her hand and tugged her over the threshold. "Let up, Bernard. She hasn't even been here a minute."

Bernard looked obstinate about it, so Kennedy turned to Sterling. "It's good to see you again."

Watching them, her gaze bouncing back and forth between Reyes and Kennedy, Sterling grinned. "Nice work, dude." She offered Reyes a high five.

Shaking his head in stern warning, Reyes took Sterling's wrist and lowered her arm to her side. "Behave."

"Never. At least not with you." She grinned at Kennedy. "I still owe him a whole lot of hassling, so you'll have to bear with me while I get it out of my system."

"Hassling?" she asked, confused by the whole exchange that had just happened.

"When I first came here, baby brother ribbed me endlessly, making me feel like a worn-out boot."

"I did not," Reyes complained, but he looked abashed as he said it.

"Come on." Sterling latched on to Kennedy's arm. "Bernard needs a few more minutes to finish up one of the most amazing breakfasts you'll ever have."

"Thank you," the stately Bernard said. Kennedy saw a definite twinkle in his eyes.

Sterling quickly propelled her through an immense room and toward a hall. "Where are we going?"

"I'll show you around. The place is big enough that, without a guide, you'll get lost." Over her shoulder, Sterling said to Reyes, "Go find your sibs. They have things to tell you. Kennedy and I will be along shortly."

Reyes didn't look happy about it, but neither did he reclaim her. No, he just let Sterling abscond with her.

Luckily, Sterling was with her, because it was true—Kennedy would most certainly get lost on her own.

CHAPTER TWELVE

"WE'LL BE EATING on the deck," Sterling said, "but no one is out there yet so we'll have a minute to chat."

Going through tall French doors, Sterling led her to a covered deck unlike any she'd ever seen. It seemed to go on forever and gave incredible views of snow-topped mountains, rocky terrain and a calm, beautiful lake.

"Wow." She could sit out here for hours, Kennedy thought. Tension seemed to seep away.

"Pretty, right?" Sterling indicated a table and chairs already set with china and a tablecloth. "It's getting chillier every day, so we won't get to sit out here too much longer. Figured we should take advantage of the sunny morning."

"You made the decision?"

Sterling laughed. "Bernard likes me, so he always gives me a choice." She leaned in a little closer. "I brag on his skills in the kitchen. Works wonders on softening him up."

That made Kennedy smile. "You like it here?" Because she felt really small, and almost…insignificant.

Turning to lean on the railing, Sterling said, "It's a little overwhelming, I know."

"Very." Moving to the railing, too, Kennedy stared out at the scenery and concentrated on conquering her nervousness.

"So…" Sterling nudged her. "You and Reyes did the nasty, huh? And judging by the way you two were ogling each other, I'd say you even liked it."

Was she really that transparent? Did she want to confide in Sterling? She glanced up—because seriously, Sterling was a tall one—and saw her friendly but knowing smile.

She liked Sterling. The woman was like an open book, tossing out her thoughts without censoring, so that you didn't have to guess what she really thought about things. It appeared Sterling liked her, and she could use another friend, so... With a mental shrug, Kennedy said, "Yes, and yes."

"Awesome." Again Sterling offered a high five, and unlike Reyes, Kennedy accepted, reaching up to smack her palm to Sterling's.

"Before everyone joins us, I'll give you a fast rundown on the family, beyond what you already know, I mean. That way, you'll be better prepared."

"I'd appreciate that."

"First, Parrish tries to be snooty, but he's not so bad. Just stare him down. He respects that."

Kennedy could easily imagine Sterling employing that tactic. Her? Not so much. "Reyes told me a few things about him."

Snorting, Sterling said, "The brothers are a little biased when it comes to their dad. He's heavy-handed, and they're not the type of guys to take kindly to that. Cade was more open in his rebellion, to the point he skipped out and joined the military. Reyes hung around and just became an annoying ass."

The insult pricked Kennedy's temper. "He's not."

"Not to you, maybe."

Okay, yeah, she'd witnessed herself how Reyes baited not only Sterling, but Cade also. "Well, from what I've seen, you bring some of that on yourself."

"Oh, for sure." Sterling grinned. "Part of the fun of being in this family is getting Reyes riled."

Unable to resist, Kennedy conceded with a smile.

"Now, Bernard, well, he's the sweetest, but he's also a tad pompous. He takes the whole butler-slash-assistant-slash-chef thing way too seriously, complete with his nose in the air and pretentious manners. Only time I've seen him rattled was when he and Reyes were battling over the cat." Sterling chuckled. "Reyes never had a chance. Bernard was so cute, cuddling the mama cat, loving on her kittens. It was something to see."

The more Kennedy learned of Bernard, the more she understood why Reyes had let him have his way. "We were actually supposed to share responsibility for the cat."

"Yeah, well, that's one instance where I can't blame Reyes. When you get to know Bernard—heck, when you see him with Chimera—you'll know what I mean. Now, the kittens, they got divvied up. One for me, one for Madison, and one for Reyes."

"There's no kitten at Reyes's house."

"I know." She smirked. "Bernard is holding out on him, claiming Chimera will be lonely if she doesn't have at least one playmate. With how busy Reyes is, he hasn't pushed it."

Probably a sound arrangement. Kennedy was honest enough with herself to admit she couldn't care for a cat now anyway. She didn't even have a home.

The despondent sigh escaped her before she could stop it.

Sterling bumped her again. "I know stuff is rough right now, but Madison's unearthed some phenomenal info. Things *are* moving along." She slanted a look at Kennedy. "You're not in a hurry to leave Reyes anyway, are you?"

In a hurry, no. Still, he had a right to the life of his choosing. "I've imposed on him for so long already." If they could get the danger sorted, then she could regain her independence and if, at that point, Reyes was interested, he could let her know without the sense of obligation guiding him.

"Eh, these guys love playing the big macho protectors. Reyes is probably getting off on it."

"Ahem."

Going rigid, Sterling winced.

Kennedy looked back to see Cade grinning, Reyes frowning, Bernard utterly unperturbed, and a very handsome older man rolling his eyes.

Parrish, she assumed.

Regaining her aplomb, Sterling turned and said, "Deny it, Reyes. I dare you."

"And ruin your fantasies about me?" Far too intently, he approached Kennedy. "Hungry? Bernard says he's outdone himself."

"I said no such thing," Bernard replied as he took steaming dishes from a rolling cart and set them on the large round table. "It goes without saying that I always do my best. Today is no different."

Parrish caught her gaze and somehow held her captive. She couldn't blink, couldn't look away...

Sterling came to her rescue. "Dude, stop trying to intimidate her. She's been through enough."

At that, Parrish glanced at Sterling. "Already defending her? Why am I not surprised?"

"Because you know I'm awesome like that?" She winked and dropped into a chair.

Cade touched Sterling's hair as if endlessly enthralled by her, then he took the seat beside her.

Reyes pulled out a chair for Kennedy, and once she sat, he started to do the same, but Parrish beat him to it. Somehow he got around the table without her noticing, then he crowded in, boldly claiming the chair beside Kennedy. She now had Sterling on her right, and Parrish on her left.

Narrowing his eyes, Reyes grumbled but moved on, choosing to sit directly across from her.

"Where's Madison?" Kennedy asked, trying to act unaffected by the musical chairs.

"My daughter gets lost in her research."

With the food now on the table, Bernard said, "I'll let her know breakfast is served."

Once he'd gone inside, Reyes chuckled. "Boy, he's really turning it on today, isn't he?"

Cade said, "He's out to impress." Shooting his father a look, he added, "Unlike some people."

"I don't need to impress," Parrish stated. Turning slightly in his chair, he held out his hand to Kennedy. "Since my son doesn't see fit to introduce us, I suppose I'll handle it myself. Parrish McKenzie. And you're Kennedy Brooks."

Like she didn't know who she was? "That's right." She accepted his handshake, not at all surprised that his hand was as big as Reyes's. She got the impression that this older McKenzie was every bit as capable as his sons, just a little more seasoned. "You and Cade share a similar look."

"It's true." With a final, gentle squeeze, he released her hand and slid his napkin from a bronze napkin ring. "Madison and Reyes have their mother's coloring."

"But still your height," Kennedy noted. "Or was she tall as well?"

"She was…" Parrish hesitated as he looked inward. A smile touched his mouth. "Average height, I suppose, but she often appeared taller because she had such presence."

"Then I suppose they inherited that from her as well."

He gave her an odd look.

It occurred to Kennedy that she'd just made it sound

like the senior McKenzie didn't have that same presence. Trying to recover, she tacked on, "And from you as well, of course."

"You're quick-witted, Ms. Brooks."

"Kennedy," she insisted.

"Do I make you nervous?"

"Yes?"

"You aren't certain?"

"I'm still taking your measure," she admitted. "I can't decide if it's being here, your attempts to intimidate, or the fact that Sterling hinted there'd be news today that has me a little on edge."

"Probably all of the above," Sterling said. "Just remember that I told you Parrish was harmless."

At that, Parrish made a rude sound. "You're the only one who thinks so."

Leaning forward to see around Kennedy, Sterling said, "Give it up already, or I'll have to switch seats with Kennedy and your son won't like that. Then he'll be butting heads with you again, and we'll never be able to enjoy Bernard's wonderful meal."

"It's fine," Kennedy said, shooting a desperate look at Reyes.

He shrugged, then lifted a lid off a covered plate. "You have a few choices here, Kennedy. Apple pancakes for starters, either with maple bacon or sausage links—"

"Or both," Sterling said, taking up the platter of meats to serve herself.

"—fresh fruit, a couple types of eggs, croissants—"

As he spoke, Reyes uncovered the feast, setting the lids on the cart behind him. Kennedy could barely take it all in. The amount of food presented was extravagant and, in her mind, wasteful.

When Reyes wrapped it up, he glanced at her and

smiled. "I guess Sterling has the right idea. I'll get you some of everything."

"Small portions," she said quickly, watching as he loaded her plate. Her stomach was currently jumpy enough that she didn't want to chance things by overeating.

Parrish stood to fill her glass with orange juice, and then her coffee cup with a rich, steaming brew. "Cream and sugar?" he asked.

"Please."

Reyes passed her plate to her, now heaping with treats. She breathed deeply of all the combined scents, and decided she was hungry after all. "Oh, this is nirvana." Just as she forked up a bite, Madison came hustling through the doors. "Sorry I'm late, but I just made the most astounding discovery."

"Does it have anything to do with a certain cop?" Reyes asked. "'Cause I have it on good authority you were flirting with him."

Madison shot a glance at Kennedy. "Maybe a little." To her brother, she said, "So what? Detective Albertson fascinates me."

That earned a severe frown from Parrish. "It goes without saying that you shouldn't—"

"Yes, I know your preferences, Dad." Pushing her plate away, she opened the laptop and turned it toward Kennedy.

The bite in her mouth turned to sawdust. Kennedy tried to swallow and couldn't. She gulped down coffee, burning her mouth in the process, and then just stared.

She hadn't been prepared. Hadn't even suspected what Madison would show her.

There, enlarged on the screen, was the very man who'd fled the wrecked car on the day she'd finally been rescued.

Memories flooded back in on her, chilling her to the

bone, then flushing her with heat. *Only a photo*, she reminded herself. *He's not here. He can't touch you.*

Reyes wouldn't let him.

She couldn't look away from his hated face. In a voice that didn't sound like her own, she whispered, "That's him."

A second later, Reyes snapped the laptop shut and circled around the table to put his hands on her shoulders. "Jesus, Madison. A little warning would have been nice."

Disconcerted, Madison rushed out an apology. "I'm so sorry. I was just excited with my find."

Kennedy managed a nod. "It's okay." It really was. She *wanted* to be kept informed. She just… The casual way they dealt with everything surprised her. "I appreciate all the trouble you're going to for me."

Sterling squeezed Kennedy's hand, and it felt like she understood. *Really* understood.

Possibly because she'd been through the same thing.

"I knew you were on his trail," Sterling said, "and that you'd narrowed down his location. But now you've found him?"

"I believe so." Madison nearly buzzed in her seat. "I'm sorry to throw more at you, Kennedy."

"I needed to know." With Reyes at her back, she felt better equipped to deal with the shock. "It's just… I had hoped he was dead."

"For sure, that'd be better," Sterling agreed.

"Eventually," Parrish said with quiet assurance.

Once she recovered from Parrish's comment—*had he just promised her that her abductor would die?*—she reclaimed her backbone. Everyone was watching her. Somehow, in the midst of this amazing meal, she'd hogged all the attention…by being pathetic.

"Where is he?" she asked Madison, trying for a note of interest instead of dread.

Now that she'd dropped her bombshell, Madison began filling her plate. "He's in Cedarville."

"Hmm," Sterling mused. "Close enough for us to come up with a plan."

"Probably chose that location for being near where I-70 and I-25 interconnect," Cade said.

"Giving him plenty of escape routes," Reyes added.

They were all so knowledgeable about human trafficking that Kennedy felt like a dunce. She'd suffered it, she'd learned what she could, but she didn't have their ease in discussing it, their quick assessment of the current situation.

"Given that he's not that far from Jodi, I'll set up surveillance around that entire area," Madison said. "I'll also get into any computers he has, see if I can find an agenda or financials or anything helpful."

"How?" Kennedy asked, both fascinated and boggled.

Madison lifted her brows. "How will I set up surveillance, you mean?" With a shrug, she said, "I'm good. I think I told you that already. I'll access any cameras in the area to see who's coming and going. They're staying at a Roadway Motel, in one of the separate cabins. Cheesy little dump, but surely they have some sort of security cameras, usually at the front and back doors, and sometimes in the lobby. Once I see what vehicle he's using, one of the boys can tag it for me. Then I'll be able to see them whenever they're on the road."

"GPS," Kennedy said, remembering that they'd done the same with Jodi's car.

"Exactly."

Bernard reappeared in the doorway, his critical gaze

taking in her still-full plate. "Ms. Brooks, you aren't enjoying your breakfast?"

It felt very much as if she'd just been chastised. "I'm sorry. Madison was discussing business and I got distracted."

"Madison is always discussing business, and if you don't wish to go hungry you need to learn to eat while she does so."

Damn, now even the butler was giving her a hard time. She scowled.

Unfazed by that, Bernard added, "Once you've finished eating, I'd be happy to let you visit with Chimera and her adorable kittens."

As far as incentives went, that was a good one.

"Thank you, Bernard. I'll get busy eating right now."

He tipped his head in a nod of acceptance and went back inside again.

Kennedy glanced at Sterling. "He doesn't eat with the others?"

"Sometimes. It all depends on Bernard's mood." She gave a crooked grin. "They treat him like family, even when he really ramps up the airs, as he's doing for your sake."

He wanted to impress her? Kennedy couldn't think of the last time that had happened. Then again, it was better than being rudely scrutinized by Parrish.

The conversation turned casual while everyone paid homage to the magnificent breakfast. When she'd finished, Bernard appeared again with fresh coffee. He refilled everyone's cups, removed the empty dishes to the cart and again excused himself.

Kennedy had just sat back in her chair, the fragrant coffee held between her hands, when Madison again opened her laptop.

"Now that Bernard is appeased, I have one more detail to share."

"Course you do," Reyes said, already frowning. "Think you can use a little more tact this time?"

"Not really, because it's a bombshell." She turned to Kennedy. "Prepare yourself."

Good Lord, what now?

With a huff, Reyes came around to her seat. Standing beside her, he said, "Let's hear it."

"Delbert O'Neil isn't alone at the motel."

Kennedy did her best not to react to that, but dread poured through her. "That's the name of the man who escaped the car that day?"

"None other."

Sterling sat forward. "I heard you say '*they* were at the motel' earlier, but I assumed you meant him and a cohort. Don't tell me he has women in that room." Before Madison could reply, Sterling pushed back her chair. "Damn it, Madison, why didn't you say so right off?"

Cade stopped her with a hand lightly clasping her shoulder.

"Not women." Cade watched his sister carefully. "Not for a second would Madison let that slide."

Madison gently confirmed to Sterling, "No, I wouldn't."

"Damn." Sterling dropped back in her seat. "Sorry."

"No apology necessary, I promise." To the table at large, she explained, "Delbert isn't alone...because he has Rob Golly with him."

Kennedy's jaw loosened. Her brain scrambled to make sense of that. *Jodi's abductor and her abductor had teamed up together?* She reached back for Reyes's hand and immediately felt his fingers close around hers. "How is that possible?"

"It seems obvious to me," Parrish said, his expression

a mask of cold rage, his tone softly lethal. "One of them knows that you and Jodi are friends, and he's looking for assistance to—"

"Don't say it," Sterling whispered.

But Kennedy already knew. Those evil men wanted revenge, against her, against Jodi. They wanted it enough that they were collaborating. Though her throat felt tight, her voice sounded strong when she said, "I understand." She stared back at Reyes. This was his expertise, after all. "What should I do now?"

Reyes gently tugged her from her seat and into his arms, where he held her close. "Easy enough." He stroked a hand up and down her spine. "You let us deal with it."

"Deal with it how?"

He shrugged. "Like Dad said, we kill them both."

FINALLY, HE'D GOTTEN AWAY. Del wiped his brow, wondering when, or if, he'd be the next target. Psychopaths didn't take kindly to having their plans disrupted.

The second Golly had left the cabin to get coffee from the diner next door, Del had pulled on his pants, grabbed a few of his belongings and dodged out to the parking lot where he got behind the wheel of his junker car.

After weeks in that deranged fucker's company, Del could practically taste the freedom. Cigarette butt clenched in his teeth, he inserted the key and turned it. Thankfully, the car started.

He realized his hands were shaking and his heart beat double time. Was this how the women felt when they were captured? Oddly enough, that realization excited him.

Usually he feared no one. When threatened, he reacted with deadly force. But the dude who'd been sharing the shack with him had too many people on his payroll, too many contacts who would know to look at Del first. He was part of a bigger machine, and if he crossed Golly...? Del knew he'd rather have cops after him than that vicious bastard.

At least the cops wouldn't torture him as payback, then dump his broken body off a cliff.

What Del wanted now was to grab Kennedy, maybe enjoy her for a day, then he'd shut her up for good—and get as far from Colorado as he could manage.

First things first, he'd call on Jodi. One way or another, she'd tell him what he needed to know about Kennedy, and then all his plans would fall into place.

AFTER REYES AND Kennedy left the deck for a stroll down to the lake, Cade glanced at his father. "What do you think?"

The senior McKenzie flattened his mouth. "Reyes isn't you. This could be nothing. Passing interest, maybe."

Sterling snorted. "Come on, Parrish. You're too sharp to believe that BS." She sipped her coffee. "I think he's in love and just hasn't realized it yet."

"Love?" Parrish dismissed that with a scowl. "That's a massive leap from mere interest."

Over the cup, Sterling narrowed her eyes at Parrish. "See, I expected *you* to have learned from past mistakes."

"Meaning what, exactly?"

Cade loved watching his wife put his stodgy, overbearing father in his place. She managed it in her frank, no-nonsense way, and even Parrish wasn't immune.

"Play nice, already," Sterling suggested. "Quit trying to alienate her, because you might just alienate Reyes, too. If she's going to be around, and I'm betting she will, what purpose does it serve to piss her off?"

Parrish gave Sterling a deadpan look. "Did I *piss you off*, Sterling, when we first met?"

"You and Reyes both," she confirmed, then she smiled

back at Cade. "Good thing he was worth it, or I'd have disappeared that first day."

God, Cade loved her. From the start, Sterling, or Star as he called her, had proved to be the strongest woman he knew—with the biggest heart. She was unique, outspoken, capable, bold, and every so often, only with him, she also showed her vulnerability.

In every way, she was it for him.

Initially Cade had avoided commitment, thinking what he and his family did would be difficult for an outsider to digest.

Star had surprised him. She'd not only accepted it, she'd been excited to take part.

The woman who'd wanted to face the world alone, on her own terms, had seamlessly joined his family.

He glanced at his sister. "No talking to Detective Albertson."

She didn't bother to look up when she replied, "I'll speak to whomever I want. You're my brother, not my boss."

Cade switched his gaze to his father, waiting for his reaction.

"Madison," his father said silkily. "I expect you to keep your head."

"As opposed to how my brothers behave?" She shot Cade a tight smile and then held up a hand to forestall any protests from the men. "Your sexism has already been exposed, so spare me."

Sterling gave a small clap of approval.

"Has it occurred to either of you that Crosby might have information we don't?"

"We are *not* going to involve the law in this," Parrish stated.

Madison ignored that to say, "You raised me to balance

what I give with what I take. Reyes and Cade aren't the only ones who can ferret out details by talking to others."

Cade sat back with a sigh. "You're literally looking for reasons to see him again."

"It's a shame that I must justify those reasons, while you and Reyes just go about doing as you please."

Grinning, Star elbowed Cade and murmured, "She's got you there."

Folding her hands on the table, Madison smiled at each of them. "Let me put it this way. I am in charge of research, and I expect the freedom to work in whatever way I see fit. I also expect the same level of trust given to my brothers." Her chin lifted. "Now, is there anything else you want to say on the subject?"

Star snickered.

Cade rolled his eyes.

After sipping his coffee, Parrish cleared his throat. And, wonder of wonders, he moved past the topic of Crosby Albertson to ask, "Have you found anything on Kennedy that we need to know about?"

"Anything that would make her unsuitable for Reyes?" Madison shook her head. "No. She has a full life that doesn't include fighting traffickers so, unlike Sterling, I can't see her teaming up with us."

"The way Reyes hovers over her," Parrish said, "I doubt he'd allow it anyway."

That earned a glare from Star. "*Allow* it? Get out of the Stone Age, will you? Kennedy is her own person and she can do whatever she wants. She doesn't need Reyes's permission, or your approval."

"Christ," Parrish muttered, "they've joined forces."

Cade sat back and crossed his arms. Overall, he agreed with his wife—but it was fact, not opinion, that Kennedy wasn't cut out for their line of work.

"As I was saying," Parrish continued, "Reyes isn't Cade. I can't see him accepting someone with your..." He paused at Star's dark look. "That is, he doesn't have the same constitution to work beside a woman he loves."

"Good save," Cade said with a grin. "Actually, I agree. Good thing Kennedy doesn't appear to want to join the business. Which brings me back to my question. What do you think? And don't try to sell me on that passing interest line, either. Just the fact that he moved her in—"

"And brought her here," Madison added while scrolling on her laptop.

"—says she's completely different to him."

"That might be true, but it becomes more and more difficult to keep our secrets contained when my children insist on bringing outsiders into things."

Madison laughed. "You already knew they weren't choirboys, Dad."

"And you?" Star challenged. "You've as much as admitted that you're going to coordinate with Crosby."

"He's been following Rob Golly for a while," Madison said without much attention. Still scanning pages on her laptop, she added, "Now that I know where Golly is, it doesn't seem fair to keep that from Crosby."

"You'll move cautiously," Parrish decreed, "and you'll keep the rest of us informed every step of the way."

"Of course." Madison smiled. "We are a team, after all." She closed her laptop and stood. "But since I have all the research data, the rest of you will just have to trust me when I say that Crosby isn't a threat to us."

As she made a grand exit, Parrish stared after her.

Cade and Star shared a look.

Apparently, Cade thought, he'd started a movement when he fell for his wife. Now he only hoped his brother and sister would end up as happy as he was.

REYES SAT ON a boulder and pulled Kennedy between his thighs, wrapping his arms around her to keep her warm. Here, by the lake, a brisk breeze sent a shiver up her spine.

He kissed the side of her neck. "Want to go back to the house?"

"No, not yet." She settled against him, her hands curling over his forearms, which he'd crossed over her breasts. "It's beautiful here."

"Yeah." He'd always liked the lake. In the warmest part of summer, he and Cade had often swum in the water that seemed to be forever icy, fed by the mountain streams. "You did well with Dad."

She turned her head so he'd see her smile. "He's a tyrant, but I think overall he's just concerned about you."

Reyes knew exactly what ailed his dad: fear of another son getting caught up in a romance. Sterling had already shaken things up. His dad probably feared losing control of the entire enterprise if Reyes got serious with Kennedy.

Thinking that, he pressed a kiss to her temple. Serious? Damn right he was serious. Serious about keeping her safe. Serious about wanting her to be happy.

Serious about...making love to her again.

Definitely serious about that.

"What will happen next?" she asked.

He wasn't entirely sure, since he'd taken her from the table before plans could be made. "Likely Madison will want a few days to figure out if the bastards have a pattern of any kind. When they're in the motel, when they're on the road, where they go and for how long. Stuff like that. Once we know, we can figure out where to grab them."

"What if..." She rested her head back against his shoulder and, after a few seconds, started again. "What if they take other women before then?"

"We'd go in sooner." Even now, Kennedy was worried

about strangers instead of herself. It occurred to him that her entire career was meant to protect others, to prepare them, educate them, so they wouldn't suffer the same fate she had. "One thing to know, babe. We never turn a blind eye to abuse. If shit happens that alters our plans, we adjust accordingly."

She sat up and turned to face him, her expression drawn in worry. "Have you ever been hurt?"

"Few times." He carried her fingers to his upper chest, near his shoulder. "Did you happen to notice the scar I have here?"

"Yes."

"Knife wound," he said. "I demolished the fucker who did that, by the way." He moved her fingers to his thigh. "The scar I have here? Graze of a bullet. Prick was trying to unman me but missed." He showed his teeth in a savage smile. "I didn't."

Her gaze searched his, and suddenly she was against him, her arms snug around his neck. "You could have been killed and I never would have met you."

Then she might have died, too, because who else could she have called on the night of the fire? No one. He crushed her closer. "I didn't, you didn't, and we're going to keep it that way."

"Sometimes," she whispered, "I'm so afraid."

He didn't want that. A healthy respect for consequences, yeah, that was good. But actual fear? She'd had enough of that in her life already. "Can you tell me anything else about O'Neil?" He'd kill the man who'd once taken her, who apparently hunted her now, and he wouldn't have a single moment of remorse. "Anything at all would be good."

Her arms loosened as she eased out of his embrace. "He was a chain-smoker." Absently she smoothed a hand along the side of his neck. "He was meaner when he drank—and he drank all the time."

Fucker. Reyes would take pleasure in ending him.

"You saw what he looks like. Faded blond hair, under six feet, I think, but I couldn't say for sure."

Because she'd been so young, and so traumatized, every man had likely felt huge. Who paid attention to little details when survival was top of the list? "Any tattoos?" he prompted. "Jewelry?"

She touched her throat, down by her clavicle. "A snake tattoo."

"What kind of clothes did he wear?"

"I don't know." Pressing her fingertips to her temples, she frowned. "Jeans usually, I think. T-shirts." Sounding shamed, she said, "I tried not to look at him."

"You're doing great, babe." Pulling her hands down, he pressed small, soft kisses to each of her knuckles. "Anything else?"

She shook her head. "I'm sorry."

"That's plenty for now." An especially cold wind blew over the lake, and Reyes decided it was time to get back to business. "Know what I want to do?"

Her eyes were big and blue, her honey-colored hair moving with the wind. "Plan?"

"Yeah, that first." He stood and tugged her to her feet. "Then I'd like to take you home and strip you naked, and spend the day in bed."

Slowly the darkness left her expression, and her mouth curled into a smile. "I like that idea."

He realized he was being a selfish ass, so he offered her an out. "Unless you'd rather take in a movie first? Or if you have any shopping to do?"

Wearing an impish smile, she pretended to think about

it. "Let me see. A movie, or you naked? Such a difficult decision."

Teasing right back, Reyes reached for her breast. "Or maybe we should just make use of this boulder? I don't think my family would spy on us, then we could head to a movie when we leave here."

She surprised him by laughing. "Don't tempt me." Holding his hand for balance, she carefully made her way down the boulder, then laced her fingers through his once they had their feet on the ground again. "Let's go get this planning over with. I can call Jodi on the way home." She flashed him a smile. "And *then*…"

"I'll show you how nice a day spent in bed can be."

Together.

He thought it, but didn't say it.

He had a lot of things to work out, including his attitude on going it alone. Kennedy might not realize it, but she'd altered his thinking on things.

Hell, she'd altered his entire existence. His habits. His convictions.

Maybe even…his heart.

CHAPTER THIRTEEN

KENNEDY AND BERNARD played with the cat and kittens while Reyes, Cade, Madison and their dad sat around a massive desk in the library making plans. She'd been confused at finding all the kittens there, until Reyes explained that his siblings always brought them along when they came to his dad's house. It was a compromise that pleased everyone, most especially Bernard.

It was decided that he and Kennedy needed to meet with Jodi again, to clue her in on the players and the risks. Kennedy wanted to make sure that Jodi knew she wasn't alone, that she had substantial backup so she wouldn't do anything reckless.

Made sense to Reyes, although that also added the risk that his father's enterprise might be exposed. Extra care, everyone agreed, was necessary.

Cade and Sterling would shadow them to Jodi's place, just to make sure they weren't ambushed. There was a good chance the goons might already know where Jodi was staying.

After all, they knew Jodi and Kennedy were friends. They'd torched Kennedy's apartment. They'd tracked them to the campsite.

So far, they'd been pretty damned determined.

Given the go-ahead, Reyes would happily move on them now. Unfortunately, his dad and Cade disagreed with that plan. Madison insisted they needed more info first, just in case other women were already targeted or even imprisoned.

It wouldn't do to kill the creeps without first knowing all the details.

Sterling, forever over-the-top, said, "We could use me for bait again."

Reyes and Madison were already shaking their heads.

Cade stated firmly, "Fuck that."

And Parrish gave her a long-suffering look. "By now, you should have realized there are better plans than putting yourself at risk. Haven't you learned anything from us?"

Grumbling, Sterling sank back in her seat. "My way is more expedient."

"Your way," Cade growled, "will never happen again."

She shot Parrish a glare. "I blame you for him being so bossy."

He dipped his head in acceptance. "I'll gladly take the credit."

While they bickered, Reyes became distracted by Kennedy's laugh. He turned to see her snuggling Chimera and one kitten, while Bernard held the other two.

The kittens were bigger now, but still undeniably cute. And he had to admit, with all the lavish attention Bernard gave Chimera, she was now a beauty.

Her all-white coat had gone from shabby to thick, and as soft as rabbit fur. Her googly, mismatched eyes—one pale blue, one yellow-green—often stared at Bernard with undiluted love and trust.

Bernard had been good for the cat. It was still a shock, realizing that stuffy Bernard had grown up on a farm and absolutely loved animals. He was too damned aloof, but with Chimera, he was a giant softie.

Of course Reyes wouldn't take the cat away. Hopefully, Kennedy understood.

In the middle of his dad and Cade going over reconnaissance for the motel, Reyes asked, "How do you feel about having the cats here?"

The two men looked up, confused. Sterling smiled and Madison kept her attention on her laptop.

"What?" his father asked, thrown by the off-topic question.

"Chimera and her three kittens. They don't bother you?"

"Bernard takes care of everything," Parrish said dismissively.

"There has to be cat hair, though, right?"

"Bernard cleans after them," Parrish reminded him, as if that explained it all.

Reyes started to mention the cat box, then changed his mind. Both his father and brother were looking at him as if he'd just announced a flight to Mars.

"Told you," Sterling said. "Totally smitten."

Now they all stared at her.

"What in the world does cat hair have to do with that?" Parrish asked.

Sterling nodded at Reyes. "He's thinking of home, hearth and pets, that's what. If not with Kennedy, then who?"

"Butt out," Reyes told Sterling, then to distract everyone, he asked, "Any news on Jodi?"

"So far she hasn't budged," Madison said. "She ordered pizza, though, and that can be risky, too."

Reyes hadn't heard Kennedy approach until she stood right beside him. "If ordering food is dangerous, how is she supposed to survive?"

Without thinking about it, Reyes tugged her into his lap. *She* thought about it, obviously, given her very rigid posture. The rest of the family did, too, as evidenced by their alert stares.

For crying out loud, couldn't a guy—

The buzzing of his phone saved him, or so he thought until he answered the call and Annette's feminine, flirty voice said, "I haven't heard from you in forever and I have a desperate *need* to see you." The emphasis on *need* plainly meant sex.

Shit. Here he was, his entire family watching him, Kennedy on his lap, and one of his regulars on his phone. Or rather, Annette had been a regular, until Kennedy had moved in with him.

"Hey," he said, stalling while he tried to think.

Sterling, who was always perceptive, cocked a brow and grinned at him. "It's a woman," she decided aloud.

Knowing he wore a deer-in-the-headlights expression, Reyes wasn't surprised when Cade said, "Probably."

He really wanted to blast them both, but he had Kennedy slowly twisting around to frown at him and Annette impatiently waiting.

He cleared his throat. "Just a sec, doll."

Even Madison looked up at that point, disapproval plain in the set of her mouth.

Right. Bad choice of endearments, but damn it, it was what he always called Annette. Habit and all that.

Before he could explain anything to Kennedy, she gave him a tight smile and jolted off his lap. "I'll give you some privacy."

Reyes watched her stride out of the room. Where she'd go, he didn't know. The house was big enough that she might lose her way if she wandered too far.

But then Sterling muttered, "Asshole," in his general direction and went after Kennedy.

Well, hell.

Annette said, "Catch you at a bad time?"

"Actually, yes." Avoiding Cade's gaze and ignoring his

father and sister, Reyes stood and, undecided where to go, headed out of the library and around to the foyer. That didn't seem private enough, so he stepped outside and pulled the door shut behind him. "So."

"C'mon, Reyes," Annette urged. "I'll make it worth your while."

Out of the three women he generally saw for casual hookups, Annette was the most affectionate, yet none of them were demanding. Of course, he usually saw each of them a few times a month.

After he'd gotten Kennedy settled in his place...well, he hadn't given other women a single thought. That realization made him frown.

Annette, Cathy and Lili didn't want anything other than convenient sex, which was why they worked out so well for him.

Until Kennedy.

Damn. He'd changed without even realizing it!

Disgruntled by that realization, Reyes said, "Sorry, but tonight is out."

"When, then?" Her voice grew a little more strident. "Or is it just that you've lost interest in me? If that's the case, hey, tell me now and you won't hear from me again."

See, this was why he avoided relationships. This crap was awkward. He started to go the route of "it's not you, it's me," but Annette was sharp and she'd see right through that.

Maybe honesty was the way to go. Why not? "Actually, I've met someone and she's occupying all my time right now."

Silence. Long, heavy silence.

Followed by...laughter?

"What the hell, Annette?" Pacing, Reyes walked along

the considerable length of the covered front porch, barely aware of dropping temps or the increasing wind.

"Oh, my God," she said around continued hilarity. "I almost peed myself."

"It's not that funny."

She went silent again, then snorted. "Don't tell me you're serious?"

Slowly Reyes blew out a breath. Snapping at Annette made him feel like a jerk. In a less annoyed tone, he admitted, "Trust me, I'm as surprised as you are."

"More like blindsided, but… Congrats?"

"It's not all that," he muttered. Or was it?

"All right. Then when it ends, give me a call. Pretty sure I'll still be free." With another chuckle, she ended the call.

When it *ends*?

Why did everyone keep bringing that up? Kennedy was always trying to figure out when it'd be safe for her to move on. Now Annette, too?

Eventually it'd have to happen, right? He hadn't changed *that* much, and for sure his vocation would stay the same. Kennedy wasn't Sterling. Even if he wanted something more with her, something…permanent? He couldn't see her accepting the family enterprise.

She had an idea of things now, but he doubted she understood the scope of it all, or the fact that hunting scumbags and freeing victims was the focus rather than a side job. Everything else centered on it.

Besides, she'd made it clear already that she wasn't looking for anything permanent, either.

He thought of her expression when Annette had called. He'd label it a mix of hurt and disappointment. Her gaze had looked distant, her smile forced.

Could that be jealousy? Or just discomfort over the situation?

He was so lost in thought he didn't hear the front door open and close until his father said, "Staying out here won't solve anything."

Reyes turned, caught his father's enigmatic expression and shrugged. "Just finished my call." He shoved the phone back in his pocket. First thing, he'd get hold of the other women and make sure they knew he was out of commission for the foreseeable future. He didn't want to go through that awkwardness again.

Parrish leaned against a stone pillar. "Anything important?"

"Nah." Glancing at the door, he said, "Sorry for the interruption."

"You're distracted. That's dangerous."

"I'm not," he denied. Hell, even if he was, Reyes knew his training would take over when necessary. Like muscle memory for a fighter, his reactions had become instinctive. He was damned good at what he did, and beyond that, he would do whatever it took, however he needed to do it, to protect Kennedy.

Damn it, his thoughts had just circled back to her again.

Parrish didn't press him. "Cade will leave soon to check out the motel."

He didn't want to, but Reyes said, "I could go with him."

"Sterling is going. It won't be too dangerous since they're only going to scope out the egresses, the security cameras and the outlying area, and see if there are any guys on watch."

"Makes sense." His dad was reluctant to admit it, mostly because he worried for her, but Sterling knew what she was about. The lady had ingenuity galore, was a little too brave, and her instincts were pretty spot-on; however, she wasn't always as cautious as she could be.

"You," Parrish said with emphasis, "need to talk to Kennedy. Whatever your personal situation might be, work it out. Now that we're involved, we'll be seeing this through to the end. But she's still an outsider and if she gets resentful and talks, it puts us all at risk."

"She wouldn't."

Parrish studied him intently. "You're sure of that?"

"Hundred percent." It was a weird thing to realize how much he trusted Kennedy. "I doubt it's necessary, but I'll emphasize to her the need to keep things private." *After* he soothed her temper—and after they spent a few hours in bed.

That is, if she was still on board for that. It was never a good idea to make assumptions with women.

Never a good idea to keep one waiting, either, especially when her imagination might be in overdrive. "Where is Kennedy anyway?"

"Off with Sterling still."

Yeah, that didn't reassure him. He wanted to charge off to find her, but his dad was still giving him the stink eye, so he waited, doing his best to act like a man without a care.

Parrish walked to the end of the porch, his gaze off in the distance. "We'll get snow soon."

"You think?" He gave the darkening skies a critical glance.

"They're predicting a few inches, but if it turns into more, it could hamper us."

For some reason, Reyes found himself scowling. "Something on your mind, Dad?"

His father, still a big man with a strong physique, relaxed a shoulder against the stone pillar. "Your mother would have been proud of you, Reyes."

What. The. Fuck. Reyes looked around, but no, there

was no one else to hear, so he rubbed the back of his neck and stepped closer. "You think?"

"She loved each of you equally." He glanced back. "Cade included."

"I know, Dad."

Cade might be a half brother, but no one in their family had ever made the distinction. He was a McKenzie, plain and simple.

Turning his gaze to the horizon, Parrish said, "Even before Cade went away, you were a wild one. Always too daring, always too quick to challenge."

More uncomfortable by the second, Reyes wasn't sure what to say. But he sensed his father needed to talk, so by God, he'd man up and listen. "I was a shithead."

A crease in Parrish's cheek told Reyes he was smiling. "That you were. All cocky bravado and such a know-it-all. So different from your reserved brother and your studious sister."

"Mom used to accuse me of giving her gray hairs."

Parrish laughed. It was a rare sound these days. "I miss her every single day."

"I know." Standing at Parrish's back, Reyes put a hand on his shoulder.

A full minute passed in companionable silence while the wind worsened and the temperature slowly dropped.

"My point," Parrish finally said, "is that I want you to know the difference a good woman can make to your life."

Because his father was often cagey, Reyes wasn't sure how to take that statement. Was he recommending Kennedy as the good woman, or cautioning Reyes that he should wait for more? "Tie the ends together for me, will you, Dad? I don't yet know if I want to be pissed or not."

Grinning, Parrish faced him. "When in doubt, you tend to go for pissed."

"Might happen now, too, so a little clarity would be nice."

"All right. I'm your father. I know you, understand you, and I sometimes see things in you that you don't see in yourself."

"Example?"

"You're different with Kennedy. You care more than you realize."

"And?"

Buffeting his shoulder, his dad said, "Relax. I'm not maligning the girl. Just the opposite, actually. I want you to know that there's more to life than vengeance, more than righting wrongs for strangers, more even than loyalty to your immediate family."

Whoa. When his dad decided to do a heart-to-heart, he went all in. Loyalty to family was a big one for him, which made it a big one for Reyes, too. "With you so far."

Parrish clasped his hands behind his back and again gazed at the tranquil surroundings. "Quiet nights in the evening with someone special—you can never discount the importance of that. Having that person to talk to when things happen…" His words stopped.

Reyes could have sworn he was struggling, and he couldn't bear it. "I get what you're saying, Dad. You had that with Mom."

"I had everything with her. In a very different way, Cade has that now with Sterling." His mouth firmed. "I want that for you."

Since that made him uncomfortable, Reyes asked, "And Madison?"

Groaning, Parrish shook his head. "Call me sexist, but no, I'm not ready to let go of my little girl yet."

"Little." He snorted, more to lighten the mood than anything else.

"Don't tell Sterling I said that. She'll eviscerate me—verbally if not physically."

True enough. He smiled at his dad, feeling an extra sense of companionship. "She's something, isn't she?"

"Beyond anything I ever expected," Parrish agreed. "And she's perfect for your brother."

"I know, right?" It still boggled his mind that his military-straight, control-freak brother had fallen head-long in love with a woman like Sterling. Boggled him, and made him happy as hell.

"Now for you." Parrish gave him a level look. "Kennedy is smart, accomplished, and she quickly adapts. I looked over Madison's notes on her, and it's astounding how she's moved on with her life, how she's always thinking of others."

"I noticed that, too. It's like she's fashioned her own existence to try to save others, not in the guns-blazing way we use, but by arming them with knowledge."

"It's admirable," Parrish said. "I respect her, and I like her. I especially like how she watches you. If she says things are casual, don't buy it. She's emotionally invested, and I think she's been through enough without adding heartbreak to the mix. If you aren't serious about her, let her go and we'll figure out some other way to keep her safe."

"No." Reyes tried not to glare, especially since he caught his dad's meaning. Parrish didn't want to see Kennedy hurt.

Reyes didn't, either. The idea that *he* might hurt her was excruciating. Still, he couldn't let her go.

Not now, not tomorrow or next week. Not ever?

Parrish again clasped his shoulder. "Figure out what it is you want, while keeping in mind what I've said. It isn't often that a woman can upend your world, and if she does, it probably means she's the one. Let the right one go, and you'll be regretting it for the rest of your life." Parrish headed for the door. "Now come inside. I'm freezing my balls off."

Cracking a loud laugh, Reyes followed his dad. Yeah, he had a lot to think about. But first he had to find Kennedy.

Dodging the rest of the family, he searched the house until he finally heard female voices coming from the kitchen. Peeking in, he saw Sterling and Kennedy sitting together at the table, and thank God, Bernard was nowhere around.

Reyes had started to intrude when he heard Kennedy say, "He has a right to his own life. If I'm not mad, you shouldn't be mad."

Sterling snorted. "There's no way you're sleeping with him and not at least a little irked that he's hearing from other women."

Right? She should be irked, shouldn't she?

Kennedy shook her head. "He's been with me nonstop, playing babysitter and protector and everything else, so I know he hasn't slept with anyone since I crashed into his life—though I did encourage him to."

Flopping back in her seat, Sterling said, "Shut the door! You can't mean that?"

"Granted, I was glad he didn't take me up on that offer. Pretty sure my imagination would have gone into hyperdrive if I'd known he was out sleeping around." Kennedy let out a huff. "But if he wants to talk to other women, if he chooses to arrange something, it's not for me to interfere. Our...association is casual at best. Once the danger's over, I'll move on and—"

"You can't be that blind."

"Not blind, no. But I'm a realist. All this?" Kennedy gestured as if to encompass the entire house with everything and everyone in it. "I'm not cut out for that life and Reyes knows it."

"Know what I think?" Sitting forward, Sterling folded her arms on the table. "I think you're usually pretty brave, but now you're being a chickenshit."

Kennedy sputtered.

Taking that as the perfect segue, Reyes strode in. "Feels a little different when you're the target of all her vitriol, huh?"

As she stood, Sterling smirked at him. "Since you're now here, instead of off chatting with some other woman, I'll leave you to it." She lightly elbowed him on her way out, murmuring, "Good luck."

"Thanks." Reyes took her vacated chair. Kennedy wasn't quite looking at him, and color tinged her cheeks. "Sterling tends to cut to the heart of the matter, doesn't she?"

"Maybe she doesn't know as much as she thinks she does."

He grinned at that. "Ah, so you're not being a chicken? You really are okay with me making a few booty calls? Because you know that's all it was with Annette, right? I didn't see her in any serious way."

"Just when you had an itch?" she asked, mocking him.

It seemed easiest to just come clean, so he said, "I slept with her, and with Cathy and Lili and, when the opportunity presented itself, a few other women as well. We had an arrangement. They didn't want anything other than sex, and neither did I."

"Yet she called you."

"Because I haven't…had an itch recently." He dipped in before Kennedy could guess his intent, and put a firm smooch on her lips. "These days, I'm only interested in sleeping with one woman."

She fried his ass by saying, "I guess there's something to be said for convenience."

Sitting back, Reyes scowled. "Now you're just trying to piss me off."

"No, I'm being serious." Leaving her seat, she went to the window to gaze out. "If I'm honest—"

"Yeah, let's try that." He stared at her proud shoulders and saw her stiffen.

"Being honest," she began again, "it'd be less awkward for me if I know you aren't with anyone else. But Reyes, I meant what I said. You're doing enough for me as it is, and if you prefer to—"

"Just so we're clear," he interrupted in a voice gone low and dangerous, "I'll be fucking furious if you think to sleep around somewhere else."

She spun to face him, her brows up in surprise, not in the least alarmed at his tone. In fact, she smiled. "That'd hardly be possible when I have to stay glued to you for safety reasons." The smile twitched. "I can't see you trailing along for that errand."

He narrowed his eyes.

"And I wouldn't presume to invite someone else into your house, so—"

Son of a bitch. He shot out of his seat and advanced on her. "I don't want anyone else, so for me it's a moot point. For *you*, if you're thinking of—"

Laughing, she pressed against him, her arms sliding around his neck, her body flush to his. "I'm glad."

"Glad?" He didn't understand her at all.

"Glad that you don't want anyone else." The smile softened. "Sterling is right. I was being chickenshit." Then she laughed again. "How could you think for even a second that I'd want another man with you around?"

"I'll admit I was stymied by the notion." While she

snickered, he wrapped his arms around her waist and kept her *right there*, as close to him as possible—where she belonged. "I can't promise to have all the answers, babe, but I know this isn't convenience for me. I don't want it to end just because the danger does. I want a chance to see where it takes us."

The humor faded away, replaced by something nearing satisfaction. "That sounds serious."

"Feels serious, too." He nuzzled her temple, pressed a kiss to her brow, then another to the bridge of her nose, and finally planted one on her sexy mouth, long and hungry and probably inappropriate for his father's kitchen.

But hey, it wasn't every day that he spilled his guts out.

When he let up, Kennedy put her forehead to his chest. Around faster, deeper breaths, she whispered, "Count me in as long as you promise to let me know if you change your mind."

"Done."

"And FYI, when it's safe, I definitely need to get my own place." When he started to protest, she spoke over him. "It's the only way we'll both know for sure."

"I already know I don't want us in separate places." Now that he'd had her with him, he couldn't imagine any other scenario.

Sleeping alone? No, thank you.

Quiet dinners without their conversations? He'd pass.

Missing her pre-coffee zombie impression? Mornings wouldn't be the same.

"Uh-huh," she said. "That's why you spent so long talking to your caller?"

Ah, there was a definite edge to her words, and damned if he didn't like it. It meant she wasn't as blasé about sending him off to other women as she pretended.

Turning her own phrase back on her, he said, "FYI,

I wasn't talking to Annette that whole time. In fact, my conversation with her was short and sweet, consisting of me saying I was off the market, and her laughing her ass off at me."

Kennedy frowned. "Why, exactly, did she laugh?"

"Because the idea of me being in a relationship is hilarious as fuck, I'm guessing." He kissed her again for good measure. "And there you have it. You're so special, so sexy and unique, you have me doing things out of character."

Her expression went through several changes, caught somewhere between displeasure and hope. Finally she sighed. "I don't understand you."

"Makes two of us." He grinned. "But I'm coming to grips with it, so I hope you do, too. By the way, I took so long because Dad cornered me on the front porch. He gave me a real heart-to-heart, the gist of which was that I shouldn't screw this up or I'd be regretting it the rest of my life. So here I am, trying to figure things out and, truth, Kennedy, I'm not getting a whole hell of a lot of help from you."

Her eyes widened. "I don't want your family to pressure you."

Laughing, he stepped back and snagged her hand, drawing her out of the kitchen. "That's what you took from all that, huh? For sure, you'll keep me on my toes." The humor swelled within him. They had a looming situation of life-and-death proportions, and still she made him laugh. There couldn't be another woman like Kennedy anywhere. "C'mon. Let's go home."

"And get naked and do all those amazing things again?"

"Now you're talking."

"I just need a few minutes to say goodbye, and to give Chimera and her babies one last hug."

Kennedy might not realize it yet, but she already fit in

with his family. She didn't need to be a computer geek like Madison, or a fighter like him, Cade and Sterling. She fit because of who she was, not what she could do.

His family liked her. He more than liked her.

Was she the one for him? It was sure starting to feel that way.

CHAPTER FOURTEEN

THE SNOW WAS already falling by the time they left. Big, fat flakes that quickly gathered everywhere, covering every surface in white. Kennedy thought it was beautiful, adding a fairy-tale feel to the terrain.

Shivering, she huddled in the passenger seat, wishing she'd brought a coat.

"Not warming up, yet?" Reyes turned up the heater.

"Getting there." He wasn't shivering, but he was probably too busy watching the road to bother with the cold.

When his cell phone rang, Kennedy jumped, then immediately scowled, wondering if it was Annette calling back, or maybe one of the other women he'd mentioned.

He surprised her by answering hands-free, so that the caller was on speaker.

"What's up?" he asked. "Make it quick, because the roads are shit."

"Sorry to bother you," Madison said. "Jodi just left the motel. Cade and Sterling are ready to go, but you'd still reach her before they do."

"What in the world," Kennedy said. "Why would she go out?"

"I don't think she's someone content to be cooped up," Madison answered. "She probably wants to face the threat, not hide from it."

"If she's alone," Reyes said, adding enough ominous

overtones to make Kennedy worry that the men had gotten to her already.

"Do you think she's been taken?" She wasn't sure Jodi would survive a second time.

"Doubtful," Madison said. "I haven't seen any movement with the men, but I still don't like it. We found her easily enough, so they could have as well."

Reyes quickly pulled over to the side of the road. "I'm on it."

Kennedy had no idea what was going on.

"Keep me posted," Madison said, and disconnected.

Reyes got out and growled over his shoulder, "Follow me."

Twisting, Kennedy saw him walk to the rear door, open it, then flip up the seat.

She got out and hustled to the back of the truck. The sound of her boots crunching in the snow seemed absurdly loud.

Reyes removed a rifle from the storage space and set it aside.

Her eyes flared. "Expecting trouble?"

"Always." He retrieved a Glock and a bulletproof vest. Turning, he handed her the vest. "Put that on."

Her heart started pounding double time. "You really think—"

"Don't know, and I won't take chances with you." He tilted his head to indicate he wanted her back in the truck. Not knowing what else to do, and already shivering, she carried the heavy vest back to her seat. After he slid into the driver's side and closed the door, he stored the rifle on the floor near her feet.

"This is nuts," she muttered aloud while struggling into the vest.

"Here, let me help you." He reached for the Velcro strips

and tightened them around her. "Look at it this way. The vest will help keep you warm." He stole a kiss then put the truck back in gear.

She made an abrupt decision. "I'm going to call Jodi."

"Not a bad idea. If she's in a listening mood, tell her to pull over someplace safe and wait for us."

Nodding, Kennedy quickly pulled up Jodi's number. At first it rang and rang without answer, until she was starting to panic. "Come on, Jodi," she urged. "Answer, damn it."

"'Lo."

Releasing a tense breath, Kennedy got herself together and affected a casual tone. "Hey, what's up?"

"Heading out for a bite to eat. Why?"

"Oh? Could you…" She glanced at Reyes, who had his attention on the road and the accumulating snow. Without coming right out and saying so, he showed that he trusted her to handle this the right way. "Do you think you could put off your meal for just a bit? I'm on my way to see you."

"Why?" Jodi asked with suspicion. "You okay?"

"Yes, fine."

"After that mess we were in, you didn't seem fine. You seemed shook." She paused, then asked, "Where's your hulk? Don't tell me he's turned on you already?"

Kennedy almost gave into an eye roll. "He's right here with me, Jodi. Now can you pull over?"

"Not that I won't enjoy seeing you, but you should be holed up somewhere, staying safe."

Exasperated, Kennedy countered, "As should you. At least I'm not alone, but you are, and really, Jodi, I thought you'd stay put until you heard from me."

"Sorry, but I was getting antsy. I felt like a sitting duck, ya know?"

Yes, she understood that well enough. Between the fire

at her apartment and Reyes taking her in, she had felt the same. "Please, pull over."

"I already took the on-ramp, but I can get off at the next exit. That's where I was headed anyway. There's a little diner that truckers use. Might take me another five minutes or so." Jodi named the exit and the diner. "How's that sound?"

Reyes held up a hand, flashing five fingers first, then two.

"I'll be there in under ten minutes. Go directly inside and wait, okay?"

"Sure, Mom," Jodi quipped. "Later."

"From what I saw of her car," Reyes said, "it's not exactly roadworthy in this weather." The wipers cleared the windshield of a continuous stream of snowflakes and ice. "I have a bad feeling, babe."

Well, hell. His bad feeling immediately became her bad feeling, too. "What's that supposed to mean?"

"Instincts kicking in."

Kennedy spotted the exit up ahead. "That didn't take any time at all."

"I know, but I didn't want to give her an exact time frame."

Because he thought Jodi might use the information to plot against them? She shook her head. "Still not trusting her?"

Reyes snorted.

Thanks to the snowstorm, the stretch of road was quiet with only a few cars present. "This is like a whiteout." It wasn't uncommon for Colorado, where the weather could be mild, then turn to a blizzard, especially at this time of year.

"At least it's not a bomb cyclone," Reyes murmured.

"And luckily it's mostly melting on the road. Guess the pavement is still warm from the earlier sunshine."

Up ahead, alone in the lot, Jodi sat in her car with her cell phone in hand.

"Why hasn't she gone in yet?"

Reyes shook his head and then pulled in with some distance between them. "Stay put while I check it out."

"She won't want to see you."

"She doesn't get everything she wants. Now will you stay in the truck?"

Kennedy nodded. "Do you need the rifle?"

"Got the Glock," he said, stuffing it in the waistband at the back of his jeans and pulling his flannel shirt over it. "Sit tight. I'll be right back." Without another word, Reyes got out and closed the truck door.

Jodi saw him approaching. Her eyes widened as she twisted to look out the driver's window, staring toward Kennedy. Her mouth opened in a warning that Kennedy couldn't hear.

Reyes stiffened, started to turn to her, and suddenly a car came careening toward him, forcing him to jump back. He landed half over the back fender of Jodi's car, then got badly jarred when the other car crashed into hers. He ended up thrown to the other side.

Horrified, Kennedy screamed his name. *What to do?* Reyes had told her to stay put, but now she couldn't even see him. What if he was horribly hurt? What if he was knocked out, making it easy for them to kill him?

In a single heartbeat she noted there were four men, three swarming out of the car and one still revving the engine as he slowly pulled away from Jodi's car.

Jodi was no longer in the front seat.

Mind made up, Kennedy removed her seat belt and grabbed the rifle. She had no idea how to use it, but they wouldn't know that. Maybe she could bluff long enough for Reyes to... She didn't know. Get his bearings? Recover?

Not die.

Just please, God, don't let him die.

She opened the door to step out—and hard hands grabbed her from behind.

DELBERT COULDN'T BELIEVE it when he got to Jodi's motel and found her driving away. He followed her to the mostly empty lot of a dive diner, staying back so she wouldn't spot him, and lo and behold, Kennedy was there. He couldn't have planned it more perfectly.

Seeing her made him want her even more. With success almost at hand, he felt the urgency burning through his blood.

Just as he pulled into the back of the lot, grateful for the thick snowfall that helped conceal him, an attack happened with a car trying to run over the big guy, no doubt to remove him so they could get to Jodi.

Didn't take a genius to know his cohort had set up the whole thing—without even telling Del about it! What a double-crossing bastard. Now Del was glad he'd bailed without a word. Let the prick have Jodi.

Del only wanted Kennedy.

Taking advantage of the chaos, he pulled up behind the truck and crept forward on foot. Thinking to use the butt of his gun to shatter the passenger window, he was stunned nearly stupid when Kennedy actually stepped out. So she wasn't a cowering girl anymore?

Better and better. He'd enjoy seeing her fight her fate.

Any second now that big bruiser could be on them, and Del would lose his chance.

While she was focused on the scene before her, he locked a tight arm around her throat, ensuring she couldn't make any noise, and jammed the barrel of his semiautomatic to her temple. "Drop the rifle or I'll kill you right now."

Her entire body shuddered, but she held on to the weapon.

The bitch had gotten a lot gutsier.

"Or," he breathed against her cheek, tightening his arm even more, "I'll tell the others to kill your boyfriend. What do you think?" She, of course, didn't know that he now worked alone, that he was as surprised as her to see men on the scene.

As she struggled for air, she dropped the rifle with a clatter.

Del looked up to see her bodyguard wasn't out of commission after all. No, he was rapidly annihilating everyone.

"Fuck." Spinning Kennedy around, Del smacked her hard in the head with his gun. Her eyes rolled back and she slumped hard into the door, shattering the window after all—and no doubt drawing attention to them.

She was a small woman, but her deadweight wasn't easy for him to lift, not with his gun still in hand.

Awkwardly dragging her, he stuffed her through the driver's door and climbed in beside her. In that single suspended moment of time, a golden-eyed gaze locked on his. Del saw his own death in those cold eyes. The big bruiser started toward him in a flat-out run.

With escape as his main goal, Del screeched out of the lot as fast as he could. He couldn't help the shudder of dread that raced down his spine. He'd seen a lot of shit in his days, but he'd never seen rage like that.

And it had been directed at him.

Glancing in the rearview mirror, he didn't yet see the big guy's truck following, so maybe he had a chance. Where to go, though? Not back to the motel where Crazy lived. That bastard would probably torture Kennedy just for amusement. By the time he finished, there wouldn't be enough of her left for Del to enjoy.

When she suddenly groaned, he glanced her way. Already a colorful knot swelled on her temple. She still looked dazed. "Be glad it's just me, girlie. If I hadn't left that crazy fuck when I did, you'd be dealing with real trouble right now." He snickered. "I mean, I'm trouble. But that other dude? Even I didn't want to deal with him anymore. I cut our association just today—and as luck would have it, I found you."

She shifted, and it occurred to him, perhaps a moment too late, that her feet were against him. Half-watching the icy road, he tried to adjust her, but then...

Drawing up her knees, she kicked like a mule, one foot catching him in the shoulder, the other in his jaw. The old car swerved on threadbare tires, sliding sideways on the slick roadway. The gun fell to the floor near his feet as he tried to keep from crashing.

Kennedy launched at him.

What the hell?

Like a pissed-off wildcat, she clawed at his face, scoring his cheek and jaw. Damn it, it hurt. Sure, he'd wanted a little fight in her, but not this berserker shit! *"Bitch,"* he roared. "You'll kill us both!" One-handed, he tried to fend her off, but she was throwing punches left and right, and somehow she managed to get him right in the junk.

Ah, *hell*.

Breath left him in a gravelly moan, and his hands went slack on the wheel. She took advantage, striking him again and again.

That did it. The car hit an icy spot and whipped sideways, slammed hard into a guardrail and then tumbled half over into a ravine.

He'd finally gotten Kennedy, only to die in the process.

A_T THE LAST_ possible second, Kennedy realized they would wreck and that it would be bad. She grabbed for the seat belt, got her hand and wrist tangled in it, but didn't have time to fasten it around her. She held on tight, trying to keep herself from being thrown around.

When the car hit the guardrail, it felt as though her entire body took the impact. Her head smacked the side passenger window, making her see stars for a moment, then she felt the car sliding over the berm and very real terror scrabbled through the angry haze that had encompassed her.

If they rolled, she didn't know if she would survive. Only her tangled grip on the seat belt kept her from bouncing from one end of the car to the other.

Delbert wasn't so lucky.

Her thigh jammed against something sharp, and her elbow hit the dash. He landed against her. She screamed, as much out of dread as pain.

When the car came to a jolting stop, they were at an odd angle, with her passenger door against the ground.

Delbert O'Neil, his face covered in blood, slumped against her, pinning her down. She clenched her teeth as she tried to move.

Please let Reyes be okay. Let Jodi be safe.

Delbert moaned, but otherwise didn't move.

Her situation couldn't be more dire. How far had they traveled? Her head split with pain, thanks to how he'd clunked her before they'd wrecked. Her wrist burned and ached, likely from how she'd held the seat belt.

Pressing a hand to her heart, she felt the rapid *thump, thump, thump* of her terror, but she also knew she was alive—and she intended to stay that way.

Looking around, she realized she saw two of everything.

She also felt like puking. That couldn't stop her, though. She had to move, right now, before Delbert came to.

If she passed out, who would send help for Reyes?

She assessed the situation as best she could and determined that first she had to get out from under his deadweight.

Easier said than done.

Little by little, she freed her trapped left arm and then her legs. Every small movement hurt, but she used the pain as an impetus. If she could escape, then she could get someone to go back to help Reyes and Jodi. That, as much as her own safety, spurred her to haste.

Getting out of the car required her climbing over Delbert. She literally held her breath and was thankful when he remained out.

As she was maneuvering, she spotted his gun jammed up between the dash and the badly cracked windshield. Getting it meant climbing over him again, but she couldn't leave him armed.

Unlike Reyes, she wasn't comfortable putting the thing in her pants, but the windows were shattered, so she tossed it out the driver's side where she'd have to exit. It landed on the snow-covered ground with a thud.

She was levering up and out, prayers on her lips, when suddenly Reyes was there, scrambling down the ravine in a hazardous race, his face covered in blood, rage in his eyes.

Hurt, but alive, and the relief nearly did her in.

He slid in the snow, recovered, then bellowed her name.

Tears welled up, blurring her vision. Damn it, she'd held it together so far, and by God she wouldn't fall apart now.

"I'm okay," she said more softly, glancing back at Delbert, hoping Reyes hadn't roused him.

She screamed when she saw his eyes open. He stared right at her.

Reyes reached in, caught her under the arms, and easily lifted her out. Standing her behind him, he withdrew his own weapon and looked in at Delbert.

Whatever he saw took some of the tension from his body. "Should I fucking kill you now?"

Unable to help herself, Kennedy peered around Reyes.

Delbert tried a laugh that mixed with a groan. Blood and spit seeped from his lips. "Might as well, because I'm dead either way."

"I have his gun," Kennedy whispered, touching Reyes's arm. "I threw it out the window."

Giving up on Delbert for the moment, he turned to her, glanced over her body, and his mouth flattened. "Come here." Sweeping her up into his arms, he took a few steps until he reached a jutting, snow-covered rock. Carefully, he set her down and brushed back her hair with a shaking hand. "If his legs weren't already broken, I'd break them slowly and with pleasure."

"What?" Delbert had broken legs? "How do you know—"

"You didn't notice the bones?"

When she quailed, he muttered, "Never mind."

Dear God. *Delbert's bones were showing*? A convulsive gag shook her, making her head ache even more.

Keeping his voice soft, Reyes supported her. "Do you need to be sick?"

"No." If she puked, her head would likely roll right off her shoulders. "No, I'm okay."

He pressed a kiss to her forehead. "Where are you hurt, baby?"

She started to say, *Pretty much everywhere*, but he looked so stricken, she whispered instead, "You're bleeding."

"It's nothing. My face hit the pavement when they tried to run me over."

"Reyes." The tears suddenly overflowed. "I didn't know if you were—"

"I'm all right. Jodi is okay, too. I left her with Sterling. Cade is right behind us."

"Actually, I'm here now," Cade said.

Kennedy jumped, felt the startle everywhere, and scowled. "Where did you come from?"

Gently Cade tipped up her face, staring intently into her eyes. "Pretty sure you have a concussion."

She was pretty sure she did, too. "I think Delbert hit me with his gun. It feels like he knocked something loose. Didn't help that I made him wreck—"

"Made him?" Reyes asked, while nudging Cade aside.

Remembering how she'd attacked him, she started shivering uncontrollably. The cold wind didn't help, sending icy snow to continually pelt her face. Tears filled her eyes again, making her madder than hell—at herself. Her lips trembled, too, and her voice emerged in an agonized whisper. "I thought you were badly hurt. I wanted to get back to you, but he was driving away… I couldn't let him do that, so I started kicking and hitting him."

"Jesus," Reyes murmured. "He might have killed you."

"That was his intent anyway, right?"

Cade's gaze swept the area, then settled on the car. "So it is Delbert O'Neil?"

Reyes nodded. "He's banged up pretty badly. Broken legs, looks like a dislocated shoulder, too. Face is scratched to hell and back."

"The last was me," Kennedy said, wanting her due. "I also punched him in the nuts."

Both men stared at her.

"That's when he completely lost control of the car."

"That could do it." After pressing a kiss to her forehead, Reyes peeled off his flannel shirt and wrapped it around her, leaving him in only a thermal Henley.

"You'll get cold—"

"Shh, babe, let me do something, okay?" He bent his knees to look into her face. "You saved yourself. You realize that, right? The least I can do is give you my shirt."

Cade cleared his throat. "Want me to do the honors?"

Reyes cupped a hand to her cheek. "We have to question him, and fast. How about you go with Cade—"

"I want to hear, too." She deserved to hear. Damn it, she felt so wretched, but she had to know it all.

"You're cold."

"No colder than you," she insisted.

After a split second, Reyes nodded and then lifted her in his arms again. With Cade at his side, he walked over to the car. Cade lifted Delbert's gun, dusted the snow off it, and then leaned into the car.

Delbert's eyes were closed but they opened real fast when Cade jostled his foot with the muzzle of the gun, causing him to hiss out an agonized breath.

"So," Reyes said. "You and Rob Golly."

The weirdest thing happened.

Delbert's eyes flared, then he managed a sickly smile. "*Rob* Golly? That's what you think?"

"It's what we know," Cade said.

"You're wrong. Rob is dead."

Held in Reyes's arms, Kennedy felt a little warmer, and yet she still couldn't stop shaking. The violent tremors racked her whole body. "I thought he was dead," she admitted, unable to look away from Delbert's battered face. *She'd done that*. Well, she and the wreck, which she'd instigated, so—

"I suggest you start talking," Reyes growled, "or I'll make you talk, and I guarantee you won't like my methods."

"I only wanted her," Delbert murmured, staring at Kennedy.

Reyes tried to put her down then, his intent obvious. Kennedy held tight. God only knew what he'd do if he touched Delbert right now.

She didn't think she could stomach more exposed bones or blood.

That didn't stop Cade from reacting. He grabbed Delbert's leg just beneath a break. "Look at her again," he whispered, "and you'll regret it."

The pain must have been unbearable, because Delbert screamed around a string of rank curses.

"Cops will be here soon." Reyes hugged her a little tighter. "You've got one minute to tell me what you know, otherwise you'll be dead when the law arrives."

Kennedy stared at Reyes, whose gaze remained on Delbert. Would Reyes kill him? She honestly didn't know— and she didn't really care.

"Rob Golly's death is what started it all," Delbert babbled. Despite the cold, sweat dripped down his white face.

"Then where's the body?" Cade asked.

"His brother took it." Delbert's breathing became shallow. "Bet you didn't know about the brother, did you?" Blood bubbled out of his mouth. "He and Rob look enough alike to confuse anyone." Del struggled with a shaky breath and his eyes sank shut. In a rasping voice, he said, "He's insane. I knew if he got to Kennedy first, there'd be nothing left…" Grimacing, he paused. "He'll kill all of you now. He wants Jodi bad for what she did to his brother. He'll make her pay. You'll all pay." They could barely hear when he whispered, "Everyone you know will pay."

Cade stiffened.

"Go," Reyes whispered, and just like that, Cade was scaling the hill back to his SUV.

Near her ear, Reyes said, "Sterling could be at risk, even in the parking lot at the diner."

So much trouble she'd brought to all of them. Her head was pounding as she made herself nod.

He lowered her, then pulled her to his side as he stepped in close to the car. "Stay right next to me, and don't interfere."

"All right."

"Where is Golly?" Reyes asked.

Delbert didn't respond. He looked like he might not be able to.

Mouth tight, Reyes snapped, "Answer me."

Delbert's eyes barely opened. "Motel."

"He's still there?"

"It's where I left him…" Head slumping to the side, he said no more.

His face was so white, Kennedy didn't know if he'd gone into shock or if he'd died. In the distance, she heard sirens.

Very softly, Reyes said, "Be glad she destroyed you, or I'd be taking you apart right now."

Surprised by that, she tried to figure out what to say. Reyes already had out his phone, and she knew who he'd called when he said, "Dad. Yeah, we're all okay." His attention moved over her with a worried frown. "Kennedy's banged up, probably a concussion… Yeah, I'll tell her."

"Tell me what?"

Briefly he covered the phone. "That you're going to need a lot of rest."

Right. She could seriously use that rest right now.

Reyes uncovered the phone and shifted his gaze to Delbert. "Pretty sure this prick just died on me and cops are almost here—What? Why is *he* coming?"

Wondering who "he" was, Kennedy hugged herself and waited, resisting the urge to collapse onto the ground.

Reyes groaned. "So it was you, not Madison? No, I'm not questioning you." He looked up the hill, prompting Kennedy to do the same. "They're here now. Later. Yeah, I will."

"Who's here?" She instinctively moved closer, pretty sure she'd already used all her reserves for dangerous situations.

"Detective Albertson."

Oh. That wasn't so bad. In fact, it reassured her a little—as long as the presence of a cop didn't get Reyes into trouble.

Sure enough, Crosby started down the hill, followed by two uniformed officers.

Reyes called up to him, "Ambulance here?"

"Yes." Using a skinny, barren tree branch for support, Crosby finished his descent. "Kennedy, are you okay?"

Leaning into Reyes, she nodded.

"She needs medical attention," Reyes said.

"Looks like you do, too." Crosby surveyed them both, then said to the officers, "Help her up the hill."

"She goes nowhere without me," Reyes stated.

Crosby accepted that, then moved to look in the car. "Jesus."

One of the officers removed his coat and held it out. Thanking him, Reyes tucked Kennedy into it and then said to Crosby, "A word?"

Scowling, Crosby moved away from the car as paramedics reached them.

Reyes, keeping Kennedy with him, stepped closer to

Crosby so no one else would hear. "That's Delbert O'Neil, scumbag trafficker."

"O'Neil," Crosby murmured, and a heartbeat later, his gaze shot to Kennedy. "That's how you're involved?"

"Medical care first," Reyes insisted. Then he asked, "You can clean up this mess?"

That earned Reyes a snort. "I can follow the law, yes." His gaze again went to Kennedy, who stood there shivering despite the layers she now wore.

She was too damn miserable to care how much attention she drew.

Sympathetic, Crosby said, "Give me the bare bones first so I know what I'm working with."

"We'd just pulled into the diner. Soon as I stepped out, someone tried to run me over. While I was diving for cover, O'Neil cracked her in the head, stuffed her in his car and took off. I was right behind him, but when Kennedy came to, she attacked him and the car went off the road." He gestured at the wreck. "This is how I found them. You saw O'Neil, with the results of the wreck."

"You didn't touch him?"

"Wish I could take the credit, but no."

As if he knew Reyes had skipped a lot of pertinent info, specifically about Jodi, Crosby frowned.

Kennedy thought he'd say more, until he again looked at her.

His expression eased from doubt to concern. "We can talk after you're feeling better. I'll be along to the hospital shortly."

"Thank you," Kennedy said, glad for the reprieve. At the moment, all she wanted was to close her eyes...after she got warm.

"Thank Madison," Crosby said. "She clued me in

enough that I'm giving you some leeway now, as your father requested. Don't abuse it."

"I'll be in touch." Reyes guided her toward the hill. "Can you walk, babe?"

"Yes," she said, though she wasn't sure if that was true.

"Good. The fewer people I have to trust, the better I like it." After waving off the paramedics who had started toward her, he casually asked, "Did you know my father is a doctor?"

"No." Yet she wasn't surprised. She'd already learned to never underestimate the McKenzie clan.

"He was a renowned surgeon, actually. He's retired now, but still one of the best."

Unsure what that meant, she asked, "Why are you telling me this now?"

He steered her toward his truck instead of the ambulance. "Because we aren't going to the hospital." He opened the door to get her inside. "That's what Dad really wanted me to explain to you."

"But Crosby—"

"Will figure it out soon enough."

He hoped Delbert was dead. It would save him the trouble of hunting him down and torturing him to death, the cowardly worm. How dare he interfere? It was because of him that Jodi got away once again.

Oh, how he'd wanted to grab her. There'd been enough chaos in the parking lot, combined with the snowstorm, that it probably would have been easy for his men to accomplish.

That is, until the other big man had shown up. That one looked as if he chewed thugs for breakfast. He had to be related to the one watching Kennedy. The size and overall facial features were the same.

Perhaps he needed a bomb, something that would indiscriminately destroy them all.

Everyone except Jodi.

When she'd killed his brother, she'd sealed her own fate.

He would always remember finding his brother broken, stabbed and bleeding in that dank basement cell, murdered by a worthless tramp.

Yes, it would be better if Delbert was dead. Then he could put all his considerable concentration on Jodi.

CHAPTER FIFTEEN

NEVER IN HIS life had he been in such a killing rage.

Once his dad had started to examine Kennedy, he'd found severe bruising everywhere. Earlier, she'd stood there in the freezing snow allowing him to prioritize everything and everyone—except her.

"She'll be fine," Parrish said as he moved Reyes out of the way yet again.

Fine, although she continued to shiver uncontrollably, wore a perpetually pained expression on her face and had obviously taken a battering when the car crashed.

Walking around the exam table, Reyes tucked the blankets over the side of her that his father had finished checking. His heart hurt. His eyes burned.

He seriously wanted to kill some bastards.

And he wanted to comfort Kennedy.

The conflict of two such disparate emotions made him shake.

He took her hand in his. She looked so small and delicate on the hospital bed, wearing no more than a loose, sleeveless gown that tied in the back.

With her eyes mostly closed, Kennedy gave him a wan smile. "Other than my ears ringing, and the pain in my head, I really am okay. I was hardly aware of the bruises."

Hardly aware. That was her being brave again. "I'm so sorry, babe."

"Not your fault," she whispered. "In fact, I should be apologizing. I brought this whole mess into your lives."

Parrish spoke before Reyes could react to that nonsense. "She has a concussion for sure, and she's going to be incredibly sore as the aches and pains sink in, but I don't think there are any fractures." After gently prodding the worst of the bruises on her thigh, he stared down at Kennedy. "How did you hurt your leg?"

Her eyes sank shut. "I don't remember."

"Hmm." Parrish gently examined her wrist and forearm. "And this?"

"I tangled my hand in the seat belt when I realized we were going to wreck."

Ever so carefully, Parrish manipulated her fingers and then her hand. "No pain?"

"Nothing too bad. Mostly my skin."

"It's like mat burn," he explained, and he put a light wrapping over it. With that done, he covered the rest of her with the blanket, all the way to her chin, then pulled up a rolling stool and sat near her. "Can you tell me what you do remember?"

She frowned for a long moment. "I saw Reyes hurt. He'd left the rifle with me, so I was getting out of the car, thinking maybe I'd scare them..."

Parrish glared at Reyes, looking furious again. "Cade grabbed the rifle," Reyes explained. "My only thought at the time was getting to her."

Nodding, Parrish turned back to her.

"Delbert told me he'd have the others kill Reyes if I didn't drop the rifle, so I did." She briefly closed her eyes. "I didn't know how to use it anyway."

"You're going to learn," Reyes said. Soon as possible, he'd teach her a hundred different ways to better protect herself. Not that she'd need to, because he wasn't ever letting her out of his sight.

"I guess he hit me, because I woke up in the car and there was Delbert." She drew a shuddering breath. "I was so afraid."

It was torturous for Reyes, seeing her like this. Yet he understood the need to have all the facts. She'd get through them soon, and then he could hold her.

She opened her eyes a fraction. "I knew Reyes had been attacked and I didn't know if he was—" Her hold on his hand tightened.

"It's okay, babe." Reyes wished he could take the discomfort for her.

"It's not okay. Look at your head."

Of all the...

"It was a small cut," Parrish said. "No stitches needed, just a few wound-closing strips. He'll be fine."

She swallowed heavily, her eyes growing damp again.

Reyes leaned in to kiss her forehead. "It's okay, baby. Take your time."

"I knew I had to do something."

"To save yourself," Parrish said with a nod of approval. "And you did."

"I wasn't really thinking of me. Not then. I just... I knew I had to somehow send back help for Reyes." She winced. "I know what I did was stupid. I could have killed myself. When it was happening, though, I couldn't reason anything out. I just knew I had to fight."

Reyes lifted her hand to his mouth. He should have been there to fight for her; instead, he'd allowed himself to be taken by surprise.

"They must have been following Jodi." He kissed her bruised knuckles. "I should have realized."

Kennedy looked at him for a long time and then gifted

him with a slight smile. "Despite what you think and what your father tells you, you can't prepare for every situation. You aren't psychic, and you aren't invincible."

"But I've been trained—"

"No," Parrish said. "She's right. Madison sent you after Jodi. Cade and I approved that plan. If you're in the wrong, we all are, but I prefer to agree with Kennedy. We can only be so prepared." He got up to pace. "Golly's brother apparently hired people to watch Jodi. We don't know why Delbert was on the scene."

"I know." Shivering, Kennedy shifted uncomfortably. "He said the other man was real trouble, and so he'd left. Something about not wanting to deal with him anymore because he was too crazy. Delbert called him certifiable."

"Hmm." Parrish lightly patted her shoulder. "Thank you for sharing that. If you remember anything else, let us know. Until then, the pain meds I gave you should be kicking in soon. You need plenty of rest."

"No problem." She closed her eyes again. "Soon as I warm up, I'm ready for a nap."

Parrish smiled, but Reyes couldn't. "We'll get you to bed in just a minute."

"When you feel better," Parrish said, "and I promise you will, stay off the phone and computer, and limit television. Reyes, you'll want to check on her every couple of hours, just to make sure she's responsive."

"We'll stay here tonight," Reyes told her.

"Here?" She blinked at him.

"Remember, I have my own suite. It'll be fine."

"But…" She glanced at Parrish, then lowered her voice even more. "I want to go home."

Home. Yeah, with Kennedy in it, his house was a home. The security was all there although the drive would be brutal for her. Just getting to his dad's had been grueling, especially with the window broken and freezing air blowing in. He hadn't seen an alternative, though.

"Here tonight," Reyes insisted, "then we'll reevaluate tomorrow. Okay?"

"You'll have privacy," Parrish assured her as he stood and walked around to Reyes, where he again checked his head.

"Ow, damn, Dad. Leave it alone."

Rolling his eyes, Parrish gave Kennedy a look. "Luckily he has a hard head, or he might've gotten more than a goose egg."

"It barely slowed me down," Reyes promised, to ease the frown of concern Kennedy now wore. "I've had enough injuries to know a serious one from a nuisance. Once I'd cleaned off the blood, anyone could see I wasn't badly hurt." Hell, the biggest ache he felt was in his heart.

A tap sounded at the exam room door, immediately followed by Cade, Sterling and Madison coming in.

Cade said, "I moved your truck into a garage bay so it wouldn't fill with snow. Tomorrow morning I'll take it to get the window fixed."

Normally Reyes would have insisted on doing that himself, but he wouldn't want to leave Kennedy while she was hurt. "Thanks."

"I brought Kennedy some clothes," Madison said. "A few T-shirts, sweatshirt and pajama pants, because she can roll those up. Sorry, but my jeans would be about a foot too long on her."

"And my butt would never fit," Kennedy said with a weak smile. "Thank you."

Sterling whistled softly as she got close. "Damn, girl. You look like you went a few rounds with a UFC champion. Your bruises have bruises." She gave an exaggerated wince. "Hurt much?"

"Mostly my head, but the meds are helping."

Sterling took Parrish's stool. "Did I ever tell you about the time I tried going out a narrow window face-first? I managed to escape a bad situation, but got a chunk of glass stuck in my thigh."

Lips parting in awe, Kennedy said, "No, but it sounds awful."

"It was. But hey, it led to Cade and me getting closer, so now it's a fond memory." Glancing at Reyes, Sterling nodded to the door, then started her story.

Ah, his opportunity to talk privately with his family. Making sure the blanket covered every part of Kennedy, he softly said, "I'll be right back."

Kennedy barely nodded. She was too enthralled with Sterling's gory tale.

Outside the exam room, he, Cade, Madison and Parrish huddled together, their voices necessarily low to keep Kennedy from hearing.

The last thing she needed right now was more to worry about.

"Do you know the bastard brother's name yet?" Now that Kennedy was safe, he could fully concentrate on forever removing the fuck as a threat.

"Of course I do," Madison replied. "He's Rand Golly, two years older than Rob was, putting him at forty-two. He has a long rap sheet, everything from drunk driving to felony assault, attempted kidnapping and arson. He got out of prison at the same time Jodi escaped. My guess is he went to see his brother right off, and found him dead."

Yeah, that could make a career criminal vindictive. Poor Jodi. The girl couldn't catch a break. What were the odds of escaping one abusive lunatic only to have another come after her? "She could benefit from one of Dad's programs."

"My thought exactly," Parrish said. "Kennedy will rest

easier if she knows her friend is clear of danger. But first we need to eliminate the threat." He added to Madison, "I want eyes on that motel room every second of every hour. We need to know if Golly moves while we formulate our plans."

"Already done," Madison assured him. "I found a few cameras that give me great access. As long as he doesn't do something extra tricky like dig his way out, I'll see him. If he does go out, I'll be able to identify which car is his, then I can grab his plates. That'll give us even more info on him."

"Now that they're onto us," Cade said, "I don't want Sterling anywhere near there when I tag the cars."

"I don't want *you* there, either," Parrish countered. "We'll get by without the GPS."

Cade stiffened. "I can handle it."

"Don't be insulted." Madison patted Cade's shoulder. "I agree with Dad. From everything I've been able to uncover, Golly has a broad network behind him."

"His connections aren't the same as ours," Cade argued.

"Agreed. We'll have to cast a wider net now, and if there's even a tiny chance that you get spotted, the rest of the goons will go to ground."

"How many people are we talking?" Reyes asked.

I've found connections to twenty, including motel owners, diner owners, truckers and a few career criminal buddies that he probably met in prison. Nothing too high-tech, but I don't want to risk missing a step and losing any—" She glanced at Reyes, stalling.

"Women," Reyes said. It was a good bet that the sick bastard had an operation going. "Agreed."

"All the more reason for the GPS," Cade argued.

Obviously, Cade didn't want to concede the point. Reyes got that. They were take-charge guys who worked best when in action. "You're the patient one," Reyes said to his brother, "so imagine how I feel. If I can stand to wait while we sort this out, you damn sure can, too."

With that reasoning, Cade nodded.

Wanting to get back to Kennedy, Reyes asked, "Where's Jodi?"

"We put her in a nice suite at Dad's hotel. We dropped off additional clothes for her, stocked the small fridge and gave her unlimited use of movies and games."

"Meaning she has everything she'd need so there's no reason to leave the room." His father's hotel was another front. Yes, it served the legit purpose of renting rooms, but the entire upper floor was reserved for situations like this. It looked like nothing more than a five-star hotel, but boasted the same security they used in their homes. Jodi would be safe there. Still… "Kennedy won't be happy to know she's alone."

Cade shrugged. "Short of kidnapping her, there wasn't much I could do. The hotel seemed like the best bet."

Would Jodi stay put? He had no idea. "Pretty sure Kennedy will insist on seeing her tomorrow, so I'll want backup." If it was just him going, Reyes wouldn't worry, but with Kennedy? Too much had already happened. Never again would he relax his guard, not for any reason.

"No problem," Cade said. "Star will insist on going along."

Parrish folded his arms. "What's happening with the detective?"

Reyes rubbed the back of his neck. "He said Madison explained enough to give us some leeway." He glanced at his sister. "Though now that I ditched him at the site, he might rethink that."

Madison stared back defiantly. "Dad and I agree that he could be a valuable asset."

"Maybe." One way or another, cops were going to show on the scene of the wreck. At least Crosby was a cop he was familiar with. "I assume Delbert is no longer an issue?"

"Dead at the scene," Cade confirmed.

Although they might have gotten more info from him, Reyes chose to see his death as a blessing. It was one less person trying to get to Kennedy.

"I'll talk to Crosby again," Madison offered. "No worries."

Reyes stopped her from walking away. "How exactly did you clue him in?"

"I told him enough that he wouldn't detain you."

Cade's eyes narrowed. "Enough being how much?"

"Overall, I mentioned the task force and a general overview of Dad's philanthropic work. Crosby was duly impressed, but now? I don't know what he'll think when he can't find either of them at the hospital."

Parrish considered things. "When I called him, it was just to say that there'd been an attempted kidnapping and it might involve Golly. That seemed incentive enough for him to jump onboard. But Madison is right. He'll want to be in control of things."

"Somehow, we need to string him along," Madison concluded. She smiled. "Leave it to me."

Becoming antsy, Reyes glanced at the exam room doors. He wanted to get back to Kennedy. "He'll have questions for me, but if you can put him off until tomorrow—"

"Impossible," Madison said. "He's a cop, Reyes, not a goon—he won't be easily manipulated. And as I keep telling you, he's on the up-and-up. His questions will be legit."

"Stick with the truth as much as you can," Parrish advised. "There were enough people in the diner to see the attack."

"And a few saw Kennedy taken," Cade said. "It'll all add up for a cop."

Madison gave a short laugh. "It's not like any of you to underestimate someone as badly as you're underestimating Crosby." Turning, she lifted her hand in a wave. "Go get Kennedy settled. I'll see you later."

"She's taken with the cop," Reyes complained.

"Seems like," Cade agreed.

Parrish stared after her thoughtfully. Finally he asked, "Do you think Kennedy will want to join us for dinner?"

Knowing her as he did now, Reyes couldn't see her lingering in bed, no matter how much she wanted to or how she needed the rest. She seemed hell-bent on proving, more to herself than anyone else, that she wasn't a burden. "I'd bet yes."

"Then I better go confer with Bernard to let him know we'll all be in attendance." He clasped Reyes's shoulder. "You did great under the circumstances."

He didn't need false praise. "I fucked up."

Giving a small shake of his head, Parrish said, "I'm proud of you." He spoke next at Cade. "And you. You've both grown into very impressive men." He walked down the short hallway that headed to the stairs.

Stunned, Reyes glanced at Cade. "What the hell was that about?"

"No idea, except that having women around is softening him. My guess is that he looks at things differently when he sees us happily involved."

A disturbing thought. His dad, softened? No, he didn't even want to consider it. "I have to get back to Kennedy."

Cade gave him a long look. "You realize you're in love with her, right?"

He wasn't stupid. Figuring out what to do about it was

the issue. "Come collect your wife, then I'll put Kennedy to bed."

Cade slowly smiled. "Be careful, brother, or you'll be softening, too."

Not likely. He was the hell-raiser sibling. The daredevil. The cocky jerk who got around.

But yeah, none of that seemed to matter a minute later when he found Kennedy drifting off to sleep while Sterling softly told another story.

Women had a miraculous effect on everyone.

In that moment, he felt pretty damned soft—in his head and in his heart.

MADISON SMILED AT CROSBY. Lord, the man was something to look at, even while scowling. They sat in her car in a deserted park where she'd arranged the meeting.

Yes, she could have handled things over the phone, but what was the fun in that? She'd told him a small fib, saying she was worried about others listening in, and so he'd agreed to the meeting.

"You're angry."

His scowl grew fiercer, making his dark-as-sin eyes glitter.

So sexy.

"Your brother is giving me the runaround. I expected to find him at the hospital or I never would have let him leave."

Ha! Clearly Crosby was underestimating Reyes, too. "I doubt that's true. You saw how badly hurt Kennedy was. She needed medical attention, so you wouldn't have delayed them. I'm even sure you realize why Reyes didn't go to the hospital, because you know how dangerous that route can be."

Frustrated, Crosby ran a hand over his sandy-brown hair, leaving it mussed.

Her fingers tingled with the need to smooth it back into place.

"Where did he take her?"

"A secure facility where she can get care and rest without worrying that Golly might find her."

His gaze never wavered. "Where?" he repeated, more insistent this time.

She dodged that, saying, "In case you were wondering, Kennedy is badly bruised all over, especially one arm and her thigh." As far as diversions went, that worked well.

"Damn," Crosby muttered. "All I'd noticed was the lump on her head, and that was bad enough."

Madison liked how truly caring he was. It appeared to really bother him that Kennedy was injured. "By the way, Rob Golly is in fact dead."

He eyed her suspiciously. "You say that as if you're certain."

"Because I am. Brace yourself, Detective, but we've discovered that it wasn't Rob causing all this trouble. It's his brother, Rand."

Incredulous now, his eyes narrowed. "You and your family have an uncanny ability to discover things."

"Yes, I know. We're good. Modesty aside, though, I'm in charge of gathering info and I'm extremely proficient at what I do."

"Do you do it legally?"

Ah, he wanted to trip her up. Then what? She smiled at him. "If you have questions for Reyes, give me the number you want him to call and I'll see to it."

"I want to see him in person."

"Yes, but Kennedy is hurt, so he won't leave her side, and no—before you ask again—I can't tell you where."

His gaze searched hers, his indecision almost palpable. "She'll be all right?"

"Certainly, though she'll be sore for a while. Before he so conveniently perished, Delbert O'Neil struck Kennedy in the head with the butt of his gun. She was unconscious long enough for him to stuff her into his car and try to kidnap her."

"Thank God he slid on the ice or he might..." He stopped when Madison shook her head. "What?"

"It wasn't the weather conditions that caused the wreck. Kennedy attacked him. She was afraid Reyes was badly hurt and wanted to get back to him. From what I was told, she kicked him several times, then punched him in a place where no man wants to be punched."

He flinched. "And that caused the wreck?"

"You could drive under those conditions?"

Shrugging, he said, "If I had to."

That amused her and she grinned again. "My brothers also, though I doubt they'd let anything like that happen."

Crosby rubbed a hand over his face. "Tell your brother that I need Delbert's gun, and that I expect to be kept informed."

"I'll tell him, but Reyes will do as he pleases on that score." No reason to explain that they all avoided involving the law whenever possible.

Snow accumulated on the windows, making the interior of the car cozy and private, not that anyone was at the park today anyway. The heated seats kept her toasty warm, and Crosby's nearness kept her on sensual alert.

"You know what?" She tipped her head at him. "Why don't you tell me why this is personal for you?"

"No." Fed up, he allowed his anger to show again. "I've let you play your games. I jumped at your father's bidding. I even allowed your damned brother to leave the scene of a kidnapping. Enough, already. If you're not going to co-operate, then I'm done wasting my time." He reached for the door handle.

"Wait." Madison didn't want him to go yet, so she drew in a breath and admitted the one thing she could think of that might keep him interested and wouldn't compromise her family. "It's personal for me, and for my entire family, because we lost someone we loved to human trafficking."

Slowly Crosby sank back into his seat. "Who?"

"My mother."

Immediately his antagonism waned. "Damn, Madison. I'm sorry."

Now, why did his understanding make her throat feel too tight? She'd lived with the loss of her mother for years now. "Dad took it especially hard." Skirting the issue of their vigilante work, she said, "That's why he funds the task force."

"To search for traffickers?"

"It's more than that, really." She didn't get to brag on her father very often, so she'd enjoy doing so now. "I know I glossed over this earlier, but Dad's involvement is actually pretty elaborate. You see, the task force he funds ensures that victims are represented legally. They get counseling and financial assistance, and they're offered access to re-covery resources."

"Like?"

Getting into the explanations, Madison leaned closer. "Many victims have no idea what to do once they're saved. Some come from bad home lives so they can't get help there. Others fear retribution. They're lost and alone and still so afraid. Through the task force they're given safe housing, offers of education or employment, and enough financial aid to get back on their feet."

While she spoke, Crosby's gaze drifted over her face—and settled on her mouth. "Remarkable."

"I'm really proud of my family and all they offer, but I'm sure you can understand that for many victims, it's a very private endeavor."

"It's not the privacy issue that concerns me." His gaze finally lifted to clash with hers. "It's the possibility of illegal activity."

"You're accusing me?" *Why did she sound so breathless?*

"All of you, actually." His voice went deeper, rougher. "Now tell me what else you're up to," he insisted, and somehow it sounded sexually suggestive.

"You know what I'd rather do?"

His dark bedroom eyes narrowed.

Madison reached for him over the console. "I'd rather kiss you," she murmured, right before her fingers slid into his cool, silky hair and her mouth settled over his.

He went still for a heartbeat, and then those strong arms closed around her, pulling her nearer as he took over. Or tried to.

Being submissive wasn't really her thing, so she angled as close as she could get and deepened the kiss.

To her surprise, he laughed.

Insulted, she lifted her head and glared at him. "You're amused?"

Smiling, his gaze tender, he stroked two fingers along her cheek, then under her chin. "Yeah, you amuse me."

"That wasn't my intent."

"I know." He leaned in for a soft kiss. "My guess is you wanted to distract me. I'm tempted, but not quite that easy."

Of all the… She dropped back to her own seat, now glad that the console kept them apart. "You think the only reason I kissed you—"

"Yeah, that's what I think." His slight smile never wavered. "I wouldn't put anything past you or your family."

"Well." Her face heated with ire. "That's insulting."

"To me, as well."

"Most especially to you," she snapped. "For your information, I don't offer those type of personal favors for my family. I kissed you because I *wanted* to. But trust me, I won't make that mistake again."

"Good. Let's keep it simple, okay?" Lifting his hip, he drew out his wallet, found a card and handed it to her. "Have your brother call me within the hour. If anything else happens, I strongly advise you to let me know."

Madison sat there, fuming, turned on and, yes, still insulted as he opened the door and got out. The wind blew back his hair and his step wasn't as sure as usual thanks to the snow and ice.

Such a gorgeous man. So...scrumptious.

Such a dick.

And he thought she'd thrown herself at him for a distraction.

The truth was that she couldn't help herself. Early on he'd intrigued her. Meeting him in person had affected her dreams.

She wanted him. Terribly.

Maybe it was better he didn't know that. Sighing, Madison hit the wipers while also turning up the defroster. As soon as the windshield cleared, she spotted Crosby.

Waiting for her to leave. Concerned for her?

Or maybe he planned to follow her? Ha, let him try.

He stayed behind her to the entrance of the park, then they each turned in different directions. Had he just been playing the gentleman?

Such a confusing man.

She didn't need him to protect her. No, she just needed him. Eventually she'd get her way. After all, she was a McKenzie through and through.

CHAPTER SIXTEEN

KENNEDY WOKE FEELING warm and comfortable in Madison's T-shirt and pajama pants. Beside her, Reyes sat against the headboard and perused his phone, the home screen reflecting in his hazel eyes.

She was snuggled against his side, part of the reason the chills had finally left her. A slight headache remained, but she could deal with that.

Loving him wouldn't be easy, not with the work he did. Valuable work, she realized, because without him Jodi wouldn't stand a chance. The police could only do so much when the law forced them to abide by a certain standard.

A standard Golly and his sick brother didn't deserve.

Suddenly Reyes looked down at her, said, "Hey," and set his phone aside. He smoothed back her hair, tipped up her chin and studied her face. "Your eyes aren't dilated anymore. That's a good sign."

"My headache is better, too." She struggled to sit up. "What time is it?"

"Almost seven."

"What?" She'd slept that long? She'd only meant to take a brief nap, not conk out for hours.

"You needed the rest, babe."

"Have you been here the entire time?"

"Did you think I'd budge?" He leaned forward to press a soft kiss to her lips, then an even softer kiss to her temple where Delbert had hit her. "You don't remember me waking you, to make sure you were okay?"

"No." She remembered crawling into his bed, but not much after that. She must have nodded off right away once she'd gotten warm.

"Are you hungry?" Reyes asked. "Bernard held dinner for us."

"Oh, no." The thought of his family waiting on her made her want to crawl back under the covers.

"Don't worry about it. It's only been half an hour. The food will be fine and no one is starving."

Using both hands, she shoved back her hair. "Is it okay for me to eat like this?" She held out the hem of Madison's shirt. "Delbert bled on my clothes."

"Bernard washed them, but yeah, they're stained. What you have on is fine. Cade and I will be in jeans. No biggie." He helped her out of the bed, then framed her face in his hands. "I found one of my flannel shirts for you to help keep you warm."

So considerate. Kennedy wrapped her arms around him and rested her face against his chest. "Thank you for taking care of me."

Tension stiffened his body. "If I'd taken better care of you, none of this would have happened."

"Even you can't predict every moment of every day."

He changed the subject, saying, "I'm so damn proud of you."

"Proud?" She leaned back to see him. "Why?"

"Why?" His expression was serious enough that it looked severe. "Damn, Kennedy. You were hurt and afraid, and still you kept your head and fought hard. Of course I'm proud."

"I caused a wreck." She still had the aches and pains to prove it.

"You disabled your kidnapper. That took a lot of guts. Most wrecks aren't fatal, especially when there's little traffic. It was a reasonable risk to take considering the alternative."

He made it sound premeditated and deliberate, but she knew the truth. "I wasn't thinking clearly at all. I just... reacted."

"Instincts," he agreed, holding her closer, his heart beating a little harder. "You knew he couldn't get you alone."

She shivered, and it wasn't from cold. It was knowing what Delbert would have done to her if he'd succeeded.

So far she'd managed to keep those thoughts at bay.

"I'm sorry." He cupped a hand around her neck and gently rocked her side to side. "So damned sorry."

Kennedy wasn't entirely sure about his mood, and she didn't want to add to his burdens or put him on the spot, but the words just sort of slipped out, maybe because they needed to be said. Or because *she* needed to say them. "I'm here with you and we're both safe. I don't have to sleep alone, and I don't have to fear anyone." She knew Reyes wouldn't let her be hurt. "You're my own personal hero, Reyes."

"God love you, girl, you turn me inside out."

Her lips parted. What did that mean?

Before she could work up the courage to ask, he stepped back, grabbed the flannel shirt and helped her into it.

"Okay?"

The material was soft, and the shirt smelled like him. "Yes." Better than okay.

"I hope you're hungry."

She gave that quick thought and nodded. "Starved."

Smiling, he said, "Come on. Bernard loves nothing more than an enthusiastic eater."

She realized that was true when Bernard joined them

for the meal in the formal dining room. Parrish sat at one end of the table, with Bernard at the other, and the siblings with Kennedy and Sterling on either side.

In deference to her injuries, the lights were kept low and everyone spoke in modulated, even tones.

It gave her the warm fuzzies to be treated so kindly. Not only that, they acted as if she were one of them. Not because she'd fended off Delbert, but because of Reyes. They saw her as his significant other.

And he wasn't objecting.

If anything, he'd doubled up on the attention he gave her, often reaching over to touch her, constantly watching her. She knew she must look wretched with the bruises and her mismatched, borrowed clothes, but clearly he didn't mind—and that made her not care, either.

Over a rib eye roast with buttery mashed potatoes and perfectly steamed vegetables, everyone caught her up on what had unfolded while she slept.

Reyes said, "I spoke with Crosby. He's pushy—"

"Like most cops," Cade added.

"—but he's all right." Reyes glanced at her. "He was real concerned for you. Wanted me to tell you he hopes you're okay, and if you need him for anything, just call."

"Why would I need him?"

Reyes, Cade and Madison all smiled.

"My thoughts exactly," Sterling said.

Parrish explained, "To his mind, the only real assistance, the *best* assistance, is an officer of the law. Dedicated cops have a difficult time accepting that their way isn't always the best way."

"He wanted to know where Golly is holed up," Madison added, keeping her gaze on her plate. "Reyes didn't tell him."

"Neither did you," Cade said. "I'm curious what the two of you discussed when you met at the park."

Parrish looked up. "You did what?"

Reyes scowled.

Sterling, who'd been mostly silent while she ate, looked up with a grin. "Sneaking out from under their eagle eyes, huh? Go you."

"My eagle eyes," Cade pointed out, "didn't miss it."

Madison affected a casual shrug. "I met with him, explained a few things, and got his number for Reyes to call. That's it." She quickly shifted the topic by saying to Kennedy, "By the way, we have everything worked out if you want to visit Jodi."

"I do." They'd already explained where Jodi was. Trying to imagine her friend in a fancy hotel left Kennedy boggled. Jodi couldn't like it. Still, according to Reyes, he'd spoken with her and she'd promised to stay put this time.

He claimed Jodi had agreed because she didn't want Kennedy stressed over it.

Kennedy didn't think that was the whole reason. The near miss had likely rattled her, too.

"When can we go?" she asked Reyes, knowing without asking that he'd accompany her there.

"Tomorrow is soon enough," Parrish answered before Reyes could. "I want you to continue resting tonight, and through the morning tomorrow. We'll reassess then."

She'd never before had such close medical care. She didn't mind being treated by Reyes's father—as long as the medical issues weren't anything embarrassing. "I feel much better, but thank you."

"Tomorrow," Parrish reiterated.

"In the meantime," Reyes said, "I don't want you to worry about Jodi. We have guards at the hotel." He reached over to cover her hand. "Even if she wanted to take off, they'd stall her long enough for us to get there."

They'd thought of everything, and it truly overwhelmed her with gratitude. Done eating, Kennedy addressed the table. "I can't thank you enough for all you've done." She smiled at Reyes, Cade and Sterling. "You've kept Jodi and me safe, and of course that's the biggie." Next she turned to Madison. "I'm in awe of your research ability, but your hospitality and kindness is appreciated, too. Thank you for loaning me your clothes."

Madison returned her smile. "My pleasure."

"And Bernard, the *food*. You are a man of many talents. I've never eaten so well."

"Hear! Hear!" Parrish said, lifting his glass of wine.

Bernard nodded regally as they all toasted him.

"Parrish." Kennedy had saved him for last, because for some reason her heart ached as she looked at him. This man had lost the woman he loved, and, instead of retreating from the world, he'd built something incredible to help others. "I owe you the most appreciation. This is all because of you. Because you cared enough to make helping others a priority." Her eyes grew damp, and for once she didn't care. She knew Parrish's relationship with his children was sometimes strained; she also knew he was the most amazing man she'd ever met. "Without you and all you've set up, I'd have no one to turn to. Jodi would be lost. We'd have had little hope at all. For us, the world would be a much uglier place."

Reyes pushed back his chair, and tugged her out of hers and over into his lap, where he hugged her. "She's right." He looked at his father, who appeared speechless. "I don't know any other man who could have accomplished what you have." He cupped Kennedy's bruised cheek. "Now more than ever, I appreciate what you've taught me."

"Agreed." With his arm around Sterling, Cade said, "If you hadn't groomed me for this job, I wouldn't have found Sterling. Thank you, Dad."

Madison grinned happily. "Here's to an amazing man who reared incredible children."

This time it was Bernard who cheered, "Hear! Hear!"

Parrish still looked flabbergasted, but he slowly smiled. "To family."

That earned another chorus of agreement. This time, Kennedy kept silent. Already, she loved this family so much. Pretty sure she always would.

Even if she wasn't a real part of it.

Not yet anyway, though she held out hope. Once they took care of Golly and she helped get Jodi settled, then she could figure out if she had a future with Reyes.

Anything less than a lifetime was unthinkable.

REYES WATCHED KENNEDY look around with interest. When he'd first brought her down to his suite of rooms, she'd been too zoned out to really pay attention. He'd guided her to the turned-down bed, then tucked her in. She'd given one big sigh and slowly drifted to sleep.

His heart had hurt then.

It hurt now.

Until he destroyed Golly and his entire network, he didn't expect the ache to let up.

"This is beautiful." Kennedy turned in a circle while looking at his living space with the couch and padded chair, a desk and PC, a bookcase and a TV on the wall. "It's like an upscale apartment."

"I didn't design it," Reyes admitted, "but I did weigh in on the choices. Same with Cade and Madison. In case of an emergency, Dad wanted us to have a place that was our own, but was also with him."

"Your father is an astounding man."

Seeing him through Kennedy's eyes, Reyes realized it was true. Funny how being reared a certain way made you overlook things. Yes, his dad could be as autocratic as a general, and he wasn't big on accepting anything less than 110 percent. But he was also supportive in ways Reyes hadn't realized until recently.

Everything he'd orchestrated, he'd done out of love.

Loving Kennedy changed things. When Reyes thought of his mother and the tragic way she'd ended her own life, he had an inkling of what his father might have gone through. How the hell had he recovered?

Not for a single day had he neglected his children. Instead, he'd given them all a new focus for their anger and grief.

It was a new focus for Parrish, as well. Without that, he might not have survived his pain. It took a strong man to forge on as his father had done. To use his grief as an impetus for good. To effect such remarkable change.

For numerous reasons, Reyes admired him greatly—now more than ever.

He snagged Kennedy's hand as she started toward the bedroom. Needing to hold her, he pulled her into his arms, breathing in the scent of her, absorbing her sweetness and insight. "Thank you."

Opening her hands on his back, she stroked him. "Reyes? Are you all right?"

"Yeah." As she'd said, she was with him. Of course he was okay. "Let me show you the rest of the place."

Though she continued to watch him with concern, she still appropriately appreciated the masculine design of the bathroom and bedroom.

"I have a dorm-sized fridge and a microwave, but I

never use them since Bernard always has something good upstairs."

"Guess I'll need to go upstairs for coffee."

"Nah." He kissed her forehead, the bridge of her nose and, lastly, her mouth. "I'll fetch it for you whenever you want." To keep her from thanking him again, he asked, "Would you like a nice warm bath?"

Slowly she grinned. "The way you say that, I wonder if you have more than a good soak in mind."

"You, naked? The view alone will be worth it."

She laughed, the sound light and easy, proving she really was recovering.

"But, babe, you're hurt, so no hanky-panky." He lifted her bandaged wrist. "The water will sting."

"It'll be worth it."

"Come on." While she watched, he prepped the bath for her and set out fluffy towels. "What else do you need?"

"A way to put up my hair? Clothes to change into?"

"Will a rubber band do? Madison left more clothes, and Bernard washed your bra and panties, so that's covered."

Her face went hot, making him grin.

"What?" he teased. "I'm sure Bernard didn't mind."

"And if I mind?"

"Too late." Strange that he could be so concerned for her and also so damned turned on. "Do you need help getting undressed?"

She gave him a look. "No."

"Then I'll get your things for you."

When he returned a minute later, Kennedy was, indeed, naked, and Reyes began wondering if this was such a great idea after all. Just seeing her made him half-hard, but he wasn't about to—

"Stop it," she said, taking the band from him, flipping her hair forward and securing it.

He wouldn't mind seeing her do that a dozen more times—when she wasn't riddled with bruises. "Er, stop what?"

"Thinking of reasons why we can't enjoy each other." She sent him a look so sultry he had to lock his knees. "Just so you know, I need you."

"Kennedy—"

Her chin lifted. "I feel safer with you. Stronger, too. Being with you is like having everything good rolled up in pleasure. I want that, Reyes. I need to feel alive, and I need you close."

Damn, he couldn't breathe. Trying to soothe her, he whispered, "I'm not going to budge from your side, but I don't want to risk—"

"Did you miss the part where I said I *need* it?" Her lips trembled before she firmed them. "I need *you*."

Yeah, that did it. Whatever control he'd had was just blown to smithereens. He watched her gingerly step into the steamy water, favoring her injured leg. He was used to seeing bruises on himself. On Cade. But on Kennedy?

A light bruise spread out over her right shoulder blade. His dad wouldn't have seen that one, or the bruise on her left hip. Kennedy had been adamant that she only show so much, and she'd promised that nothing else was hurt.

He understood what she meant. There was *hurt*, and then there was *damaged*, like with an injury. On Kennedy, he couldn't seem to distinguish the two. Even the smallest scratch pained him.

He wanted to surround her with his strength, protect her against the world. And yeah, he wanted to hold her close, sink into her, ride her gently until they both forgot about the near miss.

Ruthlessly he blocked that thought. Just because Kennedy assumed she'd be up to sex, didn't mean she was.

She sighed as she reclined back, but when the water hit her abraded arm, she hissed a breath.

"Is it bad?"

"No, it just smarts." She gave him a smile. "I won't let you slide on sex, so stop looking for a way out."

What an incredible woman. "Now, how could I possibly deny you?"

"You can't." Sinking chin-deep into the water, she said, "Oh, this is nice."

"Warm enough?" Because now that she was naked and relaxed, he was seriously sweltering. After she nodded, he stripped off his shirt and knelt by the tub.

"There's room for two."

True. He'd deliberately chosen a roomy tub for those rare occasions when he wanted a hot soak to relieve stiff muscles. At the moment, it wasn't his muscles that were stiff, and he wouldn't crowd her for fear of bumping one of her sore spots. "How about I just enjoy you, instead?"

She eyed him. "Enjoy me how?"

"You stay just like that and let me take care of everything."

She considered that for a second, then smiled again. "Mmm, that sounds indulgent."

"For both of us." Reyes picked up the bar of unscented soap—the kind he used—and worked it into the washcloth until he had a nice lather. Leisurely, he bathed every inch of her, paying special attention to key places, until her breath was choppy and need left her skin rosy.

When he reached beneath the water to touch her, she groaned. Reyes couldn't look away from her face. He loved seeing her pleasure because it spiked his own. Right now her eyes were heavy, her cheeks flushed and her lips slightly parted.

"Relax your legs, babe."

Breathing faster, she said, "Maybe we should end the bath."

"Not yet." He pressed one finger into her and whispered again, "Relax your legs."

She swallowed heavily and gradually let her thighs fall open.

"That's it." Gently he stroked her, loving the heat of her body, the growing slickness. Her nipples, puckered tight, tempted him until he shifted to lean over her, licking first one, then the other. With a soft sound of need, she locked her hands around his neck and urged him to linger.

While he circled that nipple, playing with her, he withdrew his finger, then pressed in two. Her hips lifted.

"Easy, babe. I don't want to hurt you." No matter how he burned, he wouldn't forget that she'd been injured and was recovering. "Be as still as you can."

She groaned out a curse, making him smile.

"That's it," he praised her, when she relaxed again. He rewarded her by closing his mouth around her nipple, drawing gently first, then sucking harder as he moved his fingers inside her.

He felt her rising need in the way her body trembled, the rush of slippery moisture against his fingers and the sounds she made. Ever so lightly he drifted his thumb over her clitoris, again and again.

Though she locked her fingers in his hair, disregarding his instructions, he couldn't chide her over that—and wouldn't have anyway. She was so close to release that he doubted either of them could remember caution.

When the climax hit her, he nearly came, too. Water sloshed out of the tub, but who cared? Her body clenched around his fingers. He lifted his head to watch her expression tighten in honest reaction. So real. So beautiful.

Such a freaking turn-on.

As soon as she quieted, Reyes eased away from her and pulled the drain on the tub. His jeans were soaked so he shucked them off in record time, tossing them over the puddle on the floor. Catching Kennedy under the arms, he lifted her from the tub, set her on her feet and wrapped the fluffy towel around her before picking her up again.

She smiled, her eyes still closed, and let him have his way.

On the way to the bed, he said, "I will not hurt you."

"I know." She kissed his throat, her mouth open, her tongue hot. "I trust you, Reyes."

Lowering her to her feet, he gently dried her.

She laughed at his caution. "Take off your boxers."

Every day, in some new way, she astounded him. "Not yet." If he did, it'd be over.

Frowning, she poked his chest. "No more playing, Reyes." Then in a more plaintive voice, she said, "I need you *now*."

"Get in the bed."

"Bossy much?" She crawled in as she said that, stealing his breath in the process.

"Horny much, actually." He went to the nightstand to dig out a rubber, then sprawled out beside her. Reminding himself to use ultimate care, to utilize every ounce of gentleness he possessed, he took her mouth in a deep, wet, tongue-dueling kiss while palming her breasts. Every inch of her enticed him, her silky skin, her firm bottom, the taste of her, her scent.

He kissed her throat, down to her breasts, where he concentrated for a while on getting her back to the edge, then down to her ribs and her stomach. He kissed every bruise, every small scrape, and everywhere in between as he slowly progressed down her body.

Probably guessing his intent, she made small, desperate sounds of need.

Carefully parting her thighs, he looked at her, seeing her pink flesh swollen and wet. She definitely wanted him. Whatever pain she felt, it wasn't hindering her.

"Reyes?"

There were no words for all the things she made him feel. Without forewarning, he licked over her, into her, and didn't even mind when her hips lifted. Sex had a way of obliterating aches and worries, and given how Kennedy moved now, she wasn't feeling, either.

Lifting her thighs over his shoulders, he settled in to sate himself on her taste, licking her, prodding with his tongue, nibbling with his lips. Even when she quickly spiraled into another climax, he couldn't get enough. He closed his mouth over her clitoris and suckled until she cried out, her entire body straining.

Seconds ticked by, maybe even a full minute, and his senses returned in a startling rush. Damn it, he shouldn't have pushed her like that. He was supposed to be pampering her.

Dreading the discomfort he might see on her face, he rose up and found her resting boneless across his mattress, her thighs sprawled, her arms out and limp, eyes closed and cheeks damp.

"You're mine."

Her eyelids fluttered. "What?" she whispered.

No, he didn't want to get into explanations right now, not when he was strung so tight. He grabbed the condom and rolled it on. "If anything bothers you, if your head hurts—"

"Reyes." She smiled up at him. "Have you ever known me to be shy?"

"A little."

She pressed a warm kiss to his mouth. "Not with sex." She stroked a small, warm hand over his chest.

"The bruises—"

"What bruises?" she whispered, kissing him again, and this time her lips were open, her tongue bold.

Hell, he was a goner. Slowly he moved over her, giving her time to adjust her legs in whatever way was most comfortable for her. Gripping his shoulders, she hooked her uninjured leg over his hips.

Reyes slid one hand under her sexy behind, tilted her hips and pressed into her in one long, smooth thrust.

Heaven.

It was a good thing she'd already come twice because, after all that, he was on a hair trigger.

While he kept up an easy and steady rhythm, Kennedy seemed content to kiss him senseless while stroking his back. Just when he knew he couldn't hold back a moment longer, he pressed his face into her neck and growled a powerful release. And even then he was aware of her, of how precious she was to him, how delicate. And how strong.

She'd fought a kidnapper from her past who'd had the vilest of intent. She'd persevered through injuries and fear. And she'd stolen his heart, irrevocably.

Plus, she gave him the best sex he'd ever had.

"Somehow," she whispered near his ear, "it keeps getting better."

He couldn't yet speak, but he kissed her shoulder, then rolled to his back to relieve her of his weight. She should have been crying, or at least sleeping, after her ordeal.

Instead, Kennedy immediately snuggled into his side.

They rested like that for a bit until he thought to ask, "Did I hurt you?"

"Of course you didn't. You never would."

No, he wouldn't.

She yawned. "But I am crazy tired again."

He made himself man up, but it wasn't easy. "Give me two minutes." Leaving the bed, he disposed of the condom, cleaned up and found the pills his dad wanted her to take.

He carried her one with a bottle of water. At first he thought she was already asleep, until she opened her eyes. She'd removed the band from her hair and now it tumbled over the pillow. She rested one hand on her stomach and the other, palm up, by her head.

Liking the way she smiled, Reyes sat on the side of the bed and offered her the medicine. When that was done, he straightened the bedding, turned off the light and stretched out beside her. "I'll keep you warm, okay?"

"Yes."

Holding her close with one arm, he asked, "Why were you smiling?"

"I was just thinking how funny it was that today should have been one of the scariest since I escaped traffickers, but with you, it was also one of the nicest."

Damn, she knew how to level him.

I love you. The words burned in his throat, but saying them aloud would be a commitment. Before he did that, they had a lot to work out, most especially his career. He wanted her to know that one day he would comfortably retire. He wouldn't go into his old age fighting bad guys. He'd have money in the bank, a nice house… She wouldn't have to worry about growing old with him.

Her career was another matter. He was so damned proud of her, but he knew his limitations, and he couldn't imagine letting her go off on her own without protection. Not with her past, and not with his awareness of the dangers in the world.

Would she rebel against that?

He had dozens of concerns, but voicing them would start another long conversation when what she really needed was sleep.

When he realized her breathing had deepened, he knew she'd already nodded off.

They'd make it work, he told himself. He didn't know if Kennedy loved him, but she cared. She liked being with him. She loved the sex.

He could start there and build on the rest.

And with that thought, he drifted off to sleep, too.

CHAPTER SEVENTEEN

DURING THE LATE AFTERNOON, they headed over to see Jodi. Kennedy had insisted on seeing her friend, against protests from everyone except Reyes.

He, at least, knew her well enough to understand this was something she had to do. She wanted to be close to her, to hug her, to literally be there for her.

Parrish wanted her to wear dark sunglasses because of her concussion, though, honestly, the effects of it weren't nearly as bad today. Madison had given her a puffer coat to wear, so she wasn't cold. And with Cade and Sterling trailing them, she wasn't too nervous, either.

Reyes was in full-blown protector mode, meaning he constantly scanned their surroundings without talking much.

Little by little, Kennedy was starting to grasp the complexities of their operation and how they all worked together, complementing each other's efforts, giving physical and emotional support wherever needed.

That morning, before she'd even made it out of Reyes's suite, Cade had gotten the window on the truck fixed. Soon as she and Reyes had joined the others in the kitchen for a light breakfast, Madison presented new info she'd uncovered, specifically locating a few small-time thugs with a past association to Golly. They were still local, therefore it stood to reason that they might be working with Golly again.

They'd decided it was worth checking into, and another two hours were spent going over the names, records and current residences of each of them. It was a thorough discussion, with all possibilities covered.

The process had kept Kennedy enthralled.

Reyes's family was a unit, and she admired that.

Though Madison had her information perfectly organized, she didn't seem as chipper as usual. Kennedy would bet it had something to do with the detective, but since no one else mentioned Crosby, she didn't, either.

She'd sat beside Reyes, of course, and when Madison passed him full color images that she'd printed of the thugs, Kennedy was shocked to recognize one of them.

"It's him."

All eyes turned to her. "Him, who?" Reyes asked.

"The man who was on my balcony. Remember, I told you about him?"

"You're sure?"

"Yes." She'd never forget that face, not after the way he'd terrified her.

Briefly Reyes explained about the incident that took place before the fire. "The police thought it was an attempted break-in, but Kennedy never bought that."

"Not with the way he stood there smiling at me." The memory disturbed her all over again, and she muttered, "I had my gun, but was too frozen to do anything other than aim at him."

Sterling grinned. "Likely that was enough."

"Given you have a history with him, that almost guarantees he's tied to Golly," Parrish decreed. "Which also casts suspicion on any close associates of his."

"I'm on it," Madison had promised. "I'll have more by the end of the day."

Now in Reyes's truck with the afternoon sunlight reflecting through the newly replaced window, she was glad Parrish had provided the glasses. They served the dual purpose of protecting her eyes from the glare and shielding her tumultuous thoughts from his discerning gaze. Not that she wanted to keep anything from him, but with him so attuned to their surroundings, she didn't want to distract him, either.

As if he'd just read her mind, he asked, "Doing okay?" without glancing at her.

She accepted that nothing much got past Reyes. "Much better today, thank you."

"Headache?"

"Not too bad." She looked at the bruise on his forehead. "You?"

"A-okay, babe. Like Dad said, I have a hard head." He took an exit to an industrial area.

Kennedy saw numerous restaurants, stores and a convention center. A few miles down he pulled into his father's hotel, which really was swanky with elaborate grounds now glistening under the white snow.

Driving around a small, ornamental lake, Reyes parked in a private-access garage. Her tension grew as they entered through a heavy door with a biometric lock.

"You weren't kidding about the security."

"No one other than my family accesses this part of the garage or building." With his hand at the small of her back, he steered her into a private elevator. "Nervous?"

"Anxious about seeing Jodi," she admitted. With Reyes she felt comfortable sharing her worries, so as the elevator climbed, she didn't hold back. "She's unpredictable. I don't know how she's going to react to everything."

"We'll figure it out, I promise."

We. It truly felt like they were partners in this. Having Reyes at her side meant more than she could ever express to him. She'd gotten used to going it alone…and now she didn't have to.

He saw his generosity as no big deal. To Kennedy, it was the greatest gift she'd ever been given, and was far more than she'd ever dared to hope for.

"I don't want to startle her," Kennedy said, getting out her phone. "I told her I'd text when we were here." She sent the message as soon as they stepped out of the elevator. Then she gazed around in awe. They were in a big foyer of sorts that ran the length of a long hall. Windows at one end overlooked the parking lot and main road.

She saw only one door, meaning this entire space was for the suite they'd given Jodi? Remarkable.

When the door opened and Kennedy got a look at Jodi, her stomach plummeted.

Her friend looked like a shadow of herself. Had she slept at all? Eaten? Combed her hair? She'd been afraid of this, and now she was doubly glad she'd come to see her in person rather than just calling or doing a video chat.

"Hey," Jodi said, her tone so sullen it bordered on antagonistic.

At the moment, none of that mattered. Kennedy was so glad to see her, pugnacious attitude and all, she grabbed her up in a spontaneous hug.

Predictably, Jodi went stiff.

That didn't matter, either. "Oh, it's good to see you, to know that you weren't hurt in the scuffle." To know she hadn't found a way to sneak out on her own. Of course the McKenzies had all assured her on that score, but hearing it and seeing it were two different things.

Jodi huffed. "Would have been tough for me to get hurt when your ape was busy ripping them all apart."

"I didn't rip," Reyes jokingly protested. "I demolished. There's a difference."

Jodi pressed her back. "But you?" Her gaze moved all over Kennedy's face, and when she focused on her bruised temple, she flinched. "Damn, Kennedy, you look like—"

"Hell, I know." She briefly hugged her again. "Have you heard the whole story?" She wasn't sure how much Reyes or Cade had shared with Jodi.

"Ha! They didn't tell me much of anything except that you were okay and I had to follow orders."

"That pretty much covers it." Summarizing greatly, Kennedy shared what had happened.

"I'm glad Delbert died," Jodi said.

"Same, though I would have liked to have gotten hold of him first," Reyes admitted. "Far as I'm concerned, he got off easy." With a hand to the center of Kennedy's back, Reyes began urging them both inside. "Instead of jawing out here, how about we get comfortable?"

"It's your place," Jodi said, strolling into the suite. "You can come and go as you please."

"For now," Reyes replied, "it's yours. You don't have to worry about anyone showing up without an invite."

"You two did."

Surprised, Kennedy said, "I messaged you first." Then, because she understood Jodi's attitude was part of her defenses, she quietly asked, "You don't want to see me?"

"Sure I do. Just sayin' that it wasn't my choice to be here." She shot a resentful look at Reyes, then walked across a wide entry to a beautiful living room furnished with a cream velvet couch and two armchairs. She threw herself into a chair, looking much like a ticked-off teenager.

On one side of the room was a dining table with six chairs, and behind that a wet bar and kitchenette. On the other side, an arched doorway led to a bedroom and bathroom. Through the open doorways, Kennedy saw that both rooms looked mostly unused. The couch faced a wall of windows with an impressive view of the Rockies.

Every inch of the space had top-of-the-line finishes, giving it the look of a designer home.

Though she knew Jodi couldn't be comfortable here, Kennedy tried to encourage her by saying, "Wow, this is nice."

Jodi shrugged. "In a gilded-cage kind of way."

It almost embarrassed Kennedy for her friend to be so ungrateful. "Jodi," she chided, wishing for a way to reassure her.

Reyes stalked over to stand in front of Jodi. Arms crossed and feet braced apart, he *loomed*. Kennedy had never seen him do such a thing before.

Finally he asked, "Got a death wish, Jodi? Is that it?"

Losing her slouched position, Jodi straightened as much as she could with Reyes so close. "Maybe death would be easier than waiting for fate to screw me over again."

"Nah," Reyes said. "Girl, you have to know if Golly gets hold of you, it won't be an easy death."

Appalled by that bit of verbal reality, Kennedy gasped. "Reyes!"

Both he and Jodi ignored her.

"You might not put any value on your life, but Kennedy sure as hell does. Come to that, so do I."

"Ha!"

Reyes leaned down into her space and growled, "I'd like to rip Golly apart because of what he did to you."

Anger shot Jodi out of her chair. Reyes straightened but didn't back up, so she had to tip her head way back to glare at him. Given her short stature she barely reached Reyes's shoulders, and he weighed more than twice what she did, making it a ludicrous standoff.

Full of pain and suffering, Jodi growled, "You think I

don't want that, too?" Her eyes turned red and liquid, her thin chest heaving. "Jesus, it's *all* I want. I'd gladly die if I could take that miserable bastard with me!"

"Well, you can't," Reyes said softly, laying his large hand on her narrow shoulder. "I'm sorry, so fucking sorry, Jodi, but Rob Golly is dead after all."

When Jodi would have lurched away in shock, Reyes held her still. Furious, she went on tiptoe to glare into his face. "Why would you be sorry about that? I wanted him dead! That's why I killed him."

He nodded. "You accomplished that much, and I swear, girl, I'm cheering for you."

"Then why...?" As if Jodi knew there was worse news to come, the tears spilled over and she started gulping breaths.

"Sadly, the danger doesn't end with him. But I know you're strong. You've already proven that a dozen times over. I know you're smart, too, so you'll listen to reason."

Giving one sharp, grave nod, she rasped, "Quit dragging it out. Let's hear it, already."

"What you need to know, what you have to understand, is that your life has value. Real, substantial value. Don't let Golly take that from you." He lifted his hand to briefly cup her cheek. "He's taken enough. Don't give him another damned thing."

Angrily she dashed away the tears and then, wonder of wonders, she said, "Okay."

"Thank you."

"Why are you thanking me?" she asked with another huff.

"Because Kennedy loves you, and I don't want to see her tormented by your stubbornness." He grinned a rascal's grin, dimple and all. "Now, how about we all sit down

and talk this out?" Oh-so-gently, he led her to the couch
where Kennedy sat.

Kennedy barely kept her smile contained. Every time
she thought Reyes couldn't get more wonderful, he out-
did her expectations.

"Fine." Jodi flopped back against the plush cushions
and propped her feet on the glass coffee table. "Talk away.
I'm listening."

With Kennedy on one side of her, and Reyes on the
other, Jodi was boxed in—but she didn't get jittery about it
like she usually would. Reyes had accomplished that much.

Kennedy half turned to face her. "Okay, so as Reyes
said, the good news is that Rob Golly is dead after all."

"I thought the body wasn't there, though. How do you
explain that?"

"Well..." It was so awful Kennedy hated to break the
news to her. "It seems Rob has a brother. You probably
never met him because he was in prison. Apparently, as
soon as Rand got out he went to see Rob and found his
body. I'm guessing it didn't take a sleuth to find out from
Rob's friends that he'd had you, making you the most likely
suspect."

Eyes wide in disbelief, Jodi stared at her, then laughed.
"A brother? You know, I think Rob talked about him every
so often. There was even a photo of them when they were
younger." She laughed again, the sound rusty and mean,
nowhere near humor. "I must have the rottenest luck ever.
My life has been tainted from the day I was born. You'd
be smart to stay away from me."

Kennedy sat forward in a rush. "I care about you, damn
it!"

She fell a little more in love with Reyes when he raised
his hand. "And me. I'll take it as a personal affront if anything happens to you, Jodi. So we're not going to let it."

"Terrific," Jodi said. "I have a plan."

Knowing the way Jodi thought, Kennedy groaned.

Reyes, being a little more diplomatic, said, "I'm open to ideas. Let's hear it."

"We use me as bait."

"No," Kennedy said.

"How?" Reyes asked at the same time. "Because losing you can't be part of the plan."

"You're a hotshot, right?" Jodi smirked. "You and that big, quiet bro of yours. And, hey, let's not forget the bad-ass chick he's with."

"Er, that would be his wife," Reyes said, then conceded, "although she is pretty badass."

"So I'll trust you three to keep me safe. You can handle that, can't you?"

"Probably."

"No," Kennedy said again. "Out of the question."

Still slouched in her seat, Jodi swiveled her head around to smile at her. "You're my best friend," she said. "My only friend. You matter to me a lot, Kennedy. Always know that. But I can't do this. I can't sit around and wait to see what will happen. This place might be nice, but the waiting… It makes me feel like I'm back in that damned cellar, not knowing what will happen or when."

"Then we'll stay somewhere together."

Reyes went on the alert, but she couldn't let Jodi feel alone now. "If I'm with you—"

"I'd still feel like I was crawling out of my skin. It's the waiting, you know?" She gave a small, sad smile. "It's not so much my surroundings. Not anymore. It's that I'm not in control, and I flat out can't stand it."

"They're working on it," Kennedy tried to assure her, but Jodi was already shaking her head.

"Sorry, but I can either confront things head-on, or I

can take off again. Those are the options I can live with. If I can get this over with sooner, while also having some really good backup, then hey, that's the route I'd prefer."

Desperate, Kennedy reached for her hand. "It's too risky."

Jodi slipped over to lean against Kennedy's shoulder in an uncharacteristic show of affection. "Sorry, girlfriend. Really. But it's not your decision."

Kennedy looked from Jodi's trusting expression— a sight seldom seen—to Reyes's enigmatic gaze. He was leaving it up to her, she understood that, but he wasn't objecting. "Reyes?"

He rubbed a hand over his face. "I wouldn't want to do anything unless you're okay with it."

"But?"

"I get what Jodi is saying."

Jodi grinned. "Damn, maybe I like you as a pal."

Before she could get too excited, Reyes added, "I'd need time to plan, so we're talking at least a few days." In a sterner tone, his frown aimed at Jodi, he said, "In the meantime, I'd expect you to stay put."

She crossed her heart. "No problem. I just need a light at the end of the tunnel."

Kennedy felt as though the air had been compressed out of her lungs. She didn't want to come off as a coward, but someone had to inject logic. "There's no conceivable way to plan for every possibility."

"No," Reyes agreed, "and that's something Jodi should consider."

Jodi hugged Kennedy's arm. "Don't be a pill, okay? I *need* to do this. And just think, if we pull this off, I'll be free."

Temper flaring, Kennedy demanded, "Free to do what? To continue risking yourself? To continue chasing trouble?"

"Hiding from the world," Reyes added. "Living half a life, all in the shadows."

"Hey!" Sitting up in a huff, Jodi poked Reyes in the shoulder. "You're supposed to be on my side."

"I'm not taking sides, doll. But I have a solution that might please you both."

Kennedy really didn't want to hear it, but what choice did she have? She nodded.

Jodi shrugged. "Out with it."

"We need some assurances." Sitting forward, one elbow braced on his knee, Reyes pinned Jodi with serious intent. "We need your cooperation. We need you to want to make a better life for yourself."

"You want to take over? Be my boss?" She started to rise. "Screw that."

Kennedy caught her elbow. "Can't you at least hear him out?"

Jodi was resistant, then finally flopped back in her seat. "Sure. Whatever."

So. Damned. Stubborn.

And so hurt. It seemed Jodi was part anger, part open wound and part fear, with attitude holding it all together.

Reyes didn't let it bother him. "My father funds some great initiatives for helping women who've escaped trafficking. We can go over the nitty-gritty another time, but the gist of it is that we can set you up with legit employment that you'll enjoy, plus help you with a place to stay, any additional education or training you might need, and financial assistance to keep it going until—"

Already Jodi was back on her feet and angrily stalking away. "I don't take charity."

"Wouldn't be charity," Reyes said, "unless you choose it to be. A smart person would see it as an opportunity for a leg up. A way to improve her life. Plus, you could always pay it forward. The task force needs good people pitching in."

Kennedy stood. "Jodi, please. Can't you take that chip off your shoulder long enough to accept well-meaning help?"

She stood at the big windows looking out. "Then what? You'll be rid of me?"

Catching on to one of Jodi's worries, Kennedy softened her tone. "Then you'll have a regular job with days off. We can spend time together—lunches, a movie. Shopping."

"I don't shop."

"You'll shop with me," Kennedy insisted. "The point is, I want you in my life. I want a reliable relationship that's based on mutual respect and affection, not worry or fear."

In the smallest voice Kennedy had ever heard, Jodi whispered, "You can't respect me."

Reyes asked, "Why the hell not? I do. My brother does."

Turning in surprise, Jodi stared at him. "Don't bullshit me," she said without heat.

"Doubt I could." He came to stand by Kennedy. "Now quit being such a hard case and accept a friendly offering from people who care."

"Your pa doesn't know me, so how can he care?"

Kennedy spoke ahead of Reyes. "His father, who is a wonderful man, by the way, lost someone he loved to traffickers. Believe me, he cares—about me, about *you*, about every woman who's ever been in such a horrid situation. You're not the only one who wants to make a difference, Jodi."

Reyes smiled at her with pride. "So passionate. And one-hundred percent correct."

Jodi's eyes grew glassy again. "Okay, fine. I'll do it."

"Yes!" Reyes stepped forward and swept her into a hug, shocking poor Jodi senseless. He seemed to catch himself and quickly set her back, but when he saw her slow grin, he laughed. "You're a woman of your word, so I trust you won't forget this conversation."

"No, I won't." She gestured to the door. "Now go make plans, and keep me updated. The waiting is miserable."

Obviously, Jodi wanted some time alone to digest it all.

Instead, Reyes rubbed his hands together. "Let's get pizza first. I'll send someone out for it."

Jodi eyed him warily.

His smile never slipped. "We can stuff our faces and visit. Kennedy's feeling as cooped up as you are." He turned to her. "You'd like that, wouldn't you, babe?"

Her heart felt too big for her chest. "Very much so."

"There, you see? Surely you can suffer me long enough to eat?"

It took her a second, and then Jodi laughed, not a fake laugh, or one inspired by anger, but an honest, joyous expression. "You're nuts—but okay, sure. I haven't had much appetite, but suddenly I'm starved."

"There you go." He turned to Kennedy. "This'll be fun."

She was so overwhelmed, words stuck in her throat. The best she could manage was a nod. Reyes gave her a wink and went to the phone to call the lobby.

He'd won Jodi over so easily, just by being himself. Kennedy felt caught between a good laugh—and a hard cry.

She was afraid for Jodi yet ecstatic to see her so happy, madly in love with Reyes yet anxious about the future. It felt like she was on a wild roller-coaster ride of shifting emotional extremes—and she'd never been happier in her life.

With that realization came a new fear: If things ended with Reyes, then what? Would she be able to go back to her mundane existence of writing, speaking engagements and slogging through each day without enthusiasm?

If things ended, she'd be more devastated than ever before.

Thanks to Reyes's influence, she was a stronger person now—but was she strong enough to survive that particular heartache?

Before it came to that, she'd tell Reyes that she loved him and hope it made a difference.

For now, she'd just enjoy seeing the smiles of the two people most important to her.

"YOU'RE SURE HE'S DEAD?" Rand asked. "He couldn't just be in the hospital?"

"He's dead, all right. The news interviewed some witnesses who saw the car go off the road. Said he was carried out of the ravine in a body bag."

"Did you check the local hospitals anyway?" He wouldn't leave anything to chance.

"Just like you told me. Couldn't find him anywhere. He's dead."

Rand smiled. Perfect. Delbert O'Neil had become a liability with his endless complaints and impatience. And that damned chain-smoking. The stench alone had been vile.

If Del hadn't taken off when he did, Rand would have enjoyed cutting his throat while he slept.

Pinning the small-time thug with a glare, Rand asked, "Any news on Jodi?"

"Her car was towed, that's all I know."

"Hmm." He rocked back and forth, thinking. The same behemoth who'd destroyed his men to protect Kennedy was likely protecting Jodi also. "Can you round up a few more guys?"

"How many?"

"Ten ought to do it." Added to the ten he already had, they could cover a lot of ground. "Offer them a hundred dollars a day to keep on the lookout for Jodi or Kennedy. You still have photos of them you can share?"

"Yeah, on my phone."

Rand tapped his fingertips together and prodded his tongue between his missing teeth. "Whoever spots one of them first will get a bonus of five hundred."

"Sweet deal. I'll get the word out right away." He turned to go.

Rand waited until he was out the door of the cabin before he turned to the remaining man. This guy was a little more reliable. "I need some supplies."

"Sure thing, boss."

He went down the list of necessary items. "Don't buy more than two things at any one store. Shop around in different places so you don't draw attention."

"Got it. Anything else?"

"Yes. Early evening, go by that construction site down the road and gather up anything that can be used for shrapnel. Nails, staples, broken glass. Even small chunks of rocks will do."

Eyes wider now, the guy said, "Uh, boss, are we building a bomb?"

"We?" Golly smirked. "Do you know how to build a fucking bomb?"

He shook his head fast.

"I do, so yes, *I'll* be building a bomb." It wasn't how he wanted to kill Jodi, but things were getting dicey now that Delbert O'Neil had screwed up the plans. He had to be prepared, just in case. "Get everything back to me tonight."

With that clear dismissal, Rand finally found himself alone in the cabin. He, too, was getting tired of being cooped up. Shouldn't be for too much longer, though. He'd either have his hands on Jodi, where he could enjoy his revenge, or he'd blow her into tiny bits. Either way, justice would be served.

He rocked a little harder as he imagined each scenario.

FOR TWO DAYS, they worked on the details of the trap. It wasn't easy, but Reyes convinced Kennedy that it would be better for them to stay at his father's house for now. She'd reluctantly agreed.

And she'd withdrawn.

Reyes knew it was her worry about Jodi, and maybe about him, too, that kept her mostly quiet. Soon as they wrapped it up and ensured Jodi's safety, she'd relax again.

He hoped.

To keep up appearances, they went to the gym each day. Although he'd have preferred for her to stay at home, she refused, saying she felt safest with him.

A part of him relished her trust, and another part wondered if he was seeing the future laid out for him, how she'd always react to the danger inherent in his job. For himself, he wouldn't mind. It was kind of nice having a woman who cared.

Yet he hated the idea of her continuing to live on edge—because of him.

That second day at the gym, she went to his office to look over her manuscript while he continued dealing with the public. She couldn't resume her workouts yet, especially since his dad constantly warned her to take it easy.

If Parrish had his way, Kennedy would probably still be in bed. It was pretty remarkable how she pushed through, though. More from a sheer force of will to carry on rather than in a bullheaded way meant to prove anything to others.

A personality trait no doubt learned from her past.

With the colorful bruising on her face, Kennedy had

gotten more than a few stares. She'd simply smiled and acted as if nothing had happened. So as far as he knew, no one had asked her about it. It helped that her warmer clothes covered her body, so the only mark showing was the one on her temple.

More than a little distracted with thoughts of Kennedy, Reyes almost did a double take when he heard one guy say to another, "Yeah, you just need to keep an eye out for either chick. You get paid by the day, and if you spot one of them, there's a nice bonus."

What were the odds? One guy was standing near the weight bench while another did some presses. They looked like many twentysomething guys who visited the gym, dressed in baggy sweatpants, dingy wifebeater undershirts and expensive gym shoes. Both had elaborate tats along their arms, and one had tats extending over his chest and neck. Stocking hats hid most of their hair, but judging by their brows, they both were dark.

Going for a casual vibe, Reyes whistled low as he started picking up discarded weights at the other benches to put them back on the rack, which got him close enough to glance at the small phone photo the standing guy showed to the one on the bench.

Jodi. Son of a bitch.

He didn't react as he listened a little more closely.

"No, I don't know the dude. Got the info from my buddy, Dub. You'll check in with him."

When he shared a phone number, Reyes committed it to memory long enough to get to the desk where Will, an employee, checked people in and answered the phone.

In his rush, Reyes rudely shouldered Will aside and grabbed up a paper and pen to jot down the number with the name. With that done, he murmured to Will, "Keep an eye on those guys by the benches. I'll be right back."

"Sure thing."

Will was a good worker who knew to keep his mouth shut and his eyes open. He had no real idea what Reyes did for a living other than running a gym, and he didn't ask. His loyalty had been tested numerous times already.

Reyes strolled to the office and handed the paper to Kennedy. "Call Madison and share this with her. Tell her I overheard a couple of knuckleheads talking about getting paid to look for you and Jodi."

Startled, Kennedy looked up. "What—"

"No time for questions, babe. I'll be back in a few. Stay here with the door locked. Got it?"

She nodded, stood quickly and followed him as far as the door, then closed and locked it behind him.

Thankfully, the men were still where Reyes had left them, and now they had a third man with them. He eavesdropped without hesitation.

"No shit? How many is he hiring?"

"Ten, I think, but I'm only supposed to round up five. So you in or what?"

"Yeah, sure. Where do I look?"

"We're supposed to spread out in this neighborhood, especially here around the gym." He glanced up Reyes.

Reyes nodded casually as he continued on by. When he reached the desk, in a low voice he asked Will, "You up for a side job? It's worth a day's pay."

Brows up, Will said, "Heck, yeah."

"When the kid in the gray hoodie leaves, see if you can spot his license plate number without being noticed."

"What if he's not driving?"

Yeah, that was a possibility. "See which direction he goes." Clapping him on the shoulder, Reyes said, "Thanks." He deliberately moved away from the men to the other side of the gym, where he had brief conversations with two women doing cardio, then a younger guy trying to bulk up his legs.

Though Reyes didn't stare at the men, he was aware of them the entire time.

When two of them finally left, including the one in the hoodie who been doling out info, Will moseyed out and, damn it, Reyes started to worry. If Will was too obvious, they might catch on to him and then he could get jumped later.

It was a fact that a lot of street toughs hung out at the gym. Reyes didn't discourage it. He owned the gym in this run-down section of town so that he could hear the word from the street.

So far, so good.

He was relieved to see Will cross the road to his truck, where he opened the door, got inside and rummaged in his glove box.

Good cover. He'd always appreciated Will as a smart kid, though he was probably twenty-two now.

A minute later he left the truck, locked the doors and jogged back inside. His nose and ears had already turned red from the cold, and he chafed his arms as he went to the desk, made a note and stuck it in the top drawer.

Smooth.

Holding up a candy bar that he'd brought out of the truck, he said, "Okay for me to take a break, boss?"

Will caught on quick, obviously. Appreciating how he covered his tracks, Reyes nodded.

Aware of the third man lingering inside and now watching them both, Reyes said, "No problem. I'll cover out here." Walking over to two regulars, Reyes took time to offer some instruction on a machine they were using incorrectly.

The third guy lost interest and left.

With the coast seemingly clear, the urge to check on Kennedy, to give the plate number to Madison, to follow after the knuckleheads all warred inside Reyes, but good training paid off, and he kept up the show of being nothing more than a fit gym owner interested in his clientele.

Good thing, too, because he spotted the gray hoodie goof peeking back in through the big front window.

Shame Golly had stooped to hiring scrawny troublemakers. Reyes would almost feel bad for schooling them on the error of their ways.

His issue now would be getting Kennedy out of the gym without them spotting her. He didn't doubt that at least one of them was already aware of her, but he'd prefer not to engage with them tonight. It'd be better if he could get her out of harm's way first.

Screw it. He went to the desk, picked up the landline and called Cade. His brother would be at the bar now, but he could work it out.

Making sure no one was near enough to listen in, and assuming the idiot peering in through the window couldn't read lips, Reyes explained the situation to Cade.

Of course Cade had a solution. He always did. "I can have Sterling pick her up at the back door. If you're ready to leave at the same time, you can follow behind them. Make sure Kennedy is wearing the sunglasses Dad gave her, and Sterling can bring a hat to stuff on her head."

In that moment, Reyes realized something interesting. He loved coordinating with his family.

For years he'd told himself that he did it because he'd been groomed for it, he was good at it, and it made a difference.

Now he knew it was more than that.

He thrived on this shit.

Cade would always be the older brother he looked up to, and Madison would always be the baby sister he adored.

Working with them was not only rewarding, it was special in a way few families ever experienced. They weren't just close, they routinely depended on each other. He knew his family would always have his back.

And because they understood that Kennedy was important to him, they had her back, too.

God, he was lucky—and until Kennedy, he'd never realized it. "Tell Sterling I appreciate it."

"She knows, but I'll tell her anyway."

They figured out a time for Sterling to arrive, and after Reyes disconnected, he grinned. Done playing, he went to the front door, opened it and said to hoodie-boy, "What's up, dude? You forget something?"

Like a deer in the headlights, the guy went blank. "What?"

"Saw you looking in. If you lost something, let me know. I'll look around."

Full of belligerence now, he said, "No, man. I ain't lost nothing. Can't a guy hang out?"

"Sure, no problem. It's warmer in here, though."

Lip curling, the guy turned and stalked away, going the opposite direction this time. So was he meeting someone? About a block down, he peered over his shoulder, and Reyes ducked back inside.

While he had a chance, he fetched the note Will had made and put it in his shoe. Once Will returned from his break, he thanked him again and finally went to Kennedy.

It really felt like things were coming together. Soon he'd remove all the obstacles, and then he'd tell Kennedy how he felt and ask her to stay with him.

Forever.

CHAPTER EIGHTEEN

"I WANT TO go with you," Kennedy said, and he heard a frantic note in her voice.

"Not a good idea, babe." Reyes paused in the middle of sorting his gear to press a kiss to her mouth. God, he loved that mouth. Loved her ass, too, as well as that particular obstinate expression she was giving him now.

Her soft blond hair, her blue eyes. Her stubbornness and strength.

Hell, he loved every part of her, everything about her, all the things she made him feel and the ways she'd changed him. She'd become the center of his world and he didn't mind at all.

"Reyes—"

"Kennedy," he teased back. Even if she wasn't in a teasing mood, he sure as hell was.

The day had finally come to put the plan into action. It was made easier by Golly's watchdogs, who now haunted the gym and the streets around it.

The idea was that he'd stop in at the gym with Jodi, just long enough for them to spot her. Shortly after that, once the goons had a chance to notify Golly, he'd head out to a more remote area, where they could try their luck at ambushing him again. This time Reyes planned to be ready. He'd already chosen a nice high point where he and Jodi could wait them out.

He'd pick them off one by one without hesitation or a single moment of remorse.

For the other problems, meaning Golly's cohorts, Madison had found locations for them by using hoodie-boy's plates. The girl was a whiz at tracking. Hoodie-boy met with one person, and that led them to another person, and on it went.

He, Cade and Sterling would round up all of them. With Madison on watch, none of them would get away.

Once it was over, Kennedy would be free to choose whatever life she wanted. He planned to convince her to choose a life with him.

"You have it all covered," she insisted. "You said so yourself."

"True." It was as planned out as it could be. "But we have to split up. I'll be with Jodi. Cade and Sterling will get the other creeps. Madison will keep an eye on Golly at the motel, and bam, it'll be over."

"See? It's safe," Kennedy reiterated. "You know Jodi will be more comfortable if I'm there with her."

"There are too many things that can go wrong."

"Reyes." She slipped up against him, her arms around his neck. "If it's not safe for me, how is it safe for Jodi?"

I'm not in love with Jodi. Damn it, he was so close to having it all that he didn't want to blurt out a half-baked declaration now. He wanted to do it the right way.

The way Kennedy deserved.

He settled on saying, "Jodi knows how to shoot."

"I can shoot."

He gave her a level look. "Practicing a few times is not the same as using a gun in a high-pressure situation."

"So I'll be a lookout."

Damn it, he wanted to know she was tucked away some place safe, not out in the thick of it. Yes, he was confident of his ability, but shit happened. He couldn't bear it if it happened to her again. "Kennedy—"

"I'll get her geared up," Sterling said as she stepped through the open door of the suite. "Come on, Kennedy."

Smug, Kennedy blew him a kiss and hurried after his sister-in-law.

Reyes was right on her heels. "Now wait a damn minute."

She turned, a desperate expression on her face. "I swear I won't get in your way. I won't cry and I'll follow orders to the letter."

"Ah, hon…" He closed the space between them. "I'm not worried about any of that."

Sterling stood there, arms crossed. "She wants to be with you, you dolt."

"I *know* that."

Undeterred by his dark frown, Sterling continued, "I wouldn't let Cade leave me behind."

"You," he said, "aren't natural."

"Because I'm female? Well, look at you, being all sexist."

Cursing a blue streak wouldn't help anything, but Reyes did it anyway.

Kennedy touched his face. "I keep telling you. I feel safest when I'm with you."

He glared at Sterling, hoping she'd give them a private moment. She didn't budge. Frustrated enough to make his hair stand on end, Reyes stared at Kennedy a long minute. Best-laid plans and all that. His had just gone horribly awry. "If that's true," he said, feeling Sterling's smile as she listened in, "then maybe you should plan on staying with me."

"Yes! I knew you'd see reason." She started to go.

Reyes stopped her. "I didn't mean just today, babe."

Watching her closely, he saw her eyes flare. "I mean after this is over."

"After?"

Let Sterling watch, he didn't care. Swooping in, he kissed Kennedy, taking his time, moving his mouth over hers, teasing his tongue along her lips and then into her mouth. She clung to him, and with a soft groan she reciprocated.

When he lifted his mouth, she looked dazed.

Reyes smoothed a hand over her hair, letting his thumb lightly brush the bruise on her temple. "Stay with me."

She bit her lips, then slowly smiled and nodded. "Of course I will. Thank y—"

Another kiss stopped her from thanking him.

"Ahem." Grinning, Sterling said, "Not that the show isn't great, but we're running low on time. So what's it to be? Want her in a vest and armed, or do you plan to lock her in a closet?"

Running a hand over his head, Reyes turned away, immediately paced back and cursed. "You'll stay right where I put you?"

Kennedy nodded.

"You swear you know how to shoot?"

"Adequately." She winced. "Can't promise I'll hit anything, but I can definitely return fire if necessary."

"You'll stay low, stay safe and—"

"Yes and yes." Grabbing him, Kennedy squeezed him tight. "I'll be right back. Don't you dare leave without me."

MADISON SAT IN the library, her laptop in front of her, watching all the players. Reyes, with Kennedy and Jodi, would reach the gym in the next fifteen minutes or so.

Cade and Sterling were at the back of an old house,

slowly closing in on where two of Golly's cohorts had holed up.

Golly hadn't moved from the motel, though two men had come in to see him. It was sheer luck that a camera on the connected diner caught the front of his cabin. The picture was dim, but she made it out just fine.

When the two men left, she noted that one of them carried a heavy duffel bag. Suddenly she had a very bad feeling about things. She watched the men until they got into a car, then she wrote down the license plate number and did a quick, secure search.

Matthew Grimes.

With a name in hand, she extended her search and found that the guy had a long record, similar to Golly's, and lived locally. Why hadn't she known about him sooner? Was he someone newly brought into the schemes?

Her bad feeling grew.

Her dad walked in, and, being so attuned to his children, he immediately knew something was wrong.

"What is it?" Parrish asked, hurrying around the desk to look over her shoulder.

"I don't know." Madison skimmed all the players again. The car with the two men left in a hurry. Because her father encouraged them to share misgivings—he was a big believer in instincts—she laid out her thoughts.

"This is the first I've seen Grimes. Why would Golly need a new hand at this point?" She looked at her father. "Unless his plan of attack has changed?" A terrible thought, given everything was already in the works. Both her brothers were out there, Sterling, too, and now she felt like she hadn't judged the situation well at all.

Parrish, always methodical, stared at the screen for only a few seconds before making a decision. "Call the detective. See if he knows anything about Grimes."

Glad to have a valid reason to reach out to Crosby again, Madison lifted her phone and, with the number memorized, dialed him. Knowing her father would want to listen in, she put the phone on speaker and set it on the desk.

He didn't answer until the fifth ring, and he sounded harried. "Detective Albertson."

Watching the screens, Madison saw the driver of the car take an exit that would lead him to the general area of Reyes's gym. Alarm bells went off in her head. In cases like this, she didn't believe in coincidences.

If the gym was his destination, and she'd bet it was, he'd arrive within minutes of Reyes.

"It's Madison McKenzie."

Crosby missed a beat before saying, "Ms. McKenzie. I'm surprised to hear from you."

She rolled her eyes at his absurd deference. Whether he'd enjoyed it or not, she'd kissed him. He could certainly use her first name. "You probably wouldn't have," she admitted, "not after that insult you dealt me."

Her father's brows went up.

She shook her head at him, letting him know it wasn't anything to concern him, then forged on. "The thing is, Crosby, I have a situation and I'm hoping you can help me."

"Hang on one second."

She heard movement, then the sound of a car door closing, followed by the start of an engine.

"I was just on my way out. Crazy busy at the moment, but I can talk while I drive."

"Thank you." She considered what to say, yet knew the outcome would be the same. "Now, I don't want you to get angry."

"That pretty much guarantees it right there," he growled. "What the hell are you up to now?"

He said that with so much accusation, she huffed. "Matthew Grimes. Do you know the name?"

Crosby surprised her with amped-up anger. "Damned right I know him. I'm headed to his last known location right now. How the hell do *you* know him?"

When Parrish gave her a nod, she confessed, "I'm keeping tabs on Golly. Grimes just left him."

"Jesus, Madison. You know where Golly is and didn't tell me?"

How could the man sound both hurt and frustrated by that when he'd made no effort to stay in touch with her? "We'll have to cover that later, Detective. Right now, I'm... concerned."

"As you should be. I knew Grimes hung with Golly so I've been keeping tabs on him. Last night the weasel went to six different stores buying up enough ingredients for several homemade bombs."

Madison caught her breath. *The duffel he'd been carrying.*

Leaning forward, hands flattened on the desk, Parrish spoke before Madison could. "He's headed toward my son's gym right now. How close are you?"

"Son of a bitch," Crosby exploded. "Your family has a lot of explaining to do when this is over."

"How close?" Parrish repeated in a hard demand.

"I'll call it in. Tell Reyes to clear everyone out of there."

"I'm organizing now. Don't make me regret reaching out to you."

Walking away, Parrish used his own phone to call Reyes.

Madison turned back to the phone. "Crosby?"

"Yeah?"

"Promise me you'll be careful."

He gave a gravelly laugh filled with affront. "Don't worry about me."

She'd worry if she wanted to. Irate, she glared at the phone. "Would it be too much to ask to be kept updated?"

Seconds ticked by, then he said evenly, "You haven't seen fit to give me your number."

Her heart skipped a beat. True, her calls came in as private, but she'd love for Crosby to have it. "I'll text it to you now." Why did it feel as if they'd just come to an understanding? "You'll contact me once you're at the gym?"

"I'm not going to the gym, but I'll let you know once it's been cleared."

"Then—"

"You're going to tell me what's going on," he stated, leaving no room for negotiation. "And you're going to tell me now."

REYES HAD JUST pulled up to the curb when his phone rang. It surprised him to see it was his dad calling, not Madison or Cade. Surprised him, and made him uneasy.

Making a quick decision, he pulled away from the curb and answered the call. "What's wrong?"

"Get away from the gym."

"Already doing that." He checked his mirrors, not yet spotting any trouble.

"Two men left Golly, headed your way," Parrish said, his explanation short and to the point. "Detective Albertson says the driver went shopping last night for the makings of a bomb."

"Damn." The ramifications settled in on Reyes. He had a gym full of innocents, and two women in the back seat of his truck.

"Albertson is on the way. I assume he'll alert other authorities." Parrish hesitated. "I want you to abort the plan.

Given you three are the target, stay away from the gym. Divert to Golly's motel." His voice lowered. "Get the bastard."

"You'll get everyone out of the gym?"

"It'll be my next call. Albertson will clean up that mess."

Reyes tightened his hands on the wheel. "Got it."

"Watch your back."

"Always." Before explaining anything to Kennedy and Jodi, he backtracked by going two blocks down, then two blocks over. The women patiently stayed silent.

Once he was headed in the right direction, he laid out the situation for them.

Kennedy sat forward to touch his shoulder. "Someone will tell Cade?"

"Dad or Madison, but his plans won't alter. Cade is still on to close the net."

Nodding, she sat back again, quiet as she'd promised to be.

Jodi whispered, "This doesn't feel right. Golly doesn't want to blow me up. He doesn't want me dead at a distance."

Reyes tended to agree. "It's personal for him."

Jodi's voice grew urgent. "He's trying to catch us unaware."

Yup, exactly how Reyes saw it. "But we won't let him, right?"

"No, we won't." Kennedy took Jodi's hand. "Trust Reyes. He knows what he's doing."

Damn right, he did. "I don't think anyone spotted us, but I want you two to keep watch." Giving them something to do would make them feel more in control. "Tell me if you see anything suspicious."

With no real sign of nervousness, Kennedy said, "Will do."

Jodi remained silent. He could only imagine how she felt. The girl had been all set to use herself as bait, and now the plans were upside down. Shit happened. It wasn't the first time he'd had to adjust to changing conditions, but that didn't make it easy.

When he was near the motel, he called Madison hands-free on speaker. "All clear?" he asked.

"I haven't seen Golly move. But Reyes, I don't feel right about any of this."

"I know. Same." He glanced in the rearview mirror at Kennedy's set expression. She was doing her utmost not to look unnerved. Because he knew every business on the road, Reyes said, "I'm going to put them both in a restaurant."

"No!" Jodi said, immediately objecting.

Kennedy shushed her. "Let him do his thing, okay? He knows best."

Her confidence felt good.

Madison agreed with Jodi. "Golly might have contacts in every area business. I think you should keep them close."

He hesitated but knew she was right. Away from him, either of them could get grabbed. He'd die before he let that happen, so sticking close likely was the way to go. Deciding on a quick compromise, he asked, "Where should I park so that they'll be near, but not too close, and you'll have a constant view of my truck?"

"Three spots down from Golly's cabin is best. It's the third one from the office, and I believe the other two are empty."

"Huh. Wonder if Golly rented them to ensure his privacy."

"Makes sense."

Reyes parked beneath a security lamp. Though the night was dark, the lamp hadn't yet come on. Odds were it wouldn't. Not much in the motel seemed to be in good working order.

"Kennedy?" Madison said.

Leaning forward, Kennedy said, "I'm here."

"Why don't you get behind the wheel in case a hasty exit is necessary?"

She looked at Reyes, got his nod and agreed.

The parking lot was fairly quiet. In the office, Reyes could see a desk manager backlit by a lamp, and he appeared to be alone. Seeing the place up close, he was surprised it was even still in business. What had probably been nice cabins a decade ago were now more like hovels in need of serious repairs. The gravel lot had deep ruts and potholes, and an area that should have been grass was now snow-covered weeds.

"It's a dump," he said to Madison. "You sure it's legit?"

"A grandson inherited it, and it's gone downhill since then."

Shame.

Jodi snapped, "Can't we get on with it?"

"Getting there." Reyes studied the cabin. Curtains were drawn over grimy windows. His bad feeling escalated. "I'm not going to the front of the cabin. I'll circle around back and see if there's another way in."

While watching for any sign of attack, he opened the door and got out. Turning, he motioned to Kennedy to take over as driver. She quickly removed her coat and tossed it in the back seat, then slid behind the wheel.

Jodi, he noticed, had a Glock in her hand and a stark look of resolve on her face.

"Hey."

She glanced at him.

"No mishaps with the gun, okay?"

Nodding, she went back to studying the area, her uneasiness palpable.

Knowing he couldn't put it off any longer, he touched Kennedy's chin. "Lock up behind me. If anything happens, drive away. Do not try to play my protector."

Before agreeing, she said, "Swear to me you'll be okay."

"Course I will." He stole a fast kiss. "When this is over, you and I have plans to make."

Reyes's steps were silent as he moved in the shadows toward Golly's cabin. At the farthest side of the ramshackle structure he spotted a small, high window that he guessed to be in the bathroom. Around the corner, he saw a larger window and then the door. Tightly closed curtains kept him from having a view inside.

That in itself wasn't suspicious, yet tension prickled up his spine.

He backtracked to the small window. Aging cobwebs covered the sill, and a crack traveled upward from the bottom right corner. For most, the window would be too high to be accessible. His height and overall physical fitness served him well now. Catching the ledge with his fingertips, he levered himself up for a peek.

The room was dark and it took a moment for his eyesight to adjust. The bathroom door was shut, closing it off from the rest of the cabin. He was considering how he might enter through the window when a slight movement inside drew his gaze. He levered up a little higher for a better view.

Stunned, he realized that Golly, fully dressed, was stretched out flat in the narrow bathtub. Why would he... *Shit.*

Before the thought fully formed, he understood why everything felt off.

The front door was booby-trapped, likely with a bomb.

Had he busted in, as he'd originally planned, he'd have been seriously wounded—and Kennedy and Jodi would be on their own.

Kennedy.

Silently he dropped back to his feet and, ducking low, went back to the front of the building. Gun in hand, he saw both women still in the truck, exactly as he'd instructed.

Beyond them, though, two shadows lurked.

No way would he let them get anywhere near Kennedy.

Flattening himself to the side of the building, he scanned the area, ensuring Golly didn't have more henchmen creeping around. He didn't see anyone else.

The men seemed to be waiting on something. Probably the explosion.

Picking up a rock, Reyes took aim and let it fly. It hit the man hunkering in the shadows closest to the truck. With a rank curse, he jerked around, giving up all attempts at stealth. So did the second guy.

Kennedy must have spotted them, because she put the truck in gear, prepared to move if needed. Damn, he was proud of her.

He waited, wanting the men to get just a little closer before he stepped out. Once they were within range, he'd have all the advantage he needed.

Then the unthinkable happened.

One of the men snarled, "Fuck it," and took aim at the truck, planning to shoot Kennedy and Jodi through the windows.

Terror put Reyes on autopilot. He stepped out with his gun in his hand, firing off a shot that sent the man stumbling back until he tripped over his feet and dropped. One more shot, and Reyes ensured he wouldn't be getting up.

The second man ran, disappearing into the darkness.

Furious that he'd allowed Kennedy to come along,

Reyes started for the truck, his only thought to get her to safety.

The second man had already circled back, and now he shot at Reyes. Diving for the cover of the truck, Reyes barked, "Down!" to both women, then peered around the side of the truck.

He was a crack shot, better than good. It was the one aspect of their training where his ability trumped Cade's.

Reyes watched the darkness, spotted the target peeking out, squeezed his trigger and put one right through the bastard's head.

With all the gunfire, cops would now be on their way. Even if the desk manager hadn't called them, someone would have. It'd be best if he could—

The passenger side of the truck opened and Jodi stepped out.

Alarmed, Reyes straightened enough to see her. "Jodi!" If there were more men around, she'd be an easy hit. "What the hell are you—"

Grim faced, her jaw clenched, she lifted her Glock.

At first, Reyes thought she was aiming for him, but when she fired beyond him, he immediately turned to face the new threat.

The impact of her bullet propelled Rand Golly backward against the side of an empty cabin. He must have left through the back door and moved up the yards before stepping out to the lot. Pain twisted his face and he slumped, but didn't go down.

Jodi's bullet had hit him center mass, so there was only one explanation. A bulletproof vest. Still hurt like hell to get hit, yet it wasn't a killing blow.

Slowly Golly grinned at them...and showed the bomb in his hand.

"Get down," Golly ordered Jodi. She didn't move.

Damn her, she actually took a step forward. "If I drop it, it explodes," he warned.

Curling her lip, Jodi stared at him. "An impact bomb? Really? How much reach does it have?" she asked in a dead voice. "Are you willing to kill yourself, too?"

"Yes," he hissed, his expression a morbid mix of pain and anticipation.

Kennedy, bless her practical, levelheaded heart, put the truck in Reverse and very slowly began backing away, enabling Reyes to keep pace with her. He wanted to reassure her, but he didn't dare take his gaze off Golly.

With an effort, Golly regained his feet, his twisted expression triumphant. "To avenge my brother, I'll kill all of you."

"Your brother," Jodi sneered, "was a smelly, disgusting, whiny little prick, and he sniveled like a bitch while I killed him."

Roaring, Golly straightened even more.

Sirens sounded in the distance. It was all going to hell fast.

"Jodi," Reyes said in his calmest, most even tone, despite the urgency humming through his veins. "Kennedy is going to be extremely pissed if you get hurt."

"Keep her safe," Jodi said.

Kennedy shoved open the passenger door and snapped, "Jodi, get your butt over here right now or I'll never forgive you!"

That command surprised both Reyes and Jodi.

Seeing the indecision on Jodi's face, Reyes promised her, "I've got it." When she reluctantly nodded, he said, "Now *run*."

Bolting away, Jodi sprinted for the truck. Reyes heard the truck door slam.

Golly, the bastard, tried to react in time, lifting his arm to throw the bomb—and Reyes shot him.

Deliberately, he didn't make it a killing shot.

No, he took out Golly's shoulder so that the bomb fell from his hand. A look of horror crossed his ugly face as he realized what had happened.

Satisfied, Reyes dove behind the truck.

Golly screamed a split second before the blast of sound, the rush of fire and the scattering of debris drowned him out.

Reyes heard the pellets hitting the truck, felt something sear his shoulder, and prayed Kennedy and Jodi weren't hurt.

Ears ringing, he slowly came to his feet and saw both women ducked down on their seats. Golly was on the ground, bleeding in multiple places. His sleeve was shredded—and so was his arm. It was probably the ragged, gaping hole in his neck that had killed him.

Doing a quick scan of the area, Reyes didn't spot any more threats. Other than the horrified desk manager, they were now alone.

The first sob alarmed him. Expecting the worst, Reyes jerked around and found Jodi with her face in her hands, her shoulders shaking while Kennedy tried to soothe her. She kept rubbing Jodi's back and twice hugged her.

She looked up and met his gaze, her smile sad, and gave Jodi another squeeze.

Jodi wasn't hurt, then. Likely it was an emotional overload now that the danger had ended.

Police swarmed into the lot from different entrances, lights flashing and sirens blaring.

And, damn it, Detective Albertson led the way.

Reyes set his gun aside, locked his hands behind his neck and waited.

There'd be no end of explanations to give, but the threat was now over and that's what really mattered.

Full of frowns, Crosby got out of his car and nodded toward Golly's body. "Rand Golly?"

"Yes." Reyes nodded to the other side of the lot, behind the truck. "Two other bodies in that direction. So you know, there are more weapons in my truck."

"I see." Crosby rubbed his face and said something to two of the officers. They headed for the bodies Reyes had indicated.

"I thought you were going to my gym."

"I sent others. Everything is fine there, and we now have several arrests."

Reyes had no idea what was going on, but at least his gym was safe. "I see." He frowned. "How is it you're here, Detective?"

Smile tight, Crosby said, "Your sister."

"No shit?" It wasn't like Madison to trust anyone other than family.

"I didn't give her a choice." As he approached, he took in the blood on Reyes's shoulder. "You're hurt?"

What bullshit. No one took choices from his sister. If Madison opted to share with Crosby, it was a strong indication of her trust...which meant Reyes could trust him also.

Slowly, watching Crosby in case he objected, Reyes lowered his arms. He, too, glanced at his shoulder. Blood soaked his shirt, but the pain was minimal. "Little shrapnel from the bomb. It'll be fine."

"Your brother rounded up several men, only he managed not to kill them."

"Cade is smooth like that."

Looking very much like a man in charge, Crosby took in the scene. "Golly had a bomb?"

"Threatening Jodi with it, yeah." He looked Crosby

right in the eyes and said, "He planned a lot of damage. I had no choice but to shoot him."

"Your choice could have been to notify me."

He gave a noncommittal shrug. "Didn't know he had a bomb, or I might have." A *huge* lie. "Besides, my shot didn't kill him."

"No, it just caused him to drop the bomb, as you knew it would?"

Reyes said nothing. His methods had been efficient—he wouldn't apologize for them—and he wouldn't explain further, not until he spoke with Madison and got a handle on these new dynamics. A *cop*. What the hell was his sister thinking?

Lower, so the officers wouldn't hear, Crosby growled, "Do you realize the clusterfuck your family has created?"

He sure as hell wouldn't indict his family. "You wanted Golly." He jutted his chin in the direction of the body. "Well, there he is."

Reyes waited for Crosby to arrest him, and was still waiting when Kennedy left the truck and launched herself at him.

"She's obviously upset," Crosby grumbled. "Take care of her."

Smiling, Reyes slowly gathered Kennedy close. More and more it became apparent that Crosby had a very soft spot when it came to women.

An admirable trait.

While the cops did their thing, Reyes held Kennedy, thinking of all the things he wanted to say, but first he had to prioritize. "Is Jodi okay?"

She nodded against his chest, her hold tightening even more. "She will be, thanks to you."

"And you?" It wasn't easy but he set her back enough

to tip up her chin. "I'm proud of you, Kennedy. Again." Pretty much always. "You did great, babe."

"I didn't do anything."

"Wrong. You had the foresight to back up the truck so I could use it as cover. You got Jodi's stubborn butt out of harm's way. You ducked when you needed." He pressed a kiss to her lips. "You were levelheaded and calm, and I'm *proud* of you."

Her lips trembling, she rested her forehead to his chest and mumbled something low.

"Hey, you okay?"

She took a solid step back so that his arms dropped to his sides. Her eyes widened when she saw the blood on his shoulder. "Oh, my God, you're hurt!"

"No, it's nothing."

Voice rising, she snapped, "Why is it never anything when *you're* hurt, but it's a big deal when I am?"

Wow, she'd been so calm up to that point that her agitated tone took him by surprise. Gently Reyes cupped her face. "Maybe because you mean so much to me?" He touched his mouth to hers again, lingering a few seconds this time. "Swear to God, Kennedy, it hurts me the most to see you hurt."

She hesitated, her gaze on his injury. "You promise it's not bad?"

"A tiny sting, that's all." He kissed her again. "As long as you're okay, I'm fine."

"Reyes." Releasing a long breath, she glanced around at the activity, then briefly at Jodi, who now stood beside Crosby, peering down at Golly.

Turning back to him, she gazed into his eyes and said, "I love you."

Reyes felt his face go blank. "Say again?"

"I love you. So damn much, and I know I always will."

Her lips trembled. "Seeing you hurt devastates me, but I guess it's bound to happen again."

Holy shit, the lady had terrible timing. "You love me?" He had a difficult time grasping the words, coming out of the blue like they did.

Her chin lifted an inch. "I just thought you should know."

Of all the… Slowly he grinned. "Way to blindside me, babe."

"Sorry."

Reyes hugged her off her feet, turned her in a circle, then kissed her in front of gawking officers, a disgruntled detective and her smiling friend.

"Get a room," Jodi said, laughing.

Kennedy freed her mouth. "Oh, Reyes." She looked stunned. "Despite all this, Jodi just *laughed.*"

"So she did." Jodi would be all right. The girl had a backbone of steel and a survivalist's instincts.

And she had Kennedy, the biggest asset of all.

When he realized Kennedy was shivering, he stepped to the truck, grabbed her coat and helped her into it. Then he led her over to Crosby, where the front desk manager was busy rattling off what he'd witnessed.

All in all, the dude made it sound like Golly was a lunatic and that Reyes had saved the day. Pretty accurate, really.

A cop quickly led the manager back to the office so they could talk.

Crosby looked at Reyes. "I'm guessing you know the drill."

"Arresting me after all?"

"No. But I need statements from all three of you." He gave an apologetic smile to Kennedy. "You can't keep her glued to your side."

"Wanna bet?"

Rubbing the back of his neck, Crosby said with insistence, "I gave you a few minutes, but now I need to sort this out."

Reyes was about to argue—because seriously, Kennedy wasn't going anywhere without him—when a sleek black car pulled into the lot. Recognizing it, Reyes breathed a sigh of relief. His dad had arrived.

"Now what?" Crosby grumbled.

Parrish McKenzie brought a whole lot of consequence with him. As he climbed out of the car, he looked like a stately senator and carried himself like a benevolent king. Better still, he had the instincts and ability of a warrior.

Content with how things were rolling out, Reyes said, "You can talk with Kennedy, but my dad will be with her." He bent to Kennedy's temple. "Everything is fine. I'll be back with you in just a few minutes."

Her gaze searched his, maybe because he hadn't yet returned her declaration. Soon, he promised himself. Very, very soon.

IT WAS FOUR in the morning when they finally got to bed, still at Parrish's house. Kennedy hoped she'd get a good long break now, because her system wasn't cut out for such constant cloak-and-dagger drama.

Reyes ended up with three stitches in his shoulder, and a mess of colorful bruising. *A tiny sting*, he'd said. Ha! The man had a small gouge taken out of his flesh. She supposed she'd have to accept that he wasn't one to complain.

He was usually too busy protecting, nurturing and being all-around awesome.

They'd found pieces of shrapnel from Golly's bomb scattered everywhere, including embedded in the side of Reyes's truck.

Recalling the awful shape of Golly's body, she knew she could have lost Reyes. He'd saved Jodi by risking himself, but he *had* survived. Given his personality and vocation, she'd have to focus on that.

Jodi was back at the hotel, where she'd stay for another week until a more permanent residence was ready for her, though she could now come and go as she pleased. They'd offered her alternatives, but she no longer minded the fancy suite—as long as it was temporary.

After her heartbreaking cry, she'd done an amazing about-face, looking forward to the future and, thankfully, glad to be alive. There was a new optimism about her, a zest to see what the next day would hold.

She'd be meeting with many people over the next week, including Reyes and her, to help her figure out the next steps. Kennedy was determined to make Jodi feel secure.

Just as Reyes had done for her.

Cade and Sterling had grabbed their targets without a hitch, which had led to information indicating a much larger trafficking network.

Parrish had made the decision to clue in Crosby so he could tie up all the loose ends. Kennedy discovered that the senior McKenzie had made allies with a few different people in the legal system—and some in political circles.

It seemed to her that Crosby had just been included in the hush-hush details of the McKenzie family enterprise. She knew Madison would be happy about that—if things progressed as she preferred. She'd put her money on Madison.

Now she and Reyes were stretched out in his bed, only one dim light breaking up the darkness. Tucked close to his side, Kennedy couldn't stop touching him. And kissing him. Though he kept smiling at her, he hadn't said anything about loving her.

She didn't mind. He'd had a lot on his plate dealing with Crosby, talking to his family and being very attentive to her. She didn't regret telling him she loved him, either. At that moment, she wasn't sure she could have held it in anyway. Honestly, she wanted to tell everyone, him, his family, Crosby...the whole world.

She, Kennedy Brooks, once an emotionally damaged woman forever trying to prove she was okay, disinterested in men, repelled by the idea of sex, now loved an alpha guy who epitomized danger—and she couldn't keep her hands off him.

Voice low and drowsy, Reyes said, "You beat me to the punch, you know."

"Hmm?" She loved his soft chest hair and the hard muscle beneath it. And his scent. Nuzzling against him, she breathed deeply, filling her head with that delicious smell.

"I wanted to do things right, not in the middle of chaos. Wasn't easy, but I was hanging on to my patience—then bam." He patted her backside. "You let me have it."

Smiling, Kennedy tucked her face under his chin. "Is this about me telling you I love you? Because I'm glad I did."

"I'm glad, too. Hell, *more* than glad." He fondly caressed one bottom cheek. "I love you, too, you know. I *more* than love you, actually. I want to marry you. Grow old with you. Maybe someday have little McKenzies with you."

The smile turned into a grin. "A rascal boy like you," she murmured, imagining it.

"Or a smart, strong girl like you." He kissed the top of her head.

"You really see me as strong?"

"I think you're the only one who doesn't see it. Your strength is quiet, steadfast, honorable and loyal."

He believed it, she knew…and she was starting to believe it, too.

"I want to share holidays with you, Kennedy, here at my dad's place, or even at your folks' place in Florida if you want. I will meet them, right?"

Filled with contentment, she nodded. "Yes."

"Good. So I want all that. Everything. From now until the end of time." He gave her a squeeze. "You love me enough to want that, too?"

"Yes." Teasing him, she said, "*More* than enough."

"Let's be clear here, okay? I'm the type of guy who's going to hover."

Was that supposed to be news to her? Playing along, she leaned up to look at him. "Meaning?"

"Meaning you go off on your own a lot, and I don't think I have the temperament to deal with that. How would you feel about me tagging along to play bodyguard?"

"Or sex servant?"

His slow grin warmed her. "Yeah, I can be a multi-purpose kind of travel companion." More seriously, he asked, "You wouldn't mind that? I don't want you to feel smothered, but seriously, babe, I'd turn into an old man with gray hair if I was left behind to worry about you."

She kissed his chin. "I'll be happier keeping you near. But what if I have to travel and something comes up here? Your job isn't exactly nine-to-five."

"I know. And once you're scheduled, you couldn't just change things."

Clearly he'd given this a lot of thought. "Ideas?"

"Yeah. How would you feel about an actual bodyguard?" He rushed to add, "Only when I can't go along."

"Hmm." Having lived a life where she knew how easily things could go wrong, she actually liked the idea.

"Someone low-key," he promised, "who'd blend in and

would still keep an eye on things. Someone you and I would research extensively."

"If I agree, will you agree to keep me informed of your jobs? To never keep any aspect of the danger from me?" She propped her elbows on his chest. "It'll be easier for me if I know what's going on."

Reyes trailed his fingertips down her spine. "Honestly, I never thought I'd enjoy talking shop with anyone outside the family, but with you it just comes naturally."

"That's a yes?"

"Ah, babe." He cupped her backside in both hands. "Right about now, I'd promise you anything if you'd just agree to marry me."

Giving him a thorough kiss, she murmured against his mouth, "Yes, I'll marry you."

He immediately relaxed. "Way to keep me in suspense."

"I love you, Reyes. More than I knew was possible."

"Same." This time his kiss was long and deep. "It'll be light soon. We should probably get some sleep?" He said it like a question, and judging by his wandering hands, sleep wasn't the number one thing on his mind. But as usual, he was a considerate, awesome, incredible man.

And he was all hers. "Who needs sleep?"

His hazel eyes immediately warmed. "Well, not me. But if you do—"

Kennedy straddled his hips. "I have a better idea."

"Hell, yeah, you do." He drew her close and kissed her in a way guaranteed to scorch her.

Yes, she was a little tired; she was also enormously happy, and she couldn't think of a better way to start their new life together than by making love to Reyes.

Now, tomorrow and always.

* * * * *

Read on for a sneak peek at Watching Over You,
*the next thrilling novel in the McKenzies of Ridge Trail
series by* New York Times *bestselling author
Lori Foster.*

WHEN CROSBY ALBERTSON FROWNED, he didn't just show displeasure in his incredibly handsome face. He also showed it in the rigid lines of his big body, in his tightened fists and the angle of his wide shoulders, how his feet braced apart and the way the muscles in his thighs flexed.

Honestly, Madison McKenzie thought he was downright scrumptious top to bottom, though now wasn't the best time to be admiring him.

Using her admittedly incredible digital surveillance skills, she'd been shadowing Crosby online for a while now, ever since she realized that *he* was keeping tabs on *her* family.

Granted, her family had made unique choices to combat injustice, specifically the injustice of every form of human trafficking and forced labor. She and her brothers, under their father's instruction, had become elite fighters weaponized with skill, knowledge and drive.

As a cop, Crosby had somehow caught on to them, despite how she meticulously covered their tracks.

He'd impressed the heck out of her, which wasn't easy to do, especially after he worked with them to bring down a truly heinous trafficker who'd gotten far too personal.

But Crosby was still a cop through and through, and she and her family still skirted the edges of illegal activity by pursuing their goals without involving the law.

Didn't stop her infatuation with him.

When he found out that she'd ramped up her surveillance of him, he'd likely be annoyed.

That couldn't be helped, though. No other man had fascinated her like Crosby Albertson did, and in her line of work, as her brothers had often pointed out (the hypocrites), she couldn't be too careful. She knew a lot about Crosby already, but now she wanted to know more.

Physically following him today wasn't exactly necessary, but she'd had a little free time, so why not? Never mind that Ridge Trail, Colorado, was under extremely severe weather, with a huge dumping of snow and freezing temps making the roads slick.

Her motto was that if Crosby could go out, she could, too. Overall, she figured she could do just about anything a guy could do, with a few notable exceptions. Like, she couldn't pee standing up. Then again, she had no desire to.

She couldn't get a testicular injury, so yay, score one for lady parts.

And honestly, as strong and skilled as she might be, she still took pleasure in her femininity, and knocking out a dude with one punch—something her hulking brothers managed easily—was usually out of her realm. Not that she couldn't effectively disable a guy in other ways. She *could* (hello, testicles), and yet the majority of her contributions to the family business were made behind a computer screen.

Now, with Crosby, she wanted to be a little more hands-on.

Snuggled into her chic white snowsuit, complete with a faux-fur-trimmed trapper hat and attached goggles, Madison parked her SUV behind Crosby's car, all the while wondering why he would tool around in this weather in a sedan. At least he had chains on his tires, taking some precautions.

She wondered, too, why he would stand there on the sidewalk outside a small mom-and-pop-style store and do that whole-body frowning thing. Something had angered him, but she didn't yet know what. Since he hadn't looked at her, she figured she wasn't the cause of his irritation.

After staring through the window for a flat ten seconds, Crosby went into the store, leaving her with a tingle of anticipation at seeing him again. The last time she'd been so close to him was well before Christmas, and now it was early February. She'd kissed him then…and he'd *laughed*.

Worse, he thought she'd kissed him for underhanded reasons.

She was still mad at him for that—she really was—but even though their relationship was strained at best, hostile at worst, she'd missed him.

Assuming he wouldn't recognize her bundled up as she was for the weather, Madison trudged through the deep snow and entered the quaint store. A bell jingled over the front door, drawing attention her way.

As was her habit, she immediately did a quick assessment of the small interior. Shelves lined every wall, packed from top to bottom. Besides Crosby, she noted a clerk behind the counter and a youth who'd been stocking the shelves.

Unfortunately, there were also three men in the process of robbing the place.

Well. She supposed that explained Crosby's fierce frown.

She also had the terrible suspicion that he recognized her even under all her winter gear. Had he been onto her following him all along?

His cleverness was just one more appealing trait to admire.

Guns drawn and faces hidden behind thick winter ski

masks, the robbers mostly kept their attention on Crosby and the clerk, but they did repeatedly glance her way.

Aggressively, one of the men gestured with his gun, saying, "What the hell are you people doing out on a day like this?"

Another man said, "I knew we should have locked the door."

Crosby said, "I offered, if you'll recall."

So he'd planned to lock her out? Too bad for him.

Dressed as she was, the men couldn't see much of her face or body, but she felt certain they knew she was female. It was there in the way she stood with her hands on her hips, in the long hair trailing out of her hat and probably in the way her lips smiled. "Am I interrupting?"

The man who waved the gun around barked, "Over here, now."

That suited her just fine.

As Madison started forward, her awareness of Crosby sharpened. Today he wore a dark puffer coat, thick wool scarf and padded gloves. Always, no matter the situation, he managed to look like a model. Well, except for his sandy-brown hair. He wore it just long enough for it to curl a little on the very ends. It gave him an appealingly messy look in stark contrast with his otherwise impeccable appearance.

Those dark-as-sin eyes of his never left the men standing before him, though he didn't look anxious about the situation.

Annoyed, yes. Alert, certainly. She sensed more than saw that all he needed was an opening, and he'd take on all three of the intruders.

In that, she could certainly assist.

As she strode forward, she asked the stock boy, "Would you mind ducking behind that shelf?"

Startled, the kid said, "Um…"

The robbers all started protesting at the same time, one of them barking, "No one fucking moves!"

Speaking over him, Madison said to the clerk, "If you could possibly duck down very quickly?"

Crosby issued a sound like a snarl and took a quick step to his left, which effectively shielded the clerk. The older man dropped fast behind the counter. That got the kid moving, too, and he jumped behind a shelf of canned goods.

With the two innocents protected, she set about wrapping up the danger.

"Bitch!" one of the robbers snapped, lunging for her and catching her arm in a viselike grip. Madison let him propel her forward. Deliberately crashing into him, she grabbed his wrist to control the weapon. Because the floor was concrete and could cause a ricochet, she forced his arm up and back. The gun discharged, the sound loud in the small store, but the bullet merely hit a wall of beer cases. The yeasty brew sprayed out.

Fluid, even graceful—or so she liked to think—she swung the first man's gun hand around and, since he fired again, caused him to pop the second man in the thigh, making him buckle.

Guy number two cursed a blue streak as he went down.

The dummy who'd grabbed her slipped in the beer and fell, finally releasing the gun. She wrenched it away, turned and shot him in the shoulder. His shout of pain mingled with curse words.

Crosby had already gone after the third man, making quick work of subduing him. She heard the snap of bone and knew it was the man's arm breaking. That one wouldn't be holding a gun for a while.

Furious, guy number two held his bloody thigh with one hand and took aim at her with the other.

Crosby kicked his gun away at the same time she stomped his privates. Her snow boots were heavy, her aim sure.

As if in slow motion, the dude curled in on himself, his groan low and deep.

She had just a moment to admire Crosby's skill, seeing him finish off the third man with a punch that sent him collapsing back into a display of chips.

Three men, now all wounded, two with gunshot wounds and one with a broken arm. Crosby grabbed the one she'd shot in the shoulder, stopping him from scurrying away.

He used that effective one-punch power she so often admired in her brothers and put the guy to sleep.

"Well done," Madison said, smiling at how seamlessly they'd worked as a team. Leaning over the counter, she said to the clerk, "Could you call 911, please? In this weather, it might take them a bit to respond. They'll need as much notice as possible."

Rigid, Crosby stood there glowering at her among the fallen bodies, spilled beer and scattered chips. Rage still permeated his entire being.

Those clenched fists of his? Impressive.

The rock-solid line of his shoulders under his coat? Very stirring.

"You," he whispered, the sound raw-edged with anger, "are not in charge here."

Smiling, Madison held up her hands. Unlike her brothers, she didn't mind stepping back—just a little.

He then proceeded to secure the men, rolling them one by one to their stomachs and fastening their wrists together with nylon cuffs. Had he carried those along? Obviously he'd known there would be trouble.

She kept watching him, but not once did he look at her.

Okay, the robbers hadn't unsettled her, but Crosby's attitude made her a little uneasy.

Pretending it didn't, she moved to the boy, who continued to cower behind a shelf. He looked fifteen or so, in that awkward stage of long limbs, acne and sparse facial hair on his upper lip, which he wore like a trophy.

She crouched down in front of him. "You okay, bud?"

"They were going to hurt us this time," he whispered, his face still ghostly pale.

This time? "Did they say so?" she asked, wondering what in the world she'd walked into. Maybe it hadn't been a simple robbery after all.

"They didn't have to," the boy agonized. "It was their attitudes. If Crosby hadn't showed up—"

A long arm reached past Madison, offering a Coke to the kid. She glanced up to see Crosby's set face.

With his tone sounding mild, Crosby said, "Drink up, Owen." When the boy took the can, Crosby rested his hand on Owen's shoulder. "Why don't you join your dad behind the counter? I've put up the closed sign and locked the door so you can both have a few minutes."

Nodding, Owen shot to his feet, then skirted around the downed men and the beer that now crawled across the uneven floor. When he reached his father, Madison heard the low murmur of their voices, both of them sounding shaken.

Now that Crosby said it, the two did have a similar look. "So father and son were here working together and you—"

His finger pressed against her lips, shocking her silent. When had he removed his gloves, and why hadn't she noticed? She rarely missed a single detail.

"Give me a minute," Crosby rasped, still looking somewhat savage. "Do you think you can do that?"

Madison nodded. She wouldn't mind giving him a week. Maybe a month.

Resisting the urge to lick his finger required more concentration than keeping quiet.

Crosby moved away again.

Freed from that strange and overwhelming effect he had on her, she dragged off her hat and unzipped her coat, suddenly far too warm.

Letting Crosby do his thing, she moved to stand before the counter and held out her hand. Keeping her voice very low, she said, "Hi. I'm Madison."

The older man took her hand in both of his. "Winton Maclean. Thank you for helping us."

Proving he had excellent hearing, Crosby said, "I had it in hand."

Winton smiled at him, his look almost paternal. "I'm sure you did, but a little help didn't hurt."

"Depends on the help," Crosby shot back.

Well, she liked that! Had she, or had she not, taken out one of them and helped with a second? She *had*. So...

Leaning in, Winton confided, "He's angrier when he worries."

Oh, she liked Winton. "Have you known Crosby long?"

Rubbing his forehead, Winton cast a quick glance at Crosby. "Most of his life."

Now on his phone, Crosby pinned her with a warning gaze that pretty much stated, *Don't ask questions about me.*

Fine, she'd save her questions for later. "Mop?" she asked Winton.

He was shaking his head to deny her help, but Owen said, "Through those swinging doors," then caught his dad's exasperated huff. "But you don't need to—"

"Thanks, but I'm not good with idle time." Smiling to reassure them both, she went for the mop and found it with a big bucket. Used to cleaning the sparring mats at her family's home gym, she quickly added water and cleaner, then rolled it out. Using the mop, she stopped the beer from spreading farther across the store, but she was careful not to interfere with the "scene." Cops could be prickly about things like that.

Good thing one of the robbers helped stem the flow, too; the beer was currently soaking into his side, all along his waist, hip and thigh. He tried to squirrel away, but one glare from Crosby and he went still again.

Suddenly police sirens echoed over the snowy streets. Blast, she'd run out of time. Abandoning the mop bucket, she sidled into the back room and quickly called her father. Crosby would be busy for a few minutes at least. Hopefully, everything would be wrapped up before her brothers could barge in. They tended to be overprotective where she was concerned.

Hearing the front door opening and the voices of officers, she quietly explained the situation to her father, giving him the address of the shop and assuring him it was all under control.

Never one to get ruffled, Parrish said, "So you're okay?"

"Of course."

"Are you positive you don't need any help?"

"Absolutely certain."

Her father hesitated a moment, then said, "Try not to get too involved, but if you get dragged in, let me know and I'll start covering our bases."

Yes, given their family enterprise, it was never wise to make the law too curious. Except for Crosby. Since they'd come to an understanding of sorts with him, he could be as curious as he wanted—about her.

Not the business.

One of the swinging metal doors moved and then Crosby was there, his dark gaze accusing, assessing and... more. "Calling in reinforcements?"

"Did I appear to need them?"

Instead of answering, his gaze took a slow trip down her body.

Madison struck a pose. "It's a great snowsuit, right? Soon as I saw it, I had to have it."

One side of his mouth barely twitched before settling into a hard line again.

A near smile? She wanted to think so.

"Detective Bard wants to speak to you now."

She affected a pout. "If I have to talk to a cop, I'd rather it just be you."

Without even a blink, he said, "I'm not a cop anymore, so that won't do."

It wasn't every day that he took a McKenzie by surprise, so Crosby enjoyed the rounding of Madison's bright hazel eyes and the slight parting of her lips.

Then all her arrogance rushed back in and she stated, "Impossible. I'd know if you left the police force."

"Apparently not." He took her arm and urged her from the room, not in the least surprised when her confidence melted into the mien of an untrained person. Somehow she managed to look rattled, unsure and wary all at the same time.

Crosby barely resisted rolling his eyes.

Not that long ago he'd crossed paths with the McKenzie family. For a while, he'd suspected her father of organizing vigilante justice, with her two brothers employed to see through well-planned rescue missions. Too many times human traffickers had been thwarted, practically dumped on the doorstep of the precinct with all necessary info to make a tidy sweep of the scumbag perpetrators, along with their contacts and clientele.

Crosby had appreciated the end results, but not the

methods utilized. It had taken a lot of diligence, but he'd finally found his way to the McKenzie clan. No problem.

That is, no problem except for Madison. She was the tech whiz, and he did mean whiz. Practically genius level. If she wanted to hack NASA, she probably could. Hell, even the White House might not be safe.

That alone made him uneasy, but then for her to set her sights on him? Talk about unnerving a man.

It didn't help that she was equal parts gorgeous and bold. Nearly six feet of slender femininity shot through with brilliance and wrapped in capability.

For too many reasons she unsettled him, and that was a new feeling for Crosby. Didn't stop him from wanting her, but he wasn't an idiot. That road led to trouble, and he had enough on his plate already.

Standing back, arms crossed, Crosby watched her weave her spell on Detective Bard. The poor dude never stood a chance. He bought her act, every trembling, grateful, soft-spoken second of it.

Hell, even Winton and Owen looked convinced, and they'd watched her easily annihilate a grown man.

Good thing he wasn't a cop anymore, or he'd have to set the record straight. The goons still might, but who would believe them? They each had long records of petty crimes, like trespassing, simple assault, vandalism and public intoxication. Now there was proof that they'd been harassing Winton and other small neighborhood businesses, forcing them to pay for "protection." What a joke.

Luckily, he'd just put an end to that.

Poor Madison. She'd shown off her skills with ease, but now couldn't gloat about it. Too many people were willing to give Crosby the credit for taking down all three men.

It'd be hilarious if he was dealing with anyone other than the McKenzies. Madison might be the only one on the scene right now, and God knew she was enough, but he wouldn't be surprised if the rest of the family had their noses in it before the day was over.

Once the thugs were taken away and the police left, Madison went right back to cleaning, swinging the mop with practiced ease. Swipe, rinse, wring, repeat.

Her family had deep pockets, so he hadn't expected her to even know how to clean.

Was there anything she couldn't do well?

"Whew, it's getting warm." Propping the mop handle against the counter, she dragged down the snowsuit zipper even more, down and down and down, all the way to the flare of her hips, then she peeled off the top layer and let it hang over her stellar tush.

Beneath the snowsuit she wore a black turtleneck that hugged her breasts and fit snug to her narrow rib cage. Using both hands, she gathered her long light brown hair, then asked Winton, "Do you have a rubber band or anything?"

Owen scrambled to a drawer and produced one with a flourish that left his face hot.

Recognizing that infatuated look, Crosby figured the poor kid would be dreaming of Madison for weeks.

She bent forward at the waist, quickly put her hair into a high ponytail and straightened again—still looking like a wet dream.

"I'm going to change this water. Be right back."

All three of them watched her roll the bucket to the back room.

Winton slowly turned to stare at Crosby. Owen grinned.

Shaking his head, Crosby said, "No. It's not like that, so don't get any ideas."

"Too late," Owen said, then he quickly ducked the

smack his dad aimed at the back of his head. "I'll, um, go see if she needs any help."

Crosby couldn't help but laugh. Fifteen-year-old boys—almost sixteen, as Owen said any time his age was mentioned—were made up of testosterone and determination. An uncomfortable combo from what he remembered, though it'd been twenty years since he'd had to deal with that anatomical and emotional upheaval.

"Quit frowning, Winton. He's a good kid."

"I know." Winton sighed. "And he's currently in love with a cheerleader at his school. But still..."

"Madison will handle it. No worries." Switching gears and getting down to business, Crosby added, "Thanks for following my lead."

"You know what you're doing." Bracing a hand on the counter and lifting his brows, Winton asked, "What *are* you doing?"

So much for Winton's patience. "I know her and her family. Trust me, the less she's involved, the better."

"Because?"

Unable to share the reason, he shrugged. "I knew she was following me today." She was always following him, usually online, but it figured Madison would decide to tail him in person during a snowstorm. "Warning her off wouldn't have done me any good, and I didn't want to take the time to try to reason with her." Lessons in futility weren't really his thing.

"So she wasn't part of your plan?"

Snorting, Crosby said, "Definitely not."

"That put you in a tight spot, since you knew they'd be here today."

Crosby nodded. He had good street informants. Winton's store had been targeted more than once, and Crosby had planned to put an end to the harassment. Things had gone according to plan...

Except that his initial plans hadn't factored in Madison being around. Once he'd realized she was following him, he hadn't had time to reconfigure things. Losing her would have been tough, too, with the roads so slick, some of them impassable. He'd had no way for tricky driving or fast turns.

Delaying his arrival to Winton's store could have put Winton and Owen in danger. He'd been caught in an untenable position—not the first time when dealing with McKenzies.

Emerging from the back room with Owen, Madison returned to mopping the floors, now with fresh water. "Might need to go over them one more time, so they won't be sticky."

"We'll take care of it," Winton said. "With the weather worsening, there's no point in us being open anyway."

Owen hefted the damaged case of beer and carried it into the back.

Winton began cleaning up the spilled chip display.

"I'm glad to help," Madison insisted, using the wringer on the bucket. "We'll have it all tidied up in no time."

"You," Crosby said, feeling very divided, "have some explaining to do."

She smiled and, proving she'd been listening, said, "You were right, you know. If you'd told me not to come in, it would have only sharpened my curiosity."

Winton laughed. "I'm sure Crosby could have handled it on his own, but I admit I enjoyed seeing you in action. Are you in law enforcement?"

Her gaze slanted over to Winton. "Have you ever seen a cop fight the way I do?"

"Only Crosby."

Her slim eyebrows climbed high. "Is that so?"

Always ready to sing his praises, Winton paused in his cleanup. "Before he was even Owen's age, Crosby was training. He's always been a fitness buff. Every coach at the high school tried to talk him into playing sports, but he was never interested. Said team sports weren't his thing."

"Dad says he's mostly a loner," Owen added.

"Or at least he was before—"

"Winton," Crosby warned. There weren't many things he could tell Madison that she didn't already know. She'd made no secret of researching him, using methods to open files that even cops couldn't easily access. What she didn't know she'd eventually find out, whether he liked it or not.

Winton shot him a look of apology—one that Madison didn't miss.

What concerned Crosby most at the moment was *how* Winton would tell things, with all the nuances and added affection of a father.

Winton and Owen fell silent.

Madison didn't. She returned the mop to the bucket, then folded her arms on the counter—a pose that had her breasts thrusting forward and her backside sticking out in an impossible-to-ignore way.

Deliberate, he was sure. Everything she did or said had a purpose. He'd never known a woman who was so entirely badass, a research whiz who could uncover anything, a fighter capable of leveling a grown man with ease, who also flaunted her sexiness.

It was an enticing mix, and damn it, he wasn't immune.

"I already knew he was a fitness buff," she said, using a casual tone likely meant to regain Winton's trust. "I mean, look at him."

"He's rock-solid," Winton agreed.

She turned her head to see Crosby, her glittering hazel

eyes far too compelling. "He's into fashion, too. Looks like a cover model, don't you think?"

Hooting, Owen completely relaxed again. "That's exactly what Mrs. Cline says. She always shops on Monday at six so she can time her visits with Crosby's."

"Mrs. Cline?" Madison asked, her interest no longer playful.

Winton patted her hand. "Pam is nearing seventy and just likes to flirt."

"Ah." Grinning again, Madison asked Crosby, "Have to deal with a lot of flirting, do you?"

Since it was none of her business, Crosby declined to answer. "You should get going while you still can. The roads are getting worse by the minute."

Her smile curled even more. "Not without you. In fact, I'm convinced your car won't even make it away from the curb."

Crosby opened his mouth, but again, Owen beat him to it. "He has an SUV, but Silver probably—"

Winton interrupted his son with, "Go bundle up so you can help Madison clear her ride."

Once Owen left the room, Madison took a turn eyeing each of them before straightening to face forward. With her penetrating gaze locked on Crosby, she folded her arms under her breasts. "Why is everyone trying to get rid of me?"

Crosby didn't hesitate. "We have private things to discuss that don't concern you." He saw one scenario after another flit over her features as she determined how to proceed. So damned tenacious. "Enough, Madison. It's time for you to go before Winton, Owen and I get stranded here."

Concerned, she turned to Winton. "Do you have far to travel in this mess?"

"Um…" Shifting, looking guilty as hell, Winton muttered, "No."

Damn, Winton was bad at lying, even lies of omission.

He knew the second Madison looked up that her quick mind had already put too many things together.

Golden eyes slanted in his direction with accusation. "Let me guess. They live upstairs?"

Winton cleared his throat. "I'll go see what's keeping Owen." He literally fled the shop front.

Knowing he couldn't do the same, Crosby mimicked her stance, arms crossed and expression arrogant. "Contrary to what you believe, *some* of my business is still private." It was a miracle she hadn't uncovered every bit of his life yet—including the things he'd worked so hard to hide.

To his surprise, she retrenched with a sigh, her hands falling to her sides, her expression subdued. "I've been too pushy."

That pretty much described her, always.

Two tentative steps brought her closer to him, and with her height she nearly looked him in the eye. "I'm sorry. It's a bad habit of mine."

Damn it, now he felt like an asshole. "No one is perfect."

"I want to be," she admitted. Then with surprising candor, she added, "I guess I've been competing with my brothers for so long that being anything less than perfect— perfectly informed, prepared and capable—makes me a little nuts."

Incredible insight…that made sense. "Was I wrong in thinking your brothers would show up here?" His experience had been with assertive men who wanted to take over every situation. That rubbed Crosby the wrong way, so how bad would it have been for a younger sister?

"I called Dad. He's the only one who could hold them back, and *he*," she said with emphasis, "trusts me."

Her father was an imposing figure to be sure. Crosby likened him to Batman because of the way he entered a scene to the awe of all spectators. The man definitely brought a lot of larger-than-life presence everywhere he went. His sons weren't much different. And Madison? Overall, she was cut from the same cloth.

The senior McKenzie had probably been a strict task-master. After all, he was the one who'd determined that his kids would be the alphas of all alphas, apex predators who would go up against the worst society had to offer. Each of them had incredibly honed skills and a drive to conquer.

Crosby could have easily labeled them with the criminal class, except that the more he'd learned, the more he'd... respected them.

He could label them vigilantes, true, and that definitely placed them in the category of illegal activity. The conflict for him was that they fought against human trafficking, and for that, they had his deepest gratitude.

"I see you're not going to agree."

Crosby had no idea what she was talking about.

"Trust?" When he still hesitated, she said, "Never mind. I guess it's too soon for that."

Shaking his head to gather his thoughts, Crosby asked, "Are you ready to go?"

"Guess I might as well." Disgruntled, she began feeding her arms into the sleeves of the white snowsuit. "I'll feel better about this whole cluster if you answer one question for me."

"You need me to confirm something? Seriously?"

"Oh, I'll be on my computer as soon as I get home, but given the weather, that could take a little time and it really wouldn't kill you to share one tiny tidbit."

Deliberately, he exhaled as if impatient. In truth, he had a difficult time keeping his hands at his sides when he really wanted to touch her. Just a small stroke of that long sun-kissed brown hair. Or a grazing of his knuckles over her downy cheek. Or... "What is it?"

"You're really not a cop anymore?"

"No."

"Well, why not?"

"That's two questions."

Her eyes narrowed. "I think I feel faint. Maybe I shouldn't drive? I should probably ask Winton if I could hang around for a little while to—"

"No." She didn't even try to look sickly as she said all that, but then the point was for her to prove she'd do anything to get her way. That was something that alarmed him the most.

Madison McKenzie had no idea how to give up.

"I retired," he said.

She snorted. "At thirty-five?"

Easy enough to explain. "I have an old injury that was causing me some difficulty."

Her brows leveled over her eyes. "Someone actually bought that story?"

Jaw tightening, he explained, "I was shot in the leg."

"Five years ago, but it hasn't slowed you down. Heck, I just saw you in action, remember? So try again."

"You're staring again."

"I am." Mycah switched her legs, recrossing them. And damn his too-observant gaze, he didn't miss the gesture. Probably knew why she did it, too. Not that the action alleviated the sweet pain pulsing inside her. "Does it still bother you?"

"Depends."

"On?"

"Why you're staring."

She slicked the tip of her tongue over her lips, an unfamiliar case of nerves making themselves known. Again, his eyes caught the tell, dropping to her mouth, resting there, and the blast of heat that exploded inside her damn near fused her to the bar stool. What he did with one look... Jesus, it wasn't fair. Not to her. Not to humankind.

"Because you're so stareable. Don't do that," she insisted, no, *implored* when he stiffened, his eyes going glacial. Frustration stormed inside her, swirling and releasing in a sharp clap of laughter. She huffed out a breath, shaking her head. "You should grant me some leeway because you don't know me, and I don't know you. And you, all of you—" she waved her hand up and down, encompassing his long, below-the-shoulder-length hair, his massive shoulders, his thick thighs and his large booted feet "—are a lot."

"A lot of what?" His body didn't loosen, his face remaining shuttered. But that voice...

She shivered. It had deepened to a growl, and her breath caught.

"A lot of—" she spread out her arms the length of his shoulders "—mass. A lot of attitude." She exhaled, her hands dropping to her thighs. "A lot of beauty," she murmured, and it contained a slight tremble she hated but couldn't erase. "A lot of pride. A lot of..." Fire. Darkness. Danger. Shelter.

Her fingers curled into her palm.

"A lot of intensity," she finished. Lamely. Jesus, so lamely.

Achilles stared at her. And she fought not to fidget under his hooded gaze. Struggled to remain still as he leaned forward and that tantalizing, woodsy scent beckoned her closer seconds before he did.

"Mycah, come here."

She should be rebelling; she should be stiffening in offense at that rumbled order. Should be. But no. Instead, a weight she hadn't consciously been aware of tumbled off her shoulders. Allowing her to breathe deeper…freer. Because as Achilles gripped the lapel of her jacket and drew her closer, wrinkling the silk, he also slowly peeled away Mycah Hill, the business executive who helmed and carried the responsibilities of several departments… Mycah Hill, the eldest daughter of Laurence and Cherise Hill, who bore the burden of their financial irresponsibility and unrealistic expectations.

In their place stood Mycah, the vulnerable stripped-bare woman who wanted to let go. Who *could* let go. Just this once.

So as he reeled her in, she went, willingly, until their faces hovered barely an inch apart. Until their breaths mingled. Until his bright gaze heated her skin.

This close, she glimpsed the faint smattering of freckles across the tops of his lean cheeks and the high bridge of his nose. The light cinnamon spots should've detracted from the sensual brutality of his features. But they didn't. In an odd way, they enhanced it.

Had her wanting to dot each one with the top of her tongue.

"What?" she whispered.

"Say it again." He released her jacket and trailed surprisingly gentle fingers up her throat. "I want to find out for myself what the lie tastes like on your mouth."

Lust flashed inside her, hot, searing. Consuming.

God, she liked it. This…*consuming*.

If she wasn't careful, she could easily come to crave it.

Don't miss what happens next in…
Secrets of a One Night Stand *by Naima Simone,*
the next book in the Billionaires of Boston series!

Available September 2021 wherever
Harlequin Desire books and ebooks are sold.

Harlequin.com

HARLEQUIN
DESIRE

Luxury, scandal, desire—welcome to the lives of the American elite.

A Billionaires of Boston novel from
USA TODAY bestselling author

NAIMA SIMONE

Secrets of a One Night Stand

Then: "To strangers and one night together…"
Now: She's having her new boss's baby!

Finding out her previous one-night fling is her new boss is the shock of Mycah Hill's lifetime. She can't say no to being VP for software CEO Achilles Farrell—she's finally made her career dream come true. But knowing he's so close…it's only a matter of time before she's back in his arms. It can't end well. Achilles's tortured family history means he's not up for sticking around long-term. But Mycah's surprise pregnancy is about to change everything…

Harlequin.com

Get 4 FREE REWARDS!

We'll send you 2 FREE Books plus 2 FREE Mystery Gifts.

FREE
Value Over
$20

Both the **Romance** and **Suspense** collections feature compelling novels written by many of today's bestselling authors.

YES! Please send me 2 FREE novels from the Essential Romance or Essential Suspense Collection and my 2 FREE gifts (gifts are worth about $10 retail). After receiving them, if I don't wish to receive any more books, I can return the shipping statement marked "cancel." If I don't cancel, I will receive 4 brand-new novels every month and be billed just $7.24 each in the U.S. or $7.49 each in Canada. That's a savings of up to 28% off the cover price. It's quite a bargain! Shipping and handling is just 50¢ per book in the U.S. and $1.25 per book in Canada.* I understand that accepting the 2 free books and gifts places me under no obligation to buy anything. I can always return a shipment and cancel at any time. The free books and gifts are mine to keep no matter what I decide.

Choose one: ☐ **Essential Romance**
(194/394 MDN GQ6M)

☐ **Essential Suspense**
(191/391 MDN GQ6M)

Name (please print)

Address   Apt. #

City   State/Province   Zip/Postal Code

Email: Please check this box ☐ if you would like to receive newsletters and promotional emails from Harlequin Enterprises ULC and its affiliates. You can unsubscribe anytime.

> ### Mail to the Harlequin Reader Service:
> **IN U.S.A.:** P.O. Box 1341, Buffalo, NY 14240-8531
> **IN CANADA:** P.O. Box 603, Fort Erie, Ontario L2A 5X3

Want to try 2 free books from another series! Call 1-800-873-8635 or visit www.ReaderService.com.

STRS21MAXR2